scottish brides

An Anthology

SCOTTISH BRIDES
Compilation copyright © 2018 by Glynnis Campbell
The Shipwreck © 2012 by Glynnis Campbell
The Handfasting © 2015 by Glynnis Campbell
The Reiver © 2017 by Glynnis Campbell
The Outcast © 2015 by Glynnis Campbell

Cover design by Richard Campbell
Cover photo courtesy of Armstreet, makers of medieval clothing, http://www.armstreet.com. If you like the outfit, you can own it!
Formatting by Author E.M.S.

Glynnis Campbell – Publisher
P.O. Box 341144
Arleta, California 91331

ISBN-10: 1-63480-032-X
ISBN-13: 978-1-63480-032-7
Contact: glynnis@glynnis.net

Published in the United States of America

Scottish Brides...
Like heather, these lasses are beautiful yet strong, able to brave the harsh challenge of the Highlands and blossoming only for the most wise and worthy heroes.

THE SHIPWRECK
(A Warrior Maids of Rivenloch novella)
A Norse marauder ends up shipwrecked and at the mercy of a Pictish warrior maid with a grudge against Vikings and a little girl in need of a father.

THE HANDFASTING
(A Knights of de Ware novella)
A French knight betrothed to a Highland heiress falls in love with his spirited bride, then realizes he's been tricked into wedding the wrong sister.

THE REIVER
(A Medieval Outlaws novella)
A cattle-thieving Scottish lass chooses the wrong cow to steal and tangles with a laird who heals her heart and tames her wild ways.

THE OUTCAST
(A Scottish Lasses novella)
A broken Scots warrior believes nothing can mend the wounds of war until a young lass stumbles into his cottage and heals him with the most magical power of all—love.

OTHER BOOKS BY GLYNNIS CAMPBELL

THE WARRIOR MAIDS OF RIVENLOCH
The Shipwreck (novella)
A Yuletide Kiss (short story)
Lady Danger
Captive Heart
Knight's Prize

THE KNIGHTS OF DE WARE
The Handfasting (novella)
My Champion
My Warrior
My Hero

MEDIEVAL OUTLAWS
The Revier (novella)
Danger's Kiss
Passion's Exile
Desire's Ransom

THE SCOTTISH LASSES
The Outcast (novella)
MacFarland's Lass
MacAdam's Lass
MacKenzie's Lass

THE CALIFORNIA LEGENDS
Native Gold
Native Wolf
Native Hawk

CONTENTS

the shipwreck

A Warrior Maids of Rivenloch Novella

A Norse marauder ends up shipwrecked and at the mercy of a Pictish warrior maid with a grudge against Vikings and a little girl in need of a father.

DEDICATION

For Birthe Hansen,
my dear friend and rowing partner
on the Viking longship adventure

ACKNOWLEDGMENTS

With thanks to
Tore Neve the longship captain,
Alexander Jacobson for his books,
Karen Hansen, Anna Sofie Feilberg Hansen,
Hans Feilberg Hansen, Anders Holm, Inger Holm Hansen, Trine
Holm Hansen, Sia Holm Hansen, Ruth Hansen,
Anne Hansen, Ege Franzen, and Anna Marie Sass
for their hygge and hospitality,
Chris Hemsworth, and Scarlett Johansson

CHAPTER 1

The last ominous sound Brandr heard, before the icy ocean closed over his head, blocking out the roar of the storm and the crash of the waves, was the deep crack of his longship splitting apart.

The current dragged at his sealskin cloak and boots, pulling him down. But with his one still useful arm, he managed to claw his way to the surface. Gasping frosty air into his lungs as he broke through the waves, he blinked back the stinging saltwater, trying to see in the relentless black night. The ship's lanterns had gone out. No light came from the distant shore. Even the trusty stars were hidden behind thunderheads.

"Erik!" he bellowed. "Erik! Gunnarr! Haral—"

A gulp of seawater choked off his cries. He fought to stay afloat in the paralyzing cold, turning in the water, listening for his shipmates. But all he could hear was the howl of the wind, the pounding of the sea, and the splintering of wood as his ship was dashed against the rocks.

3

A flash of lightning split the sky, zigzagging down like Thor's avenging spear to blacken the timber of the mast. Before Brandr could wonder what he'd done to offend the god, thunder rocked the heavens, and the top of the mast exploded into sparks, igniting the square sail. For a moment it looked as if the dragon painted on the canvas was breathing fire.

By the light of the flaming sail, Brandr could see the extent of the damage to his ship. The hull was broken. Ropes snapped wildly in the shrieking wind. Chests and oars slid into the sea. And his crew...

Shuddering with cold and pain, fighting the tide, he called over the roaring of the storm until he was hoarse. He found four of his men. They were dead.

The rain eventually arrived to extinguish the fiery wreckage. Brandr—beaten by the storm, devastated by loss, and too exhausted to care what happened to him—used the last of his strength to climb atop the splintered prow of his ship and resigned himself to the whim of the gods.

Death was following him. It had already come for his wife and children. Now it had come for his men. Soon it would come for him. And as far as Brandr was concerned, it could have him.

"Stay close!" Avril called after Kimbery, shaking her head as the four-year-old raced ahead of her across the wet sand. Her intrepid daughter possessed insatiable curiosity, incurable wanderlust, and a stubborn will that left her deaf to her mother's warnings.

Not that there was much to warn her about. Here in their seaside home, they lived far out of everyone's way. No one would stumble across their stone cottage or cross their stretch of beach by accident. Their exile to the eastern shores had left them in a location that was remote, isolated...and far enough from her ancestral home of Rivenloch to satisfy the brothers who'd stolen it from her.

In the distance, Kimbery squealed as she bent over some treasure along the tide's edge—probably a pretty shell or a starfish washed ashore in last night's storm. Avril kicked off her boots and hefted up her basket. With any luck, the wild tempest had stirred up something edible from the sea.

The brothers who'd banished her had probably expected her to starve, her and her "bastard Viking spawn," as they called Kimbery. Certainly, her death would have been convenient for them.

But Avril hadn't obliged them.

As willful as her daughter, she'd persisted, refusing to die. The land was hostile to crops, but she'd adapted to it. She'd learned to fish, to dig for clams, to pry mussels from rock, to snare coneys, to raid seagull nests, to make broth from seaweed and pottage from oysters. She'd even traded a silver cloak pin to her closest neighbor for a ewe that had lost its lamb, so she had milk, butter, cheese, and wool for clothing. A stream emptied into the ocean a short distance from the cottage, giving her ample water for drinking and bathing, and trout for supper.

But none of it was easy. So when the weather turned violent as it had last night and the ocean's belly roiled, spewing its contents onto the beach, Avril considered it a gift from the sea. She might find a few stranded fish not yet picked apart by the gulls, a sizable clump of kelp, a useful shell, or even an odd tool or bit of line lost from a fishing boat.

Kimbery, of course, was convinced she'd unearth a mermaid's jewels or Poseidon's trident or an otter to keep for a pet. She'd learned to relish the flash of lightning and the crack of thunder that foretold a day of treasure-hunting on the beach.

The wee lass didn't know any different. But Avril was well aware of how wrong their life of scraping and scavenging was. If she thought too deeply about what had been taken from her—her maidenhood, her lands, a proper family and playmates for her daughter, and about the fact that she'd been groomed from birth, not to dwell in a hovel, but to command a sizable holding—she'd be filled with constant rage and an unquenchable thirst for vengeance.

But there was nothing she could do. Invading Northmen had left her with child and killed her father. And once he was dead, her four younger brothers, racked with jealousy over the favoritism their father had shown her as the rightful heir, declared Avril unfit to rule Rivenloch. All the years her father had spent training her to take over his command—schooling her in the law, teaching her to wield a sword, bringing her up to be a moral, fair, honest leader—had been wasted. She was sent into exile with her daughter and what little she could carry on her back. And not a soul in Rivenloch had had the courage to face her thieving brothers and come forward in her defense.

Still, not a day passed that she didn't think about winning it all back. It was only concern for her daughter's welfare that kept Avril from taking up her sword and marching boldly to the gates of Rivenloch to demand the return of her keep.

"Mama!" Kimbery cried, draping a piece of dark seaweed over her sun-bright curls and skipping along the sea foam. "I'm a selkie!"

She smiled. She often wondered if ocean-loving Kimbery might indeed be half-seal. It was the little girl's inventiveness that kept her own bitterness at bay and kept her fighting for survival. Sometimes Avril thought that being impregnated by a Viking berserker was the best thing that had ever happened to her.

She scanned the rocky tidepools as she walked toward the ocean, searching for periwinkles, glancing occasionally up at Kimbery to be sure she wasn't straying too far. The wee lass had a healthy respect for the sea, but the tide could be unpredictable and unforgiving.

The air was calm today, and the sky was an unchanging gray, but evidence of the storm littered the beach. Avril picked up a piece of driftwood and poked at a clump of kelp on the sand. A fat abalone was attached to one of the strands, and it would make a nice supper tonight. She cut it loose, plopping it into her basket. A small purple starfish with six legs was stuck to the kelp, too. Though it was inedible, she added it to the basket to show to Kimbery, knowing she'd like its color. Closer to the water, she found a few crabs, but their shells had been picked clean by the seabirds.

She glanced up. Kimbery was hunkered down beside a tiny crab on the sand, and when the tide rushed in to cover it, the lass shrieked and leaped up, running and giggling as the ocean chased her.

Avril was still grinning when her attention was caught by something floating off the rocky point that jutted into the sea. It looked like a substantial piece of wood, maybe a crate or part of a cart, something that might prove useful. As she gradually made her way toward the point, she collected a few mussels for pottage and a large clamshell suitable for a bowl.

"Mama!"

Avril narrowed her eyes at the wood bobbing in the water. What was it? Though one end appeared to be splintered, the other sides were finished. Maybe it was a broken chest or a table.

"Mama! Look what I found!"

"In a moment!" she called back, studying the piece as it was tossed by the current.

"Mama! It's my da!"

That got her attention. Avril whipped her head around and peered down the shoreline to where Kimbery was squatting beside a furry bulk on the sand.

It looked like a dead seal.

"See, Mama?"

Of course, Avril realized—Kimbery was pretending she was a selkie, so the dead seal must be her da. The lass had a vivid imagination. "I see!" A seal was indeed a good find. If it was freshly killed, its meat could keep their bellies full a long while. And she could make coats and slippers out of its fur. "I'll be right there! Don't touch it!"

A few more yards and she'd get a good look at whatever was floating off the point. If it wasn't worth salvaging, she'd leave it be and see what she could get off the dead seal.

A broad wave caught the wood and turned it on its side. The instant she saw the design, her heart dropped to the pit of her stomach. A great round knob rose above the water. Painted on its surface in hues of red and blue was the face of a snarling dragon. It was the masthead of a longship.

Time slowed as she dropped her basket and turned toward Kimbery.

"Nay!" she screamed.

She picked up her skirts and tried to race across the beach, but the air suddenly felt heavy, and the sand dragged at her heels. Kimbery seemed impossibly distant and far too close to the body that Avril could see now was not a dead seal, but the remains of a man.

The bloody images of the berserker attack were as clear and fresh as that day five years ago...

Wild-eyed, axe-wielding giants bursting through the gates of Rivenloch, roaring and foaming at the mouth, hacking at everything in their path, smashing pottery, splitting furniture, slicing flesh...

The hounds' yelps, cut off abruptly as their throats were slit...

The steward falling as his legs were cut out from under him...

A shrieking serving woman losing her arm...

One fleeing child axed in the back while another was trampled beneath heavy boots...

A young lass, frozen with fear, snatched up and carried off, never to be seen again...

It was happening again. The Northmen had returned. Avril staggered onto one knee.

Then she looked up at Kimbery, still yards away, and bit out a curse. She wouldn't let the bastards have her daughter. She was no longer the innocent lass she'd been five years ago who'd become a victim of rape. She was prepared for them this time. Clenching her jaw in determination, she scrambled to her feet again and hurtled forward across the sand.

At last she reached Kimbery, sweeping her into her arms and clutching her so tightly that the wee lass squealed in complaint.

"Shh!" She spun, searching the boulders and clumps of sea grass lining the shore. The longship must have crashed in the storm. But what had become of its crew? Where were the dead man's shipmates?

Everything seemed normal, undisturbed. Waves lapped at the beach, leaving arcs of foam. Gulls screed and soared overhead. Crabs skittered over the rocks. No strange footprints marred the virgin stretch of sand.

"Mama," Kimbery whimpered impatiently. "Put me down."

"Hush." Avril scoured the beach once more. The Vikings had come again. There was no mistaking the origin of the carved dragon's head. But they weren't here now. Either they'd bypassed her cottage and moved inland already, or their dead bodies would be washing ashore soon. But for now at least, it appeared she and Kimbery were safe.

"Maaaamaaa," Kimbery whined.

She let Kimbery slip to the ground. The lass immediately skipped over to the dead man.

"Don't touch him," Avril repeated.

Kimbery crouched a few feet away from him, resting her elbows on her knees and her chin in her hands, peering curiously into his face. "Is it my da?"

"Nay!" Avril replied, a little too vehemently, though she could see why the lass would think that. The man's face was hidden behind strands of long blond hair that was the same pale color as Kimbery's. He was covered in a cloak of seal fur, and his sealskin boots looked much like theirs. But there the resemblance ended. He was a giant, a head taller than any man she knew. His shoulders were broad and his feet huge. A silver cuff in a dragon design encircled one thick wrist, and hanging around his wide neck from a leather thong was a hammer of silver with foreign runes carved into it.

Thank God he was dead. His kind—the invaders from the North—were bloodthirsty, vicious, ruthless murderers.

She shuddered. Despite the value of all that silver, she had no desire to loot the corpse. She didn't want to touch a Viking at all. Then she frowned in distaste. What *would* she do with the body? She didn't want it rotting on her shore. She'd have to bury it, she supposed. It was a pity it *wasn't* a beached seal. That much meat would have seen them through the winter.

Kimbery, flouting Avril's instructions, picked up a club of driftwood and began nudging the man's bloody shoulder. Avril shook her head. The lass might not openly disobey her by touching the dead man, but even at four years old, she had an annoying habit of stretching the rules as far as she could.

"Wake up!" the lass shouted into his unresponsive face.

"He's dead, Kimmie."

"Nay, he's not."

"Aye, he is," she said, though Kimbery's yelling was fit to wake the dead.

Kimbery curled her determined lip and nudged him again.

Avril raised a sardonic brow. Maybe she *could* cook him up for supper. There was probably a few hundred pounds of muscle on his large frame.

Then again, Viking meat was probably tough and foul-tasting.

"Wake! Up!" Kimbery punctuated each word with a hard poke of her driftwood.

"Kimbery, leave the poor—"

Then he groaned.

Avril froze. Shite. Kimbery was right. He wasn't dead.

"See, Mama? I told you he was—"

She snatched the lass up so fast, the little girl's head snapped backward.

The man groaned again. Avril snagged the driftwood out of Kimbery's hand and held it in front of her like a weapon.

Then Kimbery began to wail, which caused the man to rouse.

"Sh-sh-sh-sh-sh." Avril bounced the lass on her left hip, hoping to quiet her, to no avail. Damn! What would she do if the man regained consciousness? She wished she'd brought her sword. He'd swat away her driftwood club as easily as a piece of straw.

She could run. If she hurried, she could make it to her cottage with Kimbery before the man found his feet. But that would only delay him. Eventually he'd come and knock down her door, probably with one solid punch of his oversized fist.

Kimbery, enraged at being thwarted and oblivious to the danger, squirmed out of Avril's grip just as the man's eyes fluttered open.

"Run!" she screamed at Kimbery, who was already tearing off toward the cottage in fury.

Avril turned back to the man. She just glimpsed the ice-blue hue of his opening eyes before she swung around with the driftwood, clubbing him in the head as hard as she could.

CHAPTER 2

Avril was glad Kimbery hadn't witnessed her mother clouting a helpless castaway.

She winced as she used the pointy end of the driftwood to cautiously sweep aside the unconscious man's hair. Blood tricked down his temple where she'd struck him, but his pulse still beat steadily in his throat.

Thank God she hadn't killed him. True, Northmen were degenerate and insidious and evil. But slaying an unarmed man went against everything her father had taught her about honor.

Now what was she going to do with him? He might wake again at any moment. She couldn't keep clubbing him. But she had to keep him subdued. And she had to get him out of sight.

She didn't really want him in her home, but she didn't have much of a choice. She couldn't afford to have him roaming loose. At least in the cottage, she could keep her eye on him.

Dropping the driftwood, she separated out one long strand of tough kelp caught on his boot and wrapped it around his ankles several times. She wrapped another thick strand around his wrists, noting that his left forearm was bruised and swollen.

She scowled. It looked like he'd broken his arm. Then she remembered he was the enemy and it didn't matter to her if he'd broken his arm. She only hoped the bonds would hold until she reached the cottage and could tie him up with something more substantial.

Dragging him up the beach by his ankles was harder than she expected. His legs were leaden, and in his waterlogged clothing, he was as heavy as a walrus. With every backward step, the wet sand sucked at her feet, hampering her progress.

Halfway up the shore, she stopped to rest. Kimbery was safe now. She'd slammed the door behind her, and Avril could hear the little girl's muffled wailing coming from inside the cottage.

While she caught her breath, Avril wiped the sweat from her forehead and took a moment to study her captive. A light growth of beard covered his chin, but he looked considerably younger than the savage who'd raped her five years ago. His face was not unhandsome. His skin was darkened by the sun and salted by the sea, but he lacked the heavy lines of age. His nose was straight, his cheekbones were unbroken, and his brow was strong. If his size didn't give him away, the brief glimpse of his bright blue eyes confirmed he was a Northman.

She blew out a long breath and looked out to sea. In the distance, she could see refuse bobbing atop the waves and drifting toward the shore. Soon, splinters of his ship would make landfall, along with broken oars, bits of rigging, and, she thought with a shudder, the waterlogged corpses of his shipmates.

It took every bit of Brandr's willpower to play dead. He still couldn't believe the sweet-faced maiden had clubbed him with a cudgel of driftwood. But he didn't want her to club him again, not while he didn't have the strength to fight her. So he remained quiet as she began dragging him across the sand.

His head throbbed where she'd hit him, his muscles ached, and the deep-seated, dull pain in his left forearm told him he'd probably broken it.

It was still his heart that hurt the most. In the past year, he'd lost everything...his wife, his children, his ship, his men. It must be some cruel trick of the gods to keep him alive to endure such anguish.

After a while, the woman, panting heavily from her exertions, dropped his feet onto the sand and stopped to catch her breath. Even with his eyes closed, he could feel her gaze upon him like the searing touch of the sun.

What did she intend? She must not mean to kill him. Otherwise, he'd be dead by now. He figured he was somewhere along the Pictish coast, though he wasn't sure where or how he'd washed ashore. Until he got his bearings and regained his strength, he was better off feigning unconsciousness.

Which was even more challenging when the woman resumed dragging him, this time up a stone pathway and over the threshold of a cottage, jarring his ribs and banging his skull on the hard rock.

At least it was warm indoors. He thought his bones would never thaw. He heard the comforting crackle of a fire and smelled pottage simmering on the hearth. And then he heard something that wrenched at his memory—the quiet sobbing of a child.

Unbidden, the faces of Sten and Asta appeared in his mind's eye, and unbearable pain seized him as he realized he'd never see his children or his wife Inga again. The last time he'd seen them alive was when he'd set sail on a raiding voyage with his brothers, Ragnarr and Halfdan. By the time he returned, his family had been dead two months, stolen from him by a sickness that had swept through the village. His brothers' families had succumbed as well, and even though they'd never said so, he was sure his brothers regretted going on that last long raid with him.

"Shh, Kimmie, it's all right now," the woman murmured in Pictish. It was a language Brandr had learned as a boy from the slaves his father had brought home.

"You hurt me," the little girl sobbed.

"I didn't mean to hurt you, wee one," the woman replied. "But I'm very proud of you for running home. You did just the right thing. You were very brave. And you ran very fast."

The pain in Brandr's chest deepened. The woman might speak a different language, but her motherly voice reminded him of his precious Inga.

The little girl came closer, her voice hitching with spent tears. "Will my...my da...live with us now?"

"He's not your da."

"He is."

"Nay."

"Aye."

"Nay, he's not," the mother replied testily as she began cutting the bonds around his ankles. "Why do you keep saying that?"

"He *is* my da. He *is*," the little girl insisted, starting to cry again.

"Kimmie, I've told you a hundred times. Your da is dead."

"That's what you said about *him*." Brandr imagined the little girl was sticking out a pouty lip the way Asta always did when she knew she was right.

The woman, unable to come up with a suitable reply, changed the subject. "Look in the chest beside the bed and see if you can find Finn's leash."

Leash. Leash? That didn't bode well. What was she up to?

He didn't find out until it was too late. As she started sawing at the kelp bonds around his wrists, she wrenched his broken arm, and the pain was so severe that he blacked out.

When Brandr awoke again, he was bound in a leather collar and leashed tightly by his neck through an iron ring attached to the wall. His sealskin cloak was missing, leaving him sitting in his tunic, trousers, and boots. His bound legs stretched nearly to the hearth, his arms were secured to his sides by a rope around his midsection, and his wrists were tied before him.

Fury surged through his veins. By Thor! He'd come here to conquer, not to be conquered. How could he have wound up a prisoner—the prisoner of a woman?

While his rage simmered, he perused the room through narrowed eyelids. His cloak had been hung on a peg near the fire. And his captors supped at a table across the chamber, unaware that he'd roused.

He could see why the little girl thought he was her father. They shared the same blond hair. The girl was younger than his daughter, but in her dust-colored kirtle and bare feet, she reminded him of Asta.

Though he hated to admit it, the mother was breathtaking. Her hair, an intoxicating color of golden mead and ruby wine combined, hung in thick waves down her back, and her skin was as golden and radiant as flame. Her face was artfully sculpted, with generous lips and finely arched brows, and her snugly-laced, faded blue kirtle revealed pleasing womanly curves.

But this was the same lovely temptress who'd clubbed him, dragged him home, and tied him up like a dog. He wasn't about to be fooled by her pretty face.

He studied the stone cottage, which was well-kept and welcoming. Its curious furnishings appeared to be made mostly of scavenge from the sea. Odd pieces of driftwood were fitted together to form stools, and candles were set in holders made of mussel shells. A bit of fishing net tacked onto one wall held hair combs carved out of abalone, and on a shelf fashioned out of an oar sat an assortment of clamshell bowls and dishes. A fishing pole and a net were propped against the hearth. But it was what was leaned against the corner that interested him most.

It was a nobleman's sword, a magnificent blade. Its pommel was set with gems, the grip was wrapped in seasoned leather, and the guard was carved with designs that intersected, weaving complex knots. The sword looked well cared for. The steel was highly polished, the edge keen. He wondered where the man who owned the weapon was.

"Mama," the little girl said, picking up her clamshell bowl, "my da wants some, too."

"He's not your da, Kimmie, and he's not even..." She ended on a gasp as she glanced his way.

It was too late to feign sleep.

She rose suddenly, knocking over her stool. "Awake."

"He's hungry, Mama."

Brandr swallowed, and his throat clicked. He didn't feel like eating, but he was as parched as winter tundra.

The little girl started toward him with her bowl, but her mother hauled her back.

"Listen to me," she said sternly. "He is *not* your da. He's a bad man, a *very* bad man. Promise me you won't go near him."

"But—"

"Promise me, Kimbery."

Kimbery sighed unhappily and put her bowl back on the table. "I promise."

A very bad man. Brandr supposed he was that. After all, a good man would never have deserted his wife and children to go a-Viking.

Avril righted her overturned stool. Then she picked up Kimbery and sat her atop it. "You stay here."

She straightened and took a steadying breath. The Northman looked much more menacing now that he was awake. She'd already decided he was astonishingly handsome, but his fierce frown made him look dangerous as well. She glanced at the hound collar and leash, hoping they'd hold. She'd managed to keep their great wolfhound, Finn, at heel on that leash until he'd died last year. But the man probably outweighed the hound three times over. And she'd seen, once she removed his cloak, that he was all muscle and bone. She shivered at the thought of all that male strength.

Still, if her father had taught her one thing, it was never to show fear to the enemy. So she raised her chin and confronted him with a stern scowl. "You. Can you understand me?"

He glowered at her through the strands of his hair, but didn't reply.

"Your ship." She pounded one fist into her palm, then exploded her fingers outward to indicate a crash. "How many men were on board?"

He continued to glare at her.

She counted on her fingers. "How many?"

He could understand her. She knew he could. Hell, even Kimbery could understand what she was asking. But he stubbornly refused to answer.

She narrowed her eyes at him. "Damned Viking," she sneered, biting out a word he'd surely recognize.

His lip curled slowly into a grim smile.

An uneasy tremor slithered up her spine, but she refused to let him frighten her. The man was chained to the wall, after all. She had the upper hand. He was at her mercy. She was in control. She'd been trained for command, and she knew how to wield it. If only he wouldn't stare at her with those piercing blue eyes.

She picked up the fireplace poker. It felt good in her grip, like a weapon. "I know your kind," she told him, smacking the poker against her palm in threat. "You're not the first Viking I've met."

His gaze slipped to Kimbery, as if he understood her perfectly and had divined her entire sordid history. Avril's nostrils flared, and her cheeks grew hot. She leaned forward out of Kimbery's hearing to snarl under her breath. "That's right. After slaughtering half my people—men, women, and children—one of your kind took me by force and left me with a babe." She licked her lip, inventing a more satisfactory end to the story. "When I was through with him, he was unable to breed again."

A long silence followed as he stared at her, his face expressionless. She decided he must not be able to understand her after all.

She backed away, turning to jab at the coals on the hearth. "How unlucky for you, Viking," she said with a self-satisfied smirk. "You come to invade my land and end up shipwrecked on my beach. Maybe that will teach you savages to stay where you belong."

Brandr creased his brow. Where he belonged. He didn't belong anywhere. He had no home, not anymore. The place he'd once called home was full of painful memories, and he had no wish to return there.

Had he come to invade her land? Aye. Had he meant to plunder it? Absolutely. But he'd come to settle here, not to wage war. He only meant to kill if he had to. He wasn't a savage. Of course he'd taken slaves before. But none of his men brandished their weapons without good cause. And none would ever bed a woman against her will.

The Vikings who'd come before must have been berserkers. Such men ingested peculiar mushrooms that made them crazed and violent, driven to mow down everything in their path. To Brandr, they were worse than wild animals.

"I expect your shipmates will be washing ashore soon," the woman mused, replacing the poker. She gazed into the fire, adding sardonically, "I hope I have enough leashes."

Brandr tightened his jaw. He doubted any of his shipmates were alive. No one should have survived that storm. The fact that he'd been spared was proof that Loki, that mischief-making god, wasn't finished torturing him.

He didn't know what had happened to his brothers' ships. The tempest had roared to life halfway through the voyage, and the three vessels had become quickly separated. Even if Halfdan and Ragnarr somehow miraculously managed to sail into the storm and come out the other side, it was unlikely they'd end up on the same stretch of the winding Pictish coast.

"Meanwhile," the woman considered, "what do I do with you?"

She gave him a thorough perusal that ordinarily would have been flattering. But where most women gazed at Brandr as if imagining exactly what they wanted to do with him, she looked as if she hadn't the slightest idea.

"I could turn you over to the lawmen," she murmured. "If you're lucky, they'll hang you quick."

He doubted that. If berserkers had wreaked havoc here, the villagers would more likely stand in line to exact revenge on a Viking trussed up for their pleasure. They'd delight in tearing him to pieces.

"I can't keep you here," she said to herself.

She was right about that, he thought, staring straight ahead, betraying no emotion. She damned well *couldn't* keep him here. He'd allow no one to keep him on a leash, least of all a puny Pictish lass.

The woman continued to contemplate his fate aloud while, behind her, her daughter quietly inched her stool forward.

"The last thing I need," the woman said, "is a third mouth to feed."

A third. So she lived alone here with her daughter. His gaze went to the sword propped in the corner. Then whose was that? Maybe, he thought morosely, it had belonged to the *last* man she'd tied up in her cottage.

The little girl picked up the stool beneath her, toddled a few steps closer, and sat back down.

The woman sighed peevishly. "I should have tossed you back into the sea while I had the chance."

The little girl stared intently at Brandr as she tiptoed forward again with the stool.

"It would probably be a kindness to kill you," the woman muttered, "before someone with less mercy finds you here."

The little girl took two more cautious steps forward and sat down an arm's-length behind her mother, watching him fearlessly.

"And it'd be no less than you deser—" She whirled and almost tripped over the little girl. "Kimbery!" She glanced back at him, blushing, then turned to confront her wayward daughter. "I told you to stay."

"I did stay. See?" She pointed to the stool beneath her, blinking in all innocence.

The woman growled in frustration. Then a strange thing happened. The little girl flashed Brandr a conspiratorial grin, and, of their own accord, his lips curved slightly in answer. It was his first genuine smile in almost a year.

"Mama," Kimbery said sweetly, "I don't want my pottage. You can give it to my da."

The woman spoke between clenched teeth. "Once and for all, Kimbery, he is *not*—"

"Your mother's right," Brandr interjected. "I'm not your da. I'm a bad man, a *very* bad man, and you should stay away."

Avril's jaw dropped. Damn the Viking! He did speak her language, which meant he could understand her perfectly well. "You!" she spat in annoyance, at a loss for words. "You...stop speaking to my daughter."

He did. But his compliance didn't keep her from feeling suddenly threatened. She didn't know why. After all, he was bound, injured, and at her mercy. Still, that he'd been able to deceive her troubled her greatly. And the fact he was warning Kimbery away didn't fit with her assessment of him as a depraved killer. His manner—part devious, part disarming—was definitely unnerving. And she hated to be unnerved.

"Kimmie," she said over her shoulder, "go to bed."

"But I'm not sleepy."

"Go to bed. Now."

Kimbery stuck out her bottom lip, and then flounced off the stool and stomped off, whimpering under her breath.

Avril took a moment to compose herself, and then turned to him, crossing her arms over her chest. "I want some answers, and I want them—"

"Twenty."

"What?"

"Twenty." At her furrowed brow, he added, "You asked how many men were aboard my ship."

She swallowed hard. The berserkers had had at least twice that number. Still, twenty was nineteen more men than she could handle at the moment.

"Where were you headed?"

He shrugged.

"You don't know?" That she didn't believe. The Northmen were notoriously good navigators.

"I didn't care."

His words chilled her. But she supposed she should have expected as much. Barbarians like him scoured the seas, wreaking havoc wherever they landed, unmindful of the devastation they left behind, the people they killed, the lives they destroyed.

"I'd wager you care now," she said with grim threat. "You made a grave error, Viking, landing on my shore."

The doubtful arch of his brow was admittedly subtle. But Avril recognized scorn when she saw it. Men had always questioned her strength, her judgment, and her skill with a blade. At one time, it had infuriated her. Five years ago, she might have succumbed to the impulse to draw her sword to show him just how capable she was.

But she'd learned to rein in her temper. The last time she'd drawn a blade impulsively, she'd wound up at the mercy of a berserker. She wouldn't let it happen again. Besides, what satisfaction could be derived from turning a sword on a helpless captive?

He was staring at her again with his penetrating eyes. She didn't think she'd ever seen eyes so blue—as blue as a summer sky, nay, a robin's egg. Rattled, she turned aside to add another log to the fire.

"I think your arm is broken," she mumbled. Why she'd told him that, she didn't know. After all, it didn't matter. She wasn't about to fix it for him.

"It's a wonder my head isn't broken," he said with a humorless smirk.

She blushed at the reminder of her unchivalrous blow and picked up the poker again, eager to change the subject. "How is it you know my language?"

"I learned it from a Pict slave."

She clenched her teeth. A slave? She jabbed at the glowing coals, but refused to rise to the bait. Maybe she should turn *him* into a slave.

As if he'd read her mind, he asked, "What do you intend to do with me?"

She'd been asking herself that same question all morning. For the moment, she'd hold him hostage. If any of his men turned up alive, she might be able to bargain for her safety with his life. But she wasn't sure there were survivors. Even if there were, there was no telling whether he was of any value to them. The Northmen didn't seem to have the same regard for life as her people did.

"I haven't decided yet," she said.

"If you're going to kill me," he growled, "get it over with."

She frowned. Kill him? In cold blood? Obviously, he knew nothing about chivalry. She straightened with pride, planting the poker between her feet like a blade. "I can't do that. Unlike you, my sense of honor prevents me from slaying unarmed men."

He lifted a brow in mockery. "Give me a blade then," he suggested.

Avril gave him a sardonic smirk. She wasn't so foolhardy as to think she could easily triumph over a gargantuan Northman. But she didn't appreciate his insulting attitude. "I may be honorable, but I'm not soft in the head."

He half-smiled. "You look soft to me."

Her composure slipped, but only for an instant. "I assure you, you wouldn't be the first man I sent limping from the field of battle."

His eyes narrowed suggestively. "And you wouldn't be the first woman I laid out flat on her back."

CHAPTER 3

Brandr regretted his words as soon as he spoke them. He'd forgotten she'd been the victim of rape.

She winced as if he'd struck her, and then recovered so quickly he thought he'd imagined her hurt. "No doubt," she coldly replied.

For some absurd reason, he suddenly wanted to defend himself. He wanted to tell her that he wasn't a berserker. He'd never killed a man without just cause. And he'd never forced himself upon a woman. True, he'd bedded more than his share of eager wenches in his youth, but only at their invitation. And once he'd taken a wife...

Then he gave his head a mental shake. What was he thinking? It didn't matter what the woman thought of him. They were foes. She probably intended to kill him anyway. If she'd been exposed to berserkers from the North—the kind that violated women, murdered priests, and slaughtered children—she had every cause to want him dead.

And yet there were qualities about her—her independence, her intelligence, her patience with her daughter, the way she talked about honor—that told him she might not kill him needlessly. She might listen to reason.

That was why he'd volunteered the truth about his men and his ship. His fate rested in her hands at the moment. If he gave her cause for mistrust, she wouldn't hesitate to slay him. He'd do the same in her position.

But if he endeared himself to her, if he made her look at him, not as a Viking, but as a man, she'd have a harder time killing him...and maybe he'd buy himself time to overpower her and escape.

"You know, I'm not really the savage you think I am," he confided.

She ignored him, setting aside the poker and going into the kitchen.

"I had a family," he called after her, "a daughter like yours." He silently cursed as his voice caught on the words.

She froze for a moment, and then cleared her empty shell bowl from the table.

He added, "I, too, would have protected her from men like me."

She paused again, then sighed and picked up the little girl's half-eaten pottage. "It's cold," she grumbled, approaching to give him the bowl, "but it'll fill your belly."

Pain seared his cracked forearm as he lifted the bowl with his bound hands to tip the contents into his mouth. But it was better than starving to death. He finished the pottage in three gulps, and then lowered his hands to rest them limply on his lap, letting the bowl slip through his fingers and onto the floor.

The woman returned to her fire-tending. Her face glowed golden as she gazed into the flames, and her hair shone with reflected firelight. "You said you *had* a daughter." She asked casually, "What happened to her?"

It had been almost a year, but the wound still felt new and raw. "She died," he said flatly. Just speaking the words aloud hurt.

The air grew still. For a long while, she didn't speak.

Finally she asked, "How?"

He swallowed down the knot of pain in his throat. He didn't want to talk about it. He didn't know this woman. She was his enemy. Why should he tell her anything? And yet something compelled him to speak. Maybe it was the soft encouragement in her voice. Maybe it was the dewy compassion in her eyes. Maybe it was the fact that he had nothing more to lose. "Plague."

Her forehead creased, and she propped the poker against the hearth. "And her mother?"

His cruel mind conjured up Inga's precious face. "Dead," he told her woodenly. "My daughter. My wife. My son. All dead."

He heard the woman's soft gasp, but she had no words of comfort for him. There weren't any. There was nothing anyone could say to bring back his family.

After a bit, she murmured, "But you survived."

"Oh, aye." Bitter regret twisted his mouth as he sneered, "I was lucky. I was at sea."

The woman's brow furrowed. She leaned forward almost imperceptibly. For a curious instant, as she looked at him with liquid brown eyes full of empathy, he imagined she meant to touch his hand in solace.

But he'd never be sure, because at that moment, the little girl peered around the doorway. "Mama," she sang out cheerfully, "I'm finished sleeping."

"Kimbery!" the woman cried, coloring and rising briskly.

Avril felt the way she had when her father had caught her kissing the stable boy. Which was ridiculous. After all, she'd done nothing to be ashamed of. But a strange guilt lingered in the air. She'd almost reached out to comfort the Northman. And she didn't know why.

Flustered, she scooped up the empty bowl and turned to face Kimbery.

"I'm all better now, Mama," the wee lass said, using her sweetest, most cunning voice.

Avril sighed and shook her head, then carried the bowl into the kitchen.

Kimbery's wiles left Avril with a dilemma. Avril needed to search the beach to see if any more Northmen had made landfall. But it was too risky taking Kimbery with her. If there were shipwreck survivors, she didn't want to put her daughter in harm's way. And if there weren't, she didn't need her little girl seeing a dozen half-eaten corpses washing up on her shore.

She needed Kimbery to stay in the cottage. But she didn't trust the wee lass with the man she kept insisting was her da. He might very well talk her into setting him free.

She had a choice then. She could either tie up her daughter, or she could drug the Northman.

The decision took an instant.

"You must be thirsty," she called to him.

She needn't have worried he'd taste the opium powder she put in his mead. He gulped it down eagerly and wanted more. While she kept Kimbery occupied churning sheep's milk into butter, he began to get drowsy. By the time his suspicions were aroused, it was too late.

"What'd y' put...in th' drink?" he asked, slurring the words.

"Nothing poisonous," she told him. "Don't fret. You'll just sleep for a while."

With his last bit of strength, he growled at her in impotent anger, and then he slumped against the beam.

"G'night, Da," Kimbery called merrily as she plunged the dasher up and down in the wooden churn.

Avril swirled her cloak over her shoulders. "Kimmie, I'm going down to the beach. I need you to stay here and keep churning."

She nodded.

"Stay away from the man. I'll be back soon."

"Shh," she whispered. "Da's sleeping. Don't wake him up."

Avril glanced at the softly snoring Viking, who looked far

less threatening in slumber. His scowl was gone. His muscles were lax. His mouth fell open like Kimbery's when she was sleeping. With his broad shoulders, his strong jaw, and his breathtaking eyes, he was truly one of the most attractive men she'd ever seen. Indeed, she could almost imagine him, not as a treacherous Northman, but as a little girl's father. Almost.

On her way to the beach, Avril grabbed the sharpened spade from the garden. It would serve to either bury the dead or defend her from the living.

It was midday by the time she returned to the cottage. She'd found no bodies or evidence of survivors, just a few splintered planks from his longship. A lot of driftwood, however, had washed ashore from the tempest, enough to keep their hearth burning all winter. It would take more than one trip to bring it all home.

To her surprise, when she dropped her first burden at the threshold and pushed open the door to check on Kimbery, the little girl was still sitting dutifully at her post, churning butter. But then Avril glanced over at the snoring Northman. Kimbery's stuffed cloth doll was tucked into the crook of his arm.

"Kimbery," she chided.

"He was lonely," the little girl explained.

Avril shook her head. Kimbery was probably right. The man had lost his shipmates, his wife, and his children. She couldn't imagine how awful that must be. If she lost Kimbery...

It was too awful to contemplate. Her daughter was all she had now.

She took the lid off the churn to show Kimbery how all her hard work had magically separated the cream. She poured the buttermilk off into a small cask and wrapped the lump of butter into a piece of dried kelp.

But then she needed to think up a new task to keep Kimbery

occupied while she collected the rest of her scavenge. She plucked a small piece of cool charcoal from the fire and gave it to the little girl, along with the pale, flat slate they used for writing.

"Why don't you practice your letters?" she suggested. Avril's father had insisted Avril learn to read so she'd be better able to manage Rivenloch. Avril was determined to pass the skill on to her daughter.

Kimbery picked up the charcoal and, pressing her lips together in concentration, drew a straight vertical line.

"I'm going out again," Avril told her. "I'll see what you've written when I come back."

It took three more treks to collect the store of driftwood. Satisfied with her haul, which she stacked beside the cottage, she dusted off her skirts and opened the door.

"Look, Mama!" Kimbery squealed, hopping down from her stool. "Look what I made!"

Avril studied the slate. Kimbery had printed the letters D and A, and beneath was a primitive sketch of their prisoner, bound with rope, with her doll nestled in one arm.

Avril wanted to be perturbed, but it was admittedly a decent drawing for a four-year-old. "That's very good, Kimmie. Now why don't you draw a picture of a starfish?"

"Nay!" she said, covering the slate with her arms to keep Avril from wiping it clean. "I want to show him."

"But he's sleeping."

"He'll wake up."

Avril wondered. She hadn't put that much powder in his drink—certainly not much more than she did on occasions when her monthly courses became unbearable—but opium could be risky.

His arm looked awful. It was still swollen, and the skin of his forearm had a bluish cast. If he'd been someone she cared about, she would have set it and made him a splint so it would heal straight. But it seemed like a waste of time and effort when she wasn't even sure she was going to let him live, let alone recover from his injuries.

As it turned out, he slept through Kimbery's afternoon nap and their abalone supper. When Kimbery crept into bed with a huge yawn, he was still sleeping. And he hadn't awakened when Avril blew out the candles and made her way to bed.

But in the middle of the night, she was roused by the sound of scuffling in the next room, and she crept out to investigate, a dagger in her hand.

By the dim light of the banked fire, she saw the Northman beginning to wake. His movements were sluggish, and his eyelids flagged as he struggled to sit upright.

She moved forward to get a closer look, hunkering down beside him.

When his gaze alit on her, a look of wonder came over his face. His eyes lit up with pleasure and relief. "Inga," he breathed.

She frowned and opened her mouth, intending to correct him. But when she saw the affection in his eyes, she found she didn't have the heart.

"Inga." He smiled, his eyes twinkling.

She gulped, reluctant to break the fragile thread of his happy delusion.

He reached up with his bound hands and took her chin in gentle fingers. Before she realized what he was doing, he tilted his head and captured her lips with his.

For an instant she froze, stunned. Swiftly, the softness of his mouth, the warmth of his touch, the sweetness of his kiss enthralled her, and she melted into his welcoming embrace. He tasted of the sea and adventure and passion. And for one sliver of a moment in time, it was possible to believe he had feelings for her.

Then she remembered who he was and that he'd called her by another woman's name.

With a soft cry of resistance, she tore free, covering her mutinous mouth with the back of one trembling hand and holding her dagger out before her.

Oblivious to her blade, he mumbled something in his own tongue then and, with a peaceful sigh, slumped back into slumber.

Avril scrambled back, scrubbing at her lips. God's eyes! How could she have let him kiss her? He was a Northman—a savage, a barbarian, a dog. His kind were rapists and plunderers. Shite, she should have killed him while she had the chance.

Yet even though she steeled her heart against him, his taste lingered on her lips, taunting her. Returning to bed, she found it impossible to get back to sleep as unsavory memories rose to the surface of her thoughts.

It had been a long time since she'd been kissed by a man. And she'd never been kissed so tenderly.

Though she'd tried to deny it, rape had left her damaged. The loss of power, the helplessness had cut her deeply. For a long while afterwards, she hadn't been able to endure a man's glance, much less his touch. She'd wanted to crawl away in defeat, to hide in shame and lick her wounds.

But she knew that would have meant her rapist had won and that she'd bear those scars the rest of her life. So instead, she'd decided to deal with the trauma the same way she handled falling off a horse or being knocked down in a swordfight.

She'd faced her fears, diving headfirst back into the fray. Though she wasn't particularly proud of her rash behavior now, she'd begun bedding men indiscriminately, forcing them to submit to her will, enjoying a heady triumph when they surrendered beneath her. Eventually, she'd overcome her feelings of powerlessness and vulnerability.

It appalled her now to think of the men she'd seduced and cast away. On the other hand, when she'd finally realized that she was pregnant, not one of them had come forward to claim the babe and salvage her honor.

Of course, after she gave birth to a fair-haired girl who was obviously the offspring of a Viking, she was shunned by all. She'd had to face the hard truth—she'd never find a man willing to play father to a Viking's child and husband to a woman stripped of her title, her land, and her wealth.

She'd shut off that part of her that longed for family, friends, and love, hidden it away behind the locked door to her heart.

But that kiss...that kiss had turned the key in the door and stirred feelings in her she'd forgotten—feelings of tenderness, affection, and hope. And it was a long while before her restless emotions let her drift off to sleep.

Brandr wandered all night in the land between waking and sleeping. He wasn't sure what was real and what he dreamed. But now morning had arrived, and his body couldn't have felt more substantial to him. His tongue was stuck to the roof of his mouth. His eyes were gummed shut. His hands were numb.

She'd drugged him. He remembered that much. The mead she'd given him had been laced with something that had sent him into a hallucination-riddled oblivion.

If only it had left him there...

Sensing someone near, he cracked open one eyelid. In the dim light, he could see the little blonde girl crouched beside him with an empty chamberpot, studying his face.

"Kimmie!" her mother shouted, startling the child. "Get away from him!"

The little girl did as she was told, dropping the chamberpot beside him with a loud clank. Then she crossed her arms importantly over her chest and said something she'd probably heard before from her mother. "If you can't take good care of your pets, you can't keep them."

"He's not a—," she said, snagging the little girl's hand to drag her back. "I told you, Kimmie, he's a bad man."

Brandr opened both eyes now. Even mussed from slumber, the woman was lovely. Tendrils of hair had pulled loose from her braid and framed her face like seaweed draped artfully on a sandy shore. Beneath her kirtle, her rumpled white underdress was untied at the throat, revealing the subtle curve of her bosom. And her sleep-swollen lips...

He frowned. A strange memory tugged at his brain. Had he...kissed the woman?

Her fleeting glance and the guilt in her eyes confirmed his suspicion. He *had* kissed her. But when? And why?

Her gaze drifted and settled upon his lap, and suddenly he wondered if he'd done more than just kiss her. Had he taken liberties with her that he couldn't recall?

"Kimbery," she said, continuing to stare with discomfiting boldness, "bring Mama her dagger."

His breath caught. Her dagger? What did she mean to do? Surely she wouldn't...cut anything off of him in front of her daughter. Would she? He tried to ask her what she intended, but his mouth was too dry to speak.

Once she had the dagger in her hand, she approached him, and he drew his legs back defensively.

"Listen," she confided softly so her daughter wouldn't hear. "I'm going to cut your wrists free. But if you try anything, I swear I'll plunge this dagger into your throat."

He looked down at his hands, resting on his lap. No wonder he couldn't feel them. The ropes were cutting into his swollen wrists, and the fingers of his left hand were blue.

"Do you understand?" she said, narrowing flinty eyes at him.

He nodded.

She sliced him free, and he bit back a groan of pain as sensation suddenly stabbed into his fingers like a thousand agonizing needles. He felt the blood drain from his face as he fought to stay conscious.

"Kimmie, bring me a cup of water, please."

The little girl hurried to comply. Why the woman was showing him mercy, he didn't know. Perhaps it was only that she didn't want his death on her conscience. But he gladly accepted the water as she tipped the cup back for him, coughing as he drank too swiftly.

Whether she would have actually slit his throat in front of the little girl, he didn't know, but he wasn't about to put her to the test.

"Kimbery," she called over her shoulder, her blade resting against his neck. "I need you to wait in bed until I call you."

"But, Mama, I want to help, too."

"Not yet. In a moment."

Brandr didn't like the sound of that. What did the woman want to do that she didn't want her daughter to see?

"Promise?" the little girl asked.

"I promise. Now wait there till I call you."

The lass skipped off, and Brandr was left alone with the woman.

She stared at her blade where it contacted his throat, muttering irritably to herself. "I should just let you go on suffering. God knows you would have shown me no mercy." She glanced down at his misshapen arm. "If I do this for you," she said, sighing, "if I put you out of your misery—"

By Odin, she meant to kill him! His warrior instincts took over, and despite her menacing blade, despite the wrenching pain in his arms, with the last of his strength, he reached up with his good hand and roughly seized her wrist, giving it a sharp flick and sending the dagger clattering across the floor.

For an instant, their eyes met, and he saw true panic there as he gained the upper hand. But his advantage was short-lived. In the next breath, she drove her free fist forward and punched him hard in the nose.

CHAPTER 4

The Viking instantly lost his grip on her, and Avril tumbled back onto her hindquarters, cradling her bruised knuckles. What was wrong with the man? Hadn't she said she was going to put him out of his misery? The ungrateful wretch!

He was subdued now, and blood dripped from one nostril. She hadn't hit him hard enough to break his nose. Indeed, she hadn't knocked him out, only stunned him. She'd have to work quickly before he took it into his head to fight off her good intentions again.

She carefully moved his injured arm flat on his lap and pushed up his sleeve to examine it. The bone looked fairly straight, though it was hard to tell from the swelling. She ran her fingertips gently and swiftly along the edges of his forearm to check for breaks.

Nothing poked through the flesh, so it wasn't too serious. But halfway between his elbow and his wrist, there was a bulge where the bone had cracked and slipped sideways. She'd have to pull it and put it back into alignment.

Why she was showing him any kindness, she didn't know. Maybe it was because he'd lost his wife and children. Maybe it was because he was alone, abandoned, a castaway like her. Maybe it was the way he'd kissed her last night.

He was coming around again, sniffing back the blood trickling from his nose. She'd have to move fast. Seizing his thick wrist in both her hands, she thrust her foot against the inside of his elbow and pulled hard.

He bellowed, but he must have understood what she was doing. His right hand was free, and he could have flattened her with one punch. Instead, he pounded the floor with his fist.

She let go of him then and backed away. She wasn't sure what black words he spat out, for they were in his own tongue. But the rafters rang with his curses, and Kimbery couldn't resist the urge to peek around the corner at the great roaring beast.

"Mama, what are you—"

"Go!" they shouted simultaneously, and Kimbery disappeared at once.

The Northman was huffing like a wounded wolf now, and she realized he was just as dangerous. She'd set his arm. And now he might well be able to use it.

She armed herself with the fireplace poker, ready to jab him at a moment's notice. But he didn't seem inclined to aggression. His legs were bound. His upper arms were secure. The leash was still in place. He couldn't go anywhere.

"The break should heal properly now, but you'll need a splint. Move," she said, showing him the poker, "and I'll break your other arm."

Luckily she had a choice selection of driftwood just outside. Leaving the door open, she ducked out, quickly chose two fairly straight sticks, and brought them in, thinking all the while she must be mad. Mending a Viking invader made as much sense as sewing up a deer she'd shot for supper.

She rummaged in the small chest at the hearth and found a linen underdress that had grown too small for Kimbery. She ripped it into strips to use for binding. "Do I need to give you opium again to keep you calm?"

"Nay," he growled.

She still didn't trust him. "Then heed me well, Northman. Make one false move, and I'll unset your arm again as fast as I set it."

He let her splint his arm, but it proved almost as much an ordeal for her as it was for him. It felt wrong, touching him. His arm looked foreign and forbidding with its massive muscle and sprinkling of light golden hair. His tawny skin was hot beneath her fingers, as if it radiated sunlight, and her own flesh grew warm from the contact. She was close enough to feel his breath, and her pulse quickened as she remembered the pleasant sensation of his lips on hers. The kiss had been so unexpectedly gentle coming from a brutal Northman.

But she couldn't afford to be gulled by his tenderness. Besides, he looked anything but tender today. An angry furrow lodged between his brows. The corners of his mouth turned down. And his hands looked enormous and threatening beside hers. A man like him could grasp her neck in one fist and squeeze the life out of her before she could blink.

Fortunately, he didn't.

She managed to tie off the splint and then bound his wrists together again with rope. Satisfied with her work, she backed away, eager to create some distance between her and the man who was disrupting her heartbeat.

Keeping her hands occupied was easy. There were always plenty of chores to be done. She'd gathered seaweed yesterday to make a soup, and now she stood at the table with her wooden block, chopping the ruffled red strands into small pieces. Keeping her mind occupied, however, was almost impossible, especially when she felt the Viking's silent gaze on her like the intent stare of a stalking wolf.

After several unnerving moments, he finally spoke. "No chains can hold me forever, woman."

38

She continued chopping. She worried he was right, but she certainly wasn't about to let him know that.

He continued, "Have you not heard the story of Fenrir?"

She gave him a disinterested sniff.

Which he ignored. "Fenrir, the fearsome son of Loki. They tried to keep *him* chained. Shall I tell you what happened?"

She refused to look at him. "Nay. I have no wish to hear—"

"Tell me! Tell me!" Kimmie suddenly cried from the doorway. "I want to hear a story!"

"Hush!" Avril hissed. "I don't want you going anywhere near him, Kimbery."

"I won't go near him, Mama. I promise. Please?"

"Nay. I don't even want him speaking to you."

"But why?" she whined.

He answered before she could open her mouth. "Your mother is afraid I may turn you into a Viking."

"Oh," Kimmie said.

Avril let out an exasperated breath, slammed down her knife, and glowered at him. "That's not true."

"But Mama, I'm already *half* Viking," she said happily, skipping over to Avril.

Avril bit the inside of her cheek. She usually tried to forget about that half. Despite Kimbery's ice blonde hair and periwinkle blue eyes, she thought of her daughter as a sweet little Pict lass.

"Please, Mama," she wheedled, tugging on Avril's skirts, "I'll be good, I promise."

"*You'll* be good," Avril said, picking up her knife and pointing it toward the Northman. "*He*, however, is not so well-behaved."

"What do you expect I'll do?" he muttered, pointedly twisting his neck in the collar, "Pierce her with my gaze?"

Avril thought he was doing a fairly good job of that already. She felt the touch of his frosty glare like the stabbing of winter sleet.

But he was right. For all intents and purposes, he was helpless. He couldn't harm Kimbery with mere words. Besides, it *would* be useful to have the wee lass entertained while Avril tended to her chores. She'd heard Viking sagas were notoriously lengthy and convoluted, which would keep Kimmie out from under her feet for a while.

Still, she couldn't allow the Northman anywhere near her daughter. He might not be able to escape, but he could do serious damage to a little girl who wandered too close.

"I won't hurt her," he said. "I swear."

Surely he didn't expect her to trust him. A Viking's oath wasn't worth shite. "That's right. You won't. Because if you lay a finger on her, I'll carve you up with this knife."

"Please, Mama?" Kimbery pursed her lips.

Avril sighed. She shook her head, still not sure it was a good idea. "You swear on your honor, Kimbery, that you'll stay where I put you?"

"On my honor," she said, clapping a hand to her chest.

Avril put down her knife and wiped her palms on her apron. She took Kimmie by the hand and walked her to a spot near the hearth, opposite the Viking. "Stay here. And you," she said, stabbing a finger toward her captive. "Don't even cast your 'piercing gaze' on my daughter or I'll gouge out your eyes."

She didn't need to tell him that. He wasn't going to look at her precious Kimbery. His piercing gaze was reserved for the cursed wench who'd clubbed him on the head, dragged him up the beach, tethered him like a rogue hound, and punched him in the nose. He might be telling the tale of Fenrir to her daughter, but his glare and the story were meant for *her*.

"Long ago," he began, staring intently at the woman's back while she chopped seaweed, "Fenrir, one of Loki's three sons—"

"Who's Loki?" Kimmie asked.

"Loki is the brother of Thor."

"Who's Thor?"

"Thor is the son of Odin."

"Who's Odin?"

Brandr sighed. The little girl apparently knew nothing about her Viking bloodline and history. It was tempting to recite the entire lineage of the gods, an ordeal that could take hours, but his own children had always fallen asleep before he could get past the fifth generation. He settled for telling her, "Odin is a god. They're all gods. And Loki, the son of Odin and the god of fire, was always causing trouble."

"Mama says I'm always causing trouble," Kimbery told him.

"Well, not *this* kind of trouble," he said. "Loki lied and cheated and tricked the other gods."

"He had no honor?"

"Aye, that's right. He had no honor. He did, however, have three sons, creatures he'd raised up to be terrible monsters. One was a great serpent." Brandr hissed like a snake, making the little girl shiver in delighted revulsion. The woman ignored his antics.

"Odin cast him into the sea, where he grew so fast that his body coiled around the whole world and his tail grew into his mouth."

The little girl gasped with wonder. Her mother continued chopping.

"The second monster Odin imprisoned in Niflheim, a land where the sun never shines and it's always dark."

"I'm not afraid of the dark," Kimbery boasted.

"That's good."

"What about the third monster?"

"He was called Fenrir, and he was a vicious, snapping wolf." Brandr snarled loudly, startling the woman. She gasped and fumbled with her knife, dropping it with a clatter on the table. He smirked, enormously satisfied. "Odin brought him to Asgard, the home of the gods, hoping to tame him."

"Tame him like Finn?"

"Finn?"

"My dog. He used to let me ride on his back."

"I see. Nay, Fenrir was too wild to be tamed. Each day, he grew bigger and bigger, more and more ferocious, until only one of the gods had the courage to feed him. That god was Tyr, the god of war, another of Odin's sons. Tyr was brave and loyal, and every day he'd bring Fenrir his supper."

"What did Fenrir eat?"

Glancing at the woman, who had gone back to chopping, he was tempted to say "Pictish wenches." Instead, he told her, "He ate meat—cows and pigs and—"

"Sheep?" the lass asked fearfully. "Did he eat sheep? I have a sheep."

"Well...nay, I don't think Fenrir liked the taste of sheep," he assured her. "But he had a big appetite, and he grew larger every day until eventually the gods decided he was too big and too dangerous to be roaming around Asgard. They couldn't kill him, because killing was forbidden in Asgard. So they decided to chain him."

"Like Mama chained you?"

He smiled grimly. "Exactly."

The woman stiffened and paused, her knife poised in midair.

He resumed the story. "Thor, the god of thunder and Loki's brother, said he would forge a strong chain to bind Fenrir with the help of Miolnir."

"Who's Miolnir?"

"Miolnir is Thor's mighty hammer. It looks like the one I wear around my neck." He lifted his chin to show the little girl the small silver hammer.

Kimbery rose up halfway, as if she planned to walk over to get a closer look.

Like all mothers, the woman apparently had eyes in the back of her head, for she called over her shoulder, "Kimmie, stay where you are!"

"I am!" the little girl insisted, sitting back down.

Brandr continued. "Thor hammered all night on the chain. The next day, because Fenrir wasn't afraid of the other gods," he said, narrowing his eyes pointedly at the woman's back, "he let them slip the chain around his neck."

"And nobody was allowed to go near him," Kimbery guessed.

"That's right. But much to the surprise of the gods, Fenrir made one powerful lunge, broke the chain, and freed himself."

The little girl gasped in dismay.

The woman, still with her back turned, interrupted the story. "Well, they obviously didn't use a strong enough chain," she muttered, resuming her chopping.

"Then what happened?" Kimbery asked.

He smiled slyly. "The gods decided they needed a stronger chain." He saw the woman's shoulders rise and fall with an irritated sigh. "So Thor promised he'd work harder this time and make a chain that could never be broken. He hammered at his forge for three days and three nights. When he was done, the chain was so heavy that even mighty Thor could hardly lift it. This time, Fenrir was not so willing to be bound. But the gods praised his great strength and assured Fenrir he could easily break that chain as well. So he finally let them put the chain about his neck."

"Did he break it, too?"

"He gave a great shake of his head," he said, demonstrating, "and a forceful bound, and he broke free of even that chain."

The woman stabbed her knife into the block with a loud clunk, clearly displeased with the direction the story was taking. But he didn't care. He had a point to make. No Pictish woman was going to get the best of him, trying to keep him leashed like Fenrir.

"Then what happened?" Kimbery asked.

"Thor was very discouraged, and the gods didn't know what to do. Finally, Frey, the god of summer, said he would ask the dwarves who lived deep in the earth to forge a chain, for though they were small, they possessed powerful magic. Surely they could make a chain strong enough to hold Fenrir."

The little girl was enthralled now. She sat with her chin in her hands, leaning forward as far as possible. Her mother had begun chopping another batch of seaweed, but he noticed she was doing so quietly. No doubt she was hanging on his every word as well.

"It took them two days and two nights, but the dwarves fashioned a chain out of the six strongest elements they could find. They used the roots of rocks, the spit of birds, the footsteps of cats, the beards of women, the breath of fish, and the sinew of bears. They presented the chain to the gods, and though it was fine and light, the dwarves assured them the magic chain was unbreakable. Of course, by this time, the gods knew Fenrir was too clever to allow them to bind him a third time. So they invited him to join them on a voyage to a beautiful island, where they would play games together and demonstrate feats of strength."

"What's an island?"

He frowned. The little girl *lived* on an island. Didn't she know that? "Land surrounded by water."

"Like my house?"

"Aye."

"Nay," the woman countered, "it isn't the same, Kimmie. We only live *beside* the ocean."

"You live on an island," he told her.

"We do not," the woman said, turning to him with a scowl.

"It's a large island, to be sure, but—"

"We don't live on an island."

He arched a brow in challenge. "Really? How do you know? Have *you* ever sailed the seas?"

The woman gave him an affronted sniff and turned back to her work, clearly upset by this revelation.

Avril was positive the Viking was wrong. She'd traveled for days—north, south, and west—and never run into the sea. But the marauders of the North sailed great distances. If anyone knew the oceans, it was a Northman. The idea that she might live on an island was disconcerting. The idea that he knew her home better than she did troubled her greatly.

"Then what happened?" Kimmie asked. "Then what?"

"The gods brought out the chain, and they all tried to break it, but none could do it, not even Thor, who said it was so strong that surely only Fenrir could break it. Fenrir was too proud to refuse their challenge. He allowed them to place the chain around his neck on one condition—that one of the gods put his right hand in Fenrir's mouth while they did so as an act of faith, to prove they didn't mean to imprison him."

Kimbery gasped.

"The gods, of course, *did* mean to imprison him, so no one wanted to put a hand in Fenrir's mouth. But loyal Tyr stepped bravely forward and placed his hand between the wolf's sharp teeth. They put the chain around Fenrir's neck, and Fenrir tried to break it, but the more he lunged, the tighter the chain became. When he found he couldn't get free, he snapped his jaws in anger and bit off Tyr's hand."

"Oh, nay!" Kimbery cried.

Avril turned to address her daughter. "Which is why, Kimmie, we don't go near dangerous chained beasts." She lifted a smug brow at him.

He returned a smug brow and replied, "Which is why we shouldn't keep 'dangerous beasts' chained."

"Did Tyr die?" Kimmie asked.

"Nay, he didn't die," the man said. "He became a hero in Asgard because of his bravery."

"Mama, I want to go to Asgard."

Avril gave the Viking a long-suffering glower. He smiled in return.

"Kimmie," she said, "come help me wash the sloke."

Kimbery skipped over and plopped down on her stool while Avril brought her a bucket of fresh water. The little girl pushed up her sleeves and thrust her arms into the water, stirring vigorously as Avril dumped the chopped seaweed into the bucket.

The Viking's story had been completely absurd, of course. There was no such place as Asgard, no god with a hammer, no dwarves who forged magical chains. Still, the tale had been entertaining enough, and it had kept Kimmie occupied.

The man had been right about one thing, however. Avril did harbor the fear that Kimbery's Viking blood might be stirred to life one day, that she would become enthralled by the mysterious world of her Viking father, and that Avril would somehow lose her Pictish daughter to the marauders of the North.

She could feel the Viking's ice-blue eyes on her as she coaxed the fire to life and added more wood. His attention was quite disturbing. But then there wasn't much else for him to look at, she supposed. She was tempted to blindfold him, but that seemed unnecessarily cruel. If only he wouldn't watch her every move...

"That's good, Kimmie. We'll put it on to boil now and go milk Caimbeul."

It could do no harm to leave the Viking alone at this point. He seemed adequately trussed up. They'd be gone only a short while, long enough to milk the ewe and turn her into the pasture.

CHAPTER 5

The instant they closed the cottage door, Brandr began struggling at his bonds, praying for Fenrir's strength. The way he saw it, eventually the woman would tire of having him in her cottage. But she wouldn't just set him free. She'd turn him over to someone who knew what to do with a captive Viking. The last thing he wanted was to force her into a hasty decision.

He strained with all his might against the leather collar. With his arm splinted, it was even more useless now. But if he pulled hard enough, he might be able to work the iron ring out of the wall. Once that was done, he could reach the knot to free his ankles. Then he'd flee. And he'd take that magnificent sword with him.

Where he'd go, he didn't know. It wouldn't be easy for a tall, blond, blue-eyed Northman to hide in this land of dark-haired dwarves.

The leather rubbed his throat raw, and he nearly choked himself more than once, but he couldn't dislodge the ring. When they returned, he was no closer to freedom. The woman, however, suspected something, for she gave him a sharp look as she set a bucket of milk on the table.

"You're sweating," she said.

"I'm beside the fire," he replied.

She frowned dubiously and opened her mouth to speak, but Kimbery interrupted her. "I milked Caimbeul," she announced proudly. "Her name's Caimbeul because she has a crooked mouth, like this." She made a comical sneer. "Have *you* ever milked a sheep?"

He shook his head.

"Indeed?" her mother asked with a sly lift of her brow. "I'll have to teach you how when your arm heals."

He narrowed his eyes. Teach him to milk a sheep? Did she plan to enslave him? The idea was absurd. He was the son of a noble, a warrior. And unless she meant to keep him tied up, he'd easily fight his way free. A featherweight wench and her four-year-old daughter were no match for a Viking.

But this was good news. Without the imminent threat of death and with the benefit of time, he could easily lull her into a false trust. Then, when she least expected it, he'd manage his escape.

"Want to see my picture?" Kimbery asked him. She didn't wait for an answer, galloping into the bedchamber and returning with a square piece of slate.

He turned his head to look at it. "Is that me?"

She nodded.

"Did you draw it?"

She nodded again.

"What does it say?"

"Kimbery," her mother interrupted, "don't bother him."

"I'm not." Then she pointed to the letters, confiding to him in a loud whisper, "It says Da."

He couldn't help but smile at that. The little girl certainly was bullheaded.

Her mother, obviously eager to end their conversation, asked, "How is the sloke doing, Kimmie?"

Kimbery set the slate down and peered into the clay pot nestled amongst the coals. "It's bubbling, Mama."

"Good. Don't stand too close to the fire."

The little girl took a dramatic step backward and started idly twirling her braid between her fingers. Her gaze slid over to him, then to the floor, and she wrinkled her forehead in concern. Following her eyes, he saw he was crushing her cloth doll beneath his hip. He moved aside as much as he could, which wasn't very much.

"Mama," she said plaintively, "I want Maeve back."

The woman clucked her tongue. "You shouldn't have given her to him."

Kimbery's bottom lip trembled.

The woman sighed softly. "Very well. You stay back. I'll get her."

She approached carefully and crouched beside him. She smelled fresh, like sunshine and sweet grass. Her underdress was still untied, and when she bent forward, he could see the upper crescent of her breast, as pale and smooth as cream. A surge of lust rose in him, and it wasn't helped by the fact that she began rummaging under his buttock for the doll.

His uneasy grunt alerted her to what she was doing. Suddenly mortified, she seized the doll and yanked it out, unfortunately tearing its arm in the process.

Naturally, Kimbery began screaming in horror at the sight, and it took several moments before her mother could placate her with the fact that the doll could be easily repaired.

Meanwhile, Brandr was glad his hands were bound over his lap, for the sight of his rising desire would undoubtedly upset them even more. It certainly upset *him*. He'd lost his wife less than a year ago. It wasn't right that he should be aroused by this strange woman.

Eventually order was restored, though the woman had to pause in her other chores to stitch the doll's arm back on. When she was finished, the little girl studied her handiwork intently to be sure it was correct. Apparently satisfied, she took the doll into her bedchamber, chattering to it all the way.

The woman was busy the rest of the day. He'd never seen anyone work so hard. Even the thralls of his country were allowed to rest. But she labored from sunrise to well after sunset, keeping the fire stoked, preparing supper, milking the sheep, laundering linens, making cheese, mending clothes, even teaching her daughter to read and write. No wonder she wanted to make a slave out of him.

The seaweed pottage was remarkably tasty, especially after she added the fresh sheep's milk, smoked fish, and wild onions to it. It might not be the succulent roast pig he preferred, but he had to admire her ability to make delicious fare out of what was at hand. Indeed, if he'd come to Pictland for pillage and prisoners, he would have considered himself lucky to take such a resourceful woman home as a slave.

At the end of the day, the woman heated water for Kimbery's bath and undressed her. As the little girl streaked through the cottage naked, squealing that she didn't want a bath, Brandr had to bite back a smile. Eventually, her mother caught her and plopped her into a makeshift tub of a split ale cask. After a bit, the little girl's protests subsided, and she began playing in the water, singing and splashing. By the time she was scrubbed clean, her mother's kirtle was drenched, and Kimbery now didn't want to get *out* of the tub.

She kicked and screamed as her mother picked her up. Brandr, amused by the wicked little sprite's antics, couldn't help but laugh aloud.

Avril turned in surprise. The Northman was grinning. His eyes sparkled like the sunlit sea, and his teeth flashed as white as snow. But it was the low rumble of his laughter that took her breath away. She didn't realize how much she'd missed that sound. She hadn't heard male laughter in four long years.

Then Kimbery, wet and slippery, taking advantage of Avril's distraction, slid out of her grasp and began tearing around the cottage. She dodged the linen Avril held out until Avril finally gave up, figuring the little girl would dry herself off with her running.

The Viking's smile turned bittersweet then, and a faraway look came into his eyes. Avril knew at once that he must be remembering his own daughter.

She forced her gaze away, dabbing at her damp kirtle with the linen. It wasn't her concern. His people hadn't cared whose children they slaughtered when they'd raided Rivenloch. Why should she care what had happened to his daughter? And yet, against her will, words fell softly from her lips. "What was your daughter's name?"

He glanced up, as if surprised she'd read his thoughts. "Asta."

"It's a pretty name."

"She was a pretty..." He choked on the words. "A pretty lass."

She shouldn't feel sorry for him. The Vikings killed pretty Pictish lasses all the time. But there was a deep sorrow in the Northman's eyes that pulled at her heart.

"Who's Inga?" The words tumbled out of her mouth unbidden, mortifying her. She should never have asked him that. He probably didn't remember calling her by that name or kissing her anyway.

His gaze shot straight to hers.

"You...spoke her name in your sleep," she explained.

He frowned. "I dreamt she was alive."

"Your wife," she guessed.

He nodded.

He must have loved her well. That kiss had been full of tenderness and desire. As odd as it was, Avril envied the dead woman. His fortunate Inga had known the love of a devoted husband. Avril had only experienced the mindless lust of a

Viking berserker and a handful of men for whom she felt nothing.

Just then Kimbery went galloping past. Before Avril could catch her, the wee lass dove at the shocked Northman. She plopped herself into his lap and captured his gold-stubbled face playfully between her hands.

"Da!" she cried.

Avril's heart leaped into her mouth. Tiny, pale, bare Kimbery looked so vulnerable against the Viking's broad chest. Lord, he could bite off her hand with one snap of his jaws, just like that wolf in his story.

She glanced up in horror at his face. But he looked far more rattled than she was. No doubt he was unused to strange naked children leaping into his arms.

"Kimbery!" she barked. "Get away from him!"

Kimbery clambered down, looking guilty. She probably hadn't intended to disobey. She'd only been caught up in her play.

Still, Avril didn't dare let her think it was acceptable to traffic with Vikings. "Go to bed. Now."

"I didn't mean to."

"Now!"

The little girl began to weep, which made Avril feel awful. After all, she'd been so happy a moment ago. But Avril couldn't afford to let down her guard. Kimbery's life depended upon it.

Tears of heartbreak streamed down Kimmie's face. She started sobbing in earnest and shuffled sadly off to the bedchamber.

Avril bit her lip in remorse. It was hard being a mother. Sometimes she thought she would have had an easier time commanding the army of Rivenloch than she did watching over one wee lass.

But the horrible memory of the berserker hurling his ax into the child's back would never be far away from her thoughts.

Kimbery's sobs might tear at her, but at least she was alive to sob.

By the time Avril cleaned up the bath, Kimmie's crying had subsided to sniffles. "Mama?" she called tentatively from the bedchamber. "Come tell me a story."

Avril was tempted to tell her a story about vicious invading savages from the North, to cure her of her misplaced affection for their captive. But she supposed that would give the lass nightmares. Instead, she told her the story of the time she defeated all four of her brothers in combat.

From the next room, Brandr listened in rapt fascination. The woman was telling a grand, typically Pictish tale to her daughter about a warrior wench who'd disguised herself as a man and fought against her own brothers. It was a good story, like the sagas of his people—full of excitement, adventure, and retribution—and the woman had a pleasant voice, lilting and dramatic.

"The first brother, Eldred," she told the little girl, "was very arrogant and boastful."

"Arrogant?" Kimbery asked.

"Like this," she said, and Brandr heard her striding about the room, probably with her arms crossed and her nose in the air. "Anyway, Eldred had never been defeated in battle. So when this new warrior challenged him, he accepted, saluting his foe with a cocky flourish of his blade. They began to fight, exchanging blows back and forth." Brandr could hear her scuffling about and grunting as she recreated the battle with an invisible sword.

"But Eldred was so sure he would win," she said, "that he started to grow careless. And when he relaxed his guard and wasn't paying attention, his sister ducked underneath his arm. With the hilt of her sword, she delivered a hard jab to his chin and knocked him flat."

Kimbery cheered. "What about the other brothers?"

"Grimbol, the second brother, had a nasty temper and was quick to anger. Once he saw Eldred defeated, he immediately drew his sword and rushed in. He meant to slay the warrior who'd dared to humiliate his older brother."

"What's humiliate?"

"Make a fool of. She'd made a fool of his brother, and it made him angry. But his rage proved his own undoing. He began to slash haphazardly and—"

"What's hap-, hap—"

"Haphazardly, in a reckless manner, with poor aim. Most of his blows swished through empty air, and every time he missed, he grew all the more furious. But his sister used his own fury against him. When he lunged at her, she dodged aside and pushed him forward, driving him face-first into the dirt."

Kimbery clapped her hands. "Then what, Mama?"

"The third brother's name was Osbern, and he was a cheat. He'd watched the stranger outwit and outfight his brothers, and he wanted his turn. But instead of waiting for a challenge like a man of honor, he attacked his sister while her back was turned."

Kimbery gasped.

"Oh, she wasn't surprised. She knew all about Osbern's trickery and expected such shameful behavior. She leaped out of the way, and the point of his sword plunged into the mud beside her. Ignoring all the rules of chivalry, he dove at her, intending to wrest her to the ground, where he could pummel her with his fists, like the dishonorable dog that he was. But she was light and quick, and she skipped out of his reach. One clever slice of her sword, and Osbern fell to the sod with his trews around his ankles."

Kimbery giggled. "What about the last brother?"

"When it came time to battle Wilfred, her last brother, the warrior woman tossed off her helm and showed her face."

"Why, Mama?"

"Because Wilfred believed that women were made to be the servants of men, and she wanted him to know exactly who was getting the better of him."

"What did he say when he saw who she was?"

"He called her bad names."

"What bad names?"

"They're so bad, I can't repeat them."

Brandr smiled at that.

"But the other brothers—Eldred, Grimbol, and Osbern—were as angry as bees when they found out they'd been beaten by their own sister. So they yelled at Wilfred to clout her soundly."

"Oh, nay, Mama."

"But try as he might, Wilfred couldn't lay a hand on her, for she was nimble and strong. You see, while her brothers had lain lazily about, boasting of their skills, she'd spent long hours practicing. She eventually managed to smack his arse with the flat of her sword and sent him crashing into his other brothers."

Kimbery laughed long and hard. "Smack his arse!"

The woman couldn't help but laugh along, which made Brandr grin.

"Aye. And when she'd defeated them all, a servant who'd seen the entire battle ran to tell their father. Her father was so proud of her, he gave her a beautiful jeweled sword as a prize, saying that it was she who should rightfully inherit his lands."

A strange shiver ran up Brandr's spine. He glanced at the jeweled sword in the corner. Could the story be true? Pictish women were said to be able to handle a blade. But could *she* possibly be the intrepid swordswoman in the story? Surely not. Surely the tale was a work of imagination. After all, the heroine of her story had become a landed heiress. This woman lived in a humble hovel.

"Did she live happily ever after, Mama?"

There was a hesitation. "Oh, I'm sure she did."

"Mama," Kimbery announced, "I want a sword."

"You *have* a sword."

Brandr raised a brow. The little girl had a sword?

"Not a wooden sword. A *real* sword," Kimbery said.

"When you're older."

"And I want brothers to fight with," she added.

"That I can't promise you."

"I want to be a warrior just like the lady in the story."

Her mother chuckled. "You'll be twice as good as the lady in the story."

"Mama, can we practice sparring?"

"Tomorrow," she promised, "but only if you get a good night's rest."

After she finished tucking in her daughter, the woman emerged again. Brandr quickly sized her up and decided the story couldn't be true. She might be able to wield a blade, but no sweet-faced maid could possibly vanquish four seasoned warriors.

CHAPTER 6

The next morning, Brandr woke with a face full of sheep. He sputtered and reared back as far as he could, which wasn't far, since he was on a short leash.

"Caimbeul likes you," Kimbery informed him.

He grimaced as the smell of the ewe hit him full force. "Gah!"

"Don't you like her?" she asked.

He blinked the sleep from his eyes. The little girl had obeyed her mother—she was staying out of his reach—but she was holding the sheep on a rope and letting it nuzzle him with its crooked mouth.

"Shouldn't she be outside?" he whispered.

"Shh. Don't tell Mama. She doesn't like when I—"

"Kimmie," came a sleepy voice from the bedchamber. "Who are you talking to?"

"Nobody."

There was a sudden thrash of linens and the woman rushed into the room, a warning ring in her voice as she came. "You'd better not be going near that Vi-..." When she saw that Kimbery was safe, the anxiety deserted her eyes. Then she saw the ewe. "How did that sheep get in here?"

Kimbery shrugged. "Caimbeul wanted to see my da. I'm going to put her back."

"I've told you a hundred times, Kimmie, sheep don't belong in the house. And he's not your da. Now if you don't take that animal out of here this instant..."

Brandr grew deaf to her scolding as he took note of the woman's attire. By Odin, she was clad in little more than a sheer linen shift, rumpled from sleep. One side had slipped down, exposing the smooth, round cap of her shoulder. There she had a blue tattoo like those engraved on Pict warriors. It was an intriguing three-looped knot that had no beginning or end. Her hair was mussed in a careless way that reminded him of long nights tussling in bed. Her feet were deliciously bare, and her frayed shift revealed the supple curve of her calf and her ankle, which also bore an inked design, this one in the shape of a broken sword. But it was her mouth that was the most alluring. He remembered that mouth now. He'd kissed her, and her lips had been as sweet and soft as wild blackberries.

His loins tightened, and guilt made him grind his teeth against desire. But willing it away didn't make it disappear, and while the woman continued to herd the sheep and her daughter out of the cottage, Brandr fought to keep his thoughts on survival, escape, anything but the beautiful, feminine silhouette revealed by the dawning sun as she opened the door.

Avril silently cursed herself for oversleeping. Keeping Kimbery safe meant being up and about before the wee lass could get herself into trouble. She'd certainly found trouble this morning, letting the ewe into the cottage. Avril wondered if *she'd* been such a handful at that age.

From the doorway, she watched Kimmie lead the sheep back to her pen. "Make sure you close the gate," she called.

Then she turned and caught the Northman staring at her. He looked like a warrior, stern and hardened, about to march into battle. His eyes were hooded, and his jaw was tight. His chest rose and fell with a deep breath as his gaze slowly coursed up the length of her. Finally, he met her eyes.

A flash of heat like lightning seared her as she recognized his expression. She'd been wrong. It wasn't a warrior's bloodlust. It was desire, pure and direct. Her breath caught, and her face turned to flame. But his ice-blue gaze did nothing to quench the fire, instead fueling her distress.

She clenched her fists. She should curse him, clout him, kick him. Yet she did nothing. Though the urge to rebuff him was strong, the compelling lust in his eyes was even stronger.

She licked her lips. Against her will, her gaze drifted down to his mouth. She remembered the light touch of his hands upon her face, the warmth of his breath, the taste of his kiss. What scared her was that a part of her longed to feel it again.

And if Kimbery hadn't burst in upon them at that moment, she didn't know what might have happened.

"Mama! Mama!" Kimbery cried, jumping up and down, waving her wooden sword. "Spar with me! Spar with me!"

Avril cleared her throat. Of course. Sparring had always helped her when she felt emotionally out of sorts. She could take up her sword and slash away at anger, fear, and, in this case, desire, and defeat them soundly before they could get the best of her.

"You promised," Kimbery reminded her.

"I did promise. Just let me get...dressed." A blush stole up her cheek as she realized she'd rushed out in her nightclothes. No wonder the Northman was looking at her like that.

She avoided his gaze as she swept past, but she couldn't avoid hearing the conversation between the Viking and her daughter while she dressed in the next room.

"Do you have a sword?" Kimbery asked.

"I did."

"What happened to it?"

"I lost it in the sea."

"Maybe Mama can get you a new one."

"Kimbery," Avril warned, "are you talking to that man?"

"Nay," she lied. "I'm talking to Maeve."

Avril heard only whispers after that until she emerged.

"Watch me, Da!" Kimbery cried, leaping about with her wooden sword, battling an unseen enemy.

But the Northman's eyes were fixed upon Avril as if nothing else existed.

Brandr's breath caught in his chest. He'd heard legends about female Pict warriors, but he'd never seen a woman dressed, or rather *un*dressed, in such a manner. She'd foregone her confining linen underdress and wore only her sleeveless kirtle, which gave her a greater range of motion and revealed the blue design on her shoulder and her sleek-muscled arms. Riding low on her hips was a leather swordbelt carved with intricate designs. She'd tucked the kirtle back up under the belt so that it bloused halfway down her thighs, exposing a pair of long, lovely legs that were tucked into short seal-fur boots.

If he'd thought the sight of the woman in her nightclothes was alluring, it didn't compare to the vision of her dressed for battle. Perhaps that was the secret of Pict warfare. What foe could fight such a distracting beauty?

"Watch me! Watch me!" the little girl was yelling as she leaped about. It took all of Brandr's willpower to drag his gaze away from the lass's breathtaking mother.

"Kimbery, not in the house," she scolded.

"But I want Da to see me."

"We'll leave the door open." She gave him a look then that said the door would be open, not so he could watch the little girl, but so *she* could keep an eye on *him*.

Which was fine with him. After spending the night on a leash with a throbbing broken arm and waking to a stinking sheep nuzzling at his ear, he figured he deserved the reward of watching a woman cavort about half-naked.

What began as a pleasurable pastime quickly turned into torment. It had been more than a year since Brandr had bedded a woman, and his body responded as eagerly as a starving man seated at a feast. As the woman flexed and lunged in preparation for sparring, she unknowingly taunted him with her taut, slender arms and her silky thighs. Her garment clung to her body, hugging every subtle curve. Each time she twirled to change direction, her skirt flipped up, and he couldn't help but watch for a glimpse of something more.

She hunkered down beside her daughter, giving her instruction, and his gaze slipped over her rounded knees. She wrapped her arms around Kimbery, showing her how to hold the sword, and he observed the nuanced play of the muscles of her shoulder. She stood, planting her feet wide apart, and he admired her shapely calves.

"Can you see me?" Kimbery called out to him.

He gave a guilty start. "Aye," he croaked. The truth was he'd scarcely given her a glance, so transfixed by her mother was he.

"Pay heed, Kimbery," the woman warned. "Don't get distracted."

The little girl began hacking away at her mother with her wooden sword, and the woman easily defended herself, coming around slowly and carefully with her own steel blade. He'd never seen a woman wielding a sword before, and her skill surprised him. He wondered how good she was when she wasn't checking her blows.

Of course, she was no match for a Viking. But it was admirable that she was teaching her daughter useful fighting techniques. It would keep the little girl from becoming easy prey.

He continued to watch as she demonstrated proper shield technique, showed Kimbery how to dodge blows, and the two of them practiced diving to the ground, rolling, and coming up with blades at the ready.

As they sparred, tendrils of the woman's hair came loose from her long braid. Her cheeks grew rosy, her skin glowed, and her chest heaved with each exertion. She reminded him of the women he'd pleasured in his bed when he was a single, virile, carefree young man. He suddenly longed to snatch away her sword, carry her off, toss up her skirts, and ease his desires upon her battle-warmed body. And this troubled him deeply.

Avril found it difficult to concentrate when the Northman was staring at her. She didn't return his stare, but she could feel his eyes upon her. She'd left the door open for more than one reason. Aye, she wanted to keep an eye on him—she was fairly sure he'd already made an attempt to escape—but she also wanted him to see that she was no ordinary frail lass. She could hold her own with a sword. And he'd have a fight on his hands if he tried to challenge her. She'd been a victim once. She didn't intend to be one again.

"Did you see me, Da?" Kimbery yelled after she'd done a perfect forward roll and lunged forward with her wooden sword.

"Aye," he called back, "well done." But his gaze wasn't on Kimbery. He was looking at Avril again with that smoldering heat, like a wolf about to devour a lamb.

She gulped. No one had ever looked at her with such hunger. It made her knees weak and warmed her all over. Curious lightning charged the air, an uncontrollable current born of the strange attraction between them. It sucked the will from her and made her long to do things against her nature—to go to him, to touch him, to kiss him—which terrified her, because her sword was a useless weapon against her own desire.

But fear turned quickly to self-loathing and then fury. Troubled by her wayward emotions and reminding herself that he was her enemy, that his kind had murdered her people and ruined her life, she broke off her gaze and shook free with a shudder, trying to focus again on her lesson with Kimbery.

"Mama, I want to spar with Da," the little girl said, skipping in a circle.

Sweeping her blade sharply through the air, Avril barked, "Don't call him that!"

Kimbery stopped skipping. "What should I call him, Mama?"

Avril could think of a dozen names for the Viking, none fit for the ears of a child. Before she could choose one, he answered.

"Brandr," he called from the cottage. "My name is Brandr."

It was a strong name—a strong name for a strong man. But she didn't want to know his name. Knowing his name made things worse. He was easy to despise when he was simply a Viking, a Northman, a marauder. Calling him Brandr made him a man of flesh and blood.

"Can Brandr fight with us, Mama?"

"Nay."

"Why not?" Kimmie asked.

He answered before she had a chance. "I wouldn't want to hurt you, little one."

Avril smirked at that. "He's afraid he might lose."

Brandr lifted a brow and gave her a cocky smile. "Not even with a broken arm."

His grin sent a shiver through her. She hoped it was a shiver of revulsion. She feared it was something else, something that made her feel lightheaded and foolhardy, almost crazy enough to free him and let him try...almost.

But she wasn't a fool. She couldn't let him bait her.

"My name's Kimmie," Kimbery informed him, holding her sword high over her head. "And Mama's name is Avril."

Avril choked. She didn't want him to know her name. The exchange of names suggested an intimacy she didn't want to encourage.

"Pleased to meet you, Kimmie," he said with a polite nod. *Her* name, however, came out on a purr. "Avril."

She bristled. That was exactly why she'd wished to remain nameless. Already he breathed her name as if they were lovers. Already it felt like he was insinuating his way under her skin.

"Come on, Kimmie," she said, shaking off the uneasy shiver that had passed through her. "Let's show the Viking what we do to men who think they can hurt us."

She hoped to impress upon him that the ladies of Rivenloch were not to be trifled with or underestimated. But she also worried that his shipmates might show up. So she taught Kimbery some useful defensive ploys in addition to straightforward sword fighting. She showed her how to use her elbows to jab a belly, her heels to stamp on toes, her teeth to bite fingers, and her fists to punch a man where it hurt most.

So enrapt was she with teaching Kimbery survival skills that she didn't notice the figure stealing up on the cottage until it was too late. But the instant she saw the glint of metal, her worst fears were realized. It could be no one else. The Northman's shipmates must have come looking for him.

Without a second glance, she swung Kimbery up and pushed her toward the cottage door. "Go!"

For once, Kimbery didn't question her, but rushed inside.

Her Viking prisoner, however, called out, "Is it my men?"

She didn't answer him. She wouldn't give him the satisfaction. Wheeling immediately with her blade drawn and her heart racing, she faced the oncoming threat.

But it wasn't his men. It was her neighbor, the one who'd given her the sheep. She lowered her shoulders in relief. While she watched the man make his way toward her, she saw that he wielded, not a sword, but a spade.

"Erik!" Brandr called out suddenly from behind her. "Gunnarr!"

Her eyes widened. Shite! She couldn't let her neighbor find the Northman.

She whipped her head around and hissed at him. "Hush! It's not your men!"

The last thing she saw before she lunged for the door, slamming it shut, was the perplexed furrow between the Viking's brows.

Brandr bellowed out a curse. Unfortunately, he startled the little girl, who now looked as if she might burst into tears.

"Shh, Kimmie. I'm sorry," he soothed. "It's all right."

But he wasn't so sure. He wished the woman hadn't slammed the door between them. If it wasn't his men out there, who was it? Thieves? Murderers? Though he realized it was completely contrary to reason at the moment—Avril was his enemy, after all—his instinct to protect women rose to the surface, overriding everything else. Whoever was out there evidently posed a threat to her. Otherwise, she wouldn't have pushed Kimbery into the cottage.

He had to do something about it.

Kimbery's chin was trembling, and the wooden sword drooped in her grasp. "But Mama..."

"Hush, Kimmie," he coaxed. "It's all right. Shh."

"I have to help Mama fight," she decided, starting for the door.

"Nay!" She flinched at his sharp voice. "Nay, sweetheart," he said more softly. "Your mama wants you to stay here, to stay quiet. That's why she closed the door."

Yet even as he said the words, he had to wonder at the woman's judgment. Why hadn't she rushed inside as well and barred the door? What made her think she could handle the threat? The fool woman was going to get herself killed.

Hell, he thought as he strained against the leather collar, he couldn't stand the thought of a woman facing danger alone while he sat helpless. If only he could get loose, he could chase the intruders off.

He glanced at the little girl. Maybe he *could* get loose.

"Kimmie," he said, "if you help *me*, I can help your mama."

She looked skeptically at him.

"I need you to unbuckle my collar. Do you think you can do that? Do you think you can—"

"Mama said I'm not supposed to go near you."

Brandr bit back an oath. "But she needs my help. I'm big and strong, and I can fight—"

"*I'm* strong," she said. "Mama said so."

He growled in frustration, frightening the little girl again. She backed toward the door once more.

His eyes widened. "Nay, nay, nay, nay, nay." He had to keep her inside. The last thing he needed was to have *both* women out of his sight. "Kimmie, nay, Kimmie," he said urgently as her small hand touched the latch. "Come away from the door. Please. I'll..." He searched his memory. What would have convinced his own daughter to stay? "I'll tell you another story."

She hesitated.

"Aye, come sit by the fire, and I'll tell you a story about... about Muspell, the land of the Fire Giants."

She pursed her lips.

"And Niflheim, where the Frost Giants live," he added.

She lifted her brows.

"And Audhumia, the giant cow."

"Giant cow?"

"Aye. The giant cow who licked the gods to life."

She let go of the latch and walked to the hearth, and he heaved a sigh of relief. He might not be able to rescue Avril, but at least he could keep her daughter safe.

Kimbery sat cross-legged with her sword across her lap, and he began a story he'd told often to his children—the story of the world's creation. Meanwhile, he strained to hear what was happening outside, to no avail. The little girl, fascinated by the tale, edged closer and closer to him. Eventually, despite her mother's stern orders, she ended up half-draped across his lap.

CHAPTER 7

A vril thought she must be mad, covering for the Northman. Her neighbor said he'd found pieces of a Viking ship. He'd come to warn her to be watchful, assuring her in manly tones that he was on the hunt for the vermin who belonged to it, hefting up his spade as proof.

She should have turned the Viking over to him then and there. It certainly would have made her life easier. Brandr would have been out of her house, away from her daughter, off of her shoulders.

But she couldn't bear the thought of him being beaten to death with a spade, which was doubtless what her neighbor intended.

So she told the man an outright lie, saying she'd seen no sign of Northmen, but she'd be sure to alert him if she did. Thanking him for his concern, she smiled stiffly until he was out of sight.

"Brilliant," she muttered to herself. "Now I'm harboring an outlaw."

She pushed open the cottage door, cursing herself for a fool, and froze when she saw the scene before her.

She couldn't draw breath. Mother of God, she *was* a fool! While she'd been lying to protect him, the crafty Viking had enticed her daughter onto his lap. Kimbery was sprawled across his thighs like a lovesick pup. Was this the thanks she got for saving Brandr's worthless hide?

"Mama!" Kimbery cried, jumping up and running to her, hugging her about the thighs. "Da's telling me...I mean, Brandr's telling me a story about a giant cow and Frost Giants and the dwarves who hold up the sky!"

"Is that so?" Avril bit out with a shaky smile for her daughter. She clasped Kimbery close in relief, grateful he'd let her go, unharmed, but uncertain why. After all, with Kimbery in his grasp, he could have had her at his mercy and easily bargained for his freedom.

Brandr didn't seem to notice her confusion. He gave her a fierce frown, scanning her from head to toe. "Are you all right?"

She blinked, even more baffled. "Aye. Why wouldn't I be?"

"Who was outside?" The furrow in his brow deepened, and his fists clenched, as if he meant to use them.

"My neighbor. He came to tell me..." Suddenly the truth struck her. "Were you...?" She narrowed incredulous eyes at him. "You were. You were afraid for me."

He scowled in irritation, but he couldn't deny it, and something about that pleased her.

"You know," she said in amazement, "if I didn't know better, I'd say you were trying to protect me."

He scoffed. But after a moment he looked at her quizzically, lowering his shoulders and relaxing his hands. "Wait. Your neighbor?" The corner of his lip lifted in a knowing grin. "And you didn't tell him about your Viking prize?"

She stiffened.

He chuckled. "You know, if I didn't know better, I'd say you were trying to protect me."

It was useless to deny it.

He shook his head. "What a pair we are."

What a pair indeed, Avril thought. By all rights, they should despise each other. The war between their people had been going on for more than fifty years. He was a bloodthirsty Viking, and she was the Pict who'd leashed him. She'd made the cottage that he'd come to conquer into his prison. And if they'd met on a field of battle, she would have readily drawn her sword and stabbed him through the heart.

But when she looked at his twinkling blue eyes, his enticing grin, his...formidable body, she found it hard to summon up a good loathing.

"Mama, did you smack his arse?"

Avril started. "Who, the neighbor?" She shook her head. "He wasn't here to fight. He...came to see how Caimbeul was doing."

"Oh."

She and Brandr exchanged glances, and he gave her a subtle nod of thanks, something she wasn't sure she deserved. She was making a mistake, not turning him in. The longer he was here, the more difficult it would become to get rid of him. Hell, her own daughter was already clambering onto the Viking's lap as if he were her beloved grandfather.

Kimbery hopped up and down on her toes. "Mama, I want a giant cow!"

Avril eyed the Northman in accusation. What nonsense had he put in Kimbery's head now?

Brandr reasoned with the little girl. "But how would you milk her? It would take all day. And your hands are too small."

"You could do it," Kimbery suggested. "You have big hands."

Avril bit her lip. He *did* have big hands...and big feet...and big shoulders...

He chuckled. "I'm not a milkmaid," he told Kimmie. "I'm a warrior."

His words suddenly touched a raw nerve in Avril. She wasn't a milkmaid either. She was supposed to be the lady of a castle. But sometimes the world turned on people, and they had to do what was necessary to go on living.

"You know, not all of us get to choose our fate," and she said with frost in her voice. "If you're going to stay here, you'd better get used to tending animals and fishing and mending fences. It's not an easy thing, surviving in…"

She broke off at his narrowed gaze, realizing what she'd just said—*if you're going to stay here.*

What was she thinking? He wasn't an animal she could tame and tether. He was a wild and dangerous beast who'd surely turn on her the moment he was free.

Still, he could have hurt Kimbery, but he'd chosen not to. Instead he'd told the little girl some fanciful tale about giant cows to keep her quiet and safe from whatever peril lurked outside.

Why? Did he hope to persuade her to let him go? She couldn't do that. She might not deliver him directly into the hands of a neighbor armed with a spade, but neither would she turn a known marauder loose on her unsuspecting countrymen.

Kimbery waved her wooden blade through the air. "My mama's a warrior," she said. "And I'm going to be a warrior, too. When I grow up, we're going to take back Rivenloch."

"Kimmie!" Avril's cheeks warmed. She didn't need a stranger knowing all about her sordid past. "He's not interested in—"

"What's Rivenloch?" he asked.

"It's Mama's castle. I'm going to learn how to sword fight, and then we'll get an army to take the castle back from my evil uncles who—"

"Kimmie, enough! Go take your nap."

Kimbery scampered merrily off into the bedchamber. But the damage was already done. Brandr was staring at her with undisguised interest now. "Evil uncles?"

Though he'd entertained the remote possibility, it hadn't seriously occurred to Brandr that the woman and her daughter were anything but commoners, outcasts on this lonely shore due to an unfortunate encounter with berserkers.

He perused her thoroughly now, imagining her in the rich garb of a noblewoman. It wasn't difficult.

"It's only a tale," she muttered, "an invention like your giant cows and...and snow ogres."

"Frost Giants," he corrected. She wasn't a very good liar. "And the story of Audhumla is true."

She crossed her arms and smirked at him. "Really? Dwarves?"

He frowned. "How do *you* think the sky stays up?"

She shook her head as she propped her sword in the corner.

Though she tried to make light of it, Brandr couldn't let go of the feeling that there was more than a morsel of truth to her story.

Avril had had ample opportunity to kill him, even the chance to turn him over to someone else to kill. And yet she hadn't. She'd had mercy on him—feeding him, sheltering him, tending to his broken arm—when anyone else would have let him suffer. Though he was her enemy, she'd treated him with respect, wisdom, fairness, and honor. She seemed to have been raised as he had—with the qualities necessary to inspire followers and command warriors. It wasn't hard to imagine she was that woman who'd fought for the jeweled sword, that her four brothers were Kimbery's evil uncles, and that they'd taken advantage of her misfortune to seize her inheritance from her.

He and Avril must both be cursed by the gods then. He'd lost his family, his men, and his ship. She'd lost her innocence, her birthright, and her land. They were kindred souls. Against his better judgment, he found he wanted to know more about this intrepid woman.

"So in that...story...you told your daughter," he asked as she stirred the banked embers on the hearth to life with a stick, "where is this Rivenloch?"

She shrugged. "It's an imaginary place."

"Your daughter doesn't seem to think so."

She arched a slim brow at him. "My daughter thinks she's a

selkie, her sheep talks to her, and you're her father."

She had a point. "But you *are* teaching her to fight with a sword."

"Aye, so she can protect herself from..." She gave him a fleeting glance, and he was sure she intended to say "Vikings." Instead she substituted, "Attackers."

He nodded. "Where did you learn to fight?"

"All Pictish women know how to fight," she said proudly. "Don't Viking women know how to fight?"

"There's no need. They have Viking men to protect them."

"Indeed?" She gave him a cursory perusal, as if she were sizing up a horse. "And who protects them from the Viking men?"

He scowled when he realized she was serious.

Avril had felt the Northman's iron grip on her wrist. She'd seen his bulging muscles. He had the shoulders of an ox and was at least a head taller than anyone she knew. What was to keep a man like him from taking what he wanted from a woman?

"The law protects them," he replied at last, as if it were obvious.

"The law," she scoffed. "You mean the law that *men* make and enforce?"

"Men *and* women."

She lifted a skeptical brow.

He frowned. "Is it not so here? Do you not have an *althing?*"

"*Althing?*"

"A meeting of all the villagers." She waited for him to continue. "A meeting where the rules are made." At her silence, he added, "By everyone."

"*All* the villagers?" she asked doubtfully.

"Anyone who wishes to attend."

"Men *and* women?"

"Of course."

72

That gave Avril pause. She gazed wistfully into the fire, wishing it were thus with her people as well. Her father had understood. He'd believed that women were just as capable as men. That was why he'd made her his heir. But most men were like her brothers, who thought that a woman's place was under a man's boot.

"In my land," Brandr added softly, "the warrior woman in your story? She would never have lost her castle."

Avril bit her lip.

He continued. "Anyone who refused her rule would have been sent into exile."

Her throat tightened. That was how it should have been. Instead, *she'd* been sent into exile.

He went on. "And she wouldn't need an army to take back what was rightfully hers."

Tears of frustration threatened behind her eyes, but she bit them back. She couldn't think about that. What was past was past. She couldn't change what had happened. And there was nothing she could do about it now.

Mortified at the thought of crying in front of a Viking, she sniffed sharply, clapped the soot from her hands, and abruptly stood up. Unfortunately, as she did so, she stepped on the hem of her skirt, which was still partially tucked into her belt. In the blink of an eye, she tripped and stumbled sideways toward the fire.

How Brandr moved so swiftly, she didn't know. In one instant, she was falling face-first toward the burning coals, and in the next, he'd caught her with his boot and propelled her back toward him.

As she fell, she reflexively put out her hands. She managed to partially catch herself, though she heard him grunt in pain as she fell against his splinted arm. But that wasn't the worst of it. She landed with her hands on his chest, her face in his belly, and her breast in his palm.

CHAPTER 8

Brandr hardly felt the throbbing in his broken arm. It was nothing compared to the panicked throbbing of his heart. The woman had almost fallen into the fire. Thank Odin he'd had the reflexes and strength to save her. "Are you all right?"

She lifted her head to look up at him. There was a curious expression on her face, as if she were simultaneously relieved and horrified.

Then he realized what part of her was nestled against his palm, and suddenly the throbbing of his arm and his heart diminished in comparison to the burgeoning throbbing in his trousers. It had been a long time since he'd felt the soft fullness of a woman's breast. His response was unavoidable.

They stared at each other uncertainly, knowing they had to extricate themselves from this awkward predicament somehow, both reluctant to move for fear of making it worse. The moment stretched on, becoming more and more strained, and neither budged.

And then a strange thing happened. Avril closed her eyes and made a small sound in her throat, not quite a sigh of pleasure, not quite a whimper of distress, and her fingers tightened with subtle pressure on his chest. He froze, afraid to breathe.

When she opened her eyes again, it was only halfway, and she lowered her gaze to his mouth. He, too, was drawn to her lips—so sweet, so tempting, like ripe fruit just out of his reach.

He had the mad urge to lean down and steal a kiss, to taste her soft, succulent lips once again, to be reckless and bold and claim her like a marauder.

But the damned leather collar around his neck prevented him.

Hell, it was just as well. After all, it would be a mistake to do something so impulsive and irresponsible. It would destroy her trust and ruin his plans for escape.

He had to resist temptation.

She, however, didn't even try.

Lust knocked Avril over like an unexpected ocean wave, stealing her breath away, dragging her into deeper currents, drowning her good sense.

In some dim corner of her brain, she knew she should back away. But Brandr's chest felt deliciously strong and supple beneath her fingers. His breath caressed her brow. His eyes were smoky and inviting. What she really wanted to do was kiss him.

She eased forward the slightest bit, sucking in a quick breath as his hand rasped gently across her breast. She hesitated, then moved against him again, relishing the tantalizing friction as his palm grazed her. The third time, she squeezed her eyes shut in pleasure. And he responded, moving his thumb tenderly across her nipple.

There was no stopping the coursing tide then. With a soft gasp, she surged forward, caught his stubbled face between her hands, and planted her lips across his enticing mouth.

His cheek was coarse, he smelled of smoke and the sea, and his body was as hard and rough as seasoned oak. But his lips were warm and yielding, and his kiss was filled with gentle wonder.

He answered her at once, angling his face to release and recapture her lips, drawing them in with his own. He breathed passion across her cheek and gasped as she licked experimentally at his mouth. His jaw opened in invitation, and for an instant she hesitated, wondering if he'd bite her like that wolf in his story. Then yearning overrode caution, and she let her tongue venture within, enjoying the ale-sweet taste of him and the pleasing shock as his tongue answered in kind.

Her eager fingers furrowed through his hair, unmindful of his salt-crusted tangles. She pressed closer, letting her breasts chafe provocatively against his chest. They were both breathing heavily now, and she could feel her heart beating like the ocean pounding the shore.

She continued to kiss him, in too deep to turn back. She dared not stop to take a breath, for fear one of them might come to their senses and halt the exhilarating madness.

His soft groan, deep in his throat, was like the purr of a great wild animal, and it sent a frisson of strange current through her, as if he'd called to her. Lightning coursed through her body and struck at the place she most longed to be touched—that burning ember between her thighs.

He seemed to know instantly what she needed. His hand found her, even through her skirts, cupping her with a firm precision that made her gasp. She shivered as he rubbed slowly against her, easing and provoking her at the same time.

She squeezed her eyes tightly. This was mad. It was wrong. And yet it felt so right. She couldn't seem to stop. His body was a strong lodestone, and she was drawn to him like a powerless scrap of iron.

He opened her mouth wider with his, thrusting his tongue inside, devouring her, and she feasted equally on him. Her nipples stung where they brushed across his chest. And where his fingers now delved with more intense finesse, she began to swell with longing.

Desire rose like an incoming tide, too swift to escape, and soon she was swept off her feet. Higher and higher she was carried on a wave of lust, out of control, unsure of her destiny, led by a stranger. And yet she was helpless to resist.

Brandr was past thought. Otherwise, he'd never have put himself in this situation. This was the woman who had knocked him out and tied him up, and what was he doing? Pleasuring her.

Of course, she wasn't the only one receiving pleasure. It had been a long while since he'd enjoyed the attentions of a woman so enthusiastic and forthright, a woman who lustily took what she wanted. But his body hadn't forgotten how to respond to such enthusiasm.

He naturally let her have her way.

He let her kiss him like a greedy suckling lamb. He let her explore his body, run her fingers over his chest and through his hair. He let her press the supple pillows of her breasts against him. He let her arch against his hand, begging wordlessly for his touch.

And he answered her onslaught with the instinctive cravings of his love-starved body.

Blood rushed through his veins and roared in his ears as their tongues entwined and their breath mingled. Even through the layers of linen, the tempting crevice between her legs was impossibly hot, and he ached to plunge there with more than just his fingers.

Indeed, the lusty beast in his trousers was rousing, growing more demanding and frustrated by the moment. And the fact that satisfaction was so close, yet unattainable, drove him even more mad.

What made him open his eyes, he didn't know—maybe a warrior's innate sense of his surroundings. But the flicker of peripheral movement made him freeze.

The sudden tension in his body instantly alerted her as well. She stiffened, her lips still clinging to his.

"Mama!" came the little girl's scolding voice from the doorway. "I told you a hundred times, don't go near that bad man!"

Avril's eyes went wide, and she pulled away in horror, struggling to her feet and stammering. "I...I...I..."

Since she seemed too tongue-tied to come up with a reasonable explanation, Brandr offered one. "Your mama fell," he said, which was true.

"Aye," Avril choked out, straightening her garments. "I fell."

The little girl eyed them uncertainly, and Brandr held his breath, waiting. Then Kimbery shrugged and skipped off to the kitchen, plopped down on her stool and began chattering to her doll.

The air was heavy with unrequited desire, and the tension between Avril and him was as taut as a drawn bowstring. He didn't dare speak or even glance at her for fear of rekindling the volatile spark between them. It seemed like an eternity before his hunger subsided and he could draw an even breath.

Avril couldn't look at the Northman. She pressed her fingertips into her brow, hiding her eyes behind her hands in shame.

What had she done?

Hell, she'd let him kiss her, hold her, touch her. She'd shown weakness to her enemy, let him gain the upper hand, surrendered to his seduction. But she couldn't let him believe that he'd won some victory over her, that she was somehow vulnerable to him.

Making sure Kimbery was occupied and avoiding Brandr's gaze, she hunkered down to poke at the fire and whispered sharply, "Never do that again."

He barked out an incredulous chuckle, then whispered back, "What—save you from falling into the fire?"

Her lips thinned. "Kiss me," she whispered. "Never kiss me again."

He scoffed, then whispered, "I believe it was *you* who kissed *me*."

Her face grew hot at the truth of his words, but she didn't dare back down. "An honorable man would never make such..." The words stuck in her throat as she remembered the glorious sensation of his hand between her legs. "Such bold advances toward an unwilling woman."

He murmured, "I don't recall you being unwilling at all."

She gasped, casting an anxious glance at Kimbery.

"In fact," he continued, "I'm collared and bound and chained to the wall. It isn't as if I had a choice in the matter."

It was true, of course. She'd thrown herself at him. But he didn't have to come out and say it.

She felt thoroughly humiliated now. She'd made a fool of herself, attacking him with the same raw aggression she'd used on her lovers in that shameful period after her rape. Only this was much worse. This time she'd forced herself upon a man with no power to resist her. Hell, she was no better than the berserker who'd violated her.

Was that why she'd thrown herself at Brandr? Was she somehow seeking revenge upon him for what another of his kind had done to her?

As much as it pained her to admit it, she feared it might be true. She'd treated the Northman with undeserved disrespect. She owed him an apology. Swallowing hard and closing her eyes, she mumbled, "You're right. It was dishonorable of me. I'm sorry."

After what seemed an interminable length of time, he breathed, "I'm not."

Their glances collided then. And in that moment that caught them both off-guard, they were no longer Viking and Pict, no longer prisoner and captor, but man and woman.

What had made Brandr admit the truth about how he felt, he didn't know. It was reckless and unwise. The more emotionally entangled he became with this woman, the harder it would be to betray her and make his escape.

But he couldn't deny he felt…something…for the fiery Pictish lass. What troubled him was that it might be something deeper than just physical lust.

Lust he could deal with. It made sense, after all. He'd been without a woman for so long, it was only natural his body should respond at the first available opportunity. But if it were something more…

By Thor, he had to get out of this mess!

Avril, obviously discomfited by his confession, backed away and ushered Kimbery outside, ostensibly to gather cockles, but probably also to get a breath of fresh, sobering air.

While they were gone, Brandr worked at the iron ring, pulling and twisting to try to loosen it from the mortared stone. The woman might not have turned him in to her neighbor this morn, but that didn't mean she wouldn't ever. Even if she relished the idea of having captured a Viking, even if she enjoyed lording it over him as her prisoner, even if she found amusement and pleasure in his arms, eventually she'd tire of it…and him.

He shouldn't have encouraged her. True, he was collared and bound and unable to avoid her caresses. But he could have turned a cold countenance to her. He could have refused to bend to her seductive will. He could have clamped his mouth shut and made fists of his hands.

Instead, in an instant of weakness, he'd ignored reason. He'd let himself be tempted by her feminine desire, allowed himself to drift with her on an erotic sea. And for one moment, he'd almost believed that they were kindred souls floating there, that they shared a common destination and a deeper destiny.

But he had to ignore such feelings. It would only make things more difficult when the time came to play the traitor.

He yanked hard at the collar, bruising his throat. The iron ring wouldn't budge. He cursed and slumped back against the wall. How much longer did he have? How much longer would it be before Avril decided he was a bad influence on her daughter and a danger to her? How much longer before she turned him in?

CHAPTER 9

Before she even opened her eyes the following morning, Avril could hear them in the next room—Brandr murmuring, Kimbery giggling. It was a pleasant sound, a sound that reminded her of what it was like to have a real family. Her lips curved up as foolish, sentimental tears brimmed in her eyes.

She'd told herself she didn't need family. Her parents were dead. Her brothers had betrayed her. And there was little hope of her finding a husband, since she had nothing to offer. She'd convinced herself that Kimbery was family enough.

But the truth was Avril was terribly lonely.

Most days, she kept herself too busy to notice. Her mind she occupied with survival. Her heart she occupied with Kimbery.

Still, regret occasionally crept in, and she grieved for the person she used to be—the young woman who was meant to reign over a noble keep, marry a strong warrior, and have a dozen beautiful children. Most of the time that regret manifested as a righteous thirst for justice and a determination to get back what belonged to her. But sometimes, like this morn, a melancholy pining welled up in her, and she ached for what she couldn't have.

She definitely couldn't have Brandr. There was no question about that. He might have felt right in her arms. His kiss might have been sweet and tempting. His hands might have touched her with the deceptive devotion of a lover. But he was her enemy.

Barbarians like him had invaded her land for decades now. They'd razed her villages, stolen her coin, slaughtered her people. One of them had killed her father and raped her. They were brutal, ruthless savages, and they were beyond reason.

Why then was it so impossible to imagine the whispering Viking in the next room wielding an axe and charging unarmed Pictish children?

Kimbery giggled again, and this time she was joined by the Northman. His laugh was deep and warm, and it sent delicious shivers along Avril's arms.

She swallowed hard and opened her eyes to stare at the ceiling.

What in God's name was she going to do with Brandr?

She couldn't turn him in. She didn't have the heart to deliver him into the hands of an angry mob. Hell, she'd already proven that—hiding him from the man who'd come yesterday.

But she couldn't let him go either. If anything happened to her neighbors because she'd set a Viking loose, she'd never be able to live with herself.

And she couldn't keep him tied up forever. She might be a formidable foe, but she wasn't inhumane.

In the midst of agonizing over what to do with the Northman, she heard Kimbery's giggles interrupted abruptly by a low thud, a silent pause, and then a thin wail.

Avril's heart stopped. Fearing the worst, she thrashed to get free of the tangle of sheets. Cursing her own clumsiness as Kimbery's voice rose to a piercing cry, Avril tripped beside the bed, landing on one knee, her foot still caught in the linens.

What had he done to her? What had that damned Viking done to her little girl?

Fear sucked her mouth dry. It seemed to take forever before she finally managed to get free of the bedclothes and shot to her feet.

She'd kill him! She'd kill the bastard for making her daughter cry.

Desperate to reach Kimbery, she rushed forward, tripping over Kimbery's cloth doll on the floor and catching herself as she slammed against the bedchamber wall.

At last stumbling through the doorway, she froze at the sight, her eyes wide.

Kimbery was sobbing on Brandr's shoulder, and his head was inclined toward hers as he murmured soothing words against her hair.

The protective mother in Avril wanted to snatch Kimbery away at once.

But before she had a chance to move, Brandr met her gaze over Kimbery's head, and she instantly saw the truth in his compassionate eyes. He hadn't hurt Kimbery. She'd hurt herself. And she'd run to him for comfort.

Avril didn't know what to think. Kimbery had been far too trusting of the Northman, sharing her doll with him, drawing pictures of him, listening to his stories, calling him Da. And yet sometimes children had an instinct for people. Sometimes they could tell who was good and who was bad.

She stood at the doorway, watching them in tense silence.

Kimbery's sobbing subsided to sniffles, and she lifted her head to look at Brandr. "Is it bleeding?"

He narrowed his eyes, studying her brow. "A bit."

Kimbery touched the place and drew her fingers away, whimpering at the sight of the blood on her fingertips.

"It should make a fine scar," he assured her. "All great warriors have battle scars."

She stopped crying. "They do?"

"Aye."

"Do you have a scar?"

"Oh, aye, lots of them."

"Where?"

"There's one here, under my chin." He lifted his chin for her to see, though it was covered with stubble. Then he lowered his head. "And I have one on my forehead, like you."

"Did you run into a table, too?"

"Nay." He tried to scowl, but his eyes were twinkling. "That's where Thor struck me with a bolt of lightning."

"Really?"

His frown melted into a smile. "Nay, not really. My brother caught my brow with an axe."

"Is your brother evil like my mama's brothers?"

Avril's breath caught.

"Nay," he said. "It was an accident. We were sparring."

After a thoughtful moment, Kimbery rose to press a kiss to his brow. Avril's jaw dropped. "Mama says this will make it all better. Now you give mine a kiss."

Before Avril could gasp out a word, Kimbery leaned her head toward Brandr's lips, giving him no choice but to repay the gesture.

When Kimbery pulled away, she cocked her head and touched a finger to his temple, where Avril had clubbed him with the driftwood. "Is that a battle scar?"

A hint of a smile threatened at the corner of his lips. "Aye."

"My mama has a battle scar."

Avril nearly choked.

Kimbery continued, "It's right here." She pointed to the right side of her chest.

Brandr's smile blossomed into a full grin. "Really?'

Avril had heard enough. Blushing, she swept into the room. "Kimbery, what happened?"

Kimbery jumped up and ran to her. "Mama, I have a battle scar!"

"Is that so?" She crouched to inspect Kimbery's brow. There was a red bump and a tiny cut there, so tiny that she'd be surprised if it left any mark at all. Nonetheless, she frowned in concern. "And who were you battling to give you such a scar?"

"Sir...Table!"

"I see." She ruffled the top of Kimbery's hair. "And did you give Sir Table battle scars as well?"

Kimbery nodded and then leaned against her and began twining her fingers in Avril's hair. "Mama, I let Brandr kiss my cut."

And I let him kiss my lips, Avril thought. But all she said was, "Oh?"

Kimbery added in a loud whisper, "I don't think he's a very bad man."

Avril sighed, and she felt the tension go out of her. Kimbery was right. He wasn't a very bad man. He'd done nothing wrong. In spite of being shipwrecked and captured and tied up, he'd been civil and even kind. He'd told Kimbery stories, he'd eased away her tears, and been a model father to a little girl who'd never had one. He'd even saved Avril from falling into the fire. Avril slowly raised her gaze over Kimbery's shoulder and looked him squarely in the eye. "Neither do I."

Brandr should have been relieved. Avril was staring at him with complete trust now. He could tell by her eyes that she had no intention of turning him in. He wouldn't have to worry about escaping, because she wouldn't tell anyone he was here. She meant to set him free.

To his surprise, his heart sank. As mad as it was, despite his broken arm, his banged-up nose, and the cursed dog collar around his neck, he'd rather enjoyed the past few days. Avril was a fascinating woman—spirited and passionate, sensitive yet strong, and her daughter was delightful. Now that the opportunity for escape was at hand, he wasn't sure he wanted to leave.

The way she was looking at him made his heart melt. Ever since he'd lost his wife and children, there had been a deep, hollow abyss in his soul. Losing his ship and his men had thrown him farther into the chasm and made it seem impossible to ever reach the surface. But between Avril's kindhearted honor and Kimbery's innocent adoration, he'd started to believe that he could climb out of that hole, that he might be capable of caring and loving again.

Kimbery pushed away from her mother suddenly and galloped across the room into the bedchamber, announcing, "Look at me! I'm a Valkyrie!"

Avril looked askance at him, and he lifted one corner of his lip in a sheepish half-smile.

She came to hunker down beside him then, to tell him what he already knew. "I've decided I won't turn you in."

He waited in silence, not sure he wanted to hear the rest.

She turned in profile to him and lowered her eyes. "My father taught me not to judge a man by the sins of his brothers." She took a deep breath and let it out on a sigh. "You may have Viking blood in your veins. But you have nothing in common with the man who attacked me."

He held his breath, like a felon awaiting his sentence.

"I'm not sure what I'm going to do with you yet," she admitted, "but after all you've done for Kimbery...and for me..." Her glance flickered momentarily to his lips, and he knew she was remembering their kiss. *He* was remembering their kiss. He wished she would kiss him again. She tucked her lower lip under her teeth, then lifted love-soft eyes to his. "I vow I won't let harm come to you."

The naked reverence in her beautiful amber eyes took Brandr's breath away. No woman had ever regarded him with such forthright fondness or gifted him with such a heartfelt promise. The way she was looking at him made him feel he could do anything, even crawl out of his dark underworld into the light.

He opened his mouth to blurt something in return—he wasn't sure what—probably something foolish and maudlin. But Kimbery shot suddenly back through the doorway, and Avril steered her into the kitchen to prepare breakfast.

Part of him felt relief. He'd been racked with guilt all this time, cursing his misplaced affections for Avril as some weakness on his part. To know that she felt the same way about him—that her feelings went deeper than lust, that she recognized his good heart, and that she genuinely cared about him—lifted his spirits.

But the other part of him, the rational part, realized that there was one thing he feared more than Avril turning him in. And that was Avril trying to keep him safe.

Her trusting gaze filled him with dread. There had been much more than simple mercy in her expression. He'd glimpsed a dangerous combination of affection and determination in her eyes, the same unflinching adoration and steely will that had kept her daughter alive on this barren spit of shore.

The fact was she didn't want him to leave either. As improbable as it seemed, the two of them—captive and captor, mortal enemies—had somehow done much more than find common ground and an uneasy peace. They'd fallen in love. And now she naively believed she could keep him.

But she couldn't, not without endangering herself and her daughter. She couldn't hide him. Anyone with one good eye could see Brandr was a Viking. She'd never be able to explain how he'd arrived here, where he'd come from, how they'd met.

And he knew what would happen after that. Avril would be called a Viking sympathizer, branded a traitor, and probably executed. And Brandr wouldn't be able to do a damned thing to protect her.

He was cursed. Misfortune befell anyone who got close to him. As much as his heart ached with the desire to stay, as much as he knew he'd be hurled back into his familiar pit of despair if he left, he knew the only answer was to ignore the bittersweet yearning in his soul, turn his back on her—on both of them, and go.

CHAPTER 10

Avril swept through the seagrass toward the bleating ewe, a stool under one arm and her milk bucket bouncing against her thigh. She felt as light as thistledown atop a bubbling stream. She didn't have all the details worked out, but she knew that sparing Brandr's life was the right decision.

He was a decent man. Maybe he was a Viking, and maybe he'd come as an invader, but he'd shown her nothing but humanity, courtesy, and kindness, in spite of her hostility. He'd seen to Kimbery's cut and kept her from harm by telling her stories. He'd saved Avril from fire and feared for her welfare when she'd confronted her neighbor. It was obvious he felt protective of them.

Did he feel something more? Her heart fluttered at the possibility, and she grew slightly giddy, remembering the way he'd looked at her just now, not only with relief and gratitude, but with a sweet sort of devotion.

She couldn't help but smile as she pushed through the gate and closed it behind her. Plopping the stool down next to Caimbeul, she seated herself. She rested her palm on the animal's flank and set the bucket under the sheep's belly.

As she milked the ewe, she daydreamed.

What if Brandr stayed here with her, with them? He had nowhere else to go, after all. His men hadn't shown up. He was a stranger in her land. He was a castaway, stranded here with no means of survival. She could offer him a roof over his head, food, safety...and perhaps something more.

She leaned her brow against the sheep's woolly side and closed her eyes.

What if the attraction she felt for him grew into genuine love? Could he be a father for Kimbery? And—she dared to imagine—could he be a husband to *her?*

Three days ago, she would have thought it impossible. Now it seemed not only possible, but right. After all, they were both castoffs, exiled from their people. It seemed natural and fitting to seek comfort in each other's company.

She squeezed the last milk from the ewe's udders and retrieved the bucket before giving the sheep a pat to send her trotting across the pasture. Then she sat there for a moment, gazing up at the sky, where low morning clouds made a soft gray blanket that would dissolve away by midday.

Staring into the heavens, she made up her mind. She was going to let him go, set him free. In fact, she'd unleash him right now.

It was risky, she thought as she made her way back to the cottage. Once he was loose, he could physically hurt her, or he could run out of her life forever.

But she didn't think he'd do either. He'd had ample opportunity to do her and Kimbery harm, and he'd done nothing. Nor did he seem the kind of man to leave women to fend for themselves. There was no question in Avril's mind that he was a man of conscience, that she could trust him.

Now that she'd made that decision, she couldn't reach the cottage quickly enough.

When Avril left to milk the ewe, Brandr realized he didn't have much time. He began working on Kimbery at once.

"How would you like to play Fenrir, Kimmie?" he asked, licking his lips, hoping his ploy would work.

Kimbery played coy. "Maybe."

"You can be Fenrir. And I'll be Tyr, Fenrir's loyal friend."

The little girl hesitated, swaying indecisively for a moment. Then she dropped to all fours on the floor and began snapping her teeth together, pretending to be a ferocious wolf.

He spoke in the growling voice of Tyr. "You're so strong, Fenrir, stronger than any other god. I wonder if you're strong enough to break one of those sticks in two." He nodded to the kindling near the hearth.

Kimbery snarled and picked up a twig in her jaws, then took it out with her hands and broke it.

He gasped in feigned awe. "I wonder if you're strong enough to pick up that sword and bring it here all by yourself."

Kimbery hesitated at that and sat back on her heels. "Mama said wee lasses aren't supposed to touch her sword."

Silently cursing in frustration, he said in Tyr's voice, "Wee lasses? But you're not a wee lass. You're Fenrir, son of Loki, son of Odin, the most powerful of all the gods."

The little girl roared once, but then she came close and whispered in his ear. "Mama doesn't even want Fenrir to touch her sword."

Brandr sighed. Avril had her trained well, that was certain. But it didn't matter. He could get free without the sword.

"Great Fenrir," he intoned, "I wonder if you're strong enough to escape this heavy collar."

Kimbery gave a fierce growl of agreement.

"I'll take it off my neck," he said, "and you can put it around yours." He made a show of trying to break free of the collar, twisting and straining.

She became Kimbery again for a moment, whispering, "I'll unbuckle it, and then you can put it on me."

"All right," he whispered back.

As her tiny fingers worked on the strap, a feeling of misgiving weighed down his heart. He didn't want to hurt the little girl. He didn't want to betray her mother. But he saw no other way. He couldn't endanger them. And he had to leave before Avril returned or she'd tempt him into staying.

The instant his neck was free, he bent forward to untie the ropes about his wrists with his teeth.

"Put it on me!" Kimbery impatiently demanded.

"I can't until I loose my hands," he explained.

"Hurry."

He did. As soon as his wrists were free, he untied the rope around his middle, then moved aside so Kimbery could stand in his place.

He buckled the collar loosely around her neck so she wouldn't be able to follow him or hurt herself. She bared her teeth in a snarl as he struggled to his feet on legs that had grown weak with sitting.

While Kimbery growled and twisted against the collar, Brandr glanced at the jeweled sword.

In the end, he found he couldn't bring himself to take it. The blade was Avril's hard-won prize, a gift from her father, and her only defense.

He straightened slowly, groaning at the strain of his stiff muscles. Kimbery quieted. She was eyeing him uneasily now.

"You're Tyr," she said. "You're supposed to put your hand in my mouth."

He meant to leave without a word and without a backward glance. It was best if Kimbery remembered him as a bad man.

But his betrayal must have been written on his face.

Kimmie's chin began to tremble. "Nay, Da. Don't go."

He gulped as a knot of emotion rose up to choke him. He wanted to kneel before her and take her in his arms one last time, to give her the farewell embrace he'd never been able to give his own daughter. But he couldn't. He had to leave...now.

The words spilled out of him in a rush. "I have to, Kimmie. But I'll never forget you. I promise."

Then, before tears could engulf them both, he slipped out the cottage door, closing it behind him. He headed toward the sea, where Avril would never think to look for him.

Avril froze as she closed the pasture gate and noticed the distant figure limping along the shore. It took three heartbeats for her to recognize who it was and another two to realize the significance.

She dropped the bucket, and milk spilled across the ground.

Kimmie!

Fear sucked all the moisture out of her mouth as she hurtled toward the cottage.

When she threw open the door, she was relieved to find Kimbery relatively unhurt. Still, her hands shook as she rushed forward to unbuckle the collar around the little girl's neck.

"He left, Mama," Kimmie sobbed. "We were playing...and he left."

Avril wavered between humiliation and rage. How she'd been so gulled, she didn't know. But now she cursed her stupid trusting heart. She'd been right from the beginning. She should never have trusted a Viking.

"Make him come back, Mama," Kimbery pleaded as she wrapped her arms around Avril's neck, tears streaming down her face.

Avril's heart felt like a lump of lead. Brandr must have tricked her the entire time, making her believe he was decent, gentle, civil. It made her sick to think she'd ever imagined he

94

was in love with her. It made her even more nauseous to remember what she'd let him do to her.

She'd believed him. Kimbery had believed him. He'd pretended that he was different from the berserkers who'd come before, that he was noble and honorable. Yet he was no less a marauder, doing his damage and running off like a coward.

The brute had broken poor Kimbery's heart.

"I want Da!" Kimmie wailed.

Avril gave her a comforting squeeze as tears welled in her own eyes.

But as she held her weeping daughter and tried to soothe her own frayed emotions, it wasn't long before her hurt turned into anger and her anger into action.

Damn the Viking! Who did he think he was to steal away like a thief in the night? He owed her an explanation. He owed Kimbery an explanation. He'd been a father. He knew how sensitive children were. How dared he slink off out of Kimbery's life without so much as a word of farewell?

By God, one way or another, she'd make him answer to her.

She gently swept Kimmie's hair back from her sad little face and used her thumbs to wipe away the tears.

"Listen, Kimmie," she said, "I'm going to go after him. I need you to stay. Do you understand?"

She nodded.

But the moment Avril went for her sword, Kimmie panicked. "Nay, Mama, don't hurt him!"

She frowned. "I won't." At least, she *hoped* she wouldn't, though at the moment, the idea of running him through had its appeal.

"You promise?"

Avril didn't want to make a promise she couldn't keep, but she knew Kimbery would be unmanageable if she didn't. "I promise…if you promise not to set foot outside the cottage."

"I promise." Avril nodded in approval, and as she whirled to go, Kimmie added plaintively, "Bring him back home, Mama."

Home. This wasn't his home. But she couldn't deny, even after so few days, she too had begun to think of Brandr as part of her little family.

Without a word, she swept out the door and raced down to the water's edge to catch up with her quarry.

Brandr didn't realize he'd been followed until he felt something sharp jab him in the back.

"Hold it right there."

He froze. That was the point of her jeweled sword, no doubt. He knew he should have taken it. But how had she managed to find him? He was a good mile down the shore from her cottage.

Glancing down, he realized the waves rushing over the sand had only partially covered his footprints. They'd also completely covered the sound of her pursuit.

His shoulders sank. He'd hoped to avoid a confrontation. He'd hoped to escape quietly, letting Avril think he was a harmless coward like Loki—a knave who'd deserted her but wasn't worth hunting down.

"Where do you think you're going?" she demanded.

"Away."

"Without a word?" she asked, clearly vexed. "Without even saying goodbye?" She poked him with the sword, and he flinched. "How could you do that to...to a sweet little girl like Kimbery?"

Brandr could tell that Kimbery wasn't the only one hurt by his desertion. But he didn't dare let Avril know how he really felt. "She'll get over it."

His cold words hung on the air as a wave crashed on the rocks and hissed over the sand.

"Get over it?" she bit out. "You. Bloody. Bastard."

He clenched his jaw against a surge of guilt.

"She called you Da," she said.

He closed his eyes against the pain.

"Damn you, Viking," she muttered. "I would have set you free."

"I know."

Behind him, she gasped. "If you knew, then why did you sneak off like a robber? Kimbery trusted you." Her voice broke. "She...cared for you."

He furrowed his brow. He cared for Kimbery. She'd brought a welcome light back into his life, a light that had been extinguished when his own children had been taken from him. As for Avril... He was afraid his feelings for Avril went far beyond merely caring for her.

Clenching his fists, he spoke with a flippancy he didn't feel. "She's a child. She'll forget me."

He heard her sob, but she covered her hurt quickly with a jab of her sword that made him wince. "Why would you do such a hurtful thing? Why would you desert her?"

"It's for her own good," he growled.

"You son of a..." She suddenly gave his arse a punishing whack with the flat of her blade. He jerked and raised his hands in surrender. "What the hell is *that* supposed to mean?" she demanded. "You wash up on my beach, sleep under my roof, eat my food, befriend my daughter, and you suddenly decide to walk out of her life...for her own good?"

Brandr decided not to remind her that those were things over which he'd had no choice. After all, she was upset, and she had a sword in her hand. "It *is* for her own good. You said it yourself. I'm a bad man."

"You know that's not true."

"Isn't it?" It was best if she went on thinking he was a heartless brute. Leaving her would be twice as hard if she begged him to stay. "I'm a Viking, a marauder, an invader."

"She liked you. She...she loved you."

Brandr squeezed his eyes shut. He knew Avril was no longer talking about Kimbery now.

He could hear the hurt in her vexed murmur. "Damn you, did you care nothing for her? Was it all a ruse? How could you make her believe you had feelings for her and then...and then abandon her?"

Brandr didn't mean to respond. It would be better for everyone if he let it go. But the words spilled forth. "Do you think it was easy?" he choked out over his shoulder. "To walk away like that? To leave her, knowing she trusted me? Do you think it was easy abandoning her, knowing I was breaking her heart?"

"Why then?" she sobbed. "Why did you run away?"

"I had to."

"You're a coward," she said bitterly, "just like all the men I've known."

"Nay!" he insisted, unwilling to let her believe that. "The man who raped you was a coward. The man who killed your father was a coward. The men who stole your land were cowards."

"And you're not?"

"Nay! I'm trying to protect you."

"I can protect myself."

"Not from me."

"That makes no—"

"I'm cursed, Avril," he ground out. "I'm...cursed. Everyone I care about has been taken from me. My wife. My children. My village. My men." His throat closed, but he forced the words out. "I won't let that happen to Kimbery. And I won't let that happen to you."

For a moment, the only sound was the hushed whisper of the incoming tide and a single gull squawking softly overhead.

Then Avril responded with surprise to his confession. "You...care about me?"

He hung his head and sighed. Was it not written all over his face? He gave her a rueful chuckle. "Oh, my Pictish temptress," he said, shaking his head, "it's far worse than that. I fear I'm in love with you."

Avril was struck speechless. She lowered the blade from his back as his words sank in. No one had ever said that to her before. She didn't know how to respond. She'd fantasized about being Brandr's wife, about making a family with him. She'd never imagined he might already have feelings for her.

She stared in wonder at the enemy she'd discovered only days before on this very shore. His long Viking-blond hair tangled over his wide invader's shoulders and fell down his broad marauding back. But though he was definitely still a stranger, he no longer seemed a foe.

Now she saw the possibility of a bright future...for Kimbery, for herself, for the shipwrecked Northman. They *could* make a life together. They *could* find a place in the world. All she had to do was persuade Brandr of that.

He glanced over his shoulder. Misunderstanding her silence and her lowered weapon, he asked somberly, "Will you let me go now?"

She whipped the point of her blade back up so swiftly it startled him. "Not so fast, Viking." A thrill of hope suffused her even as her eyes filled with happy tears. One way or another, she'd convince the Northman to stay...even if she had to keep him leashed in her cottage for a year. "I thought you said you weren't a coward."

He didn't answer.

She continued. "You're a damned Northman! You flex your muscle, rattle your battleaxe, and speak of glorious war. And yet you'd run away from a *curse*?"

He clenched his fists, but remained silent.

"Well," she said, "I don't believe in curses. Do you think you alone are fortune's foe? I've lost everything, too. I've had bad times when I wanted to surrender. I've had moments of weakness when I wondered why I went on living. But I never gave up. Not once did I let despair get the better of me. Not once did I—"

"Mama!" Kimbery called out suddenly behind her.

Avril started in surprise.

"Kimbery!" she snapped, whipping around to give her daughter the scolding of her life. "I told you to stay at..."

But when she saw Kimmie hadn't come alone, Avril's heart plummeted, her knees buckled, and she nearly lost her grip on the sword. Her little girl was riding merrily atop the shoulders of one of dozens of Viking savages that now occupied her beach.

"Look!" Kimbery crowed, oblivious to her horror. "I'm a Frost Giant!"

All of Avril's warrior instincts told her not to show weakness, not to waver, not to beg. Five years ago, standing over her father's grave, bruised from a brutal rape, she'd vowed never to cower before a Viking again.

But five years ago, she hadn't had a daughter she'd die for.

"Nay," she choked out, "please. Don't hurt her." She prayed they could understand her words. Oh, God, she thought, what if they meant to steal Kimbery? What if they sailed away with her to the North? What if Avril never saw her again?

Quaking with fear, she moved her sword away from Brandr and set the weapon gently on the ground. "Take him. Take Brandr. Just give my daughter back to me."

CHAPTER 11

Brandr wheeled around with his fists raised and his face in a fierce scowl, ready to fight whoever was threatening the women he loved. He lowered his arms immediately when he saw who it was.

"Halfdan?" he asked in disbelief. "Ragnarr?" Relief and joy coursed through him. Behind Avril stood his brothers—whole, healthy, and grinning. By the grace of Odin, they'd come through the storm, untouched, and they were surrounded by their men. "You're alive!"

There was a rumble of celebration as he rushed forward to catch his brothers in a one-armed embrace.

"What happened to you?" Ragnarr asked, indicating his splinted forearm.

His injury was the least of Brandr's concerns. "A scratch," he said with a shrug. "But how did you find me?"

Halfdan frowned. "We followed the wreckage of your ship."

Brandr nodded. There was a long moment of reflective silence as everyone thought about those who'd been lost. Then Ragnarr cleared his throat and announced, "Your men are no doubt feasting in Valhalla."

There were cheers of agreement all around.

"But it's been days," Brandr said. "The wreckage must have drifted. How did you know to look for me here?"

Halfdan gave him a half-smile. "It might have something to do with the little girl standing in her cottage door, yelling 'Brandr! Brandr!' at the top of her lungs."

Brandr had to smile at that. Kimbery perched happily atop ferocious Axlan's shoulders as if he were her favorite uncle.

"So tell me," Ragnarr asked, crossing his arms and cocking a brow toward Avril, "how did my big warrior brother end up at the pointed end of a Pictish wench's sword?"

Brandr was so grateful to see his brothers that he didn't mind the taunt. There would be time to salvage his pride later. But when he looked back at Avril, he saw she'd gone white with fear. She didn't understand their language. She didn't know who they were or what they intended. And her gaze was fixed on Kimbery.

He switched back to Pictish. "Avril, it's all right. They won't hurt you."

Of course, he knew she had no reason to trust him. He'd manipulated her. He'd betrayed her. He'd abandoned her.

"Please, Brandr," she said almost inaudibly. "Please don't take her. Don't take Kimbery."

He furrowed his brows. He wouldn't dream of taking a child from her mother. None of his men would. That she could even think him capable of such cruelty made him want to strangle the berserkers who'd so badly damaged her.

But as he looked at her, a spark of desperate courage flashed in her eyes, and before he could see what she intended, she dove for her blade. In an instant, she swept up the weapon and trained the point at his throat.

"Put her down!" she yelled at the men. "Put her down right now!"

"Nay!" Kimmie wailed in protest.

"Put her down, or I'll cut his throat!"

Brandr froze. He probably could have knocked aside the sword with a swing of his splinted arm, but it was risky. He knew better than to come between a mother and her child.

"Avril," he said, "they mean her no—"

"Quiet!" she barked.

"Woman," Halfdan said in broken Pictish, "you are one. We are many. Put down your sword."

Avril was trembling, but her blade didn't waver an inch. "Nay."

Ragnarr frowned. "Nay?"

"Nay," she said. "Put her down, or I'll kill him."

Brandr tensed as several of the men clapped hands on their weapons in challenge.

"I mean it," she bit out. "Put her down, get back on your ship, and sail away from here, or I swear I'll cut his throat."

Most of the men figured she was bluffing. Maidens didn't kill people, especially Northmen who were double their size. Unintimidated by her threat, Halfdan drew his sword. And when Ragnarr unfolded his arms, he was holding twin axes. Disaster loomed. Brandr had to temper things before the tense standoff erupted into an ugly battle.

"Wait!" he shouted. Avril might believe she had leverage, but Brandr had seen his brothers and their men at war. No one opposed them and lived. It was up to him to prevent a violent altercation. "Don't hurt her!"

"Don't hurt her?" Halfdan echoed in amazement. "If you hadn't noticed, *she's* the one holding a blade to *your* throat."

"She won't do it," Brandr said, hoping he was right. "She won't kill me."

"That's right," Ragnarr said, "because *we'll* kill *her* before she gets the chance."

"Nay! She...she saved my life." It wasn't exactly true, but he didn't know what would have happened to him if she hadn't dragged him into her cottage. Probably her neighbor would have found him, killed him, and made a trophy out of him.

"Saved your life?" Halfdan scoffed. "She doesn't seem too interested in your life now."

Brandr sighed. Halfdan was right, of course. But if they'd shown up an hour earlier, it would have been a different tale. He would have told them how she'd set his arm, kept him fed, and protected him from a Viking-hunter. And he would have been able to explain to Avril that his brothers meant her no harm, that *he* meant her no harm.

Now, he could hardly expect her to trust him.

But maybe, now that his brothers were here, now that he was no longer shipwrecked and alone, now that he had a small army at his disposal...

A brilliant idea took form in his mind, and for the first time in a year, he began to think he might not be cursed after all.

To commit to slaying Brandr if it came to that was the most difficult thing Avril had ever done in her life. But her precious daughter was at risk. Nothing was more important than Kimbery—nothing.

"Avril," Brandr said, "listen to me. You know you don't want to kill me in cold blood. It's not the honorable thing to do. And you always do the honorable thing."

She clamped her lips together. But though her vision grew watery and a tense knot formed in her throat at what she might be forced to do, she held her ground. She realized that when it came to her daughter, Kimbery was more important than honor itself.

"Make them put her down," she said hoarsely, "or I swear I'll slay you where you stand."

He seemed to believe her. "All right." He said something to his men. They argued back and forth. But in the end, they put away their weapons, muttering in disgust as they did so.

"And Kimmie," she choked out. "Give me my daughter."

"Nay!" Kimmie complained. The wayward little sprite tucked her lip under her teeth and held tightly to the man's head. Kimbery knew she was in trouble for disobeying Avril's orders and didn't want to be punished.

But punishment was the last thing on Avril's mind. All she wanted was to get Kimbery back, safe and sound.

"I didn't set foot outside the cottage, Mama," Kimmie said. "I didn't. The Frost Giants picked me up."

"Brandr," Avril demanded, willing her voice to remain steady, "make them put her down."

He relayed her message. Despite Kimmie's protests, the man peeled the little girl's hands from his forehead and lifted her off of his shoulders.

"Come here, Kimmie," Avril said, her heart in her throat.

Kimbery reluctantly began to saunter over, and for one tiny instant, Avril lost her focus. But in that instant and without warning, Brandr used his arm—the arm Avril had splinted for him—and knocked her sword aside, and then used his good hand to wrench it from her grasp. She was still gasping in dismay when he wrapped his splinted arm around her neck, trapping her against him.

She clawed and kicked at him, but nothing would dislodge the brute's grip on her. In desperation, she cried, "Run, Kimmie! Run!"

Kimbery might be a willful little girl, but she recognized the alarm in Avril's voice. Obedient for once, she spun and began tearing across the sand toward home. The men casually watched her go.

Brandr blew out an annoyed breath. "All right," he said, "we're all going back to the cottage. Avril, you and I are going to have an *althing*. Do you remember what that is?"

She wasn't interested in conversing with him. All she cared about was keeping the men away from Kimbery. She twisted violently in his grip.

He ignored her struggles. "You and I are going to talk things over," he explained. "Together. Civilly."

With unflappable calm, he began to haul her, kicking and screaming, along the shore and back to the cottage, with his men in tow. By the time they arrived, she was hoarse and exhausted, but at least she had the satisfaction of knowing she'd put up a fight. She'd been no victim this time. She'd done everything she could to protect herself and her daughter.

"Kimmie!" Brandr called.

"Nay!" Avril yelled.

"Kimmie, come out!"

Kimbery popped her head out of the door.

"Nay!" Avril shrieked. "Stay there."

"She'll come to no harm, I promise," Brandr told her. "The men will watch over her."

He spoke as if she had a choice. The truth was she was at their mercy. Yet, when she thought about it, Brandr's men had done Kimmie no harm thus far. They could have kidnapped her when they first discovered her. They could have leveraged her life for Brandr's. But they hadn't.

She swallowed hard. "If they lay a finger on her..."

"They won't. I swear it. She'll be safe." One side of his mouth curved up. "She likes them. She thinks they're Frost Giants."

His smile of encouragement did little to assuage her fears. And to her dismay, Kimbery ran eagerly toward the man who'd hefted her on his shoulders, wrapping her arms fondly around his knees. With an uneasy spirit and against her better judgment, Avril let Brandr steer her into the cottage.

The instant he closed the door behind them, he let her go. She staggered a step and wheeled on him, ready to fight with her bare hands, if need be.

"Sheathe your claws, kitten," he said. "I only want to talk."

She scowled at him, and then, realizing her fists were no match for a sword, lowered her hands.

"I have an idea," he told her, beginning to pace pensively before the hearth.

She touched her scraped throat, rubbed raw from struggling against his splinted arm. "An idea." She couldn't imagine what he meant.

"My brothers and I came to your land, not to invade, but to settle," he said, gesturing with her sword. "All we want is a place to stay. A home. Land."

She scowled, only half-listening, wondering if there was any way she could wrest her sword from his grip. She ground out, "I don't think you'll all fit in my cottage, if that's your idea."

He gave her an indulgent chuckle, and then continued. "Nay, I have a far better plan." He stopped pacing and arched a brow at her. "How far away is Rivenloch?"

She blinked. "Rivenloch?" What was he thinking?

He smiled at her. It was wicked smile, a scheming smile.

She opened her mouth to speak and then closed it again, once, twice. Could he possibly be considering what she *thought* he was considering?

"I have an army of Northmen," he said. "Enough to take back a castle wrongfully seized from its true heir."

For a moment, she was stunned. But as she looked into his glittering blue eyes, a thrill of hope shot through her. "Are you serious?"

"I am." His face was grim now, and he suddenly looked every inch a coldhearted, bloodthirsty Viking. "Are you?"

Avril stared at him in wide-eyed wonder. Mere moments ago, she'd been sure her life was over. Now it seemed full of promise beyond her wildest dreams.

Brandr flipped her sword over in his hand and offered it to her, jeweled hilt first. She stared down at it, knowing the final decision was in her hands. He wasn't just offering her a weapon. He was offering her his sword arm. He was offering her the might of his men. He was offering her her legacy.

Unable to find words to convey her gratitude, she silently took the sword from him. As she gazed down at the glowing gems of the hilt, they winked up at her, as if eager for battle. But after a moment, she propped the weapon against the wall.

There would be time to make war later.

Now, she wanted to make love.

CHAPTER 12

Brandr knew Avril would be pleased with his offer. He didn't realize just how pleased. Nor did he anticipate how she'd choose to express her pleasure...until she nudged him backward through the doorway of her bedchamber, covering his face with eager kisses.

He shivered as she ran her hands under his shirt and over his chest, and then gasped in pleased surprise as she shoved him back onto the bed. She climbed atop him, lifting his shirt to press her warm lips to his bare flesh. These Pictish women were uncommonly aggressive, he decided. But he definitely could get used to that.

He smiled as she hooked her arm possessively around his neck and claimed his mouth with hers. But his smile fell away as her other hand ventured boldly beneath the waist of his trousers.

Caught off-guard, he sucked in a quick breath as the blood surged through him. Overcome by an unexpected rush of desire, he squeezed his eyes shut, hardening with astonishing speed at her touch.

She purred with satisfaction as her fingers curved naturally around his firm length, and he echoed the sound with a lusty growl. She slanted her mouth over his, plunging her tongue between his lips, and he instinctively reached up to clasp her face between his hands, deepening the kiss.

Her fingers scrabbled at the ties of his trousers, and he lifted his hips so she could slide them down.

With almost frantic haste, she raised her skirts and positioned herself to take him inside her.

His lust-starved body wanted her. Now. But everything was happening too fast. Though he'd imagined making love to her countless times in the past few days, it had never been like this. He had no time to seduce her, no chance to learn her body—to feast his eyes upon her breasts, to whisper in her ear, to kiss the strange design on her shoulder, to suck gently at her nipples, to part her thighs and fondle the sweet bud that guarded her womanhood.

It was too late to stop now. She seized his wrists and anchored his arms to the bed, forcefully sinking down upon him until he was sheathed to the hilt.

He groaned with pleasure as she had her way with him, riding him like a steed, grinding against his hips with a demanding rhythm that pushed him with reckless speed to the brink of passion.

If it hadn't been such a long time, if she hadn't caught him unawares, if he hadn't been so utterly swept away by his own needs, he would have forced her to slow down. But like a boy trysting for the first time, he was beyond reason and out of control.

Almost before he could draw another breath, the blood began to simmer in his veins. A flash like hot lightning seared his skin. The tide of desire rose in him, raging like a flood, filling him with need, and then bursting free in a quenching rush.

With a bellow of ecstasy, he arched up into her welcoming womb, pulsing out waves of molten fire. He heard her sigh in response, and when he was able to gaze at her from beneath his heavy lids, Brandr glimpsed intoxicating triumph on her face.

He shuddered with the power of his release while she replied with a throaty, pleased chuckle. And then, unable to formulate coherent thoughts, much less words, he simply lay beneath her, panting like a winded warhorse.

While he caught his breath, she lazily ran her fingers over the bulge of his upper arm. She bit her lower lip, flushed with longing, and he could see unrequited desire still veiling her eyes.

He wasn't finished with her. This hasty coupling had been far too swift and one-sided. But it had taken the ragged edge off of his lust, and now he'd be able to take his time with the hot-blooded wench.

Avril knew everything was going to be all right now. She'd won Brandr over, body and soul. He'd marry her now and give Kimbery a name. He'd even promised to regain Rivenloch and her rightful place of power. There was nothing as heady as being in control again. At last her world would be set to rights and she'd get her command back.

And yet she realized as she continued to gaze down at Brandr's broad chest, tracing the contours of his muscular arms and shivering at the rasp of his breath upon her skin, she felt less like the lady and commander of a castle and more like a drowsy-eyed cat longing to be pet.

The feeling troubled her. Her heart beat too fast. Her reflexes were too slow. She felt feverish and weak, as if her bones were melting. And the sensation only grew worse when she felt him begin to swell inside her again.

She knew she should withdraw. She was too exposed, too fragile, too vulnerable. If she wasn't careful, she'd leave herself open to attack. She might find herself at his mercy, the same way she'd been at the mercy of that berserker.

And yet...

She couldn't seem to pull away. Even as her mind screamed at her to flee while she still had the chance, to raise her shield, to guard her heart, as she gazed into his smoldering eyes and felt the impassioned rise and fall of his formidable chest, she was strangely drawn to him.

And when one corner of his mouth lifted in a lazy smile, when he reached up to softly brush her lower lip with the back of his knuckle, when she felt the subtle pulse of his need within her, she knew she was past escape.

Her eyes closed, and her mouth fell open beneath his touch. A curious warm glow enfolded her, softening her fear and whetting her appetite. Her fingers tightened on his shoulders, pressing into his supple flesh, as he gently caressed her cheek.

Her breath quickened as his fingers drifted down her throat, settling upon the place where her pulse now raced. She swallowed hard, knowing he could strangle her with one hand and yet trusting he would not.

Indeed, his hand moved with such sweet leisure down her neck, sweeping across her collar bone, and slipping beneath her kirtle, that she felt no desire to resist. Slowly, he teased the garment from her shoulder, running his fingers over the design inked there.

"What is this?" he whispered.

She furrowed her brow, startled that he spoke to her. The men she'd bedded before never uttered a word—not that she'd given them the chance. She hadn't wanted to know their thoughts. She'd simply wanted to use their bodies and be done with them.

It was disconcerting. Nonetheless, she managed to answer him. "An endless knot."

"It's beautiful," he murmured. "What does it mean?"

She hesitated, uncomfortable with his question. Somehow, the exchange of words made what they did more intimate. She couldn't pretend he was just another body. Speaking forced her to acknowledge he was a man...with thoughts and ideas and intentions.

Though it was difficult for her, she answered him in a stilted whisper. "The three circles are...spirit...life...and love."

"Ah." His hand left her shoulder then to brush over her ankle, which was nestled against his hip. "And this one?"

Lusty lethargy made her voice ragged and foreign to her ears. "A broken sword...in honor of my father."

He was silent for a moment. Then he asked, "Did it hurt?"

His puzzling question made her open her eyes. Then she remembered he had no such markings on his skin. Her designs must seem strange to him.

"Nay," she told him.

He shot her a dubious glance.

"A wee bit," she admitted.

He grinned at her again, and the fond shimmer in his eyes made her return his smile. Suddenly she felt more than just the sharp heat of lust and longing. There was also a gentle warmth like that of a banked fire. And as he continued to hold her gaze, she sensed he could easily stir the coals of that fire to life.

His eyes lowered to her mouth, and already she longed to taste him again. As if drawn to him by the force of his will, she closed her eyes and leaned toward him.

This time she made no demands of him, but let him lead. His kiss was tender and tentative, like the touch of a honeybee upon a blossom, and soon a pleasant buzzing filled her head. Again and again he sampled the nectar from her lips, until she ached for more.

As she gasped against his mouth, he deftly loosened the laces of her kirtle and slipped it from her shoulders. When it caught on the points of her breasts, he freed it, sliding one fingertip under the linen. When his knuckle grazed her nipple, desire welled in her like the swelling of an ocean wave, submerging her in its powerful current.

She clenched her thighs around his hips and moved against him. But he refused to engage her yet, focusing instead on her bared bosom. He kissed his way down her throat and across her breast, pausing as he reached the inch-long strip of puckered flesh there.

"Your battle scar?" he murmured.

She nodded, and he traced its length with his tongue before blazing a searing trail toward her nipple. When he sucked softly there, she cried out in wonder at the divine sensation.

Then, just when she thought she would burst from pleasure, he moved to her other breast, lavishing it with equal attention. Moans issued from her throat unbidden, and her fingers tangled in his hair as if to keep him close.

While she reveled in a languorous haze, his hand delved beneath her skirts, traveling up her thigh with silky stealth. Even knowing where he was headed couldn't prepare her for the shock that rocked her when the tip of his finger touched her at the spot where their bodies joined.

He rubbed gently there, and she squeezed her eyes shut, caught in a paralyzing tide of euphoria. She arched against him, elated yet languishing, knowing she wanted something more, something she could neither define nor understand.

This was far more potent than the intoxication of his surrender. It was a savage craving that satiated and tormented her all at once. Lost in a fog of emotions, she was nonetheless compelled to sail onward.

It was only when his arm wrapped around her shoulders and his thigh curved possessively over her buttock, when he tried to roll her onto her back, that she stiffened.

Only once had a man ever dominated her. And that had been against her will. After she'd been raped, she'd never allowed a man to toss her onto her back. She'd been helpless once. She'd vowed never to be so again.

"Nay!" She dug her nails into his shoulders, ready to resist with all her might.

To her surprise, he responded immediately, relaxing his grip on her and withdrawing his hands. She searched his face, wondering what game he played.

But there was only patient affection in his eyes. And as he lay submissively beneath her, giving her time to reason, she was forced to confront her demons. It wasn't long before she realized the truth—those demons clearly existed only in her imagination.

Brandr was not a berserker. He had no desire to hurt her, to demean her, to dominate her. He obviously cared for her. He'd confessed his love. He'd bared his soul to her. Hell, he'd even offered to fight for her. Why, then, was she reluctant to cede the tiniest bit of control to him?

If anyone was obsessed with power, Avril realized, it was she. After all, she'd held him prisoner. She'd kept him at her mercy. She'd had her way with him. What more did she want? Must he grovel at her feet, yielding to her in every way?

At her brooding silence, he smiled ruefully. "Maybe you don't truly care for me."

She frowned. How could he think that? She'd practically saved his life. She'd fed him and housed him. She'd set his arm. She'd protected him from her neighbor. How could she not care for the man who had promised to get her castle back? "Of course I do."

"But do you trust me?"

She bit her lip. It was true she'd learned to be wary when it came to trusting men. And yet Brandr had done nothing to deserve her mistrust. Even when she thought he'd betrayed her, he'd only been trying to protect her. She looked into his expectant eyes—eyes as beautiful and unclouded as a summer sky—and then lowered her gaze to his inviting mouth.

She couldn't let the damned berserker who'd raped her win. She couldn't let her wretched brothers win. She wouldn't let what had happened to her in the past ruin her chances at happiness in the future.

"Kiss me again," she murmured, certain that she *did* trust him after all.

His touch was tender and coaxing, soothing and arousing all at once. He cradled her chin and kissed her with care, as if she were a brittle seashell. He stroked her hair with the gentle caress of the ocean combing the kelp. His fingers swept over her like the incoming tide washing across the shore, exploring higher and farther with subtle stealth.

And this time, when she willingly rolled onto her back, it felt as natural as turning over in the sea on an afternoon swim. And though he rose above her, as massive and menacing as an ocean wave, she felt no panic. He moved with the steady languor of the sea, rocking her gently along the current until they floated there together in rising bliss.

Before long, she realized this was like no other voyage she'd taken. The sensual weight of his hips, the tantalizing touch of his hands, the fiery caress of his tongue took her to a place she'd never been before. Her breath expanded as an ember sparked within her, filling her with glowing heat. Her body moved of its own accord, squirming in pleasure. Her fingers pressed into the supple muscle of his buttocks, urging him closer, and when that wasn't enough, she wrapped her legs around him, arching up against the divine pressure of his belly. She closed her eyes tightly, relishing the erotic delight of his flesh on hers as he teased her lust to a fine point.

Farther and farther into uncharted waters they sailed, and Avril clung to him, half-afraid, half-obsessed, seeking... seeking...

"Look at me," he suddenly breathed.

She couldn't. She'd never felt so vulnerable, so exposed. If she let him glimpse the helplessness in her eyes...

"Look at me," he softly urged, pausing to smooth away the crease between her brows with his thumb.

With a small whimper of protest, she reluctantly complied, and her face grew instantly hot with shame. But then she gazed into his eyes—his shining, smoldering, sea-colored eyes.

As he stared down at her with pure, beautiful, unflinching love, her fears vanished. A sweetness filled her spirit, softening her, comforting her. And when he moved within her again, the tenderness between them heightened her desire.

She sailed with him on the journey toward passion, and the lovely torment in his eyes fueled her own as they grew closer and closer to the edge of the world...panting, gasping, then breathless with intensity as time froze and the earth dropped from below. Lightning struck her with stunning force, making her cry out in shock, while Brandr echoed her with a low groan.

Their shudders of release made powerful thunder, and she held tightly to him as they careened earthward again, falling...falling...back into the deep calm of the sea.

For a long while she drifted on the lazy current, miles away from care, letting waves of contentment wash over her.

Gradually, the fog of sensuality receded, and she began to notice small details like the skirt rucked up indecently around her waist, the adorable lock of hair drooping over his forehead, the rock-hard object stabbing into her spine...

With a frown, she reached behind her back and dug out Kimbery's slate and a piece of charcoal.

He lifted his head and grinned at the smeared slate. "You may have a new design on your back."

She smiled back. "I suspect it may be a drawing of you." She tossed the slate and charcoal aside and reached up to touch that irresistible blond lock. "You know, I think I could get used to these *althings* of yours."

He turned her hand to kiss her palm. "Strange, but I don't remember them ever being so...invigorating."

She lowered her gaze to his delectable mouth, and he accepted her unspoken invitation at once. They were mid-kiss when there was a loud banging on the cottage door.

Avril gasped and yanked her kirtle up to her chin.

Brandr muttered, "My brothers no doubt fear you've thrust me through with your sword." With a last light kiss upon her brow, he rose from the bed and pulled up his trousers.

As she worked hastily to repair her appearance, he retrieved Kimbery's slate and drew a few strange runes on it with the charcoal.

"What does it say?" she asked.

He gave her a sweet, lopsided smile full of affection and mischief. "Da."

Her eyes welled with joy and gratitude as she took his hand and tugged him toward the door. She couldn't wait to tell Kimbery she'd been right all along.

Rivenloch was returned to its rightful heir. And in that place, generations of Vikings and Picts intermingled and intermarried to create the sturdy stock of Scotland. The descendants of Brandr and Avril upheld the honor in which their clan was forged. Their veins flowed with the courage and loyalty of their Viking father and their Pictish mother. For centuries, they bravely defended the land from invaders with an unconquerable army, an army made strong by the marriage of their two powerful and illustrious cultures.

But one day, their courage and loyalty would be tested, for there would come to Rivenloch an enemy so formidable it would take warriors of unmatched mettle to face the daunting challenge.

These warriors would be the progeny of a centuries old Viking invader and his Pictish bride, and the fate of the clan would lie in their unlikely hands. Thus was born the legend of the Warrior Maids of Rivenloch...

The End

More books from the Warrior Maids of Rivenloch series:
A Yuletide Kiss (short story)
Lady Danger
Captive Heart
Knight's Prize

the handfasting

A Knights of de Ware Novella

A French knight betrothed to a Highland heiress
falls in love with his spirited bride, then realizes he's been tricked
into wedding the wrong sister.

DEDICATION

For all the people who weren't born perfect
and all those wise enough to
see their value anyway

ACKNOWLEDGMENTS

Heartfelt thanks to:

Suzan Tisdale and Kathryn Le Veque
for nudging me to do a holiday novella

My BFF Lauren Royal
For convincing me to find a way to matchmake
my two legendary families

Birthe Hansen for OT brainstorming

Kit Harington and Emma Watson
for inspiration

CHAPTER 1

The Highlands
Yuletide 1199

Ysenda hated Yuletide.

All around her, the clan celebrated with feasting and cheering. Lively merrymaking filled the great hall. Laughter and music echoed from the rafters.

Yet she frowned into her half-drained wooden cup.

Her loathing had nothing to do with the supper. Who could complain about the sumptuous food gracing the table each night of Yule? Tonight there were succulent boar's head, smoked mutton, roast venison, rabbit pottage, cockles, hazelnuts, cheese, and endless cups of winter ale.

She didn't even mind the drunken revelry that inevitably followed. Raucous songs chased away the gloom. Lusty lads grabbed at giggling lasses. The music of pipes, harp, and tambors filled the air. Boisterous dancing encouraged the return of the sun after the solstice.

The boughs of holly decking the hall looked admittedly festive. So did the ivy draping the great hearth. Mistletoe hung in all the doorways for good luck. Luminous tallow candles set about the room made the rough wood beams of the keep look warm and welcoming.

For once, despite being crowded elbow-to-elbow into the keep, no one in the clan was bickering. Everyone was freshly-scrubbed, smiling, and dressed in their best finery.

Even Ysenda had made an effort. She'd bathed in lavender-scented water. She'd washed her long linen leine until it was as white as the snow outside. Atop that, she wore her best gown of soft gray wool. Flowing around her waist and across her breast was an arisaid of pale gray plaid, pinned at the shoulder with a silver brooch. Her normally unruly chestnut hair was harnessed by two narrow braids at the crown, tied at the back with a ribbon, and lightly scented with more lavender.

She felt bonnie...almost as bonnie as her sister.

"Caimbeul!" From across the hall, over the top of his bellowing friends, one of the many piss-drunk ruffians snagged a squirming lass by the arm and called out to Ysenda's older brother. "Caimbeul! Why don't ye come dance with Tilda here?"

Ysenda stiffened as Tilda pulled away with a horrified blush. Everyone laughed.

That was why she hated Yuletide.

Beside her, Caimbeul grinned at their jest. But Ysenda knew he was dying inside. He wanted so much to fit in, to be like them.

Most of the time, he could pretend he was. Most of the time, Ysenda forgot he was different. When the two of them were alone, he seemed as well-made and fit as any man.

It was only when they were forced to make a public appearance, like at Yuletide—seated beside their sister and father as if nothing were wrong—that his difference was made painfully clear.

Once the crowd gathered and the ale was flowing, the taunts and the laughter began. And to Ysenda's dishonor, their father, Laird Gille, did nothing to prevent the mockery.

Why would he? The laird had disowned his deformed son at first sight. Indeed, the only reason he'd let the boy live was because Caimbeul had been six months old when the laird came home from his travels to lay eyes upon him. Ysenda's fierce mother, descended from the infamous Warrior Maids of Rivenloch, had threatened the laird's life if he touched one hair on her precious son's head.

Beside her, Caimbeul sighed and lowered his half-eaten oatcake. Ysenda followed his gaze. A group of wee lads played beside the hearth. In imitation of their older brothers, they were making fun of Caimbeul's distinctive hobble.

Her grip tightened on her eating dagger as she muttered, "Those sheep-swivin' brats. What do they think they're doin'?"

He gave her a sad, forgiving chuckle. "They're only bairns, Ysenda. They don't know any better."

"Oh, I'd be glad to teach them," she said between her teeth. "Maybe I'll spit them and roast them slowly o'er the Yuletide fire."

That made him smile. "Ach, ye sound like our ma."

"'Tis disrespectful," she insisted. "Ye're the son o' the laird."

In fact, he was the *only* son of the laird. The firstborn. He should be the heir to the clan. But he might as well be invisible. His presence was expected at holiday feasts when the extended clan filled the hall. He was allowed to sit beside Ysenda when the laird flanked himself with his daughters. But Laird Gille paid him no heed. There might as well have been a mile-high wall between Caimbeul and his father.

Still, it was insensitive of Ysenda to remind him of that. She instantly regretted her words.

To make amends and lighten the mood again, she gave Caimbeul a conspiratorial wink. Then, when their father wasn't looking, she used her dagger to steal a slice of roast boar from the laird's trencher, dropping it onto Caimbeul's.

Caimbeul grinned and dug in.

Ysenda couldn't help but grin back. How anyone could overlook the gentle humor in Caimbeul's soft brown eyes—his kindness, his loyalty, his sweet nature—she didn't know. She supposed most people never saw past his crippled frame.

Calling him Caimbeul, which meant crooked mouth, had been polite. To be honest, it seemed there wasn't a bone in his body that was straight. His back was hunched. His spine was shaped like a slithering snake. His hips were twisted. And one shoulder was higher than the other. With each passing year, his deformity had gotten worse, as if the cruel claws of a dragon slowly closed around him, leaving his body more warped and useless.

Most people assumed his brain was likewise twisted. But Ysenda knew better. He might suffer from neglect. But he was bright, and he possessed a wry wit.

Sadly, their father had deemed it a waste to teach him anything. He said the lad would die young anyway, so an education was pointless.

To make matters worse, when Caimbeul was twelve years of age, their warring mother was killed, mortally wounded by a sword. While she lay dying, she made Ysenda swear to look after her older brother. It was no small task for a wee lass of nine. But Ysenda promised she would.

Once their mother was buried, however, things changed. The laird, ashamed of his son's infirmity, banished the lad from the keep. He was sent to live in a wee thatch-roofed cottage in the farthest corner of the bailey.

Looking back, Ysenda had to admit that had probably been for the best. For when the laird was in his cups and Caimbeul was underfoot, their father tended to use his fists, taking out his frustration and rage on the lad.

At the time, however, Ysenda had felt her brother's exile was unfair. And since she'd made that promise to her mother, she couldn't let him go alone. So, heartbroken at the thought of losing both her mother and the older brother she adored, Ysenda stubbornly packed up her things, left the keep, and moved in with Caimbeul.

Her father scarcely noticed her leaving. His attention was fixed on Cathalin, the one daughter who offered him hope. Cathalin was his middle child, the bonnie one, the one who would marry and inherit the lairdship.

Ysenda had done everything she could for Caimbeul. She'd taught him what she knew of reading, writing, and keeping accounts. She'd challenged him to learn about the running of the household and every man's part in it. She'd bribed visiting scholars to tutor him in history and philosophy.

Caimbeul may not have been blessed with a powerful body. But there was much power in knowledge.

And on those occasions when he needed physical defending, it was Ysenda who came to his rescue. She used the fighting skills her mother had taught her. Many a young lad earned a black eye or a bruised shin from daring to mock Ysenda's beloved brother. A few even learned their lesson at the point of her sword.

Caimbeul nudged her with his bony elbow as she slipped him another slice of stolen meat. "Hey." He nodded toward the door with a broad grin. "I think ye've got an admirer."

Ysenda glanced up. A tall, dark, handsome man was staring at her. He wasn't dressed like a Highlander. Instead of a leine and brat, he wore a long surcoat of deep blue covered by a brown tabard that was belted at the hips. By his brown hooded cloak, he appeared to have just come in from the cold. Snowflakes dusted his broad shoulders and his hood.

A hint of a smile touched the man's lips, alarming her. But that wasn't what made her most uneasy.

The truth was she'd never seen him before.

Ysenda was certain she knew every lad, lass, and bairn in the clan, as well as most of the neighboring clans. She would have remembered this one's face. He was striking, built like a warrior. His hair was the color of coal. His gaze was intense and steady enough to pierce iron.

What was a stranger doing inside the keep?

He lowered his gaze then, and she scanned the room.

He wasn't alone. Half a dozen unfamiliar men were scattered around the hall.

Who were they? And how the devil had they gotten in?

Sir Noël de Ware loved Yuletide.

It wasn't only because the holiday happened to mark his *own* birth as well as the Christ child's. He loved everything about the season. He loved the crèches in the church and the caroles in the hall. He loved feasting on roast goose and drinking spiced wine. Most of all, he loved snuggling up in the wintry weather with a warm woman by a crackling fire.

Which was why he was unhappy.

Instead of enjoying the holiday season in France, he was stuck here in the frozen Highlands, tracking down a reluctant bride.

King Philip had promised him a wife—the most beautiful lass in Scotland, if rumor was to be believed. Descended from the magnificent Warrior Maids of Rivenloch, she was the heir to a fine Scots holding.

But she'd been delaying him with letters and excuses for weeks now.

She was ill.

She was visiting kin.

The mountain was impassable.

The river was too high.

She was grieving over a lost kitten.

Meanwhile, he'd been stuck in the Lowlands, awaiting word that he could come for her.

Finally, he'd lost patience. He was weary of waiting for the lass to decide that he merited her company.

Part of the King's reason for awarding him a Highland bride was to assure the continuing alliance between Scotland and France. King Philip had recently made peace with Scotland's enemy, England. This had naturally caused a rumble of discontent among the Scots. The fact that this particular Highland bride was delaying their marriage strained not only Noël's patience. It strained the peace between their countries.

So, as archaic as it seemed, Noël decided he'd have to formally demand his bride.

Of course, he was no fool. The Scots might be allies of the French. But Highlanders were a different breed—wild and unpredictable. He couldn't afford to be caught with his braies down in the frozen north. He'd brought only a handful of men with him. He was ill equipped to wage war.

So he decided to use his brains instead of his brawn.

He chose to come at Yuletide. At Yuletide, the castle gates would be open in welcome. The keep would be teeming with people. Ale would be flowing. Spirits would be high. Nobody would be troubled by a few stray faces among the clan.

Once they were safely inside, Noël would announce to the laird that he hadn't been able to endure one more day without his betrothed. With any luck, the romantic gesture would soften his bride's heart. At the very least, with her entire clan as witness, it would make it difficult for her to refuse him.

So far, things had gone to plan. Even now, he and his men were dispersing peacefully through the crowded hall. They'd left their armor and swords outside the gates. There was no need to appear hostile. Still, as a precaution, they'd kept their daggers close at hand.

He scanned the hall and decided that the lass seated at the laird's right hand must be his betrothed.

She was as lovely as he'd heard. Her skin was fashionably

pale. Her cheeks were fashionably rosy. Her russet hair was swept up in an amazing labyrinth that must have taken hours to braid. Her chin had a proud tilt. Her stained lips were set in a knowing half-smile. The sweeping neckline of her gown revealed firm, round breasts. Her eyes smoked with subtle, sly desire as she sipped at her ale. She would definitely turn heads, even in France, which was filled with beauties.

Then Noël's gaze drifted to the lass seated on the laird's *left* side. And his heart tripped.

He must have been mistaken. Granted, the first lass was undeniably pretty. But the lass on the left was a maid to take a man's breath away. The rumors were true. He'd never seen a more beautiful female...anywhere.

Her skin glowed with health. Her long auburn hair, shining in the candlelight, fell in simple, gentle waves over her shoulders. She had large, captivating eyes, a pointed chin, and a sweet mouth. The soft wool of her muted gray gown seemed to swirl around her petite body like Highland mist.

As he observed her, the lass stole a slice of meat from her father's trencher. Then, with a crafty grin, she passed it to the man beside her.

The corner of Noël's lip twitched in amusement. It appeared his bride had a streak of mischief in her. That pleased him.

Indeed, as he watched the wayward lass continuing to steal more food right from under her father's nose, an interesting possibility occurred to him.

Noël had always expected to have a marriage of political convenience. Like all French nobles, he served as a chess piece for King Philip. Alliances were often established through strategic marriages. Love had little to do with it. He was just as likely to be wed to a withered beldame or a mere child as to a lovely maid his own age.

Learning that his bride was renowned for her beauty had been a welcome surprise. But the idea that he might actually grow to *like* this plucky new wife of his? That was quite intriguing.

He kept gazing at her until he caught her eye.

But instead of returning his friendly smile, her grin faded, and she regarded him with suspicion.

Not wishing to make a bad first impression, he quickly averted his eyes. When he next looked up, she'd left her spot at the table and was making her determined way toward him.

He straightened and tossed back the hood of his cloak, prepared to say whatever it took to ensure that he didn't leave the Highlands without a bride. Nothing could prepare him, however, for her bluntness. Or for her big, luminous, soul-searching gray eyes.

"Who are *ye?*" she muttered under her breath in her Gaelic tongue as the merrymaking continued around them. "And what are ye doin' here?"

Noël was taken aback by her fearless and forthright manner. The lass certainly wasted no words. Nor did she seem to be intimidated by the fact that he towered over her by nearly a foot.

"I asked ye a question," she said impatiently.

He fought back a smile. What a brazen lass she was. Noël knew how to speak her language, of course. But it was important that his wife know how to speak French. For over a hundred years, since the Norman conquest, most of the English and Lowland Scots had spoken French, and he planned to take her home to France. So he replied in his native tongue.

"I've come to speak with your father, my lady."

To his satisfaction, she understood him perfectly. But she still stubbornly answered him in Gaelic. "Have ye? Well, ye didn't answer my first question. Who are ye?"

He smiled. Beautiful, mischievous, *and* clever. He was beginning to like the prospect of being wed to such a spirited lass. Indeed, he was tempted to lean down and steal a kiss from her clever mouth.

But he was no fool. He'd been put off already several times. It would be no easy task to get the lass and her father to agree to the marriage. Noël would have to be careful about how he proceeded. So for now, he would defer to her and speak in Gaelic.

"I'd prefer to answer to the laird."

She raised fine, smug brows. "Indeed? And what makes ye so certain he wishes to speak with ye?"

"By my reckonin', he does not," he admitted.

She frowned up at him. Even that expression looked adorable, like the scowling face of a wee hawk.

He gave her a wink and confided, "But I'm goin' to speak with him anyway." Now that his men were dispersed throughout the crowd, he cleared his throat to address the gathering. "May I have your attention, please?"

The musicians ceased playing, and the hall quieted. All eyes went to him. Laird Gille frowned from his seat, looking very much like the wee hawk, before he slammed his cup on the table and rose to his feet.

"Who are ye, and what is the meanin' o' this?"

Noël eyed his men, whose hands rested upon the hafts of their sheathed daggers. Then he gave the laird a respectful bow.

"My laird, I apologize for interruptin' your revels," he said. "I am Sir Noël de Ware. I've come to claim the bride I was promised by King William o' Scotland and King Philip o' France." He smiled and set a subtly possessive hand upon the shoulder of the lovely lass beside him. "I couldn't stay away a moment longer. I hoped my arrival would be a welcome Yuletide surprise for Lady Cathalin."

Ysenda stiffened. Cathalin? He thought she was Cathalin? How could anyone have mistaken her for her beautiful sister?

From the great table, Cathalin—the real Cathalin—gasped.

Ysenda had heard gossip about Sir Noël de Ware, her older sister's betrothed, for some time now. He was a noble French warrior. He meant to take her sister to France to live with him at his castle. Upon Laird Gille's death, Cathalin would return to Scotland with Lord de Ware to inhabit the keep and rule the clan.

For weeks, neither her father nor Cathalin had been happy about the arrangement. True, there was an alliance between Scotland and France. But Laird Gille didn't trust Lowlanders, let alone Normans. He wanted a Highlander to inherit his land and title. And so he'd ignored the king's command. He'd plotted to hastily marry Cathalin to a Highland laird before her Norman bridegroom arrived.

But the Highlander hadn't yet come.

And the Norman had.

And now he'd mistaken Ysenda for his bride.

Upon hearing Cathalin's gasp, Sir Noël hastened to reassure her. "There's no cause for alarm, my lady. I will take good care o' your sister, I swear." He glanced down at Ysenda with fondness. "I will honor Lady Cathalin and guard her with my life."

There was an uncertain silence in the hall.

Ysenda pulled away from the knight. This wasn't right. Her sister and her father might not want a wedding between Cathalin and Sir Noël. But it was what two kings had decreed. Ysenda would not be a party to such deception, a deception which amounted to treason.

"I'm afraid ye've made a mistake," she told the Norman. "I'm not—"

"Daughter!" her father called out.

For the first time in his life, Laird Gille had wrapped a companionable arm around Caimbeul's shoulders. Caimbeul had a look of confused hope on his face, as if his father had suddenly realized he had a son whom he loved very much.

Only Ysenda noticed the eating dagger that dangled casually from the laird's fingers, an inch from Caimbeul's throat. And there was no mistaking the threat glittering in her father's eyes.

"Cathalin, darlin'," he said, addressing Ysenda. No one in the hall corrected him. Not even Cathalin herself. She only bit her lip and stared intently into her ale. "'Tis no mistake. 'Tis the king's decree. And how fortunate ye are to have your betrothed arrive at Yuletide. The two o' ye shall have a weddin' feast fit for a king."

Ysenda blinked in disbelief. Did her father really believe he could pass her off as Cathalin? Couldn't the Norman see that her sister was the bonnie one? She waited for someone to speak up, to say it was all a jest.

But no one did. No one wanted to contradict the laird. Caimbeul was aware now that his father held a knife to his throat. They both knew if he uttered a word, the laird wouldn't hesitate to make it his last.

Finally, her sister stood and raised her cup, saying pointedly, "Congratulations, Cathalin, dear sister. No one is more deservin' o' this great honor than ye. And no one could be happier for ye than I am."

Ysenda's eyes flattened. No doubt. Things couldn't have worked out better for her sister. It appeared Cathalin would get the Highlander husband she and their father wanted. And Ysenda would be sacrificed to the Norman.

Worse, nobody in the clan was brave enough to come to her defense. She was being thrown to the wolves. And there was nothing she could do about it.

But what was her father thinking? Sir Noël had obviously agreed to marry Cathalin for the title and land that came with her. What would happen when he discovered he'd inherit neither? And what would happen when the two kings found out their alliance had been sabotaged?

It seemed Laird Gille was courting war.

Here and there, the clan folk began to cheer in tentative congratulations. The laird nodded to the musicians to resume playing. Everyone returned to eating and dancing and making merry, welcoming the Normans to their revels. And her father beckoned Sir Noël forward with an affable wave of his hand.

The Norman offered Ysenda his arm. She didn't dare refuse him, for fear of endangering Caimbeul. So she rested her forearm lightly atop his.

She tried not to panic. Surely her father wasn't serious. He wouldn't *really* defy the king. Surely he'd marry the real Cathalin to this Norman. His proud boasts of finding her sister a proper Highland laird were only that—boasts.

The laird couldn't hide the truth from Sir Noël forever. He must know that the instant Ysenda knew Caimbeul was safe, she'd confess to the Norman that she was not his true betrothed. After all, it was far better to face her father's anger than to invite the wrath of two kings.

Besides, she reasoned as she stole a sidelong glance at the knight escorting her forward, her sister should be grateful. Lots of political alliances were made with doddering old men. At least Sir Noël was fit and handsome. He had broad shoulders and thick, curling hair. His jaw was strong, and his dark eyes sparkled with life. He even spoke perfect Gaelic.

Laird Gille narrowed his eyes at the Norman. "So ye're the one who's come for my most precious prize."

Sir Noël gazed down at Ysenda. The tender sincerity in his eyes made her heart flutter. "I'm honored to have her entrusted to me."

Laird Gille guffawed at that. "I was referrin' to my castle." He picked up his cup of ale with his free hand, the one that wasn't holding a dagger to Caimbeul's neck. "But aye, I suppose my daughter is a prize worth havin' as well." He took a drink, and a foamy trickle dripped down his beard.

Sir Noël smiled at her. "She's even more beautiful than I imagined."

Ysenda's breath caught. He couldn't be talking about her. Had he even *looked* at his real betrothed? Cathalin was flawless. Next to her perfect rose of a sister, Ysenda looked like a common thistle.

By Cathalin's sour expression, she did not appreciate the slight. That anyone would praise Ysenda's looks while Cathalin was in the room was unthinkable. Ysenda could almost see the steam coming out of her sister's perfect ears.

But to be honest, it was pleasant having an attractive man gazing down at her with such appreciation. No one had ever looked at Ysenda like that before. She'd grown accustomed to hiding in the shadow of her breathtaking sister.

Of course, that bewitched look on the Norman's face would vanish once he learned his bride came with no inheritance. But she wasn't going to give him the bad tidings until Caimbeul was out of her father's clutches.

Meanwhile, her brother scowled in frustration. She could see he wanted to help her. But he didn't dare. One slip of the knife, and he'd be good to no one. Her father had been drinking heavily. He might do something foolish, something rash, something he couldn't undo...

"Why wait?" the laird bellowed. "Let's have the handfastin' now!"

Like that.

CHAPTER 2

Sir Noël couldn't have been more satisfied with the laird's idea. Preparing for an elaborate ceremony weeks in advance seemed like a waste of time to him.

The betrothal had been made. The laird had agreed to the marriage. There was already a sumptuous feast laid out at the table. Why not get the deed done?

Besides, he'd seen enough of his bride to suspect there was a splendid body under all that wool. The sooner the wedding, the sooner the bedding.

Then he glanced down at his bride.

A look of sheer panic filled her silvery eyes.

"So soon?" she squeaked.

He placed his hand atop hers in concern. Obviously, haste did not appeal to her. But why?

Surely, she'd been prepared to be a wife. It should come as no surprise. She'd known about the betrothal for some time.

Did she not find him suitable?

True, he was no golden-haired Adonis. He had a few battle scars. And he'd been told he could sometimes look fierce and menacing.

But he was young and strong, capable of defending a lady's honor. And most women found him attractive enough.

"What's wrong?" he asked her gently.

The laird answered for her. "Ach, she's only an anxious bride. All the more reason to make it quick, aye?"

His bride was growing more agitated. But she couldn't seem to find the words to adequately explain why. "Wait. I'm not... Ye can't... This isn't... Da, please... Don't ye see 'twill only make matters worse if ye—"

"Sir Noël, I should introduce ye to your kin," the laird interrupted. He turned to his second daughter, who sat fidgeting beside him. "This is Cathalin's sister, Ysenda."

"My lady, 'tis an honor." Noël made a slight bow.

The laird swung an arm out toward a red-bearded bear of a man. "That's my sister's son, Cormac." He pointed to a smaller version of Cormac. "And that's Dubne, his brother." He waved a hand toward three curly-headed maids who were whispering together. "And those wee gossips are her daughters—Bethac, Ete, and Gruoch."

"Ladies." Noël inclined his head. "Gentlemen. I'm pleased to make your acquaintance."

He lost track of all the kin. Most of them were short and sturdy. Most of them had reddish-brown hair. And most of them were half-drunk. Finally he turned his attention to the young man around whose neck the laird's arm was locked and waited for an introduction. "And ye?"

"This? This is Caimbeul."

Noël could see there was something amiss with the lad. His body was woefully misshapen. But that wasn't all. Distress furrowed the young man's brows. Maybe it was because the laird was waving his dagger about, dangerously close to the man's throat.

"Caimbeul," Noël repeated.

"Sir," the man tightly replied.

Before the laird could continue, his bride interrupted. "Da, please listen to me." Her words spilled out like the falsely calm surface over a turbulent river. "I think 'twould be best if we delayed at least till the morrow so ye can—"

"Nonsense, daughter," the laird chided. "Can ye not see how eager your bridegroom is to have ye by his side?"

"But—"

"And he's come all the way from France."

"Aye, but—"

"I'll hear no more of it. 'Tis best ye're wed right here and now." Then he turned till he was almost nose-to-nose with Caimbeul. "Wouldn't ye agree?"

Noël's bride lowered her head then. But it wasn't in submission. Her eyes were darting about madly, as if she were trying to come up with a clever ploy.

"My lady?" Noël said softly in French. "Is this not your wish?"

She lifted her eyes. They possessed all the colors of a winter sky, shifting from ominous pewter to stormy gray to serene silver. How pleasing it would be to look into those eyes every day for the rest of his life, watching their changing hues and moods.

Then she looked back at her father, who still had a possessive grip on Caimbeul.

"Da, please. Don't—"

"Ye'll do as I say, lass," the laird scolded. "Ye know your place. We all make sacrifices. Look at poor Ysenda here. Even if the unsightly wench somehow manages to snag a husband..." He paused, his eyes twinkling, and Noël was certain the laird must be jesting. The lass was almost as beautiful as her sister— even when she frowned, as she did now. "'Twill probably be no better than a Highland sheepherder. But ye... Ye'll be the wife of a Norman lord. Ye'll be Lady Cathalin de Ware."

Noël's bride clenched her hand atop his now, digging in to the muscle of his forearm. "But Da, the king will—"

"Hush! I'll hear no more!" her father interrupted as he tightened his grasp on the man, hugging him closer. "Ye should be more like Caimbeul. He knows when to hold his tongue. Don't ye, lad?"

Caimbeul lowered his eyes in anger and shame. The hand atop Noël's arm clenched even tighter.

Noël wasn't sure what was going on. Did Caimbeul object to the marriage? The man had been seated beside his bride. Was it possible he had feelings for her? And did she return those feelings? Perhaps she preferred the sweet-faced Scottish lad, despite his crooked body.

Surprised by the pang of jealousy that shot through him, Noël suddenly longed to whisk his bride away from this place. He didn't like the idea of anyone else desiring his wife.

He didn't like Laird Gille either. Didn't like the fact he seemed to be irresponsibly drunk. Didn't like the way he kept cutting his daughter off. Or how he was manhandling Caimbeul. In fact, until the laird died and surrendered his keep, Noël would just as soon remain as far away from the Highland holding as possible.

But to his own amazement, more than anything, he wanted to please his bride.

He spoke for her ears alone. "My lady, is somethin' amiss? Do ye find marriage to me repulsive? Are ye afraid o' me? I won't beat ye, I promise." Then he thought of something else. "Are ye afraid o' the marriage bed? Is that it?"

He saw that calculation in her eyes again, as if she were winnowing wheat from chaff. She turned to him with new determination.

"Aye," she decided. "That's it. I'm afraid o' the marriage bed." There was an eager light in her eyes now as she clutched his sleeve in both hands. "So if ye vow not to bed me tonight, I'll go through with the handfastin'."

She was up to something. He could see that. He doubted the intrepid lass was afraid of *anything*. But though her notion didn't please him—already his body stirred with desire for her—if it was what she wanted, he supposed he could wait another day.

"As ye wish," he said.

Ysenda sighed in relief. She'd bought herself a day. No handfasting was official until it was consummated. Hopefully, in the morn, when her father was sober, he'd realize what a grave mistake he'd made and correct it. Their sham of a marriage would be nullified, and Cathalin, the *real* Cathalin, would take her place as Noël's bride.

Part of her was not happy about that. Already she could tell that Sir Noël was too good for her sister. Cathalin was selfish and spoiled, accustomed to getting her way. Noël was considerate, noble, and polite. He'd likely try to accommodate her, and she'd end up running him ragged.

Cathalin would never appreciate his gentlemanliness. She was used to forceful Highlanders who took what they wanted. She would probably mistake Noël's kindness for weakness and belittle him at every turn.

It was a pity really. But Ysenda could say nothing about it. She was the youngest daughter, without power and without a voice.

Her father still had a dagger at Caimbeul's throat. He obviously didn't expect Ysenda to go through with the ceremony willingly.

But now that she had the Norman's promise—and she trusted the word of a noble knight—she knew she was safe, at least for tonight. So she'd oblige her father and recite the damned handfasting vows.

The ceremony would be brief, doubtless briefer than the lavish weddings of France. Highlanders had little use for religion and no patience for church approval when it came to unions. Matrimony was achieved simply by mutual consent.

Sir Noël's men made a formidable appearance as they gathered round him. They were large and powerfully built. Their manner was grave and guarded. Ysenda thought they looked ready to unsheathe and do battle if anyone so much as cocked an eye at them.

She wasn't sure why, but that gave her strange comfort.

Sir Noël had brought the marriage agreement with him. One of his men unfurled it across the table between the roast venison and the smoked mutton, along with a quill and ink. Sir Noël penned his mark on the document, as did Laird Gille.

Ysenda swallowed hard. The heavy black scrawls on the parchment made the marriage seem all too real...and permanent.

Before the ink was even dry, Laird Gille stood at the table to preside over the rite, and the hall again hushed.

"Join your right hands," he directed.

Sir Noël faced her and clasped her right hand, which felt dwarfed within his. She could feel the calluses that marked it as the sword hand of a seasoned warrior. His palm was warm and dry. She feared her own was sweaty. Yet there was something reassuring in his grip.

"Here," her sister offered, tugging a long scarlet ribbon out of her hair and passing it forward. "To make it fast."

Her father wrapped the ribbon around their joined hands, binding them loosely together.

Then she lifted her face to look at her bridegroom. She was startled. In the low light, she'd assumed his shadowed eyes were brown. But standing this close, she could see they were actually blue—a blue as deep as the ocean, as dark as the falling night. For a moment, she only stared at him, lost in the heaven of his gaze.

And then she saw he was waiting uncertainly as the silence dragged on.

"Say your piece, lad," Laird Gille urged.

A tiny furrow formed between Noël's brows. Ysenda realized he didn't know the vows for a handfasting. They probably had no such thing in France. It was up to her then.

Her voice shaking, she began. "I, Lady Ysen—" Heat flooded her cheeks as she recognized her blunder. She coughed to cover the mistake, whispering to Noël, "Forgive me. I'm a wee bit anxious." Then she cleared her throat and began again. "I, Lady Cathalin ingen Gille, Maid o' Rivenloch, take ye, Sir...Noël de Ware...to my wedded husband, till death parts ye and me. And thereto I pledge ye my troth."

She gulped. That hadn't been so difficult. And yet those simple words held such great weight.

His voice sounded much surer than hers. "I, Sir Noël de Ware, take ye, Lady Cathalin ingen Gille, Maid o' Rivenloch, as my bride—"

"To my wedded wife," she corrected in a murmur.

"To my wedded wife...till death...comes..."

She fought back a giggle. "Till death parts ye and me."

"Till death parts ye and me..."

"And thereto I pledge ye my troth," she prompted.

"Aye," he said, finishing with a triumphant smile. "And thereto I pledge ye my troth."

"'Tis done then," her father said in satisfaction, clapping the matter from his hands.

Ysenda hardly heard him. Her attention was riveted on the man before her—the man who had somehow, improbably, just become her husband. A warm twinkle glimmered in his eyes. His smile was captivating. And the thumb he stroked softly over the top of their joined hands sent a curious tingle through her veins.

The laird raised a cup of ale in salute, and the clan followed with cheers.

But Noël wasn't finished. He held his hand out to the man on his left, who placed a gold ring in his palm. Unwinding the handfasting ribbon to free her hand, Noël then gently slipped the ring onto Ysenda's third finger.

She stared down at it. It was heavy, carved with the figure of a wolf's head.

"'Tis the great Wolf o' de Ware," he told her.

She bit her lip, troubled by its scowling face. The ring was loose on her finger. She hoped that it wouldn't slip off, that she wouldn't lose it, for it rightfully belonged to Cathalin.

He bent his head down to murmur, "I vow, my lady, from this time forward, ye shall have the protection o' the Wolf."

For one foolish moment, she wished that could be true. She wouldn't mind having an army of fierce wolfish knights at her beck and call.

She gave him a faltering smile, which he returned with a wide grin that made her heart skip. But this was Cathalin's husband, not hers. And part of her burned with envy at that truth.

He was still clasping the fingers of her right hand when he lifted his left hand to cup her cheek. He tipped her head up, commanding her gaze. His dark eyes sparked at her like a smoldering coal. She had trouble drawing breath. His thumb brushed at the corner of her mouth, coaxing her lips apart. In a sensual daze, she let her jaw relax as her eyes lowered to his tempting mouth.

He was going to kiss her.

Cathalin's bridegroom was going to kiss her.

She should have stopped him. But she had to play out this fiction, for her brother's sake.

At least that was what she told herself as he closed the distance.

But it wasn't completely true.

She wanted to see what it felt like to kiss a man. And she wanted to pretend, even if only for a moment, that she was just as worthy and desirable as her sister.

When he touched his lips to hers, the cheering clan seemed

to fade away. There were only the two of them, connected by their joined hands and their searching mouths. Her eyes fell closed. His light breath upon her cheek sent a current of pleasure rippling through her.

And then he leaned closer, increasing the sweet pressure.

She expected, by his formidable appearance, that his kiss would be rough and aggressive. But the warrior somehow reined in his strength. His lips were soft, tender, and deft. His fingertips gently caressed the sensitive flesh beneath her ear, making her shiver.

As he kissed her, he entwined the fingers of his right hand with hers and drew her closer, until their tangled hands formed a lover's knot between their hearts. Ysenda felt like warm candle wax, melting into him. Her heart beat forcefully against her ribs. A quiet, joyful moan sounded in her throat as he inclined his head to deepen the kiss.

Noël never wanted the kiss to end.

It was mad—the strong, inexplicable attraction he felt to his new bride. His heart was pounding. His mouth was ravenous. He didn't dare ponder what was happening below his belt.

He supposed he should withdraw soon. He wasn't even sure public kissing was proper among the Highlanders. Yet he couldn't pry himself away.

Lady Cathalin was irresistible. Soft and sweet, young and lovely, passionate and willing.

She was the best Yuletide gift he'd ever received.

What he'd done to deserve such a treasure he didn't know.

But she was his now.

And he didn't plan to ever let her go.

CHAPTER 3

I t took the taunts and jostling of his men and the clan to break them apart at last. But when Noël, hot and breathless, peered down at his bride, she appeared as stunned as he felt.

Her cheeks were flushed. Her silvery eyes were glazed with desire. She lifted trembling fingers to her rosy lips. If he hadn't been holding her by the hand, she might have staggered backward in dizzy surprise.

The thought gave him immense pleasure. One corner of his lip curved up as he gazed down at her. He fought the powerful urge to whisk her off her feet, carry her up the stairs, and claim his husbandly rights at once.

But he'd vowed he would not—not tonight. And if there was anything that defined the Knights of de Ware more than their healthy appetites for women, it was their honor.

So he leashed the beast in his braies and stepped back with a respectful nod of his head.

"Eat! Drink!" the laird encouraged. "Ye'll need strength tonight, lad, to wield your braw claymore." He made a nasty gesture that caused a roar of raucous laughter and made his new bride blush.

Noël, with a sudden surge of protectiveness, clenched his

jaw. No one—especially not her own father—should speak so crudely in the presence of a lady.

But he didn't wish to upset her more, so he wouldn't challenge the laird for his lack of courtesy. Still, he was inclined to pack up his wife and his men and leave the keep at once.

He settled for guiding her to her place at the table and seating himself between her and her father, where he could shield her from the drunken laird's vulgarity. The last thing a skittish bride needed was more fuel for her fear.

And more delay.

Noël might agree to put off the consummation of his marriage by a day. But more than that was bordering on unreasonable. He wanted to get home. Besides, if his wife *did* harbor feelings for that young man, Caimbeul, it was probably best to make a quick, clean break of it.

Still, he knew he couldn't leave until their wedding was official. And so he intended to employ his considerable powers of seduction to ensure that, come tomorrow night, he'd bed a very willing bride.

Ysenda was still reeling from that earth-shaking kiss when Caimbeul leaned toward her, clearly upset.

"Oh, sister, why?" he whispered in despair. "Why did ye do it? Why did ye agree to marry him?"

She rested a comforting hand on her brother's forearm. "Caimbeul, I couldn't let ye be hurt."

He looked miserable. "I'd rather die than have ye wed to a stranger."

"'Twill be fine. Ye'll see," she promised in a murmur, hoping she was right. "The Norman has vowed not to touch me tonight. The handfastin' won't stand. On the morrow, Da will see the error of his ways. He'll realize he can't defy the king. 'Twill be undone faster than ye can blink."

Caimbeul didn't look convinced, especially when he glanced past her at Sir Noël. But he nodded. "Promise ye won't let him touch ye."

She gave him a scheming grin. "I'll sleep with a dagger in my hand."

But Caimbeul didn't return her smile.

In the next moment, her attention was drawn away by Noël's men. As if by magic, they'd produced a cask of wine. Noël said it was the finest from Bordeaux, which he wished to share with his new clan.

Ysenda was impressed, both by the gesture and by the wine. She'd never had wine before. In the Highlands, they drank cider, ale, and, on special occasions, mead.

Noël filled a cup for the two of them to share. She took a sip of the ruby-colored liquid. It was clear, smooth, and sweet. It was also quite strong.

She handed the cup back to Noël. He clasped his hands over hers to drink. His callused palms were warm on her knuckles. She felt that warmth travel along her arms, up her throat, into her face.

Perhaps the wine was stronger than she thought.

He gazed at her as he swallowed. His midnight blue eyes sparkled with delight.

After he lowered the cup, a droplet of red wine lingered on his lips. Ysenda fought a wild urge to steal it with a kiss. Thankfully, he lapped it up before she could do something so reckless.

His hands were still wrapped around hers on the cup. And she was in no hurry to cast them off.

"Do ye like it?" he murmured, lowering his smoky gaze to her lips.

She gulped. "Aye."

His lip quirked up into a wry smile. "Would ye like more?"

Oh, aye, she thought, gazing at his delicious mouth. She'd

like much more. More of his smiles... More of his kisses... More...

"Cathalin?" he prompted.

She blinked, then nodded, startled by the strange name and by how quickly astray her thoughts had gone.

But she didn't dare let them wander. This was her sister Cathalin's husband, not hers, no matter what vows they'd exchanged. She'd do well to remember that.

Silently toasting her serious intentions, she downed the second cup all at once.

Noël chuckled in amazement. "Ye *do* like it." Then he curved a brow in warning. "But beware, lass, 'tis a wee bit stronger than what ye're used to."

She licked her lips. It *did* seem as if her skin was growing rather hot.

He refilled her cup a third time, giving her a coy wink that made her heart race.

Her sister was damned lucky. She hoped Cathalin realized how lucky she was.

Ysenda glanced over at her. Somehow, despite the haughty lift of Cathalin's brow and the knowing smirk on her lips, she was still beautiful. Ysenda wondered if she ever looked ugly.

Sighing, she lowered her eyes to her wine. Her father was right about one thing. One of his daughters was probably going to wed a grizzled old sheepherder. And it wouldn't be Cathalin.

"Are ye not pleased, *cherie?*" Noël asked.

Cherie. He'd called her *cherie.* And the concern in his furrowed brows was sincere.

Damn! It wasn't fair that demanding Cathalin was going to win such a prize. Men like him should be loved and adored, not scorned. She felt sorry for the sweet and noble knight.

"I'm fine," she assured him, instinctively touching his chest in pity. When she realized what she'd done, she tried to pull her hand back. But he caught it and clasped it against his chest, over his heart.

"I am yours, *cherie,* heart and soul, from this day forward."

Maybe it was just the wine, but his words made tears gather in her eyes. How she wished that could be true. And how she wished she could hold on to that promise forever.

He gave her hand a gentle squeeze. "I want nothin' more than to keep ye happy."

Her heart melted. Bloody hell. Her sister was going to make mince out of the poor man.

It startled Noël to realize that what he'd said was true. He wanted to please his new wife. He wanted to watch her lovely gray eyes light up with joy and see her pretty pink mouth widen in a smile.

He wasn't the sort of man to believe in love at first glance. But there was something about his bride that bewitched him.

Meanwhile, she was draining her third cup of wine with astonishing haste, like a warrior bracing for battle. He feared the wee lass would drink herself into oblivion if she wasn't careful.

He gently took the empty vessel from her and set it on the table. Maybe a bit of fresh air would clear her head.

"Would ye like to go out?" he whispered.

"Out?"

"Outside."

"'Tis night." Her brow creased. "'Tis wintertime."

"Ye don't strike me as the kind o' lass to be put off by a wee bit o' darkness or snow. And I've got a cloak to keep us warm."

Her eyes sparked as if he'd asked her on a forbidden adventure.

Without waiting for her reply, he took her hand and nodded toward the door. "Let's go."

Most of the clan were too distracted to note their departure. Caimbeul, however, had his scowl fixed on them. Noël gave him a nod that acknowledged the man's disapproval. But that didn't stop him from taking his bride's hand and stealing out the door into the night with her anyway.

The air was crisp and cold. The snow had stopped falling. White drifts draped the ground like a linen sheet. Noël swirled his woolen cloak over his bride's shoulders as they stepped into the courtyard.

She hesitated, glancing down at her feet. He realized she was wearing soft slippers meant only for the great hall.

Without hesitation, he swept her off her feet and into his arms. She gasped, clinging to him as if she feared he'd drop her. But she was no heavier a burden than his chain mail. He sauntered easily across the courtyard, past the outbuildings nestled against the bailey wall. His boots squeaked in the newly fallen snow.

"I suppose 'tis hard to think o' leavin' the place o' your birth," he said. "But I think ye'll grow to like France. And we can return here now and then if it pleases ye."

"That's very kind."

He smiled. "So tell me, what should I know about this land we're to inherit?"

Noël knew the Highlanders followed curious customs. One was that the oldest daughter could inherit the land and become laird in her own right. His brothers had shuddered at the notion. They'd warned him that ere long, his wife would be wearing trews and he'd be forced to don a kilt.

But the idea didn't trouble him. He'd always admired capable women. In fact, he was looking forward to sharing the responsibilities of the holding, particularly since he knew so little about clan life.

"The land?" She wrinkled her brow in thought. "Well… centuries ago, 'twas settled by Vikings."

"Vikings? Invaders?"

"Nae. They were peaceful enough. They came mostly to build homes. Indeed, many o' my ancestors came from Viking stock."

"I see."

"There's little left o' their settlement now, just a few stones here and there."

"What about the land? Does it provide well for ye?"

"Aye. There are fish in the loch and game in the forest—enough to keep the clan fed all winter. We keep sheep, cattle, and chickens. And we sow oats and barley. When summer comes, there are wild berries everywhere." She thawed just a little when she mentioned summer, relaxing against him.

"I'd like to see it in summer."

"'Tis a bonnie time. The braes are cloaked in green grass and wildflowers." Then a crease touched her brow. "Though they're also full o' ankle-bitin' midges."

He chuckled. "What's your favorite place?"

"My favorite?" She mused for a moment. "The Viking well, I suppose."

"The well?"

"'Tis an old stone ruin. But some say 'tis enchanted."

Noël felt enchanted himself. His bride fit into his arms as if she were made just for him. Her voice was soft and compelling. Her body felt warm and yielding against his. "Enchanted? And why is that?"

"Accordin' to ancient legend, two lovers hid in the well from those who would prevent their marriage. A storm arose, and the lovers drowned. They were cursed to live apart in the afterlife. But 'tis said that at Yuletide, if two lovers tie together locks o' their hair, weight them, and toss them into the well, the spirits o' the ones who drowned will bless them with magic, bindin' their souls together for eternity."

"Is that so?" Noël didn't believe in magic. Everything he'd

won, he'd earned—not by magic, but by the sweat of his brow. Still, he didn't want to dampen her spirits. "And is the legend true?"

She shrugged. "I wouldn't know."

"Maybe we should go and try it."

She stiffened in his arms. "Now?" She cleared her throat. "Nae, 'tis late. And 'tis too far away. There may be wolves about."

Noël knew a feeble excuse when he heard it. He might have fallen in love with his bride in an instant. But that didn't mean she shared his sentiments. He'd just have to be patient and win her affections in time.

"Perhaps on the morrow?" he asked.

"Perhaps."

Ysenda knew she should be cold. The air was frosty. The clouds were thick. There was a dusting of snow on all the tree branches. But she felt pleasantly cozy, tucked into the knight's arms, enveloped in his cloak, snug against his firm chest.

She could feel the flush in her cheeks. Whether it was from the Bordeaux or the fact that a handsome man was carrying her across the courtyard, she wasn't sure.

But when she suddenly succumbed to the irrational desire to steal a kiss, she blamed the wine.

It happened in an instant. In one moment, they were speaking reasonably, discussing the history and resources of the land. In the next, she pulled herself up by the edges of his cloak and pressed her lips to his.

Despite surprising him, he responded with levelheaded calm. Then, as if she'd done nothing untoward, he kissed her back.

After that, Ysenda—knowing full well she had no right to do it, no claim on him whatsoever—took his head between her hands and deepened the kiss.

The liquid warmth of their tangled tongues seemed to melt the icy night. Their fervent breaths mingled, making white mist against the black.

Suddenly, her hands were acting of their own will. Her fingers spanned his wide shoulders. They caressed the cords of his neck. They wove through the thick locks of his hair.

He pulled her closer. The pads of his fingers pressed into her back. His mouth ground against hers, tasting of wine and lust. And she liked the flavor.

"Ah, *mon dieu, cherie,*" he muttered between kisses.

As they continued feasting on each other, he tilted her body, letting her slip down to stand atop his boots. He took her head tenderly in his hands. He tipped up her chin, brushing his thumbs along the corners of her mouth. Then he drew her lower lip between his own, sucking gently.

Through a haze of desire, she felt his fingers drift down her throat and across her bosom. While he clasped the back of her head in one hand, the other strayed along the neck of her gown. When he delved beneath the linen, she was too delirious with desire to refuse him. And when his hand closed over her bare breast, she sucked in an awe-filled breath at the divine sensation.

She should have pushed him away. She should have clouted him. If she'd been in control of her senses, she would have shoved him into a snow bank to cool his loins.

But she wasn't.

All she could do was float on a heavenly vessel of lust, neither knowing nor caring where she was bound.

"Ah, *mon amour,*" he murmured against her mouth. "Let's go inside."

She nodded. Anything that whisked her away from this mad and perilous place would be a wise choice. Once they were inside, surely reason would prevail.

He gave her breast one last fond caress. Then he picked her up and carried her swiftly toward the keep.

Luckily, she could blame her ruddy lips and cheeks on the cold weather, though no one paid the couple much heed as they came in. Everyone was too busy passing around the Bordeaux.

Ysenda's breast still tingled where Noël had touched her. But her gown was safely in place. She'd checked it three times to be sure.

Sir Noël excused himself for a moment to confer with her father. The laird pointed up the stairs toward Cathalin's room, and Noël nodded.

Ysenda swallowed hard. This was not going to be easy.

Her brother glowered at her, as if he could read her mind.

She glowered back.

He shook his head.

She stuck out her tongue.

Unfortunately, Noël turned at that moment and caught her in the childish gesture. She quickly withdrew her tongue, but not before his face split into a grin.

She'd hoped their escape to the bedchamber would go unnoticed. But it was not to be. Four Frenchmen gathered round with great pomp to carry Noël on their shoulders. And before she could protest, two more had hoisted her up. With the clan cheering in noisy celebration, the couple were carried up the stairs and deposited before Cathalin's chamber.

Noël opened the door. Ysenda, unwilling to risk further humiliation, hurried in. She counted herself lucky his men didn't push their way past her to make themselves welcome in the bedchamber. Noël waved goodnight to the celebrants and secured the door.

The room was dim. While she stood beside the door, he hung up his cloak and crossed to the hearth, using the poker on the wall to jab the banked coals to life. Then he added a few chunks of peat to keep the fire going.

It had been a while since Ysenda had been in this chamber. Living in her cottage, she'd forgotten how luxurious the castle was. The carved wood bed was fitted with a thick pallet of feathers and draped in a deep blue brocade canopy. A heavy chest containing Cathalin's gowns crouched at its foot. A large wooden trestle table stood against one wall. Its top was littered with vials and jars of the oils, powders, and potions Cathalin used to maintain her beauty.

The window was shuttered at the moment. But she knew it afforded a magnificent view of the distant brae and the forest where the old Viking well stood, because once, this chamber had belonged to Ysenda as well.

While she was lost in her thoughts, Noël came up behind her. When his hands settled lightly on her shoulders, she jumped.

He chuckled. "I didn't mean to frighten ye, lass."

"I'm not frightened," she scoffed. It wasn't quite the truth. But showing fear was never wise. At least that was what her warrior mother had taught her.

He slid the edges of his thumbs along the tops of her shoulders. "I'm beginnin' to suspect ye're not frightened of anythin'."

He was wrong about that. At the moment, she was a bit frightened of herself.

"Ye made me a promise," she breathlessly reminded him. "I'm trustin' ye to be a man o' your word."

"I'm a de Ware," he said, as if that should explain everything.

Then he turned her in his arms to face him, holding her in his indigo gaze. "But ye know ye can only bend a man so far. I'm your husband now. On the morrow, I won't take nae for an answer."

She nodded. His demands were perfectly reasonable. But by morn, everything would be sorted out. And tomorrow night, in this very chamber, he would claim his husbandly rights...with her sister.

The idea turned her stomach.

Her eyes lowered to his mouth. She couldn't abide the

thought of Cathalin kissing Noël. Her brat of a sister didn't deserve to wrap her arms around his neck, to taste his sweet lips.

While she continued to stare, his mouth curved up in a slow, sly smile. "Go on then."

"What?"

"Kiss me."

"What?"

"I can see ye want to."

Flustered, she gave her head a wee shake.

"Go on," he urged, crossing his arms over his chest. "I won't even kiss ye back."

Kissing him again would be a mistake. She knew that. Yet she lowered her gaze to his mouth, considering the idea.

"Come on, lass. I can't wait forever," he teased.

On the other hand, this might be the last kiss she ever got...at least until she married whatever coarse and smelly sheepherder her father lined up for her.

It was that depressing thought that convinced her to take the chance while she had it.

"I suppose I can give ye one kiss goodnight," she decided.

"O' course."

"But only one."

His eyes twinkled with laughter. "Whate'er ye can spare."

Resting her hands on his crossed forearms, she rose onto her toes. She lifted her chin and closed her eyes. He lowered his head to meet her halfway. When she felt his faint breath upon her face, she moved toward him until their lips touched.

If this was to be her last kiss, she wanted to remember it. So she focused on the supple warmth of his lips and the coarse brush of stubble on his chin. She inhaled his masculine fragrance—all leather and iron and spice. Daring to let her tongue venture out, she savored the tempting taste of his mouth. She sighed against him with bittersweet longing.

And then he began to respond.

His mouth moved over hers, gently at first, and then with more urgency, as if he sought to drink the last bit of her before she was gone.

She too was filled with a strange desperation—a craving for more of him, for all of him. A soft moan of longing built in her throat. Frustration creased her brow.

His arms came unfolded. He pulled her into his embrace.

It was utterly thrilling.

It was also dangerous.

"Ye're...kissin' me...back," she cautioned between kisses.

"Am I?"

"Aye."

"Should I stop?"

She paused. "Nae."

CHAPTER 4

Scarcely realizing what she did, Ysenda began gliding her hands beneath his surcoat. His collar bone was hard and smooth under her fingers. His pulse beat forcefully at his throat. The muscles of his chest flexed beneath her touch. She slid her palms outward. The garment loosened, slipping from his massive shoulders.

Encouraged by her boldness, he rewarded her in kind. He tugged the neckline of her gown lower and lower until it perched precariously on the tips of her breasts.

When their tongues began to entwine, she lost all hope of propriety and control. An erotic vibration began in her ears, blocking out the voice of reason. She pulled at his clothing, eager for his flesh.

He growled inside her mouth like a hungry, wild beast. And she let him feed upon her. She leaned against him, yearning to be closer. At last he pushed her sleeves down, baring her breasts so he could press his warm skin to hers.

It was heaven—this feeling—and she never wanted it to end. Where their naked flesh made contact, it seemed to melt together. Their tongues mated, creating the most intoxicating ambrosia.

She let her hands roam over him with abandon. They swept across his sleek muscles and delved into his lush hair. She tried to memorize every inch of him with her fingertips.

It wasn't enough. She wanted more.

Breaking away from his mouth, she left a trail of kisses...from the corner of his lip...along his jaw...down the side of his neck where his pulse pounded.

He groaned and then sucked a hard breath between his teeth. He drew her closer, until she could feel the rigid length beneath his tabard.

She should have been appalled. Such a blatant display was improper, crude, disgusting. Yet disgust wasn't at all what she felt as he pressed against her.

Instead, a heady thrill coursed through her, as if the Bordeaux filled her veins, warming her blood and making her drunk.

She'd done that. *She'd* made him harden like that.

But wrapped up in her exhilarating triumph was also her surrender. Her bones were melting. Her heart was softening. Her resolve was weakening.

She didn't mean to retreat toward the bed. Somehow it just happened. Suddenly the back of her knees made contact with the wooden frame.

Noël, in his eagerness, continued to advance, covering her face with kisses, not realizing she had nowhere to go.

They toppled together onto the feather pallet.

In the small sliver of her mind that wasn't drunk on wine and desire, Ysenda knew she should resist him.

But a bigger part of her mind knew there was no hope of return. They'd leaped into the raging sea and were being carried away. And every sense she possessed told her to seize the moment.

So she did.

When he was a lad, one of Noël's brothers had tricked him into sitting astride an unbroken horse. The steed had bolted off across the countryside, taking him on a wild ride. And all he could do was hang on for his life.

Which was how he felt now.

He'd resigned himself to spending a tame and quiet evening with his new bride, convincing her with reasonable examples that he'd make a decent husband.

But when she began kissing him, his good intentions went right out of his head.

It wasn't as if he'd never been kissed. He was a de Ware, for heaven's sake. But he'd never been kissed with such passion, such enthusiasm, such genuine enjoyment.

It was his clumsiness that made them fall onto the bed. And once he was horizontal, it was hard to resist doing what came naturally any time he was horizontal with a woman in a bed.

Still, he tried to resist her.

But when the lovely lass began putting her hands on him—clutching at his tabard, tearing at his surcoat—she was difficult to ignore. When she rained feverish kisses all over his face, he was compelled to answer them. And when she rolled him onto his back, all his self-control vanished.

Afraid of the marriage bed?

Hardly.

His new bride was clearly no trembling novice. He wondered what game she played, trying to make him believe she was.

Perhaps she feared he wouldn't wed her if he found out she wasn't a virgin.

She needn't have worried on that account. Noël had always preferred voracity to virtue.

He chuckled low in his throat as she moved her hungry mouth along his collar bone. Now that he knew the truth, he couldn't help teasing her a bit.

"I thought ye said just one kiss."

"Did I?" she said breathlessly.

He grinned. No longer concerned about keeping a rein on his lust, he tangled his hands in her glorious hair and opened her mouth with his. He let his tongue dance on her lips, then plunge within, relishing her wine-sweet flavor.

It had been months since he'd lain with a lover. Once he'd learned of his betrothal to Cathalin, he'd sworn off coupling with other women.

But he was paying for his abstinence now. He was as hard as stone. Indeed, he felt as if he might explode at any moment.

Which would be a mistake. Nothing would disappoint a bride more than discovering her new husband spilled his seed quicker than a twelve-year-old lad.

So taking a sobering breath, he rolled her over, sitting back on his knees to straddle her so he could have more control. He slipped his hands beneath the neckline of her gown and slid it down past her shoulders, leaving kisses along the way. Then he pulled her garments lower, to her waist, trapping her arms beside her.

"Ye're so beautiful," he murmured. "They said ye were the bonniest lass in all Scotland. They were right."

She gasped as he slowly ran the pads of his thumbs down her soft breasts until they rested above her taut nipples.

Noël smiled as she arched up to force his touch, brushing the peaks of her breasts against his thumbs. Then he lowered his head to replace his thumb with his tongue, flicking lightly at each nipple before drawing the lovely nubbin into his mouth.

She groaned and clenched her fists.

Desire surged between his legs. But he had to temper his lust, at least until hers matched his.

He glided his hands slowly up her silken legs, raising her skirts. She lifted her head and jerked her arms as if she might try to stop him. But her hands were caught in her sleeves. And judging by the smoldering gray smoke of her gaze, he could see she didn't truly want him to cease.

Sure enough, when his fingers crested the tops of her knees and continued upward, she dropped her head back onto the pallet with a sigh of rapture.

When he reached the crease of her thighs, he pushed back her gathered skirts. There he stole a glimpse of heaven. Dark, curling hair made a small, perfect triangle against her fair skin. His loins ached with longing as he perused her lovely body.

Swallowing back his ravenous desire, he gently urged her legs apart. Slipping his fingers into her nest of curls, he opened her as tenderly as a flower.

Ysenda sucked a sharp breath between her teeth. Why was she letting him do this to her? She didn't know. But she couldn't form the words to stop him. Nor did she want to.

She wanted this.

Nae, she didn't want it. She *needed* it.

Yet it wasn't hers to have. He didn't belong to her.

Still, she wanted him so badly.

And when she felt his mouth upon her...down there...all rational thought abandoned her. Stricken by erotic lightning, she could form no words. His lips caressed her with delicious intimacy, flooding her with heat. His tongue bathed her with care, making her gasp in blissful wonder.

She squeezed her eyes closed, too ashamed of her own pleasure and weakness to face him. But her shame came with a curious joy. A powerful force began to build within her. Her veins filled with brilliant fire. Her blood surged with glorious energy. Her flesh warmed and swelled and longed.

Just when she thought she would burst with craving, the world seemed to stop for a timeless instant. Then, with a silent scream, she lost control.

She was rocked by waves of ecstasy as the most divine sensation encompassed her. It seemed she sailed along on a deep ocean of pleasure.

But it lasted for only a moment.

And then he plunged into her.

She cried out, feeling the sudden searing heat of his trespass like a knife.

Noël bit out a curse and froze. What the devil?

He'd been so sure his new bride was not a virgin.

Ah, god, he'd made a terrible mistake. An unforgivable one.

"Oh *non, non*," he lamented. "I'm so sorry, *cherie*."

Her knuckles were white. Her eyes were tightly shut. And her lips were compressed into a tense line.

He ached with remorse. He'd give anything to undo what he'd done.

But he couldn't.

All he could do was to withdraw and leave her alone, as he should have done all along…as he'd promised her he would.

Yet if he withdrew, it would only make things more difficult. The next time, she would be even more reluctant, and with good cause.

That was no way to start a marriage.

Nae, if he wanted to repair the damage he'd done, he had to help her through the pain and bring her back to pleasure. So he remained within her.

"I'll make it better," he promised, smoothing the hair back from her troubled brow. "I didn't mean to hurt ye, lass. Truly I didn't."

He tugged her sleeves off, freeing her arms. Her hands relaxed. But she still wouldn't look at him. And it broke his heart. He had to fan the flames of her desire quickly before his own subsided.

"Ye aren't afraid, are ye?" he asked. "Because if ye are..."

That got her attention. She opened her eyes and furrowed her brow. "Nae."

She *was* afraid. He could see it in the way she sucked her lower lip under her teeth. But she wasn't going to admit it. And he rather admired her for that.

"I can make the pain go away," he said, "if ye'll allow me."

She looked doubtful. Then she gave him a nod.

Holding himself up on his elbows, he lowered his head to kiss her. But this time, he kissed her softly, tenderly. And when she answered too eagerly, he drew back. It was essential this time that she be completely ready.

It didn't take long. Soon she was reaching for him. She clasped the back of his neck to hold him close. She gasped against his throat and arched up until her bosom grazed his chest.

Then, to his relief, she began grinding her hips slowly against him. He closed his eyes as a ripple of desire coursed through his loins. Even a virgin instinctively knew the dance of love.

The sweet friction was almost too much to bear. He clenched his teeth against his release as she sought her own.

When she finally stiffened, opening her mouth in joyous awe, he groaned her name and drove deep within her. Together, they shuddered out their bliss.

For a weightless moment, Ysenda felt like a hawk, soaring high in the sky. There was no more pain, only freedom. Then she dove through clouds of pure pleasure, plummeting down so swiftly that her wings shivered on the air.

It would have been a moment of perfect bliss...if only he hadn't cried out her sister's name.

The word struck her like a slap in the face, snapping her back to reality.

Bloody hell! What had she done?

Noël, utterly spent, sank down upon her, careful to support his weight on his forearms. He heaved a contented sigh against her neck.

"Ah, lass, I'm so pleased to be your husband."

Ysenda gulped, wrapping her arms around him in an awkward hug.

She didn't know what to say.

She couldn't even pretend this was his fault. She'd encouraged him. She'd been the one who had to have that goodnight kiss. If he hadn't kept his promise, it was only because she'd led him to believe she was no longer holding him to it.

He'd done nothing wrong. He'd only made love to the woman he thought was his wife.

But Ysenda had committed a sin. She'd knowingly and intentionally consummated a counterfeit marriage.

"Are ye all right, *cherie*?" he murmured, lifting his head to look at her.

Nae, she was not all right. She'd behaved like a wanton. And she'd stolen her sister's bridegroom.

But she didn't dare confess to him. So she gave him a bleak smile and nodded.

He eased away to lie beside her, still holding her close.

"The next time," he promised, "'twill be better."

The next time? There could be no next time.

She bit her lip. She supposed she was ruined now. But she wouldn't make Noël pay the price for that. On the morrow, when her father came to his senses and handed over Noël's *real* bride, Ysenda would do the right thing, the merciful thing. She'd deny she'd ever bedded him.

The handfasting would be broken. Noël and Cathalin would be free to wed. He'd whisk his new wife away to his castle in

France. And Ysenda would probably never see him again.

She glanced over at the handsome knight with the dazzling smile and the kind heart. If he hadn't drifted off to sleep, he would have seen the childish tears gathering in her eyes.

It was silly, she knew. But she wanted him for herself. She didn't care that he wasn't a Highlander. She didn't care that he was Cathalin's. She didn't even care that she had nothing to offer him—no castle, no land, no title.

She'd given him her maidenhood already. And if she believed for an instant that he'd take it, she'd offer him her heart as well...for she was sure she'd fallen in love with him.

As mad as it sounded, it was true. Though she'd known him only a few hours, she knew he was everything she'd ever wanted in a husband. He was loyal, brave, sincere, fair. He commanded the respect of men and earned the admiration of women.

But her heart wasn't what Sir Noël had come for. He'd come for a political alliance. Besides, a man like him could have any maiden he chose. Why would he choose Ysenda when he'd been given the most beautiful woman in all of Scotland?

She turned away and sulked herself to sleep.

CHAPTER 5

Ysenda woke before the sun. In her sleep, she'd somehow wrapped her arms and one leg around her bedmate. She paled, realizing she had to untangle herself both from Sir Noël and from the mess her father had created before it was too late. She also had to make sure nothing bad had happened to Caimbeul.

She carefully extricated herself and glanced at the man sleeping beside her. She couldn't resist a fond grin. One side of his face was distorted where it was smashed into the downy mattress. His hair stuck out every which way, like a tree struck by lightning. His mouth hung open, and great snores issued forth. The noble knight didn't look quite so noble now. And yet his unguarded sleep made her adore him all the more.

How pleasant it would be to wake up each day to such an endearing sight...to hear the reassuring sound of his breathing...to peruse the sculpted contours of his...

She almost choked when she beheld the bold silhouette poking up the linen sheet. How could that be? How could he be aroused when he was fast asleep?

Her cheeks flaming, she crept out of the bed before things could get worse. She cast one last despondent glance at the man she was leaving behind. Then she left the chamber to seek out her brother.

"Where is he?" she demanded. "What have ye done with him?"

The laird grimaced as her sharp words pierced his aching head. "He's fine." He shooed her away and continued to poke among the kitchen stores for something to soothe the pain.

She found the vial of willow bark extract and shoved it into his hand. "Father, listen to me. What happened last night was a mistake. Ye can't go against the king. 'Tis..." She glanced around the cellar, even though it was too small to conceal spies. Then she whispered, "'Tis high treason."

"Ach!" he scoffed. "The king won't come marchin' all the way up here to enforce one wee marriage." But Ysenda detected a hint of uncertainty in his eyes. "Besides," he said, uncorking the vial and sniffing at the contents, "'tis too late now."

"But that's just it. 'Tisn't too late." She licked her lips, hating to lie. "We didn't...that is...there was a weddin'...but there was no beddin'."

He screwed up his face in disbelief. "What?"

"The handfastin' can be broken now. He'll be free to marry Cathalin."

He stared at her as if she were stupid. "He's not marryin' Cathalin."

Ysenda's heart plummeted. "But he has to. The king decreed it. Ye signed the papers yourself."

"I'm not givin' my land to a Norman, no matter what the king decrees."

"But my laird...Da...don't ye see? Ye've been given a second chance."

He narrowed his eyes. "Ye wily wench. Ye refused him on purpose."

"Aye, I did. I did it for the good o' the clan. I could see ye weren't in your right mind last night. And I knew if I didn't—"

The back of his fist cracked suddenly against her cheek, rocking her head and making her stagger sideways. She caught herself on the shelf, knocking over a row of bottles that clattered on the stones.

She blinked in shock and worked her jaw, making sure he hadn't knocked out any teeth. Her instincts told her to repay him with a solid punch of her own. It wouldn't have been the first time she'd given as good as she'd gotten from a man.

But for once she had to resist the urge.

After all, he was the laird.

He was her father.

And he had Caimbeul locked away somewhere.

"How dare ye speak to me like that," he snarled. "I know what's best for the clan. And 'tisn't havin' a laird that's not even Scots."

She ignored her stinging cheek. Somehow she had to convince him he was making a mistake. "But Da, he must be a decent man. The king himself chose him. He'll be good to Cathalin and provide for the clan as well as—"

"Nae, 'tis settled." He took a tiny sip from the vial, wrinkling his nose. "Cathalin's bridegroom, her *Highland* bridegroom, is due to arrive any day now. I'll simply say we couldn't wait any longer for their Norman knight, that by the time he arrived, her weddin' had already taken place."

"You'd lie to the king?"

"'Tisn't a lie. 'Tis a stretch o' the truth."

"And what will ye tell Sir Noël when this Highlander arrives?"

"He'll be long gone. Your husband seems very keen to get home." He toasted her with the vial, took a generous swig, shuddering at the bitter taste, then stuck the cork back in. "Ye know, ye should count yourself lucky, lass. In France, ye'll be a proper lady."

"But Sir Noël will find out I'm not Cathalin."

"Not unless ye tell him."

Her thoughts raced. "And what if I tell him now?"

"Oh, I don't think ye'll do that."

"And why not?"

"Because I'm holdin' that hunchback pet o' yours, and ye don't want to see anythin' bad happen to him."

Ysenda clenched her hands at her sides. She wanted to think he was bluffing, that he wouldn't do anything to harm his own flesh and blood. But she knew better. The laird had been wanting to get rid of his embarrassing son from the moment he'd first seen him.

Laird Gille chuckled. "Ye know, ye're just like your ma. Strong-willed and weak-hearted. Don't think I don't know about your sneakin' in tutors to teach that halfwit."

"He's not a..." She managed to stop herself, but only because she knew it was hopeless.

"Ye'll do fine in France. And if ye get too headstrong for Sir Noël's taste, he has an army o' braw lads at his command to keep ye in line."

If he was trying to scare her, it wasn't working. She trusted Sir Noël completely. What she couldn't anticipate was his reaction when he discovered he'd been gulled by her father...and by her, for that matter. Would he believe the truth—that she'd been in fear for her brother's life? And if not, what would he do to exact revenge? Would he toss her aside and demand his true bride? Would he make war on the clan and lay siege to the keep?

A voice came from beyond the door. "Good morrow?"

Ysenda sucked in a quick breath. It was Sir Noël.

Her father arched a brow. "Your husband's callin' ye." He smirked. "Probably comin' for somethin' ye forgot to give him last night."

"Cathalin?" Noël called.

Ysenda winced.

Her father snickered.

"In here," she called back, swinging open the door.

Noël was even more magnificent than she remembered. He'd finger-combed his hair. His face was freshly scrubbed. He was dressed again in his dark blue surcoat, which set off his sparkling eyes.

Unfortunately, he looked nothing like a man who'd been forced to spend his wedding night in unrequited passion. And the memory of what they'd done washed over her like a warm wave, heating her cheeks.

"Ah. Good morn...son," her father said. Somehow he managed to make the word sound like both an insincere welcome and an insult. He'd never called Caimbeul "son." Not once.

"My laird," Noël replied with a nod. Ysenda got the distinct impression Noël didn't care to call Laird Gille "Father" either.

Already there was animosity between them. If Lord Noël found out that the laird had tricked him, it would get ugly. She couldn't afford to let that happen, not before Caimbeul was safe.

"Have ye broken your fast, Sir Noël?" she asked, taking his hand, eager to separate the two men. "Are ye hungry?"

"Aye." Noël was hungry, to be sure. He wanted to feast on his wife's lovely body again.

His wife. He loved the sound of that. And to think he'd been dreading meeting his Highland bride.

When he'd awakened to find her gone, he feared it might have all been a dream. But the rumpled sheets smelled like her—fresh, warm, and womanly—and that scent had stirred him to life.

Now, walking beside his lovely new wife, he had to resist the urge to sweep her up the stairs, toss her onto the bed, and make love to her...all day long.

"There should be bannocks in the bakehouse," she said, ushering him out the door of the great hall.

The courtyard was still covered in white. But the sun had peeped out this morn. Icicles dripped from the thatched roofs of the outbuildings. The snowy expanse twinkled like crystals.

His bride was still in her slippers. So he scooped her up to carry her toward the bakehouse.

She squeaked, startled.

He grinned down at her. Then he noticed something that made his smile vanish. One side of her face was red, as if someone had clouted her.

He stopped walking and tipped up her chin to examine the mark. He clenched his teeth. "Your cheek—did someone strike ye?"

She frowned, tugging her chin away. "Nae," she told him. "I probably just slept on it."

He suspected she wasn't telling him the truth. "Ye know that I'm your protector now." Indeed, he was surprised by just how fiercely protective he felt. "If anyone touches ye, he'll have to answer to me."

Her eyes went all soft and dewy when he said that. But he was serious. Any man who laid a hand on a defenseless woman deserved to be beaten to a bloody pulp.

"'Tis very chivalrous," she said. "But ye know *I* come from a long line o' warrior maids."

"So I've heard."

Still, he had a hard time believing his wee wisp of a wife could fend off a grown man. If someone *had* struck her—and he suspected it might be her father—perhaps it was a good thing he was taking her away from this place.

He carried her to the bakehouse. As she'd promised, there were oat bannocks, fresh out of the pan. They were warm, buttery, and filling. He ate three of them. But he saved his last bite for her. He fed her from his hand, letting his fingertip linger on her lip.

He'd appeased one hunger, but the other still nagged at him. He stared at her beautiful mouth. Then, not caring whether it was proper in Scotland, he pulled her close, lifted her chin, and placed a soft kiss on her lips.

She responded at once, letting her eyes drift closed. Her lips were pliant beneath his as she dissolved against him. He pulled her closer, reveling in her warmth. Her arms traveled up around his neck. And then he felt a strong surge of lust in his braies, one he had trouble concealing.

She gasped lightly, and he knew she felt it as well. Without another word, he finished the kiss, nodded to the baker, picked up his bride, and headed back to the keep.

Thankfully, no one stood in his way—not her unpleasant father, not Noël's knights, not the Caimbeul lad. He climbed the stairs and pushed open the door to her chamber.

Then he stopped. Her sister was there, rummaging through Cathalin's clothes.

"Oh!' she exclaimed in surprise, looking back and forth between the two. "I...I just needed to...borrow a gown...from Cathalin. Is that all right...Cathalin?"

Ysenda had never felt more awkward. There was no question now. They were all conspiring together to fool the Norman knight. When he found out...

She glanced at him and gulped. Considering the breadth of his chest, his powerful muscles, and the formidable men who followed him about...she didn't want to be there when he found out.

But there was nothing she could do about it now. As far as Cathalin, it seemed that as long as her sister was granted access to her extravagant gowns, she wasn't in the least perturbed that Ysenda might be swiving the man who should have been *her* husband.

"Cathalin?" her sister prompted again.

"O' course," Ysenda said. "Help yourself."

She gave them a knowing smirk. "I can come back later if—"

"Nae," she said. "We're only—"

"Aye," Noël said simultaneously. "Come back later."

Cathalin left with a wink, coyly waving the stockings she'd picked out.

This was a disaster. Ysenda had still hoped she could persuade her sister, if not her father, to see reason. Surely Cathalin wouldn't wish to be the target of two kings' wrath. But now it would be impossible to convince her sister that she'd never consummated the handfasting.

Noël didn't seem to note her distress. He had only one thing on his mind. And the longer Ysenda gazed into his smoldering azure eyes, the more she had to agree that nothing else seemed important.

What started as feathery, inviting kisses grew urgent and demanding. Against her better judgment, she began caressing his flesh and then grasping at his clothes. By the time they tumbled headlong onto the bed, they were already half undressed.

She told herself it didn't matter if they made love again. After all, they'd consummated the handfasting. What difference did it make whether they coupled once, twice, or a dozen times? A lie was still a lie.

But the truth was she was too overwhelmed by desire to think straight. She wanted him. She wanted this. And when Noël peeled off his surcoat and tossed it aside, the sight of him left her breathless.

There was no time for the play in which they'd indulged last night. They both knew what they needed. There was no reason to delay.

He pushed up her skirts and smoothly sheathed himself inside her. She welcomed him with shivering desire.

This time it felt like they were running together up the slope of a great brae. They panted with exertion as they neared the top. When they reached the peak, they paused to admire the beautiful glen below. Then they tumbled down the other side as fast as a waterfall, rushing over the rocks and diving into a deep, refreshing pool.

Afterward, as they caught their breath, Ysenda thought she'd never felt as contented as she did, lying in Noël's arms. A brilliant glow seemed to surround them, protecting them from regret and guilt and sorrow. She closed her eyes and enjoyed the peace of utter satisfaction.

But all too soon, it faded away. Then she was left with remorse and worry.

What would he think when he found out she was a pretender? Would he think she was no better than a wanton harlot who had used him for her own gratification? Or just a heartless betrayer?

She bit her lip as an even worse thought occurred to her.

What if he'd gotten her with child?

He leaned on one elbow, gazing down at her with adoration and gratitude, two things she knew she didn't deserve. But she forced a smile to her lips.

"Let's get out o' here," he said with a lopsided grin.

"Now?" For an awful instant, she thought he meant to leave immediately for France.

"Aye." He brushed her hair back from her brow. "Why don't we pack a wee feast, and ye can show me this wishin' well o' yours?"

She let out the breath she'd been holding. Brilliant idea. She needed to get away from the temptation of the bedchamber. There was still a chance that Cathalin would decide to do the right thing and agree to wed her intended husband. Ysenda didn't want to jeopardize that possibility any more than she already had.

Still, it was with great regret that she donned her sister's warmest clothing and boots. She bid a silent farewell to the downy bed and to the ecstasy she would never have again...yet never forget.

Noël knew his men were restless, eager to be home. And now that the handfasting had been sealed, there was no reason to remain in Scotland. If they left on the morrow, there might even be some of the holiday left to enjoy.

He smiled at the thought of sharing his new bride with his family. He couldn't wait to show Cathalin the beautiful Christmas crèches. He wanted her to see the jongleurs performing caroles in the hall. And on his birthday, he wanted to drink warm mulled wine with her beside the fire.

Still, he didn't wish to appear rude to her clan. One day, all of this would be his, and he hadn't even given it a decent inspection. So as much as he'd prefer to lie in bed with his delectable wife all day, he decided he should do the proper thing and make a tour of the land.

Now, as they slogged through the snowy field toward the forest, Noël had to admit he was surprised by just how extensive the holding was. It appeared the king had been quite generous. They'd been hiking for some time.

"How much farther is it?" he asked.

"Not far. Just through those trees, in the clearin'."

Her cheeks were rosy with the cold. Her breath made fog on the air. And her gray eyes shone with excitement. It almost seemed a pity to tear her away from the land she loved so much.

"There," she breathed when they finally reached a small clearing in the wood where stray beams of sunlight seemed to cast glittering gems in the snow.

The well wasn't much of a well anymore. It was a ruin. A winding stream ran into what was left of the stone walls and trickled down the other side. Ferns grew up around the moss-covered rock. Snow-laden pines crowded near, their tops bent inward as if to shield the well from intruders. If Noël didn't know better, he'd say it *was* a magical place.

As they drew near, he saw a curious stone disk sitting askew atop the well. It looked like a dislodged lid.

"There's an inscription on top," she told him. "See the Viking runes?"

"What does it say?"

"'Tis a blessin'. For a quiet journey, joyful days, and strong deeds for Odin."

"Odin?"

"The Viking god." She ran her fingers across the carved runes. "And here it says, 'May your love stay true to your noble heart'."

He nodded. "That sounds like a good blessin'." He drew his dagger. "Do ye think we should try it? Shall we cut locks of our hair and—"

"Oh, nae!" she blurted out. "I don't think so."

Her response set him on his heels. Yesterday he expected her to have some qualms about staying true to a man she'd never met. But they were properly married now.

And they'd made love.

Twice.

"Nae?"

"'Tis just...I guess..." she said, stumbling over the words, "I guess I don't much...believe in wishes."

"Hmm." She wasn't being completely forthcoming with him. But he supposed it didn't matter. Wish or no wish, he intended to stay true to his noble heart. And he intended to keep his new bride so satisfied that she wouldn't even *think* of straying.

He sheathed his dagger, and then peered over the stone lid

and into the abyss of the well. It seemed like a perilous thing to leave open. A small child could fall in and drown. *Their* small child.

"'Tis deep," he said with a frown. "If I were laird now, I'd seal it up."

"Oh, ye mustn't do that."

"And why not?"

"Because the spirits will be trapped inside. Besides, at this time o' year, all the lasses toss their wishes in it."

"I thought ye didn't believe in wishes."

"Well, *I* don't, nae," she said, coloring a little. "But the others..."

"I see," he said with a grin. He crossed his arms over his chest. "Ye know, ye're quite bonnie when ye blush like that."

She gave him a teasing push. "I'm not blushin'. 'Tis only the cold."

"Well, I'll have to warm ye then, won't I?" He didn't wait for an answer. He opened his cloak and swept it around her, enfolding them both. "Better?"

Ysenda nodded. She had to admit it *was* better. But not because she was cold. She had the thick blood of a Highlander, after all. And her sister's fur-lined wool cloak and sturdy leather boots were good protection against the snowdrifts.

It was better because she felt...protected...in Noël's arms.

She could protect herself, of course. Her mother had passed on enough of her fighting skills to ensure that her daughter wouldn't be left vulnerable.

But there had never been anyone to champion Ysenda. She'd fought against the prejudice of her father. She'd battled the arrogance of her sister. She'd defended her brother when he was too weak to defend himself. But she'd always fought alone. No one had ever stepped in and taken her side.

Now, for the first time, snuggled in the arms of this Norman warrior, she felt absolutely safe.

"How long have ye been a knight?" she asked.

"I'm a de Ware. I was *born* with a sword in my hand."

She chuckled and gave him a poke in the ribs. "That must have been painful for your mother."

"Oh, aye, the poor woman had eight of us wee knights."

"Eight? 'Tisn't a family. 'Tis an army."

"France's best," he said proudly. He wrapped his arms tighter around her. "I can't wait to show ye off to my brothers."

He began to rattle off their names, too many to remember, giving a humorous description of each. And with each name, Ysenda grew more and more despondent. They sounded so wonderful. But she was never going to meet them. And she had to face that fact.

Indeed, the reason she wouldn't wish at the Viking well was that she didn't want to indulge in the false hope that she could somehow keep him for herself.

As she watched the stream in silence, her eyes mirrored the well, filling with water. A secret tear trickled down her cheek as she longed with all her heart for that which she couldn't have. Then, ashamed of her selfishness, she quickly wiped it away.

His voice was full of affection as he continued speaking about his family. Meanwhile, the water gurgled over the rocks. The ice at the edges of the rill made soft cracks as it yielded to the sun. Snowmelt dripped from the trees.

Ysenda closed her eyes, wishing she could stay here forever, enfolded in his arms.

She wished a lot of things.

But what she'd said was true. She didn't believe in wishes.

CHAPTER 6

Noël spent most of the morn with his new bride, hiking across braes and moors, through the pine forest and past a great loch. They stopped along the way to share the small feast of oatcakes and soft cheese they'd packed, washing it down with cider.

Afterward, she pointed out the best fishing place and the spot where the lasses liked to bathe in summer. She showed him the rotting remnants of a Viking longhouse where she used to play and the holly grove where her mother had once frightened away two wolves. He saw how much she loved the land. It made him love it as well.

But there was also a touch of sorrow in her gray eyes. He wondered... Was it the idea of leaving her home that saddened her? Or something more?

He thought again about the young man who'd sat next to her at the table. They'd seemed very close. Did her heart belong to him? Jealousy pricked at Noël again.

He supposed it didn't matter. They'd journey to France in a day or two, leaving everyone she knew far behind.

Still, that didn't change the way she *felt*. And Noël wanted his bride to be in love with *him*.

The idea was laughable. He'd come to Scotland for one purpose—to make a political alliance. Falling in love had never been part of his plans.

But that didn't change the fact that he wanted to win her heart now. He wanted to make her smile. He wanted to bring the joy back into her eyes.

"So, lassie, when was the last time ye made a snowwoman?" he asked.

She quirked her brow at him. "I've made a snow*man.*"

"Oh, aye, everyone's made a snowman. But have ye made a snow*woman?*"

She gave him a skeptical grin. "I don't see how there could be much difference."

"What? O' course there's a difference. Come on, I'll show ye."

Together they piled and packed the snow until they had a vertical mound that was about her size. He rounded the top into a ball for a head. She formed two stubs to serve as chubby arms. Then she sought out two small pine cones to make eyes. He made a small snowy nose, and he stuck a curved twig under it, turning it into a frown.

"Why is she so unhappy?" she asked.

"Because she looks like a snow*man.*"

"I told ye there was no difference."

He scowled and stroked his chin, studying the sculpture. "Perhaps if ye found some beautiful flowin' hair for her."

She perused the glen and found golden drifts of fallen pine needles near the trunks of the trees. While she was busy gathering them, he set to work. He patted together two small globes of snow and plucked a holly berry to perch in the middle of each one. These he affixed strategically to the front of the body. Then he waited for her return.

First she gasped. Then she giggled. It was a delightful sound.

"Shame on ye, Sir Noël," she scolded, unable to keep the laughter from her voice.

"Shame?" he asked, all innocence. "Why?"

Her silvery eyes danced as she came up beside him. "Ye aren't goin' to leave her like that."

"Like what?"

She gave him a chiding elbow. "Undressed."

"She'll be fine," he assured her. "She won't get cold. She's a snowwoman."

"'Tisn't the cold I'm talkin' about, and ye know it."

He reached out and turned the frowning twig into a smile. "But look how happy she is now."

She shook her head. "Ye're a naughty lad."

He winked at her. "Ah. Wait till ye see my snow*man*."

For a moment, she only stared at him. Finally her eyes went wide, and her mouth formed a shocked "O." She started pelting him with the pine needles.

He laughed and shook off the deluge. Then he caught her about the waist and hauled her to him.

Kissing her felt as natural and instinctive as breathing. Her lips opened to his as readily as a lock to a key. Her laughter spilled into his mouth, and he lapped up her joy. Their tongues touched, and the current bolted through him, making him instantly hard and eager.

If it were summer, he would have spread his tabard on the soft grass and made sweet love to her, right there and then.

But the world was wet and frozen.

So, between kisses, he gasped out, "Let's go back...to the keep...before I turn *ye*...into a snowwoman."

Shaking off his lust, he took her hand and began the short hike home, happy he'd made her smile. But by the time they emerged from the wood, in view of the keep, he was already thinking about her warm bedchamber.

"I'll race ye," he said.

"What?" She giggled.

"Come on. Whoever is first to the gate gets to undress the last."

She was still puzzling out whether it would be better to win or lose when he bolted off across the snow.

"Wait!" she cried. "Ye cheated!"

"Hurry up!"

"But ye never said go!"

"Go!" he yelled.

He gained several good yards. But then he made the mistake of turning around to gloat. While he was running backward, his heel caught on a tree root, and he fell smack on his arse.

She burst into laughter, charging past him as he scrambled to get up.

"Come back here, wife!" he bellowed after her.

"I don't think so!" she crowed.

"But a wife's supposed to obey her husband!"

She only laughed.

Chuckling, he dusted the snow off of his surcoat and let her get a short distance ahead. He was enjoying the view, after all, watching her bustling backside and catching a glimpse of her lovely calves as she picked up her skirts to scurry through the snow.

He couldn't get over the fact that she was his. That breathtaking, vibrant, fresh-faced Highland lass belonged to him. How he'd gotten so lucky, he didn't know. But he didn't intend to let her get away from him. Now or ever.

In the end, he let her win, but only by an instant. He nipped at her heels the whole way, making her squeal in panic one moment and giggle at his antics the next. By the time they collapsed against the gate, they were breathless from running and giddy with laughter.

He grinned into her shining gray eyes and bent to give her a bold kiss, deciding he didn't care whether it was proper or not. What should it matter if a few curious clansmen saw how much he loved his bride?

Her lips were cool. Her tongue was warm. Her breath

mingled with his as they kissed, then caught their breath, then kissed again.

"You win," he whispered, cradling her face with his palm. Then he stepped back with his arms outstretched. "Go ahead. Undress me."

She gasped in delighted shock, shoving at his chest. "Ye're a wicked, wicked man."

She'd add a few more "wickeds" if she could read the lusty thoughts coursing through his head right now. Of course, he wasn't about to act on any of them. By now there were several sets of eyes on them.

Instead, he escorted her politely through the gate, walking hand-in-hand with her.

The courtyard was bristling with Yuletide preparations. Cooks roasted haunches of mutton on a great spit. Maidservants tied together clumps of evergreen with red ribbon. Kitchen lads carted baskets of bread into the keep. And in one corner of the yard where the snow had been shoveled away, his men were sparring, providing lively entertainment for the laird and for the wee lads gathered round.

When Noël lifted his gaze, he saw someone else was watching. At the highest window of the tower, intently studying the knights, was Caimbeul.

"They're very good," his bride exclaimed as she saw his men crossing blades.

He smiled. "Aye." The Knights of de Ware were the best swordsmen in France.

He peered up again at the window. Caimbeul had spotted him. The young man was staring back at him with a venomous glare.

Noël frowned. Was that jealousy? He had to find out. He might not be able to mend the lad's broken heart. But he could at least try to make peace with him and make the truth—that Cathalin was his wife now—easier to bear.

"Would ye like to watch them for a bit?" he asked her.

"Aye, if ye don't mind."

"Not at all." Kissing her knuckles and releasing her hand, he glanced up again at the scowling Caimbeul. "I'll be back. I've somethin' to attend to."

Ysenda admired good swordsmen. It was a trait she'd doubtless inherited from her mother. And the Knights of de Ware were far superior to any fighters she'd seen in Scotland.

But that wasn't the real reason she wanted to watch them.

She mostly wanted to avoid going to Cathalin's bedchamber.

Ysenda's will was weaker than ever now. Not only did she desire this Norman knight with the handsome face, unruly black hair, and dazzling blue eyes. But now she also adored him.

He made her laugh. He made her feel beautiful. He made her feel loved.

She glanced down at the Wolf of de Ware ring on her finger. Giving him up was going to be painful. And the more intimate they became, the harder it would be.

Cathalin was watching the knights battle as well. Maybe if Ysenda could get her sister alone, talk to her, she could make her see reason.

After Noël left, she approached.

"Cathalin," she whispered, tugging on her sleeve.

Cathalin whipped her head around. "Don't call me that," she hissed. "They might hear ye."

"We need to talk."

"There's nothin' to talk about."

"'Twill take but a moment. We likely won't see each other again for years. Can we not at least say farewell?"

Cathalin rolled her eyes. "Ach, very well. I've grown weary o' watchin' these French bairns playin' with their wee blades anyway."

Wee blades? Their broadswords might not be as big as a Scots claymore, but Ysenda was sure an agile Norman with a light blade had a definite advantage over a Highlander with a heavy sword.

They retreated to a spot along the back wall of the keep.

Cathalin crossed her arms over her bosom. "What did ye wish to say?"

"I need ye to think about what ye're doin'."

"I know exactly what I'm doin'. I'm marryin' a Highlander. And he and I will inherit the castle and rule the clan when Da is gone."

"But don't ye see? The kings won't allow it. They've betrothed ye to a Norman because they want a Norman to hold the land."

"It doesn't matter if they'll allow it. 'Twill be done. I'll be wed ere they can have their say." She smirked. "Besides, ye've already made good on the handfastin'."

"We can say I haven't," Ysenda said, clutching her sister's sleeve in desperation. "We can say 'twas never consummated. Then ye'll be free to..." She almost choked on the words. "To wed Sir Noël."

"I don't *want* to wed Sir Noël."

"Ye must. 'Tis the will o' the king."

"I don't care," Cathalin said with a pretty pout. "Besides, Da said the royals wouldn't dare come to the Highlands to—"

Ysenda grabbed her sister by the shoulders. "They *will* come. They'll send men like those," she said, pointing toward the Knights of de Ware. "And they'll kill everyone in the clan if ye don't do as the king wills."

Cathalin pried Ysenda's hand from her shoulder. "Then ye're goin' to have to keep pretendin' *ye're* Cathalin. 'Tis the only way to keep the peace."

Ysenda sighed in exasperation. "He'll find out. Even if I say nothin', it won't be a secret for long. As soon as Da dies, the secret will be out."

Cathalin straightened with pride. "By then my Highland husband will have raised an army to defend the keep." She scoffed. "His men will slaughter every last one o' these wee bairns with their wee blades."

Ysenda could only stare at her sister, mortified. How could Cathalin be so delusional, so reckless? She would bring destruction down upon their clan. And for what? So she could wed the man of her choice? A man she'd never even met?

She wanted to wring her sister's perfect neck.

But maybe she could try a different approach. Ysenda had no intention of going to France in Cathalin's stead, leaving Caimbeul and their clan behind to be killed by the king's army.

"Ye know, Sir Noël would be a very good match for ye." The words were hard to push past her throat. "He comes from a wealthy family. Ye'd live in a beautiful castle. Ye'd have everythin' ye desire. Servants at your beck and call. All the new gowns ye want. Jewels, furs, falcons. Sir Noël would grant your every wish, I know. And your bairns... They'd be the most beautiful children in all o' France."

"That may be." Cathalin sniffed. "But I refuse to marry such a blind and stupid man."

She blinked. "What do ye mean?"

Cathalin lifted her haughty chin. "How could the fool have thought *ye* were the most beautiful lass in all o' Scotland?"

While Ysenda stood with her mouth agape, Cathalin picked up her skirts and stalked off in a vexed huff.

Ysenda could only stare off after Cathalin. She couldn't argue with her. That *was* what Sir Noël had thought. And once Cathalin's pride was insulted, there was no way to assuage her feelings.

Hell. Now she didn't know what to do.

Noël rapped lightly on the door. "Caimbeul?"

There was no answer. But he heard a startled scrape on the other side.

He slowly opened the door, preparing to defend himself if necessary.

Caimbeul was sitting on the floor below the window, scowling up at him.

"I need to speak with ye," Noël said.

Caimbeul's frown turned mistrustful.

Noël closed the door behind him. Caimbeul made no move to rise, but perhaps the young man's twisted frame made it difficult for him to stand. He obliged the lad by hunkering down before him.

"I think 'tis best we speak plainly," he told him, "so I'd like the truth from ye. Do ye have...feelin's for my bride?"

Caimbeul's face twisted. "Feelin's? What do ye mean?"

"Romantic feelin's."

Caimbeul's eyes narrowed with rage. Before Noël could dodge aside, the young man shot out a furious fist. Fortunately, it missed Noël's nose, but only because a heavy iron chain around his wrist brought it up short. Still, Noël instinctively recoiled, falling backward onto his hindquarters.

"How dare ye!" Caimbeul yelled. "She's my sister, ye horse's arse!"

Noël didn't know what shocked him more—the fact that Caimbeul packed an impressive punch for a crippled man, that he was chained like an animal, or that he was his bride's brother. He held up a hand in peace.

"Wait. Ye're her brother? The laird's son?"

"Aye," he ground out.

Noël sat forward, resting his forearms on his knees. He

189

remembered the laird's attitude toward Caimbeul at the table. He'd never introduced him as his son. And he'd treated him with a distinct lack of respect.

"Is your father the one who put ye in chains?"

Caimbeul didn't answer. His frown of shame was answer enough.

Why would the laird do such a thing? Was he afraid his son would interfere with the wedding? Maybe Caimbeul thought he was protecting his sister.

"Tell me, man to man," Noël said. "Do ye disapprove o' me? Do ye think I'm not good enough for your sister?"

Caimbeul's eyes burned with silent anger. "Which sister?"

It was a strange question. "The one I'm married to, o' course."

Caimbeul stared at him in silence for a long while, as if deciding whether to say anything further. Finally he did. "Ye're not married to the right one."

"What do ye mean?"

Instead of answering, Caimbeul focused on the ground and said tightly, "Ye've slept with her, haven't ye?"

Noël let the lad's words sink in. What did he mean, "the right one"? Was it possible he'd married the wrong sister?

"She's Cathalin. Aye?" he asked, fearful of the answer.

"She's not."

Noël felt the breath freeze in his chest. How could that be? How could he have wed—and coupled with—the wrong sister?

Then he glanced again at the young man. Perhaps Caimbeul was mad. Perhaps he was confused. Perhaps that was why his father had chained him up.

"Are ye certain?" he asked.

"O' course I'm certain. I know my own sisters. Ye've wed...and bedded," he added with a sneer, "Ysenda, not Cathalin."

Noël couldn't comprehend it all. He rose slowly to his feet. "But why would..."

"My father wanted a Highlander, not a Norman, to inherit his land."

"But 'tisn't up to your father. Two kings have decreed this marriage."

"Aye, and ye've seen it through. As far as ye know, ye're wedded to Cathalin."

"But that's ridiculous. If she's not the real Cathalin, then when the laird dies—"

"Ye'll inherit nothin'. The land will go to the *real* Cathalin and her Highlander husband."

Noël was astounded. "That can't be true. Every member o' the clan would have to be privy to the deception in order for—"

"No one said a word when you mistook Ysenda for Cathalin. They were too afraid to gainsay the laird. My father was overjoyed. Ye played perfectly into his hands."

All the air went out of Noël's lungs. How could this have happened? Had his honest mistake become an act of rebellion? He shook his head, which was spinning as he recalled the events of the past day.

"Your father was afraid ye'd speak out," he realized. "That's why he had a knife at your throat."

Caimbeul nodded.

"And why he's put ye in chains now."

"Aye."

"Then he mustn't know I came to speak with ye." Noël straightened and placed a hand of reassurance on Caimbeul's forearm. "I don't know how, but I promise ye...brother...I'll make everythin' right."

With that, he left the chamber. But his mind was far from settled. And as he descended the stairs, he began thinking—not like a suitor, but like a warrior.

By offering him the wrong bride, Laird Gille had intentionally broken an oath to two kings. By rights, Noël should drag him before the royal court.

But the clan would turn on him if he made a prisoner of their laird. That was the last thing he wanted to do, considering that some day these people would be his responsibility. He'd always ruled his knights, not by force, but by earning their respect. And that was how he wished to rule the clan.

Besides, he'd only brought a small contingent of his men. True, they were Knights of de Ware. But they were no match for a hundred angry clansmen.

There had to be another way. And he was determined to find it.

Still, that wasn't the most troubling aspect of the deception for Noël. The worst part was knowing his bride had lied to him. She'd held his hand, kissed him, spoken the handfasting vows.

His brow creased as he remembered she'd asked him not to consummate the marriage. Perhaps she'd had one moment of regret then.

But they *had* consummated the marriage. She'd let him... Nae, he corrected, he'd imposed himself upon her. It had been an accident, but it *had* been his fault. Maybe she hadn't wanted for it to happen.

Still, she'd never told him the truth—that she was not his real betrothed—even though there had been ample opportunity for her confession.

She'd laughed with him.

She'd slept with him.

She'd made him fall in love with her.

Was it all a lie? Did she have no feelings for him?

He frowned, swallowing down the lump lodged in his throat.

It didn't matter, he told himself. They were not intended to be husband and wife anyway. He would find some way to annul the marriage. No one had seen them in the bedchamber. He could claim he'd never consummated the handfasting. That way she could continue her life, unburdened by their sin.

But his heart felt like it was breaking in two. He couldn't get her laughing gray eyes out of his mind. Nor could he think about the other sister, the one he was supposed to marry, without a shudder of distaste.

He would do his duty, for king and country, no matter how painful it was. But he would never be happy about it.

CHAPTER 7

Ysenda watched with the rest of the clan as the Yuletide bonfire was lit in the courtyard. Sir Noël stood beside her. The flames illuminated his face. But his expression was still inscrutable, as it had been since he'd returned from the keep. She didn't know what was wrong. Somehow he seemed...distant.

It was probably just as well. After failing to convince Cathalin to do the right thing and marry Noël, Ysenda figured her only hope was to make Noël fall in love with Cathalin. Once he saw her sister in her best light, surely he couldn't help but be charmed by her. All men loved Cathalin. And of course, Cathalin would fall madly in love with him, for what woman would not? Maybe then Ysenda could repair the damage that had been done.

Of course, the whole idea made her sick at heart. She couldn't bear the thought of losing Noël, especially to her spoiled sister. But for the sake of her brother, whom she'd vowed to protect, and for her clan, to whom she owed allegiance, she'd make the sacrifice.

"Ysenda!" she called softly to her sister, nudging her when she didn't respond to the unfamiliar name.

Cathalin scowled.

Undaunted, Ysenda touched Noël's forearm and smiled back at her sister. "I was goin' to tell Sir Noël about the time we tried to save the pups in the pond."

Cathalin stared silently back. Finally she shrugged and said, "Go on then."

Ysenda gave her sister a pointed look. "But ye tell it so much better."

Cathalin sighed. "What's to tell? We saw the pups in the pond, and we jumped in to pull them out."

Ysenda's face fell. "Aye." She turned to Noël to explain. "But 'twas silly, because the mother hound was only tryin' to teach them to swim." She grinned. "We didn't know they could swim, so we dove in to save them. And when Ca-, my sister found out, she was furious, because she got her new gown soakin' wet."

Cathalin managed a small smile then. "After 'twas ruined, I gave *ye* that gown."

"So ye did," Ysenda said with a chuckle.

She glanced at Noël. His expression was one of polite interest, no more.

Ysenda tried again. "Your hair looks lovely tonight, dear sister."

That worked. Cathalin touched her locks. "Do ye like it? It took Tilda half the morn to braid."

"'Tis beautiful. Don't ye agree, Sir Noël?"

He nodded.

Cathalin, clearly annoyed by his lack of praise, pursed her lips.

Ysenda wrung her hands. What more could she do? What would impress Noël?

"Ye know, Sir Noël, my sister is quite skilled with a needle."

Noël lifted a brow. "Sewin' cloth or jabbin' people?"

With a huff of irritation, Cathalin picked up her skirts and whirled away to stand beside someone else.

Ysenda turned to Noël in accusation. "Why did ye do that?"

"She's like a spoiled hound. Someone needs to bring her to heel."

Ysenda thought about his words as the flames flickered high into the night sky.

"Someone like ye," she decided. "Someone who could take her in hand, teach her patiently, bring out the best in her." She gulped. "Do ye think ye could be happy with...someone like my sister?"

His mouth tightened as he stared into the fire. "Not nearly as happy as I am with ye."

Ysenda's eyes filled. She tried to blame the smoke. But her heart was breaking.

"I... I've grown tired. I'm goin' to go up to bed."

She didn't wait for his reply. She needed to get away before she burst into tears. Maybe Noël would speak again with Cathalin. Maybe not. But she would at least give them the opportunity.

After she left, Noël tried valiantly to fall in love with Cathalin. He stared at her from afar in the bonfire's glow, admiring her perfect profile, her creamy skin, her pouting lips. He watched her laugh when someone whispered in her ear. He saw her toss pine cones onto the fire with delicate grace.

But she wasn't her sister. She didn't have Ysenda's honest face, her sweetness, her endearing awkwardness and innocent charm. Cathalin was haughty, coddled, and hopelessly vain. Life with her would be unpleasant.

Noël watched his chance at happiness float away, like one of the bright sparks from the bonfire, rising and becoming swallowed by the black sky. All he could think about was the irresistible lass who waited in her bedchamber even now, less than a hundred steps away.

She'd pledged him her troth. She'd spoken the words to bind them as man and wife. At least, that was what she wanted the world to believe. And if she wished to keep up that appearance, why should he deny it?

If tonight was to be their last night together…if tomorrow he would confront the laird and demand his true bride…then perhaps he should seize what joy he could before he resigned himself to a lifetime of misery.

He gave the woman he was supposed to wed one last glance. She was beautiful. There was no doubt. But she was no match for the lass he'd married.

Against his better judgment, he took those hundred steps to the bedchamber.

When he softly entered the room, his wife was crouched by the fire, stirring the coals. She shot to her feet in surprise. The flames crackled to life behind her, illuminating the sheer linen of her leine, leaving nothing to his imagination.

"I thought ye were stayin' below a while." Her voice was cautious.

His eyes never left her as he closed the door behind him. "And I thought ye were goin' to bed."

"I was. I am."

This woman had lied to him. She'd deceived him, earning his trust now so she could exploit it later. Worst of all, she'd made him fall in love with her. By all rights, he should feel hurt and betrayed.

But seeing her in the hearth's soft glow—her face alit, her eyes shining, her lips so tempting—made him feel only longing.

Had her affection for him been a ruse? Did she feel nothing for him?

He had to find out.

"Then let's go to bed *together*," he said.

She gulped. "Don't ye want to watch the Yule fire?"

"Nae. I've seen enough." He took a step toward her.

She fidgeted with her gown. "They make a circle round the outside..."

He took another step.

She licked her lips. "And they walk..."

He took a third step.

"In the direction o' the sun, so..."

His fourth step brought him close enough to detect the smoky desire in her eyes. And when he lowered his gaze, he could see the sweet curve between her breasts where the linen gapped away.

"Tell me somethin'," he whispered, almost afraid of the answer.

"Aye?" Her voice cracked.

"Do ye love me at all?"

As she stared up at him, her eyes filled with tears, and her chin began to tremble.

He felt his heart crack. She might not want to say the words. But the answer was there in her silence.

He clenched his jaw against bitter disappointment.

But just as he would have turned and left her alone—perhaps to drown his sorrows in a barrel of Bordeaux—she collided against his chest with a great sob.

"Oh, aye, god help me, but I do, Noël. I love ye so much."

She rained kisses and tears on him in equal measure. The warmth of her admission was a soothing balm to his heart. He held her close, too lost in relief and joy to think beyond the moment.

Their kissing quickly fanned the flames of love from affection to desire, then from desire to desperation. Noël didn't want to think about tomorrow. Or his king. Or his *real* bride. All he wanted was one beautiful night with this irresistible woman who, aye, loved him.

Ysenda knew she was playing a perilous game. Yet she brazenly continued, like the lads who leaped through the Yule bonfire. She couldn't stop herself.

The situation was impossible. She hadn't been able to make Cathalin fall in love with Noël, any more than she could make *herself* fall *out* of love with him.

And now that she'd admitted she cared for him, she couldn't confess that she'd deceived him. It would break his heart.

Yet even as the deadly knot of lies and deception wrapped around her, all she could think about was making love to him. She didn't want to think about her sister. Or Noël's return to France. Or what would become of Caimbeul. All she wanted was to live for this moment.

Somehow their clothes fell away. Somehow they wound up on the bed. In a delicious tangle of limbs, they let the rest of the world disappear.

His lips kissed away her guilt. His fingers caressed away her cares. And with his bare flesh pressed to hers, there was no room for remorse.

She floated in heavenly oblivion. For now, all that mattered were the two of them and their compelling quest for pleasure.

This time, it was more than mere coupling. She wanted to show him how much she cared for him. She wanted him to feel her love in the deepest recesses of his soul. And she wanted to feel cherished in return.

When he pressed gently into her, she sighed in relief. Looking up at him with a languid gaze, she saw the same sweet satisfaction in his midnight eyes.

When he began to move within her, she met him, thrust for thrust. Just as they had hiked hand-in-hand across the snowy fields, they traversed the landscape of desire together.

His gaze burned into hers. His breath sent shivers along her skin. His tongue bathed her with intoxicating nectar. His fingertips teased and coaxed her to greater heights.

Wanting to keep him with her forever, she wrapped her legs around him. She dug her heels into his buttocks, making him groan with bliss.

He laced his fingers through hers, anchoring her to the mattress. She caught her breath as her lust sharpened to a fine point. Then it exploded into a hundred beautiful fragments. She arched up and clenched her fists in his.

He answered her, surging into her with a ragged cry of release.

Then she stiffened.

He'd called her by name.

Her *real* name.

She sucked in a panicked breath, but he wouldn't release her. His fingers were still entwined with hers. And when he slowly opened his lust-glazed eyes, she saw the truth.

He knew who she was.

He knew everything.

For a long moment, they only stared at each other.

"How did ye find out?" she whispered.

He didn't answer her. Instead, his gaze hardened. "How could ye lie to me?"

"I had to," she confessed. "I had no choice."

He was still holding her down. She wasn't afraid of him, not really. He was a man of honor, a knight who'd never harm a lady. But she could see by the glower in his brow and the strength in his arms that he could be a fearsome foe.

"When did ye plan to tell me?" he demanded.

"I've wanted to tell ye all along. I tried to stop the handfastin'. I never meant to consummate it. I hoped to convince my sister to wed ye." She added quietly, "I still do."

"Why didn't ye just tell me that first night?"

She swallowed hard, lowering her eyes. The truth was humiliating. But she owed it to him. "The laird said if I told ye, he'd hurt Caimbeul. He's been wantin' to kill my brother ever since he was born. He can't abide havin' a son who's...who isn't perfect. When my mother died, she made me vow to look after Caimbeul. I've always taken care o' him."

His fingers loosened around hers. The grim line of his mouth relaxed. "Ye could have told me. Your father wouldn't have known."

She gave him a rueful smile. "And what would ye have done then? Insisted on marryin' my sister? And when my father refused, would ye have taken on the whole clan with your six knights?"

He compressed his lips.

"I never wanted to deceive ye," she told him. "'Tis pure madness to go against the king. I've tried to tell my father so. But he won't listen. He wants a Highlander to hold his lands."

"When the kings find out—"

"They'll send an army to quell the clan. I know. My father refuses to believe that. And my sister thinks her Highland husband will bring men to defend the keep."

"So he'd rather start a war than see a Norman inherit his lands."

She nodded.

He unlaced his fingers and rolled off of her then, lying on his back to stare at the ceiling. She pulled the linen sheet up over her breasts.

It pained her to say the words, but she did. "I wish my sister loved ye."

He didn't hesitate. "I could never love her. Not the way I love ye."

Her heart flipped over. And then it sank. "What are we to do?"

"*Mon dieu,* I don't know."

A good night's sleep solved nothing.

Noël wished he'd never learned the truth. He could have lived happily in France with his counterfeit bride for years before her father died. By then, it would be too late to undo what had been done. Not that he even wanted to. He'd begun to dream less about inheriting the Highlander's land and more about stealing off with the man's daughter.

But, short of kidnapping her, he still didn't know how to solve the problem of his marriage.

One problem he *did* know how to solve. A young lass like Ysenda shouldn't be burdened with watching over her brother for the rest of his life. This morn, Noël intended to prove to her that Caimbeul was not some helpless creature who needed to be hand-fed and fussed over. If Noël could do nothing else, he could at least give Ysenda the gift of freedom.

He crept out of the bedchamber without waking her. Most of the clan were in the great hall, breaking their fast with buttered oatcakes. He approached Laird Gille.

"My laird, I haven't seen your man, Caimbeul, about lately."

The laird grunted. "Why should ye be interested in him?"

Noël shrugged. "I was wonderin' if ye think he'd be up for a wee bit o' sport this morn."

The laird's eyes lit up. "Sport?"

"Aye. My men have issued me a challenge. They say I can't make a fighter out of a cripple. I say I can."

"Indeed?" The laird stroked his beard in speculation. "And have ye put coin on it?"

He waved away the idea. "Nae, 'tis only a matter o' pride."

The laird's eyes were glittering now. "Pride? Ach! There's coin to be made on a wager like that."

"Perhaps."

Laird Gille chortled. "Not to mention it could be an amusin' sight—Caimbeul with a sword."

Noël bit back his distaste. "So do ye think he'll agree?"

"Oh, aye, I can get him to agree."

"After breakfast then? In the courtyard?"

"Aye." The laird gleefully rubbed his hands together and left to fetch Caimbeul.

Noël didn't tell Ysenda what he was up to. She'd only try to interfere, to protect her brother. She'd find out soon enough anyway.

The knights were exercising in the courtyard, and the sun was dancing along the tops of the distant pines when Caimbeul, no longer in chains, came limping and lurching briskly across the yard, leaning on a gnarled staff.

Noël studied him. But instead of noting the flaws in his gait, he looked for the man's strengths.

Of course, Noël's men hadn't really issued that challenge. They knew Noël well enough to realize he could turn any man into a fighter. Instead, they welcomed Caimbeul onto the field with open arms and ready blades.

Laird Gille had servants bring him a chair so he could sit on the sidelines. He probably imagined he was about to see a horrific and entertaining spectacle. A small crowd of men gathered around. Noël could see them exchanging coins, betting on the outcome.

By the time Caimbeul reached Noël, his face was an angry shade of red, and his eyes were full of rage.

"Is this how ye repay me for tellin' the truth?" he bit out. "By makin' sport o' me?"

"Not at all, brother," Noël said in quiet reassurance. "I'm goin' to teach ye to fight properly...so ye won't have to be afraid o' your father anymore."

Caimbeul blinked in surprise. For an instant, hope flared in his eyes. Then they darkened with cynicism. "I'm a cripple. I can't fight."

"Ye threw a fair clout at me last night. If it hadn't been for the shackle, ye would have flattened me."

Caimbeul almost looked pleased at that.

"Come on," Noël urged, clapping him carefully on the shoulder. "Let's show your father what ye've got."

The lad fell a few times. His father laughed. But each time, Noël and his knights bolstered the young man's courage and heart, assuring him he was making good progress.

And he was. He might not have the stature to wield a broadsword with great precision, power, or speed. But he had surprise on his side.

Anyone looking at Caimbeul would imagine he couldn't defend himself. But even with his twisted frame, he could thrust forward with a dagger, cuff a man squarely on the nose, and kick an attacker's legs out from under him.

Indeed, Laird Gille started to frown as Caimbeul managed to not only stay on his feet, but to knock a few of the knights off theirs.

It was then that Ysenda arrived.

But to Noël's chagrin, the wide grin of triumphant pride and cheery salutation he gave her was withered by her scowl of pure fury.

CHAPTER 8

Ysenda's heart had fluttered in panic when she'd awakened to find Noël gone. Had he decided it was too painful to say goodbye? Had he simply left without a word?

Even though that would probably be best—even better if he'd absconded with Cathalin—she hoped with all her heart he had not.

She scrambled to the window and peered out through the shutters. Noël's men were still here, sparring in the courtyard below.

With a sigh of relief, she turned back toward the bed. Her gaze caught on the foolish prize she'd collected last night while Noël lay sleeping—the black curl she'd snipped from his head and tied into the red handfasting ribbon.

She tucked her lip under her teeth. She'd forgotten about that. It had been a childish gesture. But she'd wanted a memento of him.

Someone scratched at the door. With a little gasp, Ysenda snatched up the incriminating lock and stuffed it down the bodice of her leine. She opened the door to Cathalin and her maid, come to choose Cathalin's attire for the day.

After they'd gone, Ysenda threw on her own gown and went downstairs. She meant to make one more attempt to convince her father to make things right. She grabbed a buttered oatcake in the great hall, and made her way outside to speak to the laird, who was watching the Norman knights practice.

Now she'd reached the edge of the field where her father was seated. She halted in her tracks.

What she saw made her jaw drop. She let the oatcake fall to the ground.

In the midst of the fighting stood Caimbeul. He was dragging a sword behind him as he hobbled toward two of Noël's men.

He suddenly swung the weapon around. The first knight dodged it. The second shoved Caimbeul aside with his shield, pushing him off balance.

Caimbeul tumbled backward onto his arse. Beside her, her father snorted in laughter.

Her blood boiled.

Clenching her jaw, she strode forward. She shoved her clansmen out of her way, stealing a sword from one of them before he even realized it, and kept charging.

Caimbeul had recovered now and was back on his feet, hacking away at his attackers. But it would only be a matter of time before he fell again.

She elbowed aside one of Noël's knights. He instinctively drew his blade. Then, seeing she was a woman, he sheathed the sword and backed away with his palms raised.

"To me!" she yelled at the knights attacking her brother.

Like most strangers to the Highlands, the French knights were unaccustomed to facing a woman with a weapon. Startled, they turned to her. One of them lowered his shield. The other was forced to raise his when she came at him with a blow forceful enough to lop off his head—had it landed.

Jarred by the impact of his shield on her steel, Ysenda staggered back a step. But she recovered quickly enough to intervene between the knight and her brother and took another swing.

From across the field, she heard Sir Noël shout, "Nae!"

Too late. She gave his man a punishing clip on the shoulder. He stumbled backward, clutching his bruised arm, while his companion quickly retrieved his shield.

But then she was caught around the waist from behind. Before she could squirm away, her sword was wrenched from her grip. An instant later, her captor swept her off her feet with a swift kick to the back of her heels. Instead of letting her fall, he caught her on his arm and lowered her with exaggerated care onto the wet grass.

She immediately rose on her elbows, scowling up in sputtering rage. But her anger vanished when she saw who had disarmed her.

"Caimbeul?" She blinked in astonishment.

He grinned down at her. "Good morn, sister."

"What did you...? How did you...?"

It seemed impossible.

He gave her a wink. "'Twould appear ye're not the only one whose veins run with the blood o' warriors."

She was still speechless with wonder when Noël hunkered down beside her. His brow was heavy.

"*Mon ange,* are ye hurt?"

She glanced back and forth between the two men. Noël's eyes were filled with concern, Caimbeul's with gleeful pride. "What the devil is goin' on?" she snapped.

"She's fine," Caimbeul assured Noël.

Noël looked doubtful. "'Twas quite a spill she took."

Caimbeul shrugged. "I've seen her take worse."

Noël shook his head. "How can ye bear to watch your own sister fight?"

"She's tougher than she looks."

Noël's brows raised. "Is that so?"

"Oh, aye. And 'tisn't the first time she's fallen on her arse."

Ysenda frowned. "That'll be quite enough, ye two. I'm right here, ye know. I can hear ye."

She struggled to her feet, batting away their helpful hands.

Noël murmured, "Are ye sure ye're all right?"

"I'm fine," she bit out, though her pride was bruised. "Now one o' ye had better tell me what's goin' on."

"Sir Noël's teachin' me to fight," Caimbeul said.

"Oh, he is, is he?"

Her eyes burned as she turned slowly to face Noël. Then she seized him by the front of his tabard and dragged him out of Caimbeul's hearing. "Teachin' him to fight?" she hissed. "Against battle-tested knights? A...a cripple?" She hated to use that word, but there was no other term for it. "Why? Did ye think 'twould be entertainin' for my father?"

Noël's eyes grew dark. He lowered his cool gaze to rest on her fists, still clenched in his tabard. His unspoken message was clear. He wouldn't allow her to belittle him in front of his men and her clan. And he wasn't going to reply until she unhanded him.

So she did.

But she still needed an answer.

"How could ye be so cruel?" she whispered. "Can ye not see how the laird mocks him?"

"He's not mockin' him now."

She glanced at her father. Noël was right. The laird wasn't gloating. He was glowering.

"Your brother is more capable than ye think. He's more capable than even he believes."

"Ye don't understand. He's...he's crippled."

"He's a wee bit twisted up," Noël admitted. "But he can still fight. He knocked *ye* on your arse." One side of his mouth lifted in a smile.

"Maybe he can trip up his sister. But he can't fight against seasoned warriors." A wave of dread washed over her as she considered the consequences. "If ye make him believe he can, ye'll get him killed."

"And if *ye* make him believe he cannot, ye'll keep him weak."

Her shoulders drooped. "I can't let harm come to him. I made a vow."

His eyes softened. "Ye were children when ye made that vow. He's a grown man now. He can take care o' himself."

Ysenda bit her lip. Part of her wanted to believe that. But Noël didn't know Caimbeul like she did. He didn't see how Caimbeul had been mocked and belittled all his life, how he longed to be normal. He couldn't understand her brother's pain.

"Watch him for a wee bit," Noël suggested. "And if ye don't agree that he can fend for himself, ye can go back to wipin' his arse."

She gave him a shove for that remark, but it only made him grin. Then she peered past his shoulder at Caimbeul, who was already back to sparring with one of Noël's knights. She couldn't remember a time when her brother had looked so bright-eyed, eager, and alive.

It was a difficult decision. But she finally nodded her assent. Noël returned to the field.

Her knuckles were white as she clenched her fists in her skirts, resisting the urge to rush forward in Caimbeul's defense while he dodged slashes from men with arms as thick as oaks. She gasped several times when a blade narrowly missed his head. And her heart dropped to the pit of her stomach when one of the knights sent him sprawling in the grass.

But then, in the midst of the fighting, Noël called out a few instructions. Caimbeul suddenly executed an unexpected spin to duck backward under one man's sword arm, pushing him forward into the second attacker.

As the two knights fell in a tangle of chain mail, Caimbeul crowed in victory. Noël rushed forward to clap him on the back.

"Well done. Ye see? Your best weapon is the element o' surprise."

Intrigued now, Ysenda watched as Noël continued to train her brother with a unique style and technique. Of course, once Caimbeul began to improve and his antics were no longer amusing, the laird lost interest and retired to the keep. But Ysenda remained to watch in fascination, glimpsing a side of her brother she'd never seen before.

Gradually, over the course of an hour, Noël transformed Caimbeul into an impressive and lethal fighter. Even more significant, the Knights of de Ware became Caimbeul's companions in arms. They challenged him, jested with him, boasted and cursed together. Her brother finally had friends who treated him as an equal.

Yet to what end?

Her heart sank. The knights might be his brothers now. But soon they would desert Caimbeul to return to France. Then he'd be left once again with clansmen who mocked him.

It wasn't fair. It was bad enough that she had to surrender a perfect husband to her selfish sister. It was beyond cruel to make Caimbeul sacrifice his happiness as well.

She had never felt more like fortune's foe.

In the shadows of the armory, Noël unbuckled his sword belt and tossed it aside. He was filled with regret. As if choosing between his duty to his king and the dictates of his heart wasn't difficult enough, now he had to grieve over losing a young brother whom he'd quickly come to admire.

Noël had never had a more enthusiastic and attentive student than Caimbeul. The young man not only learned fast, but he was clever and inventive. If only Noël had more time with him, he was confident he could mold him into a respectable warrior.

Noël slipped his tabard off over his head, then bent forward to shiver off his chain mail, letting it pool on the ground.

Behind him, he heard someone enter the armory. The uneven gait—the stab of a staff and the foot dragging across the floor—was instantly identifiable.

"I came to thank ye, Sir Noël," Caimbeul said quietly, "for givin' me somethin' no man's ever given me before." He stopped in the middle of the chamber. "Hope."

Noël's shoulders lowered. Hope? He feared he may have given Caimbeul only *false* hope. What would become of the lad once the knights left? Would he go back to cowering before his father?

"Ye've made me see that I'm more than just a cripple," he continued. Emotion thickened his voice. "I'll never forget that. And I'll never forget ye."

Noël nodded and turned to Caimbeul. But he couldn't look him in the eyes. "I'll never forget ye either."

However, another pair of eyes floated into his thoughts. Eyes that glowed like soft gray fog. Eyes that shimmered like the sleek silver sea. They were eyes he'd never be able to banish from his mind. With a sigh, he sank down on the wooden bench and hung his head.

Caimbeul limped over and sat beside him.

"Ye love her, don't ye?" he guessed. "Ysenda?"

Too weary to lie, Noël nodded.

"And ye don't want to leave her."

Noël swallowed back despair and answered gruffly. "'Tisn't my choice. I'm honor-bound to do the king's will."

Caimbeul shook his head. "'Tis my own damned fault. If I hadn't told ye ye'd wed the wrong sister..."

Noël smile ruefully. "'Tisn't like sparrin', Caimbeul. Ye can't feint and fool and deceive your way through life."

"Can't ye?" he grumbled.

Noël shook his head.

"But if ye truly love my sister, isn't that all that matters?"

Noël clucked his tongue. "Ye've got skills with a blade now. But ye still have much to learn about duty and honor."

Caimbeul heaved a sigh. Then he drew his dagger and began idly carving the top of his wooden staff.

"Besides," Noël said, "would ye not prefer I take the real Cathalin and leave Ysenda here? I know ye're very close to your sister. And she loves ye very much."

Caimbeul continued carving in silence, but Noël saw his lips compress with an unasked question.

"Ye were hopin' to come with us," Noël guessed, "weren't ye?"

Caimbeul shrugged. "Maybe." He dusted the wood chips from the top of his staff. "I could make myself useful now."

His words broke Noël's heart. There was nothing worse for a man than not feeling useful. He wished he *could* take Caimbeul with him.

But if he did the right thing and married the real Cathalin, he had to leave Caimbeul behind. He couldn't be so heartless as to steal Ysenda's brother from her.

With a growl of frustration, he shot to his feet, raking his hands back through his hair.

The abrupt movement spooked Caimbeul, who lurched from the bench in surprise and almost fell. As he grabbed Noël to regain his balance, his dagger grazed Noël's neck.

"Ach!" Caimbeul cried. "Forgive me. Ye startled me. Are ye all right?"

"Aye," he said, clapping his hand to his bloodied neck to make sure his head was still attached. Then he gave the lad a wink of reassurance. "'Tis only a scratch. But ye'd better put away your weapon before your warrior blood gets the best o' ye."

"Sorry." Caimbeul sheathed his dagger and bent to retrieve his dropped staff. "Are ye sure ye're all right?"

Noël sighed. Nae, he was *not* all right. He was brokenhearted and discouraged. He could see no way out of this predicament.

There would be no happy ending...for anyone.

After Caimbeul limped off and Noël was alone again in the armory, his thoughts began to drift.

The Viking well suddenly materialized in his mind. Why, he didn't know. He didn't actually believe in enchantments. Only a fool would imagine an ancient ruin held some magical power.

Yet Ysenda's words haunted him. What had she said? That the well could bless two lovers, binding them together for eternity.

Which was ridiculous. But he supposed every place had its local legends—the Highlands probably more than most. For the superstitious, all it took to keep such a legend alive was enough inexplicable coincidences.

Noël, however, was neither superstitious nor gullible. Shaking his head over his absurd imagination, he left the armory.

As he entered the great hall, he glimpsed Ysenda near the far wall. She looked as beautiful as...as a Viking goddess.

He frowned. A Viking goddess? What had made that pop into his mind? He knew nothing about Viking goddesses.

He straightened and made his way through the crowd toward Ysenda.

Her smile was melancholy. Her eyes looked like heavy clouds about to loose their store of rain as she murmured, "I can't thank ye enough for what ye did for Caimbeul."

"He's a good fighter. If he puts his mind to it, he'll one day be a great Viking warrior."

"A what?"

Noël furrowed his brows. What had made him say that? "Highland, a great Highland warrior."

Ysenda's eyes were moist. He could see his praise of her brother meant a lot to her. But the longer he looked at her, the more miserable he felt. Standing beside her was torture when he knew he couldn't keep her.

He had find an excuse to get away, if only for a moment.

There was a keg of ale at the opposite side of the hall.

213

"I'm goin' to fetch myself a drink from the well. Would ye like me to get one for ye?"

She gave him a quizzical look. "From the well?"

"What?"

"Ye said ye were fetchin' a drink from the well."

"Nae, I didn't."

"Aye, ye did."

Had he said that? What was wrong with him? "I'm fetchin' a drink from the keg there, on the far...wall. Aye, that's what I said, from the wall."

That wasn't what he'd said, and he knew it. But he couldn't explain why his mind was fixated on that damned Viking well. And he didn't want to try.

Without waiting to see if she wanted a drink, he left to fill two cups.

By the time he brought her ale back, he'd forgotten all about the well. He nodded toward her father. The laird was speaking to three of the de Ware knights and Caimbeul.

"It looks like your father has new respect for his son."

"Aye," she replied, taking a sip, "at least while he's surrounded by your men."

The reminder of Noël's imminent departure brought a scowl to his face.

Just then, Cathalin breezed down the stairs and into the great hall. Not a hair was out of place. Not a wrinkle creased her gown. Even his own men, accustomed to the great beauties of France, turned their heads as she entered the room.

But looking at her only made Noël's heart sink. A weight descended on his shoulders. And he knew he had to do something about it.

"We need to talk," he told Ysenda.

"I know."

"We need to decide what to do. I planned to leave today, and—"

"Today?"

"Waitin' any longer won't make it easier."

"I know."

She was trying to be brave. He could see that. But her eyes were wet. And it was making his throat ache.

A tendril of her hair fell forward against her cheek, and he brushed it back, tucking it behind her ear. But his gaze locked on it in speculation.

A lock of her hair and a lock of his, tied together with a ribbon.

He frowned. He was *not* going to do it. It was a silly ritual. A waste of time.

And yet, he thought as she clamped her jaw to keep her chin from trembling, what harm would it do? He'd tried everything else. Why not try this? As long as no one caught him at the well, no one would be the wiser.

But how would he get a lock of her hair?

"And who will ye be leavin' with?" she choked out. "My sister? Or me?"

She was on the verge of tears. He knew she didn't want to cry in front of her clan. So he took her hand and guided her toward the stairs.

When they reached the shadows of the stairwell, he swept her into his arms. He kissed her deeply, passionately. It was a bittersweet embrace of loss and longing, of fond farewell and ill-fated desire.

It was also an opportunity for Noël to sneak out his dagger and steal a wisp of her hair. Feeling foolish, he nonetheless managed to collect it without her knowledge. He closed it in his palm and then broke off the embrace to hold her at arm's length.

"I need to be alone for a wee bit...to think."

She nodded.

He looked into her eyes again, imparting his love for her with a glance. And then he left.

CHAPTER 9

After he'd gone, Ysenda's eyes filled and spilled over. Sobs lodged in her throat, too painful to swallow away.

She never wept—at least not where anyone could see her. Weeping was a sign of weakness. Or so her mother had always believed. So she sat on the step, indulging her sorrow in secret.

Was there no way to undo what had been done? Was there no choice that would satisfy everyone? Was there nothing she could do to change their destiny?

As she continued sniffling into her hands, she felt an itching between her breasts. With tear-damp fingers, she reached into her bodice.

The lock of his hair. She'd forgotten it was there.

She withdrew it by the red ribbon and stared at it. Suddenly a strange tingling started at the back of her neck. A wee hope blew through her soul like a stray wind.

Locks from each lover's hair, tied together with a ribbon.

Was it possible? Could she call upon the magic of the Viking well?

She didn't even know if she believed in the magic. Some of

the clan swore by it. But she didn't put much faith in old legends and ancient enchantments.

On the other hand, something had compelled her to snip the lock of his hair last night. Why else would she have done that? She must have known, deep in her heart of hearts, that she would end up visiting the well.

She ran her thumb over the silky strands of black hair. She was being childish. It was only a Yuletide story, after all. Nobody even knew if the story was true. Going there was probably a reckless waste of time.

Still...what was the harm? She had to try.

Wiping away her tears, she went upstairs and donned her cloak. She didn't want Noël to see her going. He would guess what she was up to. And he would think she was a fool. So she left the keep quietly and took a roundabout path to the well.

Halfway there, she stopped to rest. Drawing her dagger, she cut off a small piece of her own hair and tied it together with his. Her auburn and his black made an interesting contrast. She couldn't help but think about what their children's hair might look like.

She gulped. What if a child was already growing in her belly? The thought was at once thrilling and horrifying.

Closing the precious strands in her hand, she continued on her journey, hoping no one would catch sight of her.

In fact, she was so busy making sure she wasn't followed that when she arrived, she didn't notice at first that she wasn't the only visitor to the well. A mere ten paces from the stream, she finally saw she wasn't alone.

She gasped in surprise.

Noël glanced up with a frown. "Ysenda?"

"What are *ye* doin' here?"

He hid something behind his back and cleared his throat. "I could ask ye the same thing."

She realized she was holding the bound locks of hair where

he could easily see them. But she couldn't exactly tuck them back into her bodice. "I needed...fresh air."

He wasn't fooled for an instant. And his gaze went immediately to what she was holding in her hand. "What have ye got there?"

A dozen lies crossed her mind. She opened her mouth to speak one of them. But none of them were believable. So she closed her mouth again. She might as well confess. She shook her head. "Locks o' hair."

"Whose hair?"

She raised her chin in challenge. "Yours and mine."

She expected him to make fun of her. He'd doubtless have a good chuckle at her expense. And just as she anticipated, he began to laugh.

But then he held aloft what he had behind his back. "Like these?"

She frowned. He was holding strands of black and auburn hair tied together with a green ribbon. Her hand went instinctively to her head as she wondered when he'd stolen a lock of her hair. "How did ye...?"

"While we were kissin'." One side of his mouth curved up in a grin. "And ye?"

She gave him a sheepish smile. "While ye were sleepin'."

He shook his head. "Come on." His eyes twinkled as he summoned her with his free hand. "We may as well get it over with."

She joined him where he stood over the well. "Do ye think 'twill work?"

"I have no idea, but 'tis worth—"

There was a sudden movement through the trees. They both froze. Someone was coming their way. Damn! The last thing Ysenda wanted was an audience for their foolishness.

But after a moment, she blinked in surprise. She recognized the lurching motion of the intruder.

Noël recognized it as well. "What the devil? Caimbeul?"

Caimbeul was struggling through the snow. His staff slipped on the slick surface. He was out of breath. But he had a wide smile on his face.

"Caimbeul!" she said, handing the locks of hair off to Noël before rushing forward to meet her brother. "Are ye all right? How did ye walk so far? And in the snow?" As far as she remembered, he'd only been to the well once before, and he'd had to ride part of the way on a vendor's cart.

He shrugged off her questions to ask his own. "What are the two o' ye doin' here? Are ye wishin' on the well? Is that what ye're doin'?"

"Nae," she said.

"Aye," Noël said.

Ysenda frowned. She wasn't exactly proud of what they were doing.

But Caimbeul only laughed and hobbled forward, then dug something out of his satchel. For an instant, Ysenda couldn't speak.

"Is that what I think 'tis?" Noël asked.

Caimbeul grinned. "Locks o' your hair? Aye."

Ysenda blinked at the white-ribboned bundle. "I'm beginnin' to think I'm lucky I haven't been plucked bald. How did ye...?"

"Remember when I knocked ye on your arse in the courtyard?" Caimbeul asked, clearly acting the braggart. "I might have stolen a few strands while ye lay helpless."

Noël narrowed his eyes and nodded. "And ye took mine when ye had that 'accident' in the armory, didn't ye?"

"Ye said trickery was my strength." Caimbeul beamed with pride. "So what do we do now?"

It had seemed silly enough when Ysenda was thinking of making the wish by herself. Now, with three of them reciting the wish, it seemed absolutely ridiculous.

On the other hand, what did they have to lose? The fact that they all wanted the same thing touched her. And it made her more than willing to indulge the two most important men in her life.

"I suppose we weight them with rocks and drop them into the well together," she said.

Noël nodded. "That should give our wish three times the power."

Once they'd secured small rocks to each bundle, they stood together over the well.

"What are we supposed to say?" Noël asked.

"I'm not certain," Ysenda admitted. "I suppose we wish for a way to bind our two spirits together for eternity?"

"I'll do it," Caimbeul offered when they stood above the well. "I think ye should hold hands." They did. "In the name o' the unfortunate lovers who once drowned in this well, I make this Yuletide wish that the two souls to whom these locks o' hair belong to be blessed in their marriage and joined together forever and aye."

They all nodded, pleased with his choice of words. And then they dropped their tokens, one by one, into the water, where they disappeared into the inky depths.

The heavens didn't open up to let angels descend.

The air didn't stir with the breeze of faerie wings or fill with the sound of ancient pipes.

No Viking ghosts appeared.

Indeed, the moment was remarkably unremarkable.

"What do we do now?" Caimbeul asked.

Noël answered. "I suppose we wait."

As the moments crept by, Ysenda became more and more despondent. Nothing was happening. The spell wasn't working. She should have known better than to believe in magic.

After an uncomfortably long silence, she finally spoke. "Maybe we should be gettin' back."

"Do ye think it worked?" Caimbeul asked.

"Nae." The word scraped across her throat, like a sword blade on a sharpening stone.

Caimbeul's brows came together. "So what do we do now?"

Noël's chest was tight. He'd hoped he wouldn't have to answer that. He'd hoped, impossibly, that somehow the well would give him an answer. But there had been nothing.

"What we must," he decided.

Caimbeul straightened, as much as his crooked frame allowed. "Whatever happens, I'm goin' to France with ye," he blurted out. "That is," he amended, "if ye'll have me."

From the corner of his eye, Noël could see Ysenda had clenched her jaw.

He shook his head. "I can't take ye from Ysenda, Caimbeul. Ye may be her younger brother, but now that ye're grown, *she* needs *your* protection."

Caimbeul scowled, simultaneously disappointed and flattered. In the end, all he did was mutter, "I'm not her younger brother. I'm the oldest."

There was a long, melancholy silence.

Finally, Caimbeul's words sank in. Noël blinked, wondering if he'd heard wrong. "What? What did ye say?"

"I'm older than Ysenda. Three years older."

He frowned. "Ye are? And what about Cathalin?"

"I'm two years older than Cathalin."

He rattled his head. Surely that wasn't right. "Ye're the oldest?"

"Aye."

Noël closed his eyes. Was he missing something? "Ye're the *oldest?*" he repeated.

"Aye," the siblings said together.

"The oldest, as in the rightful heir to the laird?"

"Oh. Well, nae," Ysenda explained. "The laird has never…he's never claimed Caimbeul as his heir."

"Hold on." Noël's heart started to race. He didn't want to get prematurely excited. But something was awry here. "Are ye sayin' ye're the next in line?"

"In principle, aye, but—"

"Nae, nae, nae, nae," Noël interrupted. "Not in principle. In actual fact." Now his heart was pounding. This could be his answer. "Exactly why has he not claimed ye? Are ye not his son by blood?"

"I am."

"Are ye a bastard?"

"Nae."

"Why then?"

Caimbeul flushed and lowered his gaze.

Ysenda answered for him. "He's never claimed Caimbeul as his son because he's a cripple and unfit to rule."

"But he's not unfit," Noël insisted, beginning to pace eagerly now as he considered this new piece of information. "Ye saw him on the field. Not only is he bright and clever, but he can even hold his own with a sword."

Ysenda and Caimbeul stared at each other. Clearly, the thought of contesting the inheritance had never crossed their minds.

He supposed he could see why. The Highlands were so remote that a clan laird was essentially the ruler of his own domain. The Scottish king might lay down the law of the land. But the laird felt he had the power to bend that law as he saw fit.

In truth, however, laws were a matter of record. No man could alter what was written down by a king to suit his own wants or needs...not even a laird.

"It doesn't matter whether the laird wishes to claim him or not," Noël explained. "Caimbeul is his son. As long as he's fit to rule—and anyone can see he is—by law, Caimbeul is the true heir."

"So ye're sayin' the holdin' doesn't rightfully belong to

Cathalin," Caimbeul mused aloud, "no matter who she weds? It belongs to me?"

"Exactly." Noël crossed his arms over his chest in satisfaction. "Which means—"

"Which means we can all have what we want," Ysenda gushed. "We can stay married and go to France. Cathalin can wed her Highlander..."

"And I can come to train with your men," Caimbeul inserted, for fear he might be excluded.

Noël gave him a slow grin. "Aye."

Caimbeul rubbed his jaw, thinking this over. Then his brow creased. "It doesn't seem possible. Do ye truly think 'twill come to pass? My father is very strong-willed. And the Highlands is a long reach for the arm o' the law."

"Which is why the king sends men like the Knights o' de Ware to enforce the law," Noël said.

"Ye'd do that?"

"Aye, o' course. Ye're one of us now."

"But what about the clan?" he asked. "I don't want war with the clan."

"They're my clan as well," Noël assured him. "When the time comes, we'll find a way to keep the peace. Ye're a clever man. Ye'll think of somethin'."

Ysenda's beautiful silver eyes shone with hope. But there was wisdom and caution in her voice. "'Twill all have to be kept a secret. If the laird suspects that Caimbeul has a claim to the holdin'..."

She didn't finish the thought. But they all knew the risk. Laird Gille wouldn't hesitate to eliminate his heir if Caimbeul proved to be...inconvenient.

"Aye," Noël said. "'Twill be a secret between the three of us."

They nodded in solemn agreement.

And then, with a soft cry of victory, Ysenda threw herself into Noël's arms.

He chuckled with pleasure and held her close.

But as their lingering embrace went on and on, Caimbeul finally rolled his eyes and turned to leave.

"Where are ye goin'?" Ysenda asked him.

"Back to the keep," he said over his shoulder. "There's somethin' I've been meanin' to do for a long while. But don't fret. By the time ye get finished...celebratin'...ye can catch up with me."

Noël bid him farewell. Then he grinned and kissed the top of his lovely wife's head. "It looks like we'll have our whole lives to celebrate."

"Not just our lives," she murmured. "Eternity."

"It worked, didn't it?" he asked her softly. "The Viking well. It granted us our Yuletide wish."

She nodded. Then she gazed up at him. Her smile was as sweet as mulled wine. Her eyes glowed with the warmth of Christmas candles. "For ever and aye."

epilogue

eaving her Highland home to travel south with the Knights of de Ware, Ysenda had never felt so well protected. Of course, that hadn't kept her from packing her own chain mail and weapons. Old habits were hard to break. It would be a long while before she'd grow to accept that she had an army of knights at her command and that her brother could take care of himself.

Caimbeul had certainly proved that upon their return to the castle.

Ysenda had had a lot of time to think on the way home from the well. Now that she was no longer beholden to her father, years of anger over Caimbeul's mistreatment began to fester within her. All the laird's past abuses—his mocking, violence, and cruelty—congealed into a single, hard knot of rage and injustice that stuck in her craw. With each step she took toward the castle, fury flowed hotter in her veins.

When they finally arrived at the keep to face her father, he was alone in the great hall and deep in his cups. His drunken sneer as the three of them approached only added fuel to the almost irresistible desire Ysenda had to pay him back for all the pain he'd caused.

But she'd held her tongue as Sir Noël explained that they wished to take Caimbeul with them to France.

Her father's eyes lit up. "Ach, aye!" he crowed. "I've heard the French courts like to use dwarves and such for entertainment."

Ysenda longed to curse her father for his brutal words.

But then she heard the echo of her mother's voice. Above all, the warrior maid had taught Ysenda to maintain control of her emotions. Losing one's temper was never wise. Besides, she and Caimbeul would leave soon and likely never see the laird again. There was no point in stirring up trouble. So she tensed her jaw against the urge to fire off a biting retort.

The laird eyed Caimbeul speculatively over the top of his cup. "Or maybe ye're plannin' to sell him along the way? The lad has a decent voice. No doubt a singin' cripple could bring ye a good price."

Ysenda clenched her teeth until they hurt. But she kept mentally repeating her mother's advice. One must take a deep breath, harness all the anger, and choose one's battles wisely.

The laird took a drink and then smacked his lips. "He's probably got another five or six years o' life at most. Still, ye'll get your coin's worth."

That made Ysenda's blood boil. But no matter how much she yearned to claw that smug smirk off of the laird's face, no matter how gratifying it would be to tear the beard from his chin, no matter how her fist ached to...

Crack!

Ysenda lifted a brow as her father's head snapped back under Caimbeul's solid punch. The laird staggered backward, dropping his cup and clutching his nose.

As Ysenda stared in wonder, Caimbeul shook his bruised knuckles. Then he grinned in satisfaction. "That's for a lifetime o' sufferin'...Da."

Those had been Caimbeul's last words to the laird, who'd

shuffled off to have someone tend to his bloodied nose. Ysenda had never been prouder of her brother. And she thought their mother would agree that he'd chosen his battle wisely.

Now they were headed to France—to freedom and to family. As impossible as it seemed, Ysenda thought Caimbeul looked taller as he traveled beside his new companions-in-arms. Perhaps he no longer felt crushed by the weight of his infirmity.

As for her husband, though his men laughingly insisted Noël was the ugliest of the de Ware brothers, Ysenda could not have been happier to be wed to such a handsome, kind, noble, brilliant, and honorable man. Noël had promised that when her father died, he and his men would return with Caimbeul to help him claim the Highland holding without shedding a drop of blood.

Their path from the keep took them past the Viking well. Ysenda requested a private moment before they continued on their journey to visit one last time. Gathering her cloak about her, she clambered across the snowdrifts until she reached the silvery stream and the crumbling stones of the ruin.

There, she ran her fingers over the ancient runes carved into the lid of the well. She whispered thanks to the lost lovers for granting her wish. Then she sent up a silent prayer of her own—that somehow, some way, no matter how long it took, the doomed couple might eventually have their own curse lifted.

By the time she returned to the company, the knights were speaking with a dozen strangers—travelers headed in the opposite direction. The band of ragged Highlanders said they were on their way to the keep of Laird Gille.

The wee lad at the fore licked his chapped lips and raised his beardless chin, boasting in his high, sweet voice that he was going to marry the bonniest lass in all of Scotland.

Ysenda's brows lifted. But she wisely held her laughter. She wished she could see her sister's face when Cathalin beheld the bridegroom she'd wanted so badly—all four feet of him.

Instead, she smiled up at Noël, whose lips were twitching with amusement. He gave her a wink, and she sighed with pleasure.

This was going to be, without a doubt, the best Yuletide ever.

The End

More books from the Knights of de Ware series:
My Champion
My Warrior
My Hero

ᴄʜᴇ ʀᴇɪᴠᴇʀ

A Medieval Outlaws Novella

*A cattle-thieving Scottish lass chooses the wrong cow
to steal and tangles with a laird who heals her heart
and tames her wild ways.*

ÐEÐICATION

*For Barb Batlan-Massabrook
and Deborah Stewart,
two of the toughest "Scottish" lasses I know*

ACKNOWLEÐGMENTS

My sincerest thanks to
my sisters in The Summer Star,
Tanya Anne Crosby and Laurin Wittig,
for inspiring the legend;
my niece Rayna Barden
for sharing her knowledge of livestock;
my husband Richard Campbell,
for taking me on the best adventures;
my amazing Readers Clan,
for their love and support;
and Michelle Rodriguez and Chris Pratt
for their inspiration.

CHAPTER 1

Brighde felt the star coming long before anyone spied it in the night sky.

She could feel it in the way she felt the brush of a spider's web or the faint caress of a breeze, the distant drone of honeybees or the delicate kiss of morning mist.

Every seventy-five years it came. Like a spark struck from a smith's anvil, it streaked across the black night. For several days it hung in the heavens, sweeping close to the earth, lighting up heath and braes.

Some feared it would drop from the sky and set the world ablaze.

Brighde knew better. The star's course never strayed.

But it did possess a singular magic—the power of transformation. And that power was dangerous, for it could be used for either good or evil.

Some claimed the star brought bad luck. They blamed it for fire and flood, famine and misfortune.

But those who believed in the goodness of the star were

granted rebirth, renewal, redemption—a chance to begin again.

Brighde smiled as she tossed her shimmering golden locks over her shoulder and pulled the tap, filling her patron's wooden flagon with ale.

Two lost souls whose fates would be changed by the star were about to cross Brighde's path. She could feel it in her bones. One, the lass, was coming later this eve. The other was already on his way.

She turned toward the gap-toothed old soldier who'd plunked his coin down for a pint and gave him a brilliant smile.

"There ye go, lad," she sang.

If he gave her a quizzical look for calling a man who appeared to be twice her age "lad," she didn't pay much heed. Her attention was centered, not on the soldier, but on the door. In another moment, *he* would arrive.

Brochan Macintosh didn't really know why he was stopping at the inn. After all, he needed to get home to his young sons. He'd been gone for hours. And he hated to leave Colin and Cambel in the hands of his already overworked housekeeper.

For the last several weeks, he'd inhabited the tower house on the holding he'd inherited from his uncle, the former Laird of Macintosh. But the old laird must have grown daft or penniless over the last few years, for when Brochan arrived, the keep was deserted and half in ruins.

Brochan was doing most of the repairs himself—fixing leaks in the roof, replacing cracked timbers, rebuilding rotted stairs—while his two faithful servants swept out the moldy rushes, chased mice from the buttery, kept the household fed, and watched over his sons.

To have five of his cattle go missing in the last week only added to Brochan's long list of problems to solve. He'd searched for hours today for the lost cows, scouring acres of the thick woods that made up the border of his property, to no avail.

Perhaps that was why he felt he deserved to stop for an ale at the roadside inn before he trudged home.

Throwing back the hood of his gray tartan brat, he ducked under the thatched roof and pushed open the heavy door. The inn was cheery inside, lit by tallow candles and a lively peat fire. He nodded a greeting to the old man seated by the hearth, the only patron in the inn at this hour. Then he untied the wooden cup from his belt and approached the bar.

When he set down his cup, he almost knocked it over, so rattled was he by the tavern wench beaming at him from the other side. She was as bright as an angel and as beautiful as a goddess. Her golden tresses spilled over her perfect bosom like honey. Her skin glowed as if lit from within. Her smile was as open, pure, and enchanting as a child's.

But that wasn't what made his cup stutter on the bar. Her eyes, like rare crystal, caught the light and reflected it back in mutable shades of green and blue.

"Good day," she said. "I'm Brighde, at your service. What will ye have?"

Her voice was as lovely as her appearance. And yet he couldn't help but compare her to that other beauty, the one who'd been taken away from him. No woman would ever measure up to his lovely wife, the mother of his sons. She'd been dead for five years. But his heart still ached when he thought about her sweet freckled face and her sky-blue eyes.

"Ale, please," he said quietly.

Brighde took his cup and started filling it from the tap. "What are ye up to this fine summer's day?"

"Not much," he said.

"Indeed?" Her expression was amused, skeptical.

He reconsidered. Maybe the tavern wench had information about his lost cows. "Actually, I'm searchin' for my cattle. Some o' them have gone missin'. Ye haven't heard anythin' about any coos runnin' loose, have ye?"

Brighde handed him his full cup. "Coos," she mused.

He pulled a coin from his pouch for the ale and set it on the bar, then tossed back a healthy swig.

When Brighde picked up the coin, her eyes were twinkling. "'Tis a band o' reivers after your coos," she told him.

"What?"

"Reivers have stolen your cattle."

He frowned. "Reivers? What reivers?"

"Och, that I can't tell ye."

"Then how do ye know 'tis reivers and not—"

"They're comin' again tonight."

"What?"

"The reivers. They're comin' again. Tonight."

Brochan lowered his brows. The lass seemed very sure of that. What wasn't she telling him? "Look, lass, if ye know somethin'..."

"Aye. I know somethin'." Her eyes had taken on an unsettling silvery shade now, as if she were gazing into another world. "Watch for the reivers to return tonight. Ye'll get your coos back...and more."

More? What the devil did that mean?

Before he could ask her, she captured his eyes with her own, burning into them with blue-green fire, and the words suddenly fled from his mind. She murmured tenderly, "And ye'll no longer be lonely."

He gulped. Lonely? What made her think he was lonely? Brochan wasn't lonely. He was rarely ever alone. He had his two sons. His two servants. And, until recently, a whole herd of cows. The woman must be mistaken.

Tearing his gaze away, he scoffed, "Lonely? I'm not lonely."

Yet something about the way she'd spoken snagged at his heart. Something about his reply was empty and false. And something about the way she was gazing at him now—compassion softening her eyes to a gentle gray—made him believe she was peeking between his words of denial, peering at the truth. A truth he refused to admit, even to himself.

Her eyes lost all their frost then, darkening to a friendly blue, and she smiled. "Ye know, your stars are about to change, lad."

He lifted a dubious brow. Had the young miss just called him a lad? "My stars."

"Aye. But 'tis up to ye whether ye lay claim to that fate," she intoned, "or let it pass ye by."

He took another cautious sip at his ale. "I see." He didn't see, not at all. Indeed, he was beginning to wonder if Brighde's great beauty was compensation for a lack of wits.

"The star has chosen ye," she said.

"The star," he repeated.

The poor lass *was* mad. All stars did was light up the night sky.

He sighed. He knew he shouldn't have wandered into the inn.

He finished his ale in a gulp and tied the empty cup back onto his belt. But before he could turn away, Brighde seized his hands in hers.

It startled him, especially when a warm vibration began to flow up his arms. Yet, even more startling, he felt no panic, no desire to pull away.

"Remember," she whispered, gazing into his eyes with blue-green intensity. "Your destiny is in your hands."

When she released him, he felt shaken to his core. But he wasn't about to let her know it. Instead, he thanked her for the ale and turned to go. Faith, he had to get back home, back to people who believed destiny was determined, not by stars, but by hard work.

Still, as he plodded down the road toward the tower house,

he wondered if Brighde's comment about reivers had merit. It hadn't occurred to him that his cows might have been intentionally stolen. But considering the chilly welcome Brochan had received from the local folk on moving into the tower, it was entirely possible that a couple of the hostile neighbor lads had thieved his cattle.

He decided there was naught to be lost by keeping a watchful eye on his herd tonight.

Cristy Moffat picked up her inconvenient skirts, cursing her throbbing ankle and struggling to keep up with her cousins. Her lungs were burning. But she didn't want to get left behind.

The lads were always leaving her behind. It was bad enough that, even at eighteen, she was a wee lass and couldn't match their long stride. But ever since she'd twisted her ankle at supper, every step sent a twinge up her leg.

It had been a stupid accident, entirely her fault. Serving her uncle pottage, she'd tripped over her cousin's stray foot and slopped the soup into her uncle's lap.

She supposed she deserved the clout he'd given her for her clumsiness. And it wasn't the first time he'd called her a worthless lass. At least the black eye and the insult didn't hurt like her ankle did.

Of course, she wasn't about to let her cousins know she was in pain. If she did, they'd tell her she had to stay home. And more than anything, she wanted to come along.

Each of the five lads had taken a turn, creeping out at night to reive a cow from their new neighbor, Macintosh. Tonight was her turn. And she didn't intend to miss her chance.

Her uncle didn't much care for Macintosh, the new owner of the tower house and land adjoining his. Her uncle didn't like strangers, especially those with more cattle than he had. So he'd crowed with glee over his sons' stealth and trickery, happy to add another cow to his own herd at Macintosh's expense.

Cristy was determined to show her cousins that she could reive cattle as well as any lad. And she meant to prove to her uncle that he was wrong, that she wasn't entirely worthless.

"Come on, runt!" Fergus yelled back at her as they headed toward the starlit inn. "We haven't got all night."

She heard Doug mutter, "I told ye this was a mistake."

"Shite, Cristy!" Morris jeered. "Ye won't even catch a calf at that speed."

Hamish grumbled, "She'll probably go for the bull and break her neck."

"I'm comin'," she insisted, hobbling forward. "I'm just...I'm savin' it for tonight."

Archibald, the oldest, shook his head. "We shouldn't have brought her. I've got a bad feelin' about this."

Cristy raised a determined chin as they gathered outside the inn. "I can do it. I'll show ye."

"Sure ye will," Morris sneered.

"I *will*," Cristy insisted.

"If ye don't get a coo," Hamish threatened, "that's it. No more taggin' along like ye're one of us."

His words crushed her. But she'd learned to hide that kind of pain long ago. The pain of not belonging.

He was right. She wasn't one of them. But after the death of her parents seven years ago, her uncle and her cousins were all she had. If she lost them...

She gulped back her fear.

She couldn't afford to fail. So she forced a cocky smile to her lips. With a confidence she didn't feel, she said, "I'll do it. Ye just watch me."

Rolling his eyes, Fergus pushed open the door of the inn, and they all crowded inside.

Last to enter, Cristy closed the door behind her and tossed back the hood of her brown arisaid, dragging out her long black braid. A merry fire crackled on the hearth. A handful of patrons sat at tables, laughing and drinking foamy cups of ale. Her cousins were quick to claim the largest table against the wall.

Before she could slide onto the bench beside Archibald, Hamish flipped a silver coin onto the table in front of her. "Be a good lass, and fetch us all ales."

They unbuckled the wooden cups from their belts and set them on the table in front of her.

Cristy snapped up the coin, took the five cups by their handles, and headed across the room to the bar, where the tavern wench was pulling ale.

She set the coin and the cups on the bar, adding her own.

When the woman turned toward her, Cristy gave a little gasp. She was the most beautiful lady Cristy had ever seen. Her skin glowed like a candle, and the tresses framing her face shone like spun gold. Her lips curved up as if she kept some delicious secret, and her eyes sparkled like the surface of a stream, in varying shades of blue, green, and silver. It was hard to say how old she was. She looked both as fresh as a newborn babe and as worldly as an ancient sage.

Obviously, Cristy's cousins hadn't seen the breathtaking wench. If they had, they'd have fallen all over themselves for the privilege of speaking to her.

"Good even," the woman said. Even her voice was beautiful, like the soft, melodic tones of a harp. "I'm Brighde, at your service. What will ye—" She broke off abruptly. Black lightning flashed in her gaze, then vanished as quickly as it had struck. She was staring at Cristy's bruise. "Where did ye get that?"

Cristy raised her fingers to her cheek. She'd all but forgotten about her injury. She supposed she should have kept her face hidden so as not to trouble anyone.

"'Tis naught," she said with a shrug. "Just an acci—"

But Brighde suddenly seized her wrist and pulled her forward. "Let me see."

Cristy scowled. How dare the woman grab her? And why was she making such a great fuss? It was only a black eye, after all.

She tried to pull away, but Brighde was having none of it. The woman lifted Cristy's chin to take a closer look. Then her eyes softened to the color of fog.

Cristy wished she wouldn't look at her like that, with kindness and pity. It made her uncomfortable. She squirmed out of Brighde's grasp, avoiding the woman's eyes. "Six ales, please."

With a nod, Brighde set out a tray and began to fill the cups from the tap. As she did, she dispensed an unwelcome bit of advice along with the ale. "Ye shouldn't let them treat ye like that, orderin' ye about like a servant."

Cristy blinked. What concern was it of a tavern wench's how her cousins treated her? Unsure what to say, she smirked and shrugged. "They're kin."

"Did one o' them give ye that mark?" she asked, nodding at Cristy's eye.

"Nay," Cristy said defensively.

Brighde began filling the second cup. "But 'twas a man. A man with a hot temper, aye?"

Cristy frowned. She owed the woman no explanation. But somehow the words came tumbling out before she could stop them. "'Twas only my uncle. I tripped and spilled pottage on him."

Brighde placed the full cup on the tray, arching her perfect brows. "He clouted you—for an accident?"

"I suppose so." It did sound wrong when she said it like that. But Brighde didn't know the situation. And Cristy didn't feel like explaining that she'd always been a clumsy fool.

Brighde was silent a long while as she filled three more cups. "So what are ye and your lads up to this even?"

"Cristy!" Morris yelled. "What's takin' ye so bloody long?"

"Comin'!" she shouted back. Then, because she was impatient with Brighde—who seemed to be taking her time and sticking her nose where it didn't belong—Cristy snapped, "I don't think 'tis any o' your bloody concern what I'm doin' this even."

Instead of the shocked gasp Cristy expected, Brighde glanced up at her with a curious smile on her lips. "Well, they haven't crushed *all* your spirit yet, have they?"

Cristy furrowed her brows. What was that supposed to mean?

"Ye know, lass, it doesn't have to be like this," Brighde said, placing the last cup before her.

"Like what?"

She leaned forward to whisper, "Tryin' so hard to belong."

A queer tingling started at the back of Cristy's neck. Brighde's glittering eyes seemed to change color, shifting from green to blue and back again. Cristy felt as if the woman was reaching inside her mind, inside her soul, reading her thoughts and heart.

"Change is on the horizon," Brighde told her, penetrating deep into her eyes. "Your stars are about to transform. Fate hangs in the balance. *Your* fate."

Cristy had no idea what the woman was talking about, but something about Brighde's words and the way she was staring made her shiver.

Brighde reached out then and seized Cristy's hand, placing it between both of hers. Cristy gasped. The woman's palms were charged with some mysterious current, like the crackle of static in the north wind that preceded a shock. But Cristy couldn't pull away.

She knew she should be afraid. She could feel Brighde's strength, her will, her force. And yet, gazing into the woman's exquisite and kindly face, she felt no fear.

"The star has chosen ye," Brighde softly intoned. "The rest is in your hands. 'Tis up to ye whether ye seize the day..." As if making her point, she released Cristy's hand, "Or let it escape through your fingers."

Cristy glanced at her hand, half expecting it to be transformed into something else.

With a gentle smile, Brighde placed the mugs full of ale on the tray and handed it to her. "Your future beckons," she murmured. "Follow it, and ye may change your fate."

"Cristy!" shouted Hamish. "Move your arse!"

She winced. "Comin'!"

She turned to thank Brighde for the ales. But the woman had already moved away and was attending to a pair of gape-jawed drunks.

Cristy picked her cautious way to the table. She didn't want to trip over her own feet again.

"What took ye so bloody long?" Archibald demanded, passing out the ales. He added in a mutter, "'Twill be midnight by the time we get to Macintosh's."

He didn't expect an answer, and she didn't give him one. But as the lads gulped their ale, elbowed each other, and made ribald remarks about the toothsome tavern wench they'd finally noticed behind the bar, Cristy was lost in her thoughts.

Even after they left the inn for the long walk to the Macintosh holding, she couldn't get the curious woman's words out of her head.

What had Brighde meant?

What future was she talking about?

Was she some kind of seer?

Or was she only mad?

They continued along the road by the long-lasting light of summer until they reached the narrow burn that divided the two properties—her uncle's and Macintosh's. From there, they'd leave the main road so as not to be spotted. It was still a long hike over heather-covered braes and through soggy bogs to reach the place near the tower house where the cattle bedded down for the night.

But if what Brighde had said was true—if Cristy's fate would change tonight—she didn't intend to let anything, even her twisted ankle, prevent her from making the journey.

CHAPTER 2

"Where are ye goin', Da?" wee Colin asked as Brochan buckled on his sword over his white leine and black trews. The lad's brows were furrowed, and his five-year-old eyes looked fretful.

Brochan hunkered down and clasped the lad's wee shoulder.

"Nowhere. Just out to the fields. Now I'm countin' on ye lads to keep watch while I'm gone." He reached over to squeeze Cambel's shoulder as well. Then he glanced up and gave his man, Rauf, a wink.

Cambel didn't look convinced. He glanced at Brochan's sword. "How long will ye be gone, Da?"

"Och, not long at all."

Brochan exchanged a meaningful look with Rauf. He *hoped* he wouldn't be long. If they returned, he was determined to catch the damned reivers tonight.

He was convinced now the tavern wench was right. It *was* reivers who'd taken his cows. The nasty thieves had already stolen five of them in as many days. Tonight he would stand watch over the herd. If the villains tried to strike again, he'd be ready for them.

"Why can't I come, Da?" Colin asked, his green eyes serious. "I'll be careful around the coos."

"Me too," Cambel chimed in. "And I'm not afraid o' the dark."

Brochan smiled and ruffled the twins' unruly auburn hair that looked so like their mother's. "Ye're two brave lads, that's for sure. But I need ye here. After all, ye can't expect Rauf to watch o'er the keep all by himself."

"That's right," Rauf said, lowering his gray brows to give them a stern frown. "'Tis up to us to guard the house."

Rauf's wife, Mabel, called out from where she was tending the fire. "I'm countin' on ye braw lads to keep me safe."

Brochan grinned at that. Keep her safe indeed. Mabel was as big as a tree, as strong as an ox, and as unyielding as iron. If required, she could probably roust the entire English army from the tower house.

In fact, once she heard about Brochan's intentions to waylay the reivers, Mabel had offered to go after the good-for-naught knaves herself. But Brochan wasn't about to let her tangle with outlaws. She was too valuable as a cook and a nursemaid to his sons to be risking her life over such nonsense.

Brochan was grateful Rauf and Mabel had come with him to this new holding. The loyal servants had been with him since the lads were born. He didn't know what he'd do without them.

This battle with the reivers, however, was Brochan's. He was fairly sure that reiving his cattle was his unfriendly neighbors' attempt to chase him off.

It wouldn't work. He was determined to stay. He'd come too far and surrendered too much to go back now. He wouldn't let a few hostile neighbors frighten him away, especially since he had no intention of returning to the place where he'd met and married his beloved wife. There were too many painful reminders of her there.

It was best he make a fresh start. On this sizeable plot of land with its grassy, rolling braes and its thick forests, its lovely winding burn and its crumbling-but-reparable tower house, he could raise his sons in peace—far away from their mother's kin, who, though they never spoke of it aloud, silently blamed the twins for her death.

Brochan gave Cambel and Colin a kiss on the brow. How anyone could blame his two precious sons for anything so tragic, he didn't know.

"Ye do what Rauf tells ye now," he reminded them.

The lads nodded. Brochan straightened, adjusting his sword belt. He wore his sword out of habit. He doubted he'd need a weapon. The reivers were likely just a couple of lads up to mischief.

They would quickly learn that Brochan Macintosh was not a man to sit idly by while his cattle were picked off. A stern word from him about the foolishness of stealing from one's neighbor and the return of his cows should set the matter to rights.

The evening air was mild and pleasant. The sky was still not fully dark as he headed down the steep slope of the motte toward the glen where the cows usually spent the night. The dark green pines of the forest were etched in jagged silhouettes against the violet sky. Stars were just emerging, sprinkled like salt across the heavens. Thistles of starlit purple studded the grass like gems.

The crickets stopped chirping as he hiked across the spongy loam. In the well-grazed pasture, he could make out the rough, dark shapes of horned black cows slumbering on the sod.

Angling across the brae, he found a good vantage point where he could hide in a clump of tall heather and view the whole glen. He settled onto his seat on the damp ground, rested his arms on his raised knees, and narrowed his eyes at the herd below.

The crickets gradually resumed their singing. Now and then a cow would stir, raising its shaggy head and lowering it again. Brochan sat as still as stone while the moon slowly moved across the sky.

As always, when he was alone and unoccupied, memories of his wife seeped into his thoughts. Even after five years, he missed her. He hated to admit it was getting harder and harder to remember her face. But the features their sons had inherited from her—her reddish-brown hair, her freckled nose, her stubborn chin—haunted him. It was a blessing the lads had been born with green eyes like Brochan's, for he didn't think he could endure seeing his wife's merry sky-blue eyes every day.

He still wasn't past blaming himself for her death. Recalling her pale and shivering body as she delivered their second twin with her last breath, he felt crushing guilt, even though he'd done everything he could to save her life. Everything except stay away from her bed in the first place.

He swallowed the lump in his throat. It was too late for regrets now. She was gone, and he'd never find another like her. He had to do the best he could for their sons on his own.

As he surveyed the great glen that was now part of his holding, his eye caught on a curious star he hadn't seen before above the distant brae. It was lower than the others. And though it appeared motionless in the sky, a long stream of light trailed after it like a tail.

A comet, he realized in wonder. He hadn't seen a comet since he was a lad. He'd never seen one so vivid nor so close to the earth. Now he wished he *had* brought Colin and Cambel out to the field with him.

He narrowed his eyes. If it was like the comet he'd seen before, it would appear every night for several days as it slowly crossed the heavens. He'd be sure to show it to his sons tomorrow night then, just as his father had done for him all those years ago.

Most people believed that comets were a portent of things to come. Some thought they brought bad luck. Some thought they were harbingers of good fortune.

Brochan figured they were no more than an interesting feature in the night sky that men could only partly understand, like falling stars or eclipses. Still, if the comet wished to bring him good luck, he'd be grateful for the return of his cattle.

His eyes shifted suddenly as they caught movement coming from the edge of the woods. He stiffened. He could make out the shadowy shapes of six cloaked figures stealing out of the forest, not forty yards away.

Brochan moved his hand to the hilt of his sword. Maybe it was good he'd brought it after all. Never had he imagined he'd have to deal with an entire army of reivers.

At the edge of the trees, they all stopped, all but the smallest one. That one continued to slowly advance. The reiver had chosen his target carefully. The lone cow was at a little distance from the rest of the herd, at a good distance from the bull, and she had no calf with her.

In the same way the reiver meant to separate the cow from the herd to make it easier to capture, Brochan could separate the lad from the rest of his companions. If he could steal down the brae without being spotted, he could easily grab the thief and use him as leverage to quell the rest of his fellows.

The reiver clearly knew what he was doing. He took his time, letting the cows adjust to his presence, and headed in a straight line toward his target. Though Brochan couldn't make out the words, he could hear the lad's low, soothing murmurs as he calmed the cattle.

Slowly, Brochan eased up from the ground, creeping forward through the heather, keeping his eyes trained on his prey.

Then a curious thing happened. The reiver stopped abruptly, went silent, and straightened.

Brochan realized the lad was staring at the sky.

He'd seen the star.

Brochan glanced toward the other reivers. They were pointing at the comet and jostling each other, as though arguing over it.

Finally, one of them hissed at the lone reiver in the moonlight, beckoning him.

But the reiver stood frozen in the field, awestruck.

While they were thus distracted, Brochan made his swift way down the rise.

He was no more than twenty yards away when the tallest reiver spotted him. The lad cursed and shoved at his companions, and the lot of them retreated under the trees.

All of them but the reiver in the field, who paid no heed to their calls or Brochan's presence. The lad lingered in the moonlight, transfixed by the comet, as Brochan crept closer and closer.

Cristy stared, struck dumb by the vision in the heavens.

What was that? A star? Or something else?

It wasn't moving. Yet a long, feathery tail stretched out behind it as if it were flying across the night sky.

She'd never seen such a thing.

"Cristy, come on!" Archibald hissed from the trees. "Now, damn ye!"

She ignored him. She didn't care about the cows now. She could catch a cow another night. This was far more intriguing.

Suddenly she remembered what the tavern wench had told her.

Change is on the horizon. The star has chosen ye. Follow it, and ye may change your fate.

She shivered. Was this her star? Had Brighde truly foreseen her future?

In one moment, she was gazing at the star in wonder.

In the next, she was hurtling toward the ground.

When her shoulder hit the sod, her first thought was that the bull had charged and knocked her over.

But when she tried to scramble out of harm's way, a heavy arm held her down—a human arm.

248

"Archibald," she bit out, for she was sure it was her oldest cousin, "let me up."

"Hold still."

Cristy's eyes went wide. It wasn't her cousin. She didn't recognize the voice.

"Ye'll frighten the coos," he warned.

If it wasn't her cousins, it must be one of Macintosh's men.

Shite! She couldn't be caught. Reiving cattle was a serious crime.

Deciding she'd rather take her chances with the herd of frightened cows than with their vengeful owner, she spat out a curse, then struggled and bucked and kicked and scratched, trying to free herself from the clutches of her captor. But he was very persistent and very strong.

Through the strands of her hair, she glimpsed her cousins hiding under the trees. Why weren't they helping her? She grimaced as the arm around her waist tightened.

And then she heard the cattle. All the noise was disturbing them.

Good, she thought. Maybe the restless cows would distract the beast attacking her long enough for her to escape.

She took in a deep breath, ready to yell for all she was worth.

Her cry was cut short by the clap of a huge hand over her mouth.

"Hush!" the man hissed against her ear. "Ye'll get us both killed if that bull charges."

Cristy glanced again toward the trees. Her cousins had vanished.

Her heart sank. If they'd abandoned her, she was as good as dead. So what did she care if the bull killed her?

She renewed her struggles.

In the end, it was no use. Her captor, whoever he was, had a grip like iron and a will to match. He hefted her up like a fleece of wool in one powerful arm, muffling her cries with his sweaty palm, and packed her off across the field toward the tower house.

Her last thought as she caught one final glimpse of the strange star in the sky was that Brighde had only promised her a change of fortune.

She hadn't said it might be a change for the worse.

Brochan realized about halfway through subduing the reiver that the scrappy firebrand he'd caught was a lass. But by then, it was too late to let her go. She was already riling up the cattle. He had to get her away from them.

The cows were by nature fairly calm. Brochan let his sons pet the shaggy beasts, as long as they were with him. Twice a day, the lads milked the two cows that had lost their young in the byre. But some of the cows in the field had young calves they were protecting. And the bull was unpredictable.

Even if Brochan had wanted to let her go, the wee reiver's companions had deserted her. And he wasn't about to let a lass roam the countryside by night all alone. He'd never be able to live with himself if she were attacked by wolves or miscreants.

So, regretting his rough handling of the lass, he proceeded to remove her from the field as efficiently as possible.

Any regret he had was cut short when, halfway up the brae, the minx bit into the soft part of his palm.

With an outcry that was more aggravation than pain, he yanked his hand away.

She took a breath.

No doubt she meant to curse him.

Or cry for help.

Or scream at the top of her lungs.

He couldn't have her doing any of those. So he stuffed a wad of her arisaid into her open mouth before she could make a peep.

But like plugging a wasp's nest, his actions only served to agitate her further. She thrashed and twisted in the prison of his arms. Her anger erupted in frustrated squeals behind the stifling wool.

She was still fighting him and screaming into her arisaid when he climbed the motte and reached the tower house door. But he didn't have a free hand. So, grimacing in anticipation of her curses, he uncovered her mouth long enough to reach for the handle.

She didn't disappoint. As he swung open the door, she spat the wool from her mouth and emitted a string of oaths vile enough to make the devil blush.

Even the stalwart Rauf, who rushed forward to close the door behind them, blinked at the foul curses.

Eager to be rid of his noisy burden, Brochan carried the lass into the hall and set her abruptly on her feet, so abruptly she nearly tripped on the hem of her kirtle.

She tossed her head, and her long black braid slapped him in the face. He had just enough time to see her snarling white teeth—the teeth now imprinted upon his palm—before she did the unthinkable.

While he was disentangling himself from the hissing she-cat, the lass laid her hands upon the hilt of his sword and pulled it from its sheath.

Brochan leaped back just in time to avoid the edge of the blade. It whistled past, missing him by inches.

Before he even had time to curse himself for his carelessness, she stabbed forward. He fell back, grabbing a lit sconce from the wall to use as a weapon.

"Put the sword down," he warned.

She glared at him through damp strands of her dark hair, but still she held the blade aloft in both hands.

"Put it down," he repeated.

When she refused to comply, he lunged forward with the sconce, forcing her to skitter back.

With a determined growl, she slashed again and again at the space between them. Her swings were reckless and wildly unpredictable.

Defending himself with the sconce, he managed to keep her from doing too much damage.

"Nay, Rauf!" he barked at his man, who was trying to sneak up on the lass. "Stay back!"

He didn't want anyone injured by a stray blade. Besides, if Brochan couldn't handle this minikin of a lass on his own, he didn't deserve to be laird of the tower house.

"Whoreson!" the lass spat. "Satan's spawn!"

Brochan frowned. He wondered if she kissed the lads with that filthy mouth.

She took another swipe at him, and he fended it off with the sconce, extinguishing the candle.

He could have brought the heavy piece down on her head at that point and knocked her out. But he hated to resort to such violence when it wasn't necessary.

Besides, the way the lass was fighting—with all her pluck and every bit of her strength—she couldn't last much longer. He'd just wait for her to tire.

"Ye hedge-born bastard!"

Brochan shook his head and deflected another wayward swing.

As he did, he caught a glimpse of Cambel and Colin, who'd heard the noise and come downstairs. They peered out from the shadows of the stairwell with their wooden swords in hand, ready to do battle.

He grimaced. They'd probably witnessed the whole sordid incident and were hanging on every blasphemous word.

CHAPTER 3

Cristy dared not show it, but she'd never been so scared in her life.

The evening couldn't have gone more wrong.

Her cousins had deserted her.

She'd been captured and spirited away by the enemy.

A fiery star was headed for the earth.

And now she was fighting with a weapon so heavy she could scarcely wield it—against a man who looked as big as an ox.

He was going to kill her. She knew it.

He'd caught her going after his cattle. And now he was going to make her pay.

Her heart was pounding. Her palms were sweating. But she knew she couldn't show an ounce of fear. For if she did, he would surely finish her on the spot.

So she tossed her braid over her shoulder, kicked her skirts out of the way, and attacked again, cursing at him with courage she didn't possess. "The devil rot ye *and* your coos!"

"Na-a-a-a-y!" A high-pitched war cry announced a young child in a long white leine as he came running out of the shadows toward her, wielding a wee wooden sword.

253

She hesitated an instant, and a second child followed, looking like a mirror image of the first.

Before she could even blink in astonishment, the man she'd been fighting bellowed, "Nay!"

In one sudden movement, he dropped the sconce and lunged for her, heedless of her sword.

His momentum knocked her backwards so hard, she was sure her head would crack upon the stones. But at the last instant, he turned with her, cushioning her head with one hand and landing mostly on his shoulder.

"Stay back, lads!" he called out to the children.

His warning was unnecessary. The fall had loosened her grip on the sword. It had clattered out of reach on the rushes.

He rolled her quickly on her back, straddling her and pinning her wrists to the floor.

Now she was helpless. And frightened. If she wasn't careful, she'd erupt in full-scale panic, which would give him even more of an upper hand.

But then she peered at the man through the disheveled veil of her hair. The blood had drained from his face. He had a fretful look in his eyes. He looked as if...as if he'd expected her to run those children through with the sword.

Now her fear gave way to outrage and anger.

She frowned and spit a lock of her hair from her mouth. Did he really believe her capable of such violence? She might reive a cow or two, and she would definitely stand up to an ox like him. But she didn't slay innocents in cold blood.

"God's eyes," she muttered, "I wouldn't have harmed them."

He stared down at her with such ferocity that she couldn't look away. "Hurt my sons," he bit out so softly she could scarcely hear it, "and I'll kill ye."

She gulped. A dark fire burned in his emerald eyes, searing her soul. His sons. He must love them fiercely to make such a vow.

Finally, growing apprehensive beneath his intense glare, she mumbled, "What kind o' monster do ye think I am?"

"Ye were thievin' my coos," he pointed out.

"Thievin' coos isn't the same as murderin' bairns."

"I'm not a bairn," one of the lads pronounced with indignation.

"I'm not a bairn," the other mimicked.

The man's furrowed brow softened fractionally, but his grip was still steel-hard.

What were his intentions? She shuddered to think. In some parts, cattle reivers were punished as severely as murderers.

"What do ye mean to do with me?" she challenged him, though her mouth was dry with fear as she spoke.

He didn't answer her. He only continued to stare at her in silence while his flinty green eyes seemed to entertain a host of grim possibilities.

She nervously licked her lips, her mind racing. He obviously cared deeply for his sons. He was protective of them. She wondered...

"Ye wouldn't kill me in front o' *them*, would ye?" She glanced at the two lads, who were staying obediently back, but who still clung to their wooden swords. "Ye won't let them watch while their father slays a helpless lass."

It was a risky bluff. He might be the sort who wouldn't hesitate to demonstrate to his sons what happened to people who reived their father's cattle.

On the other hand, when he'd knocked her to the ground, he'd turned onto his shoulder to soften the blow. That proved he wasn't without mercy.

"Are ye goin' to slay her, Da?" one of the lads asked.

"Da wouldn't do that while she's unarmed," the other assured his brother. "'Twouldn't be chivalrous." Then he added, "He'll give her a sword. Right, Da?"

Cristy doubted that. Still, the lads' words had served to

diminish the vengeful fury in their father's eyes. In fact, she would almost swear she saw a glimmer of amusement in his gaze as he let out his breath on a sigh.

A pounding footfall announced someone coming up the stairs from the lower level. Eager for any kind of distraction that might allow her to twist free, Cristy tossed the hair from her eyes to get a better look. Out of the shadows emerged a hefty woman with iron-gray hair, snapping eyes, and a heavy black skillet.

"All right!" she bellowed as she came. "Where's that connivin' cattle reiver? I'll give him such a wallop that he won't..."

The woman stopped in her tracks when she laid eyes on Cristy. She lowered the skillet, knitted her wiry brows, and then gasped. Handing the skillet off to the gray-haired man who'd answered the door, the woman rushed forward to peer down at Cristy. Her expression transformed swiftly from outrage to motherly concern and then back to outrage as she looked at Cristy's captor.

"What the devil are ye doin', m'laird?" the woman demanded.

Cristy's eyes widened. M'laird? Was this Macintosh himself?

"Can't ye see the poor lass is hurt?" the woman said, clucking her tongue.

Cristy almost choked in surprise. The last thing she expected from the skillet-wielding giantess was pity.

"Hurt?" Macintosh scoffed. "This is the lass who's been reivin' my cattle."

The woman bent forward to stare down at her with kindly eyes. "Was it ye who gave her that black eye then?"

"What?" He peered down at Cristy, apparently noticing her bruise for the first time.

It was tempting for Cristy to let everyone believe Macintosh had struck her, intentionally and cruelly. But she was reluctant to blame an innocent man for what her uncle had done.

Still, she wasn't stupid. She needed whatever advantage she could grasp.

"I'm sure ye didn't *mean* to do it," she hedged.

He wasn't fooled for an instant. "I didn't touch ye, lass, and ye know it. That's an old bruise."

The woman parked her hands on her hips. "Is that true, lass?"

Cristy caught her lip under her teeth, reluctant to answer. God only knew what Macintosh's punishment would be for reiving his cattle *and* lying to him.

Brochan shook his head. More than anything, he hated being blamed for things he hadn't done.

All his life, he'd followed the code of chivalry. He'd tried to be a decent man. He'd always done the honorable thing. He'd taught his sons right from wrong, leading by his example.

He had willingly and singlehandedly accepted responsibility for his children, his servants, a herd of cows, and this new holding with its derelict tower.

It was bad enough that anything that went awry was his fault. But to be accused of doing something as heinous and reprehensible as clouting a lass when he'd never dream of raising his hand to a woman...

"Da would never hit a lady," Colin said.

"Aye, thank ye, Colin." At least one person in this hall trusted his character. Brochan looked down at the bonnie reiver with smug satisfaction. "That's right."

Then Cambel added, "But sittin' on one is perfectly fine."

Rauf sounded like he was strangling on laughter.

Brochan sighed. The frankness of wee lads was both a blessing and a curse.

The lass beneath him arched her brow in challenge, awaiting his reply.

"Nay, Cambel," he admitted. "Sittin' on a lady is *not* perfectly fine. Not usually. But as laird, 'tis my duty to make sure she isn't goin' to hurt my clan."

"Why, Da? Is she dangerous?" Cambel asked.

He gazed down at his captive. *Was* she dangerous? He had her at his mercy now. But he had to admit, getting a closer look at the lass, that she was dangerously *attractive*. And between the feral beauty of her face, her arching bosom, and her insistent squirming between his thighs, the wee, wild wench was making him feel dangerously *awakened*.

"Is she, Da?" Colin echoed.

"Dangerous?" Brochan cocked his head at her. "Well, lass, are ye?"

"Ye'll find out just how dangerous if ye don't let me go."

Her words were harsh and threatening. But Brochan detected a flicker of fear in her eyes. He decided she was about as dangerous as a cornered kitten with tiny claws and her fur on end—all hiss and spit.

"I'd be a fool to let ye go," he told her gently. "But give me no trouble, and I'll do ye no harm. Once I get my cattle back, I'll return ye, good as new."

She looked horrified. "I'm a hostage?"

He winced. "I wouldn't say so much a hostage as a..." He couldn't really think of a better term.

"I'm a bloody hostage," she bit out, renewing her fight to get free. "Ye son o' the devil!" She twisted beneath him. "Damn ye to hell!"

"Ooh! She's goin' to have to clean the garderobe, Da," Cambel announced.

"Aye," Colin agreed, telling the lass, "Da says if ye use foul words, ye have to do foul work."

If he weren't so busy battling the wee wildcat beneath him, Brochan would have grinned in approval at his sons' comments.

The lass's brown eyes smoldered with fury. "Let. Me. Go."

"What's a hostage, Da?" Colin asked.

"A hostage is someone you hold on to...for safekeeping," he said pointedly, "until the person who wants her back pays the price."

Cambel crept a bit closer. "What price?"

"Stay back, Cambel," he said. He didn't think the lass would hurt the lad, but he couldn't be sure. She seemed very desperate, despite his reassurances. "Her price is the five coos she stole from us."

"Who wants her back?" Colin asked.

"That's a very good question, Colin. How about it, lass? Whose clan do ye belong to?"

She froze for a heartbeat, and what he saw in her wide brown eyes spoke volumes. She didn't want to say.

"I don't belong to a clan," she lied.

She renewed her struggles, forcing Brochan to tighten his thighs around her. He sincerely wished she wouldn't do that. It was having an undesired effect, one he was sure she didn't intend.

"Ye had a whole gang o' lads with ye," he said. "I saw them."

"Could be the Moffats," Rauf suggested. "They own the adjoinin' property. There look to be five or six young men."

The reiver's brow creased, and Brochan could tell Rauf was right. "Are they your brothers then?"

She clamped her lips closed, obviously unwilling to say.

"Come on, lass," he reasoned. "If ye don't tell us, we won't be able to collect the ransom. Ye'll be stuck here."

"Ye can't keep me here," she said, adding with a sneer, "unless ye plan to sit on me all night."

That idea *did* sound pleasant to less honorable parts of his body, parts that hadn't been used in more than five years.

But he had other plans.

"That won't be necessary. I have shackles."

Mabel gasped, as if he'd said he was going to string the lass up by her braid.

Consequently, the lass, sensing an ally in Mabel, pressed her advantage. "Ye'd put me in shackles? Like a common criminal?"

"Damn it all! Ye *are* a common criminal," he argued, aroused and exasperated that he was aroused. "Ye were reivin' my bloody coos."

"Da!" Colin cried with glee. "Now *ye'll* have to clean the garderobe!"

Cristy half expected Macintosh to turn on his son and backhand him across the mouth for his impertinence. That was what her uncle would have done. But the laird only muttered more oaths under his breath, mostly cursing himself.

Meanwhile, Cristy agonized over her predicament. It was bad enough that she'd been caught by the very man whose cow she'd been trying to steal, Laird Macintosh himself. But when her uncle found out...

Not only would she lose any hope of gaining his respect. She'd probably get a beating for her carelessness. She supposed it was no less than she deserved. But her cousins would never let her accompany them again.

She couldn't let that happen. She had to find a way to escape.

As much as she hated how helpless she felt, at the mercy of the self-satisfied brute—the way his hands dwarfed her wrists, how his eyes burned green fire, the unsettling weight of his body on top of her—she couldn't let him put her in shackles. Then she'd never be able to flee.

Perhaps it was in her best interests to go along with the laird after all. If she could get him to trust her, convince him she was harmless, maybe he would let down his guard. Then she could outwit him, escape, and return to the Moffat keep before morn.

Fighting all of her instincts, she relaxed beneath him, as if surrendering to his will.

She sighed, lowering her eyes. When she spoke, it was in the soft voice of defeat. "'Twasn't my idea to reive your coos, I swear."

The old woman took the bait at once. "Did they force ye, lass?" She clucked her tongue. "'Twas one o' them gave ye the black eye, wasn't it?"

Cristy nodded.

She felt the pressure on her wrists ease up the slightest bit.

"I knew it," the woman said. "'Twas those Moffat lads, aye?"

She nodded again.

When Macintosh spoke once more, his voice was gentle, compassionate...vulnerable. "What's your name, lass?"

"Cristy."

"And ye're a Moffat?"

"Aye." There was no use hiding her identity. Besides, honesty would serve to gain his trust. "They're not my brothers. They're my cousins."

As predicted, his grip on her loosened. "If I let ye up, ye won't do anythin' foolish, will ye?"

The temptation was great. But every scenario she ran through her head—lunging for the sword, elbowing back the old woman, diving for the door—ended with Macintosh back on top of her.

So instead, she obediently shook her head.

He released her cautiously, rocking back on his haunches. As if he'd read her mind, he immediately slid his sword across the rushes, far out of her reach.

He held out a hand to her. She resisted the urge to spit on his palm, instead taking his hand and allowing him to help her up. To her consternation, he didn't let go. And to her annoyance, his grip felt possessive and commanding.

"She's very bonnie," one of the lads said in a very loud whisper.

"Aye," whispered his brother.

"Lads," Macintosh warned them. Then he turned to his man. "Rauf, I'll write a missive to Moffat, demandin' the return o' my coos in exchange for his niece. Ye can send it with Brother William in the morn."

"Right," Rauf replied. "And I'll stand watch o'er the herd tonight, in case the Moffat lads return for the lass."

"Good." As Rauf headed outdoors, Macintosh nodded to the old woman. "Mabel?"

"M'laird?"

"Can ye see to the lads?"

"O' course. Are ye sure ye're..." The woman glanced at Cristy, as if she suspected Cristy might have mischief in mind.

Cristy *did* have mischief in mind. But she lowered her gaze and tried to appear suitably humbled.

"I'll be fine," Macintosh assured her. "But be sure and close the lads' chamber door."

"Kiss us, Da," one of them said.

"I'll come and kiss ye when ye're in your bed," the laird said.

For an instant, Cristy felt a pang in her heart. She couldn't remember the last time anyone had kissed her goodnight.

"Goodnight, bonnie lady," the other lad called from the stairwell.

Caught completely off-guard, Cristy mumbled back, "Goodnight."

Hand-in-hand with Mabel, the lads climbed the stairs, disappearing into the dark.

And then there were just the two of them in the great hall.

Now that she could get a good look at the laird, she realized how tall and formidable he was. He stood a full head above her, and his shoulders were nearly as wide as a doorway. It must have taken yards of linen to make a leine broad enough to span his chest.

"Cristy, is it?" he asked.

She nodded.

"Ye can call me Brochan."

"Brochan."

"Aye."

He was still holding her hand. It felt very improper now. With the casual air of a courting gentleman, he escorted her across the hall, stopping in front of a great cupboard.

"Listen, Cristy, I don't want ye to fret." He gave her hand what was probably supposed to be a comforting pat. "I truly mean ye no harm."

It took all of Cristy's willpower to appear docile and obedient, resisting the urge to snatch back her hand.

Until he opened the cupboard door and pulled out the shackles.

CHAPTER 4

Brochan hadn't been fooled for a moment by the lass's meek and mild behavior. She might appear to be tamed. But he'd seen the intrigue seething behind her innocent eyes.

He'd raised twin sons, after all. He'd encountered every manipulation known to man.

As predicted, once she saw the shackles, she began screaming in fury.

But he was prepared for her resistance. And now that his sons were safely upstairs, behind a closed door, he could ignore her screams. While she tugged back frantically on her captured hand and batted at him with her free one, he simply bent down and slipped one of the shackles around her ankle.

Then he lifted up the wee cursing lass, carried her to the hearth, and clapped the other shackle around the heavy iron fireplace crane.

"I may be kindhearted," he told her, "but I'm not a fool."

He gave the long, thick chain between the shackles a shake, testing its strength. Then he removed all the fireplace tools she might consider using as weapons.

While she called him every foul name he'd ever heard, he

returned to the cupboard for a chamber pot. From the oak chest against the wall, he pulled out several thick sheepskins.

She was practically hoarse from screaming by the time he dumped her amenities beside her.

"Now ye have a choice," he said between her curses. "Ye can either stop your squallin', or I can fetch a gag to stuff betwixt your teeth. So what'll it be?"

That stopped her cries. But her dark eyes contained such smoldering hatred that he almost felt singed by her glare. Her hands were curled into tight fists. Her jaw was clenched as tight as a cockle. And her whole body heaved with the passion of her anger.

For a brief moment, he thought it was a shame she was so full of fury. She was actually quite a lovely lass. Her hair was as black as night, and the tendrils that had come loose from her long braid curled gracefully over her shoulders. Her eyes matched her woolen kirtle—a deep, rich brown, like the color of a brook trout in a shadowy loch. Her skin looked as smooth and sun-kissed as honey, and her lips were a soft, inviting pink.

In the next moment, her dark bruise caught his eye, and he wondered what kind of heartless brute would clout such a bonnie lass across the face.

Then he realized it was none of his affair. His hands were too full, raising his own lads, to be concerned with how the Moffats treated their cousin. Even if he did feel sorry for the lass.

Nodding to approve her choice of silence, he returned to the cupboard for a sheet of vellum, ink, and a quill. Then he sat at the trestle table.

"Your uncle's name?" he asked, dipping the quill.

She glared at him in silence. The lass was decidedly more stubborn than his sons.

"Fine. Ye have another choice to make. Ye can either tell me, I'll write the missive, and then I'll leave ye in peace," he said, "or I can stay here, waitin', until ye feel the need to use the chamber pot. Maybe then ye'll tell me."

She glowered at him in disgust. "Douglas," she spat.

He wrote. "To Laird...Douglas...Moffat."

While he finished penning his demand, Cristy arranged the sheepskins to her liking and flounced down upon them, deliberately facing away from him.

He picked up the candle on the trestle table.

"Goodnight, Cristy. I'll send this out at dawn. If all goes well, Moffat will return my coos, and ye'll be back home, safe and sound, by midday."

She didn't answer him, but he doubted she was asleep. As vexed as she was, she'd probably toss and turn half the night before she finally drifted off.

Carrying the candle, he started toward the stairs. He'd promised his sons a goodnight kiss. It was something the lads insisted upon. And he was glad to do it. One day, they'd grow too old for the ritual. And he'd miss it.

As curious as it was, when he passed by the lass, he was tempted to stop and give her a kiss as well. She might be fierce and angry, but he sensed that beneath the surface, there was something vulnerable, some sad, neglected part of her that was starved for affection.

Again, it was not his affair. He couldn't save every small, suffering creature that crossed his path. He had too many other things to look after.

Colin and Cambel were sleeping back-to-back in their big bed when he eased open their chamber door. It was still odd to him that strangers couldn't tell the difference between the lads. To Brochan, they were as different as night and day.

The stars shone through the narrow window. It was a balmy evening, so he left the shutters open and banked the coals of the fire.

When he bent down to press his lips to Colin's brow, he

suddenly remembered the comet. He glanced out the window, but it wasn't visible from here. He'd have to take the lads out to see it on the morrow.

He leaned over farther to kiss Cambel's brow. And it was then he recalled the tavern wench's prophecy.

She'd told him he could change his *stars* tonight. Was it just a coincidence that she'd chosen that word? Or was it possible she'd seen the comet as well?

It was accepted knowledge that comets foretold change. Brochan didn't really believe that. But it was admittedly eerie to have a tavern wench predict that his destiny would hang in the balance, this night of all nights, when a stranger had just entered his life.

Cristy thumbed away the stupid tear trickling down her cheek and gazed into the blurry flames on the hearth. There was no use in weeping. There was naught she could do now to change what had happened. Or what was going to happen.

Brochan Macintosh was going to get his cows back. What other choice did the Moffats have but to return them?

Her uncle would be furious. Her cousins would be disappointed. She was dreading their banishment almost more than the beating Douglas Moffat would give her.

After Macintosh had headed upstairs, she'd tried to free herself. She'd struggled with the shackle until her already twisted ankle was scraped raw. But it was no use. She couldn't escape.

She supposed it could be worse. Macintosh could have run her through with a sword. He could have hanged her. He could have decided to keep her prisoner. At least he was willing to ransom her.

And it wasn't so terrible here. He'd given her sheepskins to lie on. They were softer and warmer than the scratchy wool coverlet she used at home. The fire was pleasant, though the summer air was mild enough not to need its warmth. And he'd left her a chamber pot.

She rolled onto her back and peered around the great hall. It looked a bit unkempt. But he'd only lived here a short while. And it appeared his only servants were the pair he'd called Rauf and Mabel. With so few inhabitants, it was no wonder her cousins had been able to steal his cattle so easily.

The Moffat clan had at least a dozen servants, and four alone were in charge of the cows—two lads to watch over them and two maids to milk them each day and night. How Macintosh managed to keep track of his herd, which was double the size of theirs, she didn't know.

Maybe his sons worked in the field. They were young, but they seemed clever enough to watch over cows.

She'd never seen two lads who looked so alike, with matching russet hair and freckled noses. They must be twins. She'd never seen twins before. She wondered if Macintosh ever got them confused.

One of the wee lads had said Cristy was bonnie.

She smirked. Nobody ever said that about her. Her hair was too black. Her eyes were too fierce. Her skin was too dark. Obviously, the lad hadn't seen many lasses.

She wondered where the lads' mother was. Since the old woman had put them to bed, maybe their mother was dead like hers.

They were lucky at least to have a father—a father who kissed them goodnight and taught them not to curse and would brave the edge of a sword to protect them.

She gazed into the slowly dying fire, watching the flames double and blur as moisture again filled her eyes.

Despite the fact he'd lain awake half the night, Brochan rose at dawn, as he did every morn. And as usual, he scrubbed the

sleep from his eyes while mentally reviewing what he needed
to do for the day.

First he'd wake Colin and Cambel and send them out to milk
the cows. Mabel would be up already, baking oatcakes. Rauf
was supposed to help him rebuild the stone wall around the
garden this morn, and Mabel had promised to see what she
could salvage of the overgrown herbs there. Brochan also had
to tally the payments his uncle owed to the local vendors, for
the old man had neglected to pay for some of the goods and
services he'd received in the last year.

Then there were the stores that needed to be tossed out—
broken crockery, soured ale, mouse-riddled grain. Once that
was done, he'd have to account for what remained and replace
what was necessary to survive the winter. It was going to be a
long day.

Sitting up and swinging his feet over the edge of the pallet,
he scratched at his stubbled jaw and blinked against the rising
sun.

All at once he remembered the lass.

Damn. His well-ordered day was going to be even longer.
Before he did anything else, he had to get his cows back and
return Cristy Moffat.

Fully alert now, he threw on his leine and trews and raked
his hands back through his hair before descending the stairs.

When he came into the great hall, what he saw at the hearth
took his breath away. And then it took his heart away.

Cristy Moffat—sprawled like a queen across a mountain of
sheepskins, coverlets, and furs—was snoring blissfully away
beside the fire. Tucked around her, fast asleep—one on the left,
one on the right—were his sons.

His chest tightened with fear, seeing Colin and Cambel so
close to the woman who'd come at him with a sword last night.

Then he looked at the tangle of coverlets and realized they
belonged to his sons. They must have sneaked down sometime

in the middle of the night. A thick knot lodged in his throat. The fact that the lads were curled up around the lass like orphan pups tugged painfully at his heart.

He heard Mabel coming up the kitchen stairs behind him.

She whispered, "Forgive me, m'laird. I didn't have the heart to disturb them. But I don't think she'd hurt the lads."

He nodded.

Then she stepped beside him and cocked her head at the sight. "I fear the wee things miss havin' a mother."

Brochan clenched his jaw. It wasn't the first time Mabel had brought up the subject. She nagged him at every opportunity about getting a mother for the lads. She seemed to think Brochan could easily solve the problem by just snapping up some convenient wench to be a mother to his sons. It didn't seem to occur to Mabel that the lass would also be his wife. And that Brochan would never find a wife to equal the one he'd had.

He murmured through clenched teeth, "Don't ye have breakfast to attend to?"

Her cheer undiminished, she replied, "Aye, and I've made a hearty frumenty for our guest. The poor thing looks half-starved."

Brochan scowled at Mabel as she wheeled merrily and scurried back downstairs to the kitchens.

Frumenty? The old woman never made frumenty for *him*.

And guest? Cristy Moffat was definitely not a guest. She'd said it herself. She was a hostage. Brochan needed to get his cows back, and she was simply the means to achieve that.

Still, as he leaned a shoulder against the wall and continued to watch the dozing threesome, he couldn't help but smile when the delicate lass emitted a decidedly unladylike snort. Colin raised his sleepy head once to check on her and then shut his eyes and snuggled closer against her hip. Cambel turned over in his sleep and draped an arm over her thighs.

Brochan felt the familiar burden of guilt settle onto his

shoulders. Was Mabel right to nag him? Was he being cruel to his sons by not remarrying? Were they hungry for maternal affection?

He perused the lovely lass. Could he be happy with someone like her?

Of course, no one would ever compare to his dear departed wife. And certainly a lass who reived cattle was not the sort of woman a proper laird should wed.

Contrary to what Mabel had said, the lass didn't look half-starved. She had a gently rounded bosom and a small waist, and where she'd kicked off the covers, her dark chestnut skirts had slipped up to reveal long, graceful legs.

Then his gaze lowered to the shackle he'd fastened around her ankle. He scowled, pushing off from the wall in concern. The skin around the iron ring was broken and bloody. She must have tried to squeeze out of it.

He couldn't understand why. After all, he'd assured her he didn't intend to hurt her. He'd shown her kindness and mercy. He'd promised to return her as soon as he had his cattle. Why should she be so determined to escape?

Then he remembered that someone had given her that black eye.

While he was pondering all of that, she must have stirred. When he lifted his gaze again, she was staring at him. He wondered how long she'd been awake.

Startled, he blurted out the first thing that came to mind. "Did ye sleep well?"

He could have cursed himself for asking such a thing. Of course, she hadn't slept well. She was a hostage. She was lying on the floor of a stranger's great hall. Her ankle was bloody. And she was serving as a pillow for two presumptuous five-year-olds.

She must have agreed it was an inane question, because she didn't reply. And when she rose up on her elbows and frowned down at Colin and Cambel, Brochan panicked for one brief instant as he realized she could easily wrap the shackle chain around one of the lads' throats.

But she didn't seem vexed or violent. Instead, she appeared puzzled. And when she moved to sit up, the lads woke.

Eager to defuse the volatile situation, Brochan motioned to his sons. "Wake up, lads. 'Tis past time to milk the coos."

Cambel apparently felt he had to explain the circumstances. "We were worried about m'lady, Da."

"We didn't want her to get cold," Colin said, discreetly pulling Cristy's skirts back down over her legs to protect her modesty.

It took all Brochan's willpower not to grin at his son's gentlemanly gesture.

Brochan cleared his throat. "I'm sure she appreciates your concern, lads. But I fear a couple o' coos need some attention as well. Be off with ye. They'll be lowin' soon if ye don't tend to them."

The lads jumped up and, without even fetching their boots, scrambled out the door.

As they did, Mabel arrived with a steaming bowl of frumenty. "Ah, ye're awake. Here, lass," she said, passing by Brochan to deliver the breakfast. "This should warm your bones and put a wee bit o' meat on ye."

Cristy licked her lips as she looked at the bowl. Maybe Mabel was right. Maybe the lass *was* half-starved.

With a quiet word of thanks, Cristy dove into the bowl of oats, cream, berries, and spices as if it were the food of the gods.

Mabel seemed pleased. "'Tis my own grandma's recipe, passed down to me by my ma." She confided with a wink, "The secret is a wee bit o' honey."

As Mabel continued to expound on her grandmother's formula to their guest—their *hostage*, he corrected—Brochan couldn't help but wonder where *his* frumenty was.

Then he realized he really didn't have time for frumenty. He already had too much to do today, and this whole ransom situation had thrown an extra cog into his normally smooth-running mill.

"Did Rauf give the missive to Brother William?" he asked Mabel.

"Aye, m'laird. He said he saw neither hide nor hair o' the Moffat lads last night. So he sent your letter on to the laird with the monk. I've put Rauf to bed now so he'll be rested to help ye later today."

Brochan nodded tersely. He'd forgotten that after being on watch all night, his man would need to sleep. That meant Brochan's work was going to take that much longer. He definitely didn't have time to break his fast.

"Hopefully Rauf will be up and around by the time the coos come home," he said, thinking aloud. "I could definitely use an extra pair o' hands today."

"Well, he's an old man," Mabel admitted. "He needs his rest." And then, as if the brilliant notion suddenly occurred to her, she said brightly, "But as long as she's here, why not have the lass lend a hand? I'm sure she has some sort o' valuable household skills."

Irritated by Mabel's poorly disguised attempt at pointing out the lass's wifely talents and peeved at having to miss breakfast, Brochan muttered, "Ye mean other than reivin' cattle?"

CHAPTER 5

Cristy supposed he had every right to say that. But it hit a nerve.

Her uncle always said she was useless.

Cristy wasn't useless.

"Fie, m'laird!" Mabel protested. "O' course. Surely she can churn butter and shell peas," she suggested. "Och, and mend the lads' trews. Can't ye, lass?"

A child could do those things. Cristy suspected she was being flattered into menial labor. Nevertheless, her pride and boredom made her reply, "O' course."

"Excellent!" Mabel cheered with far too much enthusiasm. "I'll just take that bowl if ye're finished and bring a needle and thread."

Cristy could have eaten another bowl of the frumenty. It was the best thing she'd tasted in weeks. Her uncle never served such tasty fare. He had rather simple tastes and preferred oatcakes and watered ale to break his fast.

Mabel took the bowl and hurried down the stairs, leaving her alone with Macintosh.

He looked rather different in the light of day—younger and less menacing. She realized he wasn't much older than her. His sleep-mussed, chestnut-colored hair made him look as boyish as his sons. And though his eyes were shadowed from lack of sleep, she could see they were gentle and kind, just like Colin's and Cambel's.

"The missive should be delivered soon," Macintosh assured her. "Ye won't have to spend the whole day mendin' the lads' trews."

She nodded, though now that she'd passed a night unscathed in the house of the enemy, she wasn't particularly looking forward to going home. Naught awaited her there except her uncle's cruel tongue and hard knuckles.

She shrugged and said pointedly, "'Tis the least I can do to thank your *sons* for their charity."

He could not have missed her point. But he managed a smile anyway. And she was struck by the warmth in his face in spite of her sarcasm.

"I'm not certain ye should thank them for accostin' ye in the middle o' the night and stealin' half the covers," he said. "But I'm sure they had good intentions."

The truth was she hadn't minded them at all. When she'd first awakened in the middle of the night to hear the lads' worried whispers in the dark hall, something had melted inside her. When they threw coverlets over her shoulders and nuzzled against her, she'd never felt so cared for and so needed. A tiny part of her wished she could spirit the sweet lads away with her.

Of course, stealing Macintosh's lads would be far worse than reiving his cattle. She could see that he loved them more than life. Besides, he needed them here. With so few servants, someone had to milk the cows.

Brochan's brow furrowed briefly, and he went to the cupboard. Opening the door, he ran a finger along a shelf of small clay jars, stopping and taking one down. Then he came to hunker down beside her and gave her the jar.

"Healin' unguent," he explained, nodding to her ankle, "for your..."

He locked gazes with her, and her breath caught. This close, she could see his face clearly for the first time. Not only were his eyes the most beautiful and startling shade of rich green, but they were deep and expressive. In a single glance, she could see the whole history of his emotions written there—joy, grief, humor, hurt, strength, love.

Suddenly disarmed, she was at a loss for words. He seemed to be tongue-tied as well. But when his gaze lowered to her mouth, her heart made a queer flutter in her breast.

Before Cristy could wonder what was happening, Mabel came stomping up the stairs. Brochan moved away as fast as a spooked cow.

"I'm goin' to the garden now," he announced, his voice cracking over the words. "I've got to repair the wall."

"Aye, fine, m'laird," Mabel sang. "Don't ye worry about our wee guest. I'll keep her properly occupied."

Cristy watched him leave, seeing him with new eyes. The young laird seemed to bear the whole weight of the world on his shoulders. And yet he still had room left in his heart to care for his sons and to make sure his hostage was comfortable.

She felt bad about stealing his cows now. And she was glad he was her neighbor. The old Laird Macintosh had been a sour and miserable man. This new laird seemed good-natured.

As Mabel handed her a pair of torn trews and tools to sew them, a silly hope sidled into Cristy's mind. Perhaps, after all this mess with his cattle was straightened out, she would come and visit on occasion. She liked Colin and Cambel. And she could even lend a hand to Brochan, just until he got his keep in order.

The lads returned an hour later, as she was taking the last stitch in Cambel's trews. At Mabel's prompting, they thanked Cristy, whom they insisted on calling m'lady, and dutifully took the trews and the coverlets they'd dragged down the stairs back up to their own chamber.

When they returned, they'd changed into the repaired trews. Mabel gave them each a couple of oatcakes and cups of fresh, warm milk. Colin insisted on sharing his milk with Cristy, boasting that he'd milked the cow himself. So she obliged him with a sip, though it was a strange taste to her, since she was much more accustomed to ale.

Mabel brought out the full butter churn and a basket of peas, returning to the kitchens to start the supper pottage. The lads took turns churning the cream, while Cristy shelled peas into a wooden bowl. It was soothing work, and the lads were good company.

They chatted about their old home, how there had been more kin living in the keep, but that they liked this big empty tower house because it was all theirs. Colin especially liked the cows. And Cambel enjoyed exploring, especially down by the burn.

Cristy told them she lived on the other side of that burn with her uncle. She explained that her parents were dead. And she learned from the lads that they'd never known their mother.

She asked them what it was like to have a brother who looked so much like them. They told her a few of the tricks they'd played on their kin. But they mostly found it disappointing that people couldn't tell them apart.

Cristy said she thought that was ridiculous, as ridiculous as not being able to tell cows apart. She assured them that even though she'd known them less than a day, already she could tell the difference between them. The lads brightened at that.

And then they began to ask more difficult questions.

Cambel stopped churning and wiped his brow. "Why did ye steal our da's coos, m'lady?"

Cristy almost dropped a peapod. How could she explain that?

She sighed. "'Twas a foolish trick, I suppose, maybe like the tricks ye played on your kin. I wanted to show off for my cousins."

"But stealin' is bad," Colin said.

"Aye."

"Are ye sorry?" Cambel asked.

"Aye."

"And are ye goin' to be punished?" Cambel asked.

"Probably."

"By our da?" Colin asked.

"Nay, by my uncle."

"What will he do?" Cambel asked.

Cristy didn't want to talk about it. She shrugged.

Cambel suggested to Colin, "Maybe he'll make her muck the stables."

Colin whispered back, "Mabel said Laird Moffat probably gave her the black eye. Maybe he'll hit her again."

Cambel straightened. "But that's not right. Da says ye should never hit a lady."

Cristy sighed. She was liking Brochan Macintosh more and more.

Colin took over Cambel's spot at the churn then, and Cambel added a block of peat to the fire.

"Do ye know any stories, m'lady?" Colin asked as he pumped the churn. "I like stories."

Cristy thought about it. Her mother had told her stories when she was a wee lass. One of her favorites was from the Bible—the tale of the shepherd David fighting the giant Goliath.

She regaled the lads with a rousing rendition of the battle, complete with a demonstration of David's sling, using a pod to fire a pea across the hall, which made the lads erupt in laughter.

"Will ye come back to visit us, m'lady?" Cambel asked.

"Aye, will ye?" Colin chimed in.

She was saved having to answer when the door opened and Brochan returned from working outside. The lads leaped up and ran to him.

"Da!" Cambel cried. "Do ye know the story o' Goliath and wee David?"

"M'lady fixed my trews. See?" Colin turned his back and bent over so Brochan could view the mended seat of his trews, nearly splitting the seam again.

"We've been helpin' churn the butter."

"She can come visit us anytime, right, Da?"

"Lads, let me catch my breath," he told them.

Cristy could see Brochan was overwhelmed. He must have been working hard on the garden wall. He was dripping with sweat, and his forearms were smudged with mud. Yet he was still as aggravatingy handsome as the devil. And as tired as he must be, he had hugs and a smile for his sons.

"Mabel!" he called out. "Have ye got a spare ale?"

From the kitchens below, Mabel yelled, "Aye, be right up!"

Then his gaze fell on Cristy, and something caught in her throat. Brochan looked so content, standing there with an arm around each of his sons. She couldn't help but feel a sort of bittersweet envy.

Then Colin said exactly the wrong thing. "Ye aren't goin' to let m'lady go back to that bad man who beats her, are ye, Da?"

The awkward indecision in Brochan's eyes crushed her. Yet what could he say? All he knew about her was that she'd stolen his cows. What happened between her and her uncle wasn't his concern.

"Well...I..."

She came to his rescue. "I have to go home, Colin. But maybe I could come and visit now and then."

Brochan was clearly relieved. "Aye, if ye like. Would ye like that, lads?"

They jumped up and down and cheered.

Mabel came up the stairs with a tray of cups for everyone. "What's all this fuss?"

Colin replied, "M'lady is goin' to come and visit us."

"Is that so?"

Brochan clarified, "After the…situation…is resolved."

"No word yet?" Mabel asked, handing out the ales.

Brochan shook his head. "Ye're certain he gave the missive to Brother William this morn?"

"Och, aye. He said the monk was makin' rounds today, reassurin' the folk who were frettin' o'er the star last night."

"What star?" Colin asked.

"Och, lads," Brochan said, "I must show ye the star tonight. 'Tis a special star with a tail, called a comet. 'Tis quite spectacular."

So it hadn't been a dream, Cristy thought. The strange star was real. She'd begun to wonder if she'd imagined it.

"Can m'lady come see it with us?" asked Cambel.

"Well…Miss Moffat is most likely goin' home today," Brochan explained.

The lads' faces fell, and Cristy had to admit she felt the same disappointment.

"That's all right," she told them, "I've seen the star already."

"That's right, ye have," Brochan said, no doubt remembering that her distraction by the comet was how he'd been lucky enough to catch her.

"If ye wash up, I can bring us all pottage," Mabel said.

Brochan shook his head. "I just came in for an ale. I'm only half done with the wall. Is Rauf up and around yet?"

"Nay, m'laird, and 'twill be a while. Don't ye have accounts to go over? Why don't ye come sup with us now and do your outdoor work later? Rauf can help ye finish the wall this afternoon."

Brochan rubbed the back of his neck, considering the idea. Cristy was astounded that he was hesitating. He hadn't broken his fast, as far as she'd seen. Did the man take no time to eat?

Mabel said, "Ye can bring your work to the table, slay two birds with one stone."

"One stone?" Colin tugged on Brochan's trews. "That's just like David, Da."

"I suppose 'tis." Brochan smiled and ruffled his son's hair. "Fine. I'll go wash up. But I'm countin' on ye lads to help me with the accounts."

When he returned and Mabel began to serve supper at the table, the lads made more trouble.

"Da," Cambel whispered, just loud enough for Cristy to hear, "we can't make m'lady sit on the floor to eat."

"Aye," Colin agreed. "'Tis unchivalrous."

"Can't ye take off her chains?" Cambel asked.

Brochan replied in a murmur. "Lads, she's our prisoner. If we let her escape, she'll go home, and we'll never get our coos back."

Cristy stared into the fire, pretending not to hear, though she was hanging on every word. Would they unshackle her? Was escape still possible?

Colin tried to convince Cambel. "Da's right, Cambel. We have to get our coos back."

"But 'tis dishonorable," Cambel argued. He frowned and crossed his arms over his chest. "I won't eat my pottage unless she's allowed at the table."

Cristy feared Cambel was begging to be clouted for his impertinence. But Brochan answered him with patience and consideration.

"Indeed?" he said. "Then what would ye suggest?"

"I know," Colin said. "She could give us her word she won't flee."

"Her word?" Brochan almost choked. "And how do ye know ye can trust her word?"

"She's a lady," Cambel said, as if it were obvious.

Brochan smirked. "Ye've much to learn, lads. But if ye think 'tis the right thing..."

Cristy's pulse raced.

Colin and Cambel answered in unison, "Aye."

Brochan went to the cupboard and brought back a key. He dropped to one knee beside her. "Do ye swear ye won't try to escape?"

"Aye."

"Do ye give the lads your word on it?"

"Aye."

He sprang the shackle and held out a hand to help her up. For one tense instant, she thought about racing for the door, despite her oath. And as if he read her mind, he clasped her hand firmly in his and led her to the table, wedging her strategically between his two sons, to whom she'd just given her solemn word.

The pea and barley pottage Mabel served in a crust of coarse maslin was just as delicious as the frumenty. Cristy thought she'd be glad of an excuse to visit every day if the food was always so appetizing.

While they ate, Brochan looked over several documents he'd brought to the table. Then he slipped a page toward the lads and asked them to recite the numbers in a long column while he checked them off on another page.

Cristy was astonished the young lads could decipher the marks on the page. She wished she could. Women were seldom tasked with anything requiring such knowledge. But she often wondered how much more power she would have if she could read and write.

In a flight of whimsy, Cristy imagined coming here every day to learn from the lads how to recognize numbers and pen letters.

When Brochan no longer needed the lads, Mabel put them to work, sweeping up the rushes on the floor of the great hall.

The old woman said she planned to see what crops she could salvage from the overgrown garden.

Meanwhile, she quietly brought a ripped leine to the table and asked Cristy if she wouldn't mind mending it.

Brochan glanced up. "That's *my* leine," he murmured to Cristy. "Ye don't have to do it."

"I don't mind," Cristy said. Otherwise, she'd be bored, with naught to do. "I promise I won't even sew the sleeves shut."

He snorted at that.

The afternoon was the most peaceful Cristy had passed in a long while. Between the fire crackling on the hearth, the laird quietly scrawling figures, the whispery sweep of the rushes, and the soothing repetition of stitching, she felt calm and restful.

She'd just made a final knot in the thread when she glanced up to see Brochan slumped atop the table. His pen was still in his hand. His head rested on his forearm. And his open mouth was making a soft sawing sound. She smiled. He looked more like his sons than ever when he was asleep.

All at once, a dangerous thought occurred to her. Mabel was outside. Rauf was in his chamber. Brochan was asleep. And she was no longer shackled. She could easily send the lads on some errand upstairs and slip out the door. Her heart raced as she considered the possibility.

Then she thought about Mabel, who had made her a bowl of frumenty and treated her like a guest. She glanced again at the poor overworked laird dozing on the table. She watched his kind and dutiful sons, piling rushes near the door.

She'd given them her word. She'd promised she wouldn't flee. And though it might mean a beating for her if she didn't escape, she couldn't stomach the thought of betraying the sweet lads. Or their father.

So, silently cursing herself for a fool, she carefully set his mended leine aside so as not to wake the laird. Then she glanced around the hall, wondering what else she could do to make herself useful.

Brochan woke to the sound of Rauf coming downstairs. Startled and disoriented, the laird lifted his head, nearly upsetting the vial of ink. Then he frowned and gave his head a good shake, dispelling the fog from his brain.

Had he fallen asleep at his work? Again?

He had to stop that. There was too much to do for the luxury of dozing.

The rushes were gone from the great hall. The lads must have finished their chores. But where were they now? And Cristy...

His blood turned to ice as he realized the lass was missing. He stood up, knocking the bench over with a great thud.

"M'laird, what's wrong?" Rauf said as he stepped into the hall.

"Where is she? Where is the Moffat lass?"

Rauf looked befuddled. "I've only just awakened, m'laird. I thought she'd be ransomed by now. Do ye want me to look for her?"

Brochan was too troubled to answer. This was his fault. His lads were missing, and his hostage was gone. He should never have trusted the word of a reiver.

With his heart in his throat, he strode toward the door.

It swung open before he could reach it. In came Colin, Cambel, and the lass, their arms overloaded with great clumps of sweet-smelling green rushes.

Unable to see where she was going, Cristy barreled forward and collided with him, dropping rushes everywhere. She would have fallen backwards from the impact, but he reached out and seized her elbow to steady her.

"Da! Ye're awake!" Colin called as he dropped his rushes.

Cambel dropped his as well. "M'lady took us to cut new rushes. See?"

It was then he noticed that Cristy was holding a scythe, the scythe he kept by the front door. He narrowed his gaze. Last night she would have tried to use the thing to cut him off at the knees.

But today when he looked at her, the smoldering hatred he'd seen in her face before was gone. Her dark eyes danced with delight. And her wide smile revealed beautiful white teeth. Colin was right. She *was* a bonnie lass.

Apparently, the bonnie lass had kept her word. She hadn't kidnapped his sons after all.

"Well, Da?" Cambel asked. "Are ye goin' to give m'lady a proper thank ye?"

He was standing close enough to her that he could see the pink kiss of the sun across the bridge of her nose and smell the fresh summer air on her loose hair. As his gaze fell to the gentle upward curve of her lips, he was sorely tempted to give her an *im*proper thank you.

The thought was disturbing. In five years, he'd thought of no one in that way. He'd clung to the memory of his wife, remembering her touch, her embrace, her kiss. That he was daydreaming about kissing another woman troubled him.

So he set her at arm's length and gave her a nod of gratitude. "Thank ye, m'lady."

Rauf stepped forward then, clearing his throat. "If ye're ready to take a look at that garden wall, m'laird..."

"Aye," Brochan said, eager to evade temptation. "I can come back to the accounts later. I've got the wall halfway done, and I want to finish before dark."

"Then when 'tis dark," Colin told Rauf, "we're all goin' out to see the great comet."

"Are we?" Rauf raised a brow at Brochan.

Brochan shrugged. "I promised the lads I'd take them out."

"And m'lady is comin' as well," added Cambel.

Rauf's brow lifted even higher.

"We'll see, Cambel," Brochan said. "Her laird is likely worried about her and will send for her soon."

As it turned out, Moffat must not have been very worried about his neice after all. He sent neither the cows nor a message back with the monk. Brother William passed by on his way home, taking a moment to admire the newly repaired garden wall. But though he assured Brochan he'd delivered the missive into the laird's hands himself, he reported that Moffat had simply scoffed and sent him on his way.

Brochan was glad Cristy wasn't around to hear that. It would no doubt break her heart. But then he guessed that a man who considered it acceptable to strike a woman might also think it acceptable to torment her by delaying her ransom. And that thought made him feel ill.

So he penned another demand to send with the monk, this one a bit more threatening. For each day of delay, Brochan would add one cow to the price of Cristy's return. Surely that would get Moffat's attention.

Later, when Cristy asked if there was news from her uncle, he told her that Moffat was negotiating fiercely for her return, but that Brochan didn't feel he was offering what she was worth.

She seemed mildly disappointed. No doubt she expected Moffat to return the cattle at once to ensure her safe return, not to negotiate for a lower price. But Brochan was glad he hadn't told her the truth. It would have crushed her.

When it began to grow dark, Mabel announced that she and Cristy had a surprise for everyone. Brochan shook his head in amusement. He hadn't seen the old woman so full of life in a long time. Apparently, she was intent on impressing their "guest." He'd heard the busy clattering of pots and pans from upstairs when he sent the lads out for the late milking. Now, as he sat finishing up the accounts by candlelight, he smelled the savory aroma of something baking in the kitchens.

What the ladies had planned was dinner under the stars on the crest of the motte surrounding the tower house. From there, they could view the heavens in all their splendor, as well as keep an eye on the herd below.

Rauf spread a wool cloth on the grass for them to sit on. Of course, the lads had to squeeze in beside Cristy. Under the evening sky, they dined on flaky pork coffyns, oatcakes spread with soft ruayn cheese, and crispels with cloudberries. Mabel said that Cristy had found a dusty-shouldered bottle of Port in the corner of the buttery, so she poured everyone a cup, even giving the lads a few drops.

The sky darkened until the stars popped out, one by one. Then Brochan pointed out the comet near the horizon to the lads.

"See how it has a long tail streamin' out behind it?"

"Why does it have a tail?" Cambel asked.

Colin asked, "Where is it goin', Da?"

"Is it goin' to crash into the earth?"

"Are the coos afraid of it?"

Brochan chuckled. "The coos don't *seem* afraid of it. Do ye think they are?"

"Nay," Colin decided.

Mabel added, "Some *folks* are afraid of it."

"Why?" asked Cambel.

"They say such a star can bring bad weather or bad luck," Mabel said.

"What do ye think, Da?" asked Colin.

Brochan frowned. "I don't think a faraway star, way up in the sky, can do us any harm down here."

"What about ye, m'lady?" Cambel asked. "Do ye think it brings bad luck?"

Brochan nearly spat out his oatcake. The star had certainly

brought Cristy bad luck. If she hadn't been staring at it, he wouldn't have caught her so easily.

But Cristy sounded pensive. "I'm not sure." And when she continued, her words echoed what the tavern wench had said. "I've heard the star has the power to change one's fate. But I don't know if 'tis good or bad."

"I think 'tis good," Cambel declared. "After all, the star brought ye to us, m'lady."

Brochan saw him give her a squeeze of affection, and his heart pinched at the gesture.

"'Tis a very kind thing to say, Cambel," she replied.

"I think so too," Colin said, not wishing to be excluded.

She gave him a hug as well.

Brochan didn't know what to say about that. He was fairly certain what had brought Cristy to them was not the star, but a cattle reiving gone awry.

Nevertheless, the night felt magical as they continued to watch the heavens and the unique star perched in the sky. Somewhere deep in his heart, Brochan made a wish—a secret wish on the star—that he could always feel this content.

CHAPTER 6

When Brochan rose the next morn, he was sure he'd find his sons tucked around the reiver lass again. He'd heard them last night when they thought he was asleep, stealing down the stairs and dragging their coverlets with them.

He should probably have stopped them. After all, it would serve no purpose to let them get close to her. It would only make it all that much harder for them when she left.

But he didn't have the heart to call them back. And in truth, he envied their daring. He wished he could creep down and crawl under the furs with the lass.

Mentally chiding himself for such reprehensible thoughts, he continued down the steps. But when he entered the great hall, fragrant now with fresh, sweet rushes, the coverlets were stacked neatly away, and the hearth was deserted.

Where were his sons? Where was his hostage?

Unwilling to resort to premature panic, Brochan descended to the kitchens to find Mabel.

"Good morn, m'laird," she sang out.

"Where have the lads gone?"

"Och, they've taken Cristy out to milk the coos."

289

He let out an invisible sigh of relief. Then he blinked. The lads rarely got up before dawn. Perhaps having a guest was giving them a sense of responsibility.

The scent of warm cinnamon was making his mouth water. He nodded to a tray full of freshly-made pastries. "What are these?"

"Almond frytours."

He reached out to take one, and she gave his hand a smack. "They're for supper, a special treat for Cristy."

He scowled. "Ye've never made these for *me*."

She told him matter-of-factly, "Well, honestly, m'laird, ye've never seemed to care if ye were eatin' capercaillie or collops."

He raised his brows. Was that true? He supposed he hadn't expressed much interest lately in what he put in his mouth, as long as it filled his belly. Half the time he was too busy or tired to eat. The other half, he shoved down his food as fast as possible so he could get back to work.

He furrowed his forehead in disappointment.

"Och, here," Mabel said, looking sorry for him. She handed him a couple of frytours and poured him a cup of watered ale. "I'll make up another batch."

He returned to the great hall to eat, mentally reviewing his tasks for the day. The frytours *were* delicious. Perhaps he should tell Mabel so. Perhaps then she'd make them more often.

Now that he'd figured out how much he owed to the various vendors, he had to count out the silver and send Rauf to deliver the payments. Mabel said she'd accompany Rauf so she could purchase food supplies. While she was away, Brochan planned to clear out the goods in the pantry that were beyond use. And with any luck, sometime today Moffat would arrive with the Macintosh cattle to exchange for his niece.

By the time he finished counting out the payments he owed and enclosing them in pouches with the receipts for Rauf, the sun was already streaming in to the hall. He wondered what was taking the lads so long. He could use their help today, sealing cracks in the dovecot. He'd promised Colin he could keep chickens, but first he had to make sure the dovecot was in good repair.

When he wandered outside, the cows had already been milked. The wooden buckets were brimming, and the pair of milk cows were ambling slowly back toward the rest of the cattle. But where were Colin and Cambel?

Shielding his eyes with his forearm, Brochan gazed down the slope.

In the midst of the herd, acting as if she was impervious to the great beasts, stood wee Cristy, as bold as a knight. She had Cambel and Colin with her.

Brochan's heart staggered. His sons never visited the cattle without his supervision. It was too dangerous. Cows were unpredictable, and they spooked easily. Did the lass know that? Did she understand cattle at all?

Shite.

His first instinct was to yell at them to get away from the herd. But he knew that would be a mistake. Naught would set off a stampede like a sudden loud bellow. He rubbed an anxious hand across his chin.

Where was the bull? Thankfully, at the other end of the field, peacefully chewing his cud.

But there were still several protective cows with young to worry about.

Moving as swiftly as he dared, he slipped down the brae.

What the devil was the lass thinking? Why had she let the lads wander into the thick of the herd? What was she doing?

God's eyes, he had neither the nerves nor the time for this.

Halfway down the slope, he slowed his pace. As he continued to watch, he realized what Cristy was up to as she held the lads' hands to keep them close, moving purposefully between the cows, herding them, isolating one from the rest.

Bloody hell. The mischievous minx was teaching his sons how to reive cattle.

"That's it," Cristy murmured. "Go slow enough not to spook her. But not so slow that she thinks ye're a wolf. Once she starts walkin' in the direction ye want, move with her so she keeps goin' forward, but keep your distance."

The lads did just as they were told. She was impressed. They were learning fast. She hadn't been much older than they were when she'd first learned to handle cattle.

They moved steadily alongside the cow until it was separated from the rest of the herd and walking at a good pace.

"Ye did it!" she quietly cheered. "If ye wanted, ye could walk her wherever ye liked now. She's—"

"Psst!"

Cristy jumped. Brochan had startled her, coming up behind her that way. But she didn't want to panic the cows, so she instructed the lads, "Just keep calm."

"What do ye think ye're doin'?" Brochan's voice was hushed, but she could feel the intensity of his anger in the bite of his words.

"Quiet, Da," Cambel warned.

"We're reivin' Eufemie," Colin whispered.

"I can see that," Brochan muttered.

Cristy, recognizing the impatience in his tone, suggested, "Why don't we put her back with the rest o' the herd now, lads?"

"But I want to take her to your keep," Cambel said.

Cristy arched a brow. "Now, Cambel, I told ye before—"

"Is that what ye intended?" Brochan said between clenched teeth. "Were ye goin' to reive my coo *and* my sons?"

Her jaw dropped. She stopped in her tracks, halting the two lads and the cow. Then she craned her head toward him. "How could ye think that?"

The dark fire in his eyes told her exactly how he could think that. He saw her only as a cattle reiver, a lass who'd attacked him with a sword and might be a threat to his sons, a lass who someone had given a black eye, and who probably deserved it.

The hurt she felt was unexpected. Normally, her skin was as thick as chain mail. It had to be. If she showed a hint of weakness, her cousins would swoop down on her like a hawk on a mouse. But to her horror, the accusation and condemnation in Brochan's gaze made her eyes well with moisture.

She tried to transform the hurt to anger, but her voice broke when she spoke. "I gave ye my word."

"Your word? The word of a..." He left the sentence unfinished, apparently not wishing to berate her in front of his sons. Then he looked away. His mouth was working as if he battled with his emotions.

Cristy steeled her chin, trying to still its trembling. She'd been so happy a moment ago, carefree and content, holding hands with two endearing children, playing in the sunshine, teaching them a useful skill.

Now she was good-for-naught Cristy the reiver again.

Colin and Cambel peered up at her. Colin spoke. "Are ye all right, m'lady?"

Cristy choked back the pain. Somehow she managed to nod. At least *someone* believed her. At least *someone* thought she was worthy of trust.

"We're all goin' back to the byre," Brochan proclaimed, his voice gruff. "There's to be no more reivin' o' cattle today."

"Och, Da," Cambel complained. "M'lady said we're good at it."

Brochan made a strangling sound deep in his throat.

"And Eufemie doesn't mind," Colin said.

"No more reivin'," Brochan insisted. "Ye lads know better."

Colin sighed. "I'm sorry, Da."

"I'm sorry, Da," echoed Cambel.

No one spoke on the way. The lads were still holding her hands when they reached the byre. And by then, Cristy's armor was back in place.

"Ye lads take the milk in to the house," Brochan said. "I need to speak with Miss Moffat alone."

Cristy's breath caught. She didn't want to let go of the lads. She knew once they were gone, Brochan would feel free to unleash his anger on her.

But if they disobeyed him, that anger might be unleashed on his sons.

Cristy could deal with a man's rage. She'd had plenty of practice. But she feared the lads didn't have such strong armor. So she gave them a forced smile of reassurance and reluctantly released them.

As soon as the twins were well on their way to the tower and out of hearing, Brochan turned on her. "What the devil were ye thinkin', endangerin' my sons like that?"

"They weren't in any danger."

"The hell they weren't." He started pacing. "There's a bull out there and coos with young. Do ye know what they'd do if they felt threatened?"

"Aye, o' course."

"Aye? Then why would ye take my lads out there?"

"God's bones! Do ye think I don't know cattle? I've been around them my whole life. I know how to stay out o' harm's way." Miffed, she added pointedly, "At least from coos."

Brochan stopped in front of her, and for an instant, she cursed her own waspish tongue, wondering if he would clout her after all. He might have told his sons that it wasn't right to hit a lady. But they weren't here to see him now.

Besides, it was obvious he didn't think she was a lady, not really.

He didn't hit her, but he did curse. "Shite. Teachin' my sons to be outlaws."

She creased her brow. Was that what he thought? No wonder he was angry. "What? I wasn't teachin' them to be outlaws."

"They were reivin' a bloody coo."

"'Twas their own bloody coo. They weren't reivin' her."

He let out an exasperated sigh. "'Twas Colin who put ye up to it, wasn't it? He wanted to know how to reive cattle."

Cristy stiffened. She wasn't about to let sweet wee Colin take the blame for it, even if that *had* been the lad's idea.

"'Twasn't his fault. 'Twas my idea. And I wasn't actually teachin' him how to reive cattle, only how to herd them." That much was true. Learning how to separate a single cow from the rest was a useful skill. "Don't hurt the lad."

"Hurt him?" He pulled away, aghast. "Ye think I would hurt Colin? My own flesh and blood?"

Cristy bit her lip and looked at him uncertainly. She was Douglas Moffat's own flesh and blood, and it didn't stop him from hurting her.

Brochan searched her face, shaking his head as if he were trying to figure out the strange workings of her mind. Then he reached out toward her hair.

Out of instinct, she flinched away.

Too late, she realized he didn't mean to clout her.

"Och, lass," he said in disbelief, his hand still raised, "are ye afraid o' me?"

She lifted her chin, putting on a brave face. "Nay."

But he didn't believe the lie. And the fact that he'd scared her made him look utterly crestfallen, so much like his wee sons that it squeezed her heart.

"Well," she amended, "ye *are* very angry."

He lowered his hand and stared down at his feet for a moment. "I *am* angry." Then he scoffed at himself. "I *was* angry." He lifted his head and locked gazes with her. His eyes were earnest and impassioned. "But I've never raised a hand in anger to my sons. And I would never, *ever* hurt a lady."

She gulped. Somehow in her heart she knew that. It was only habit that had made her duck away. Brochan was not at all like her kin. He was kind and noble and just.

He approached her again, this time with caution, as if she were a wild cat. "May I?" He lifted his hand, slowly.

His fingers in her hair were almost soothing as he plucked out a stray piece of straw. Then he locked gazes with her.

She held her breath. She couldn't remember the last time a man had looked at her with such compassion or touched her with such tenderness. She felt herself drawn into the deep verdant pools of his eyes.

It was a wee bit frightening.

She'd worn invisible armor for years now. It served to protect her against her cousins' subtle cruelty. It might not be strong enough to ward off her uncle's fists, but it kept her safe from his demeaning words.

Now, the way Brochan was touching her with measured care, looking at her with affection and concern, it felt like he was gently stripping away that armor, link by link.

A new fear fluttered in her breast.

But it wasn't dread.

It was anticipation.

Her gaze fell to his mouth, and she couldn't help but wonder what it would be like to press her lips to his, to melt into his welcoming arms, to feel perfectly safe and protected.

She let out the breath she'd been holding. It came out on a tremble.

She was going to do it. She couldn't help herself. She was going to kiss him.

Brochan couldn't believe he was going to kiss her. Every instinct told him not to. No good would come of it. He could think of at least a dozen good reasons not to do such a reckless thing. And he would list them all...right after he finished the kiss.

Their attraction was as inevitable and unavoidable as the pull of steel to a magnet. The distance closed between them with natural grace. When their mouths met, it felt like coming home.

Her lips were soft, warm, and vulnerable as she pressed them tentatively against his mouth.

She was shaking. Perhaps she'd never kissed a man before. But since he hadn't kissed a woman in five years, he too was out of practice.

Yet instinct swiftly took over. He moved his hand to cup her silky cheek, drawing her closer. He closed his eyes, angling his head to capture her lips between his.

She responded with a soft gasp. She placed her hands on his chest—not to push him away, but to clench her fists in his leine.

The long-banked coal of his desire flickered to life.

He threaded his fingers through her silken hair. He circled her ear with the pad of his thumb, deepening the kiss.

She answered instantly, seeking out his mouth, striving to get even closer.

Encouraged by her response, he circled her waist with his other arm and drew her up against him. He groaned at the familiar and divine sensation of a woman's body pressed firmly to his—the supple yielding of her breasts upon his chest and the sweet curve of her hips below his palm.

Then she slipped her tongue out to taste him.

Like lightning striking dry grass, his passion flared to life. Hot blood raced through his veins as he opened his mouth, granting her access.

His tongue danced with hers, lightly at first and then with more devotion, and they sang the music of desire. Like a starving man, he feasted upon her, and she drank his greed as if it were wine.

Suddenly her hands were everywhere, skimming his chest, roving over his shoulders, weaving through his hair. He explored her beautiful contours as well, delving his fingers into her inky tresses, tracing her delicate throat with his fingertips, and venturing lower, daring to brush his palms atop the sensitive tops of her breasts.

The breath she raked in was so raw with need that he felt the surge in his trews like the powerful wave of a stormy sea.

All the lust that had been bottled up for the last five years streamed through his veins at once in a brilliant flare, blinding him to reason. He tore away from the kiss and nudged her up against the wall, wanting her so badly he could scarcely breathe.

Somewhere in the depths of his soul, he knew he was behaving like an animal. But what he glimpsed in her eyes wasn't pain or fear. It was a desire as strong and pure as his. She wanted him. She wanted this.

In another moment...

"Hallo!" he heard from outside the byre.

Cristy's eyes went wide.

Brochan stepped away, silently using every foul oath he could think of.

Curse Brother William. Naught could douse the flames of passion faster than the voice of a monk.

Yet Brochan's fire was far from extinguished. The evidence of his lingering desire displayed itself as proudly as a pennant pole in his trews. With a look at Cristy that was half apology, half exasperation, he turned his back to her, made the necessary adjustments, and prepared to face the monk.

"I'm in here, William."

As William entered the byre, Brochan suddenly remembered that the monk might have news that could upset Cristy.

He turned to her. "Will ye go see to the lads?"

She seemed glad of an excuse to leave, especially when she

saw their visitor was a man of the church. She gave him a curt nod in greeting, picked up her skirts, and scurried off.

"Was that..." William began.

"Aye, Miss Moffat." He didn't feel like excusing his lack of an introduction...or detailing why they were alone in the byre...or explaining why the woman he was holding hostage apparently had free range of the property. "What news?"

"I've brought a missive from her laird," William said, handing over a small rolled parchment.

Brochan hesitated, stricken by an urge to destroy the thing without reading it. Part of him would rather leave things just as they were, with the lovely, sweet-lipped lass under his care.

But he was a man of honor. He'd offered a fair exchange. He had to be true to his word.

So he popped the seal and opened the document.

On it were scrawled three words.

Keep her. Moffat.

Brochan kept staring at the letters. He couldn't be reading that right. There had to be some mistake.

But no matter how many times he read it, the message was as clear, raw, and brutal as it could be. He tightened his fist around the missive as rage slowly burned inside him.

"Is somethin' wrong, m'laird?"

Beyond speech, Brochan clenched his jaw and handed the parchment to the monk.

William frowned as he read the note. "I don't understand. 'Tis only five coos. Surely he wants the lass back."

Brochan's heart twisted with fury and sorrow. How could a man be so cruel? Did he truly value his cattle above his own niece? Was he so apathetic about the lass that he would casually cast her aside? What a monstrous man he must be.

"How will I tell her?" he wondered aloud. "How will I tell her her own uncle doesn't think she's worth five coos?"

William shook his head. "'Tis a travesty. She looks to be a

lovely lass too. Most men would trade a whole herd o' cattle for a beauty like her."

Brochan had to agree. With her night-black hair and deep brown eyes, she was as bonnie and enticing as a dark faerie queen.

He rubbed his hand across his mouth, wondering how he was going to break the news to her. "Wait. What did ye just say?"

"I said she was a lovely lass."

"Nay, after that."

"Most men would trade a whole herd o' cattle for a lass like that."

"That's right. They would." Suddenly inspired, he snatched the missive from William's hand. Then he clapped his palm on the perplexed monk's shoulder. "Thank ye for takin' care o' this, William. I'm grateful for all ye've done."

After bidding the monk a hasty farewell, he headed toward the tower house. Halfway to the keep, he ripped the missive in half and tossed it away. By the time he reached the door, he'd weighed all the consequences and made up his mind.

It was completely reckless and irresponsible of him to keep Cristy in his home. His sons were growing too fond of her. Mabel was growing too fond of her. And *he* was growing too fond of her.

Cristy was a dangerous temptation. There was every reason to return her as soon as possible, whether or not he got his cows and whether or not her uncle wanted her back.

Keeping the peace between clans was the right thing to do. Holding on to her and risking a clan war with his own neighbor was rash and reckless.

Fortunately, Brochan didn't mind being rash and reckless.

CHAPTER 7

I t took all Cristy's willpower to keep up a calm appearance for the lads when her emotions were writhing around her brain in a tangled mess.

Kissing Brochan, she'd never felt so alive. One moment in his arms, and all her cares had vanished. He'd opened a locked chest inside her and revealed a treasure of new feelings.

It felt like a sultry wind had blown through her soul and awakened every fiber of her being. Yet within that sharp and wakeful clarity was a mist that softened the edges of reality, making it seem like the inside of a dream. Her sense of reason might be muted, but the rest of her senses had been heightened to dreamlike intensity.

Then that cursed monk had ruined everything.

In one moment, she'd felt like a warhorse primed to charge across the field.

In the next, she'd felt an abrupt backward pull on the reins, preventing her from moving.

And now she had to pretend that naught had happened, to speak to the wee lads as if she hadn't just been dallying with their father in the byre.

Colin shook his head. "I should never have asked ye to show

us how to reive cattle," he said, his voice full of regret.

"And I should have protected ye," Cambel said ruefully. "Da says gentlemen are supposed to protect ladies."

Cristy gave them each a fond squeeze. But she was only half listening, trying to settle her rattled nerves with a cup of ale as she stared into the fire.

"What do ye think he'll do to us?" Colin asked his brother.

"He might make us scrub the chamber pots," Cambel gravely decided.

"Or pick up the coo pats," said Colin.

"Or wear stick tails," Cambel said with a shudder.

"What?" Cristy asked. What were the lads going on about?

"Once," Cambel said, "we tied a stick to a hound's tail for fun. Da tied stick tails onto our belts and made us wear them for two days."

"To shame us," Colin explained.

"Aye, to shame us."

Cristy blinked. If her uncle ever picked up a stick, it was to beat her.

"What about ye, m'lady? What do ye think he'll do to ye?" Colin wondered.

A dozen wildly inappropriate ideas popped into Cristy's head, and she almost spat out her ale.

Cambel suggested, "Maybe she'll be rescued by her uncle before Da has a chance to punish her."

Cristy hoped not. After that blissful embrace, she'd be willing to clean chamber pots, pick up coo pats, *and* tie a stick around her waist just to see where that kiss would lead.

Still, the reminder that she didn't belong here was sobering. She wondered if the monk had brought news from her uncle. Was he going to return the cattle today?

"I don't want ye to go," Colin admitted.

"I don't want ye to go either," Cambel said, leaning against her thigh.

A lump lodged in her throat. She knew how they felt.

At that moment, Brochan came in, stomping the dirt from his boots at the door.

Cristy was afraid to look at him. She was afraid of what she might see in his eyes. What if the monk had brought bad news? What if Brochan was still upset about the cows? Worse, what if he regretted kissing her?

Brochan wondered if Cristy was sorry she'd kissed him. She stood near the fire with her eyes downcast. But it was hard to believe she hadn't felt the same world-shattering desire he had, the longing that didn't seem to be going away any time soon.

He wouldn't do anything about it, of course. As pleasurable as the kiss was, it had been impulsive and improper. It was dishonorable to seduce innocents. Besides, he owed his loyalty to the mother of his sons. Didn't he?

Those sons flanked Cristy at the moment like knights standing guard, ready to defend their lady. The sight almost made him wish he could just forget about their disobedience. Almost.

"Ye've all had time to consider your actions," Brochan said with forced calm, closing the door behind him. "So tell me, which o' ye deserves the punishment for this?"

"I do, Da," Cambel volunteered. "I should have been watchin' o'er the lady so she wouldn't get hurt by the coos."

"Nay, 'twas my fault," said Colin. "'Twas my idea to reive Eufemie."

"Nonsense," Cristy said. "Ye're only wee lads. 'Twas my fault for takin' ye out to the coos without your Da's consent."

Brochan tried not to smile. He was actually very proud that his sons were willing to take the blame. It proved they were men of character.

And the fact that Cristy too was trying to protect them warmed his heart. He was glad he'd made the decision he had about her.

"And what do ye think your punishment should be?" he asked.

"Pickin' up coo pats?" said Colin with a sigh.

Cambel shuddered. "Cleanin' out the garderobe?"

Cristy glanced up and opened her mouth. No words came out. But he didn't think he'd be able to understand them anyway. Seeing her rosy lips again heated his blood and scattered his thoughts.

He cleared his throat. "I think ye all bear a wee bit o' the blame. So here's your punishment." He didn't tell them it was a task he'd intended for the lads all along. "The doocot is in need o' repair. The cracks need patchin' so the wind won't get through. So on the morrow, I want ye to mix up a batch o' clay, straw, and coo dung. Then ye'll have to daub it into the chinks to seal the walls from the weather."

Watching his sons try to hide their excitement over their punishment was amusing. They loved to be helpful, and repairing the dovecot was a chore that appealed to their sense of worth and independence. For Colin, especially eager to get his own flock of chickens, it was all the lad could do to keep from jumping up and down with glee.

Cristy, however, had a puzzled look on her face. "What news did the monk bring from my uncle?"

He hesitated. Of course, she expected she'd be going home before the morrow.

"M'lady doesn't have to go home, does she, Da?" Cambel folded his hands in supplication.

"She *has* to stay till the morrow," Colin declared, "for her punishment."

His sons apparently liked having her here almost as much as he did.

Cristy lifted her chin in challenge, but he could see her face had gone pale. "What did he say?"

Brochan straightened. He was now positive he was doing the right thing. "Your uncle agreed to return the five coos today to ransom ye," he lied.

He saw her jaw tense.

The lads wailed in protest.

He held up his hand to stop them. "But I told him I've changed my mind. I've decided five coos isn't nearly enough for a lady o' such quality."

"What?" Cristy was startled.

"I told him the ransom was now thirty coos."

Thirty? *Thirty?*

Cristy's jaw went slack. She couldn't believe Brochan had made such a demand. There was no way her uncle would pay such a price for her. That was over half of his herd.

She wanted to tell him so. She wanted to tell him his price was too dear.

But Brochan's words didn't escape her notice. He'd called her a lady of quality. That made her glow inside.

While the twins cheered and leaped for joy around her, she couldn't help but smile at Brochan. As hopeless as his demand was, it was immensely flattering.

The secret smile he gave her in return took her breath away. Suddenly she imagined she was back in the byre, pressing her fevered lips to his, brazenly exploring him with her hands, tasting the hot, wet length of his tongue, and longing for more.

Lust shadowed his eyes and flared his nostrils. He wanted her too.

Unfortunately, there were wee lads dancing about them at the moment and a dozen tasks he probably had to finish before the day was done.

If she helped, they'd go faster.

Then maybe she'd steal another kiss before she broke the news to him that her uncle was never going to send him thirty cows.

Beside her, Colin was counting on his fingers. "Thirty?" His eyes went round. "Are we goin' to get thirty coos, Da?" Before Brochan could answer, Colin took his brother by the shoulders and shook him with joy. "Cambel, we're goin' to get thirty more coos!"

Of course, the lads had overlooked the fact that they'd be trading Cristy for those cows. But her uncle wasn't going to send that many anyway, so it didn't matter.

"Now, lads," Brochan chided. "What is it Aesop said?"

Cambel said, "Slow and steady wins the race?"

"Well, aye," Brochan said, "but I'm thinkin' o' the *The Milkmaid and Her Pail.*"

"Och!" Colin cried. "Don't count your chickens ere they're hatched."

"That's the one," Brochan said.

Cristy had no idea what they were talking about, although not counting chickens until they're hatched seemed like a good suggestion.

"Do ye like Aesop's stories, m'lady?" Cambel asked.

"I don't know Aesop," she said.

"Da will tell ye some o' his stories," Colin confirmed. "Won't ye, Da?"

Cristy could see Brochan had a dozen things on his mind already. "Maybe later?" she suggested. "I fear your da is very busy today."

"I'll make ye a bargain," Brochan said. "Ye three come help me clean out the pantry ere Mabel gets home, and I'll tell ye some of Aesop's stories while we work."

Unlike the much smaller buttery that Mabel used daily, the pantry was deep, dark, and cool. When Brochan brought down a candle stand so they could see better, the lads discovered an abundance of cobwebs and mouse droppings. It seemed that parts of the storeroom hadn't been touched by anything but vermin in years. Thick dust coated clay jars filled with unidentifiable substances that, when the corks were popped off, made the lads' noses wrinkle in displeasure. A few earthenware vessels had fallen, and shards of pottery were scattered on the floor. Mushrooms had sprouted on a few of the shelves, and the sack of barley slumped against the corner had long ago been chewed at the bottom, strewing grain everywhere.

Cristy would be surprised if anything was salvageable. Still, it had to be cleaned up to make room for the supplies Mabel was bringing home. So she pushed up the sleeves of her kirtle and grabbed the broom perched in the corner, determined to set the place to rights.

Brochan hauled in a great bucket of water, along with rags so they could clean as they went. He took the items off of the uppermost shelves and set them in the middle of the pantry. It was Colin's task to wipe away the dust and read the letters on the vessels to identify their contents. Cambel had the responsibility of peeking inside to determine if they were empty, rotten, or usable.

"Da, ye said ye'd tell us a story," Colin reminded him.

"Which story do ye want to hear?"

"The Lion and the Mouse!" Colin cried.

"Aye, *The Lion and the Mouse!*" Cambel echoed. "Ye'll like this one, m'lady."

While Cristy swept, Brochan told the story. "Once, a long while ago, a great lion was sleepin' in the woods..."

"Do ye know what a lion is, m'lady?" Cambel interrupted.

She smiled at his concerned expression. "Aye."

"As I said, a great lion was sleepin' in the woods. His enormous head was restin' on his paws, and he was snorin' as loud as...well, as loud as Rauf."

The lads giggled.

"Meanwhile, a timid wee mouse, payin' no heed to where she was goin', came upon the dozin' lion. In her hurry to get away from the dangerous beast, she accidentally ran straight across the lion's nose."

Cambel gasped dramatically, mostly for Cristy's benefit.

"O' course, the lion awoke at once, and, seein' the mouse, raised his big paw, intendin' to kill the wee beast that had disturbed his sleep."

The lads were enrapt and no longer toiling. Cristy, too, slowed her sweeping, transfixed both by the tale and by the sight of Brochan lifting heavy vessels off the top shelf, which made the impressive muscles of his back strain against the cloth of his leine.

"But then the mouse cried, 'Spare me, I beg ye!' 'Why should I spare ye?' said the lion. 'If ye spare me,' said the mouse, 'one day I shall repay ye for your kindness.'"

Cristy bit back a grin at the wee voice he'd given the mouse and the loud boom of the lion. No wonder his sons like the tales. Brochan was a gifted storyteller.

"Well, the lion didn't believe the mouse for one moment. After all, how could such a wee creature ever help a big and powerful lion? Nevertheless, he was amused by the minx of a mouse, and so he let her go."

Colin was squirming with anticipation. "Wait till ye find out what happens, m'lady."

"Many days later, the lion was chasin' after his supper in the same woods when he was caught in the tangle of a hunter's net. Unable to free himself from the ropes, no matter how much he twisted and turned, he let out a huge roar of anger."

"Do it, Da, do it!" Cambel cried.

Brochan gave Cristy a wink. Then he emitted a loud roar that left her heart in her throat, so savage was the sound.

The lads were giggling.

"Don't fret, m'lady," Cambel said. "'Tis only Da, not a real lion."

"Miss Moffat's not afraid o' lions, are ye, Miss Moffat?" Brochan asked.

If she was, she wasn't about to admit it. She lifted the broom. "Not while I have my trusty lion spear by my side."

The lads went wild with laughter then, which made her laugh in turn. She suddenly felt more giddy with joy—in a dark storeroom, holding a broom like a weapon, telling stories with two wee lads, admiring their father's hilarity and hindquarters—than she'd felt in years.

"Go on, Da," Colin said. "Tell m'lady what happens."

"Where was I? Och, aye, the roar. The mouse heard that roar and came at a run to find the lion strugglin' in the net. So, bein' a mouse o' her word, she nibbled and nibbled at the ropes until the grateful lion was free."

Colin clapped.

Brochan finished with, "The mouse said, 'Ye see? Even a wee creature like me can be o' help to a lion.'"

"Did ye like it, m'lady?" Cambel asked.

"Och, aye." Cristy could take the story to heart. For much of her life, she'd been made to feel like a mouse—wee, insignificant, useless.

"Now, lads, what's the moral o' the story?"

The lads recited, "Kindness is ne'er wasted."

Cristy smiled. It was a good moral.

"Tell us another, Da," Colin begged.

Brochan cocked an eye at them. "Ye finish those last few vessels, and then ye can start on the bottom shelves."

They hurried to do his bidding. Meanwhile, Cristy tied a damp rag around the handle end of the broom and swabbed away the cobwebs along the plaster ceiling.

"Will ye tell the story o' *The North Wind and the Sun,* Da?" Cambel asked when they started on the lower shelves.

Colin pouted. "But it doesn't have animals."

"'Tis a good story, though."

Colin shrugged. "I suppose."

"M'lady would like it."

"Would ye like it, m'lady?" Colin asked.

Cristy thought she'd happily listen to Brochan reciting the hours of the day, so pleasant was his voice. She nodded.

"Lady's choice 'tis," Brochan declared as he wiped down the top shelf. "One day, long ago, the North wind and the sun were bickerin', tryin' to decide which was the strongest. While they were arguin' in the road, a traveler happened to pass by."

Cambel gave his father a sly smile. "Did the traveler have a name?"

Brochan returned the grin. "Aye, as a matter o' fact, she did. Her name was Miss Moffat."

Cambel beamed. Apparently, it had been his plan all along to feature *her* in the story. She was enchanted.

Brochan continued. "The sun said to the wind, 'I know how we can settle this dispute. Whichever of us can strip the arisaid from that traveler—'"

"Miss Moffat," Cambel interjected with a giggle.

"Aye...'from that traveler, Miss Moffat, will be the strongest.' The North wind agreed and, all at once, blew a cold blast of air toward Miss Moffat."

"Do it, Da!" Cambel urged.

With a sheepish smile, Brochan pretended to blow out a long blast of air toward her. Caught up in the spirit of the play, Cristy feigned being blown backward by his North wind, which delighted the lads and made even Brochan laugh. So she continued to act out his story.

"Harder and harder the wind blew. One corner of the arisaid flew up, then the other. But Miss Moffat wrapped it close about her. The fiercer the wind blew, the tighter she held on to the arisaid. And finally the wind had to surrender."

Everyone was laughing at her antics. But it was Brochan's grin that made her melt.

He continued. "Then 'twas the sun's turn. The great yellow ball began to shine, very gently at first. Miss Moffat enjoyed the warmth after all the bitter cold o' the North wind. In fact, 'twas so pleasant that she unpinned her arisaid and loosened it a wee bit."

Cristy saw where the story was headed. And, feeling the way she did at the moment—lusty and daring—if she were alone with the laird, she might be tempted to actually remove her clothes, layer by layer. She settled for miming the actions, which seemed to satisfy the lads.

It also seemed to satisfy their father, whose eyes had taken on a shadowy cast.

"Warmer and warmer the sun burned," he said, "until Miss Moffat tossed back the hood o' her arisaid and mopped her brow."

She complied, wiping her forearm across her brow.

"The sun continued to blaze," he said, his voice a bit hoarser. "Cristy loosened the arisaid until it hung from her shoulders."

As she pretended to loosen her arisaid, Cristy watched Brochan. He might have been reciting a story, but his mind was clearly elsewhere. He was gazing at her with the same hunger she'd glimpsed in his eyes before, a hunger that sent a thrill through her.

"And then what, Da?" Colin urged.

Brochan licked his lips, staring at Cristy. "Then...then she...cast the arisaid away, because..."

From the level above came Mabel's voice. "Are ye down there, m'laird?"

Cristy clapped her hand to her bosom, as if she'd been caught disrobing.

"Aye!" His voice came out on a squeak. He cleared his throat. "Aye! In the pantry."

"We've brought the goods," she called down. "Can ye help Rauf unload them, m'laird?"

"I'll be right up."

"Da, ye have to finish the story," Colin said.

"Och, aye," he said in a rush. "So she tossed her arisaid aside, which meant the sun won. Now ye lads help Miss Moffat finish up the pantry while I unload the cart."

"But the moral, Da," Cambel reminded him.

"Right. What's the moral, lads?"

They replied, "Persuasion is better than force."

Cristy sighed as Brochan disappeared up the steps, her gaze lingering on his snug trews. Persuasion? It wouldn't take much to persuade her to kiss the irresistible laird again.

Brochan was glad of the heavy physical work, because it helped to take his mind off the enchanting lass in the pantry.

He was ashamed that he'd let lust take such control over him. For years, he'd kept it at bay, focusing on taking care of his sons, making a good life for his motherless lads. He felt he had to honor their mother's memory, and he'd never been tempted to look at another woman.

It was bad enough that he was drawn by Cristy's feminine lures—her lush black hair, her shining eyes, her succulent lips, her winsome figure. But now he was also attracted to her charming nature.

She was most remarkable, a lass of fascinating contrasts. Her spirit had been damaged in some ways, yet there was a willing playfulness about her. On the one hand, she seemed as innocent as his sons, yet on the other, she was worldly and wise beyond her years. She could be frail and fearful at times, fierce and frisky at others.

He liked her. It had been a long while since he'd said that about anyone. But he genuinely liked her.

And hours later, as they all sat together under the light of the comet—Cristy happily cradling both lads' sleepy heads in her lap—he wasn't sure "like" was a strong enough word.

CHAPTER 8

"Does your da always punish ye like this, with chores?" Cristy asked the lads the next morn as they skipped hand-in-hand toward the dovecot. She still thought it was the most curious form of chastisement. Her uncle always backhanded her and her cousins when they did something wrong. But the lads seemed genuinely excited to do the work.

"We haven't done daub in a while," Colin said.

"Usually 'tis chamber pots," Cambel added.

"Does he never clout ye?" she asked.

The boys looked at her as if she were mad.

"Why would he clout us?" Cambel asked.

"That would be ungentlemanly," Colin said.

Cristy frowned. "But what's to keep ye from disobeyin' him again if ye're not afraid to be clouted?"

The lads looked at each other, pondering the question.

"'Twould make Da unhappy," Colin finally decided.

"Aye, and 'tis dishonorable," Cambel added.

"Da would never use force against us," Colin assured her.

"Aye, that's it!" Cambel said. "'Tis like the story about the North wind and the sun."

Together the lads said, "Persuasion is better than force."

Cristy lifted her brows. Was that true? Had Brochan *never* clouted his sons? Had he managed to raise these two wee gentleman with their kind manners and courteous speech without raising his hand to them?

She shook her head in wonder. Perhaps persuasion *was* better than force.

Daubing the dovecot might not have seemed much like punishment to Cristy, but it promised to be dirty work. So once inside the stone structure, she brought the back of her skirt between her legs to the front, looping it up to tuck it into her belt like the crofters did. There was no point in getting the hem any filthier than it already was.

"Ye'll have to show me how to make the daub," she said.

Colin and Cambel took pride in demonstrating their very precise recipe. They showed her exactly how many handfuls of straw, clay, and cow dung to use, though she insisted they employ a spade to measure out the cow dung. They mixed it all in a large wooden bucket, stirring it with a stick until it made a thick paste.

Then, using a few small spades, they began to daub the mixture into every cranny where the sunlight streamed through.

"Da says we can get chickens when the doocot is repaired," Cambel said.

"I can't wait to get chickens." Colin wiped his cheek, leaving a streak of daub there. "I'm goin' to be in charge o' collectin' the eggs every day."

"I'm goin' to be in charge o' the pigs when we get them," said Cambel.

"What are ye goin' to be in charge o', m'lady?" Colin asked.

"I..." she began awkwardly.

Cambel elbowed his brother. "She's goin' home, Colin. Remember? Da said when we get the thirty coos, she's goin' home."

Colin pursed his lips in a sad pout. "I don't want her to go home."

"But ye like coos, Colin."

Colin's chin trembled. "I don't like coos as much as I like m'lady."

Cristy felt her heart cave in at his words. No one had ever said such a sweet thing. She bit her lip to keep from crying.

Cambel consoled his brother. "But she promised she'd come and visit us, right, m'lady?"

She didn't trust herself to speak, so she just nodded, hoping she could keep her promise. She knew it was only a matter of time before the ransom was paid. It wouldn't be thirty cows. That was a preposterous number. But her uncle would at least return Macintosh's own cattle. And then she'd have to leave. But it wouldn't surprise her if Douglas Moffat forbid her from venturing to the Macintosh holding after that.

It took over an hour to use up the first bucket of daub, though a good portion of it seemed to have found its way onto their clothing. While the lads were mixing another batch, Cristy surveyed the dovecot. The interior was dimmer, now that they'd filled in the lower crevices. She decided they should have the door open for light.

As she swung the door wide, something fluttered out of the path. It looked like a scrap of crumpled parchment. She bent down to pick it up. As she did, she noticed another piece. She compared them. They fit together. Someone or something had torn the parchment in half. There was scrawling on one side, but she couldn't read it.

An inexplicable tingling suddenly traversed the back of her neck, as if she'd backed into a spider's web.

"Lads," she said, wandering back into the dovecot, "do ye know what this is?"

They glanced at the two pieces.

"Parchment?" Colin guessed.

"Can ye tell me what it says?" she asked.

They frowned in concentration as they bowed their heads over the two scraps, deciphering the letters.

"Keep her," Colin said. "It says 'keep her.' But I can't read *this* word."

"'Tis too messy," Cambel said.

She stared closer at it. She'd seen that scrawl before. "Moffat."

Cambel shrugged. "Maybe."

Keep her. Moffat.

The letters blurred as she continued to stare at them.

Suddenly she felt dizzy. Then sick. Then numb. Her blood congealed in her veins. And her heart seemed to shrivel in her chest.

Cristy's worst fears were confirmed. She didn't belong. She wasn't wanted.

"What does it mean?" Colin wanted to know.

How could she answer him?

What it meant was that she was alone in the world. That her own uncle didn't care about her. That nobody cared about her.

"Are ye all right, m'lady?" Cambel asked, resting a dirty but concerned hand on her skirt.

She looked blankly down at him.

But that wasn't right. Someone *did* care about her. These two lads cared about her. They thought she was bonnie...and better than cows.

And then, as she let the pieces of parchment flutter to the ground, she realized someone else cared even more about her.

Brochan.

This note was for him. He must have read it. And he must have torn it in half.

He'd lied to her.

There had been no fierce negotiations. Her uncle hadn't been willing to trade for her at all. And Brochan hadn't demanded thirty cows for her return. He'd only said that because he knew there was going to be no return.

He'd made all of that up to keep her from being hurt. He'd tried to protect her feelings.

Her deflated heart slowly filled again—with wonder, with warmth, with joy.

The Macintoshes cared about her. The lads called her "m'lady" and snuggled with her at night and laughed at her playacting. Brochan treated her like a guest, guarded her heart from pain, and kissed her with tenderness.

She dared to wonder if she might make a home here, if she might be able to find a place in their kind and loving household.

She would do whatever it took to earn their trust and be deserving of their love. She'd empty the chamber pots, scrub the garderobe, and pick up coo pats every day if it meant she could be part of their clan.

With a trembling smile, she placed a hand atop Cambel's sweet head. "I'm all right. Everythin' is goin' to be all right."

Her spirits renewed, she straightened and looked around the dovecot. There were still a lot of gaps to fill, but the sooner she finished, the sooner her darling wee companions would be able to get their beloved chickens.

Her ambitious plans were curtailed when the lads started quibbling.

"Don't!" Colin snapped at Cambel, ducking his head away.

"I'm just tryin' to get the daub off your face," Cambel argued.

"Nay, ye're not! Ye're puttin' more on!"

"Lads," Cristy chided.

They ignored her.

In perceived retaliation, Colin dipped his finger in the daub and smudged it on Cambel's cheek.

Cambel's eyes went wide in disbelief. "Colin! For shame!"

Colin giggled.

Cambel dipped his whole hand in the bucket then and put a handprint in the middle of Colin's white leine.

Colin's jaw dropped.

"Lads!" Cristy scolded, planting her hands on her hips.

In return, Colin grabbed a fistful of daub and smeared it across Cambel's leine.

Cambel gasped.

Then began the melee. The lads started reaching into the bucket and firing sticky handfuls at each other as if engaged in a deadly battle. Soon, brown splats covered their hair and clothing and stuck to the walls of the byre.

"Lads!" she shouted.

Then one of the twins—she wasn't sure which one—happened by chance to fire a daub missile straight at her. It caught her on the forehead.

All three of them froze in horror as the daub began dripping down her nose.

Cristy didn't know what got into her. She acted on instinct. With a vexed growl, she reached both her hands into the bucket and smacked the mischievous lads in the face with daub.

Unfortunately, that only escalated the fight. Colin accused Cambel of attacking Cristy, and Cambel accused Colin. They began pelting each other again. And Cristy found herself elbow-deep in the battle.

Not long after that the giggles started.

Brochan smiled as he strode down the brae toward the dovecot. His penitents didn't sound very penitent. He could hear laughter coming from inside. The sound of his sons laughing always lifted his spirits. But hearing Cristy's giggles mingled with theirs was like listening to merry music.

He wondered what had made them so full of cheer.

The door was open, so he poked his head inside. "What's goin' on, my wee merrymak-?"

His question was cut short by the smack of something against his chest. Something wet and brown and sticky.

"What the...?"

Frozen before him, looking as filthy as pigs and guilty as sin, were his sons and his hostage. It didn't escape his notice that Miss Moffat's skirts were hitched up like a crofter's, leaving her mouthwatering legs indecently bare, albeit coated with nasty-looking mire. Indeed, if he weren't so appalled by the mess, he might have been aroused.

He lifted his fingers to his chest and drew them back with a scowl. Daub. One of the three miscreants before him had thrown daub at him.

"I can explain," Cristy said. At least he *thought* it was Cristy. It was hard to tell under all that muck.

"I'm sorry, Da."

"We're sorry, Da."

For the first time in his life, Brochan wasn't sure which twin was which. Their faces were covered in mire, and straw stuck out at all angles from their hair.

He shook his head in disbelief. It looked as if they'd been having some sort of full-scale daub war.

Then Cristy snickered.

The lads covered their mouths, stifling giggles.

Brochan glowered at them from the doorway, his arms crossed sternly over his chest—just below the splash of daub.

But the mischief-makers couldn't contain their laughter, and soon the rafters of the dovecot were ringing with the sound of unfettered glee.

Brochan narrowed his gaze and gave them a dire warning. "If ye think I'm goin' to let ye get away with this, ye're mistaken."

He then proceeded to do what any wise laird would do to

maintain the upper hand and establish his dominance. He joined in the battle and defeated them all soundly.

When they ran out of munitions, they collapsed in a laughing heap on the floor of the dovecot. Daub not only caked their clothing and stained their skin. Muddy splats also decked the walls and littered the floor.

But it was worth it to hear their laughter. For the first time in too many days, now that he had an extra helping hand, Brochan felt he could spare a few moments for frivolity.

Of course, the mess had to be cleaned up. And the lads needed to be scrubbed from head to toe before he'd let them into the tower house.

"Ye know what this means, lads," he said.

One of them sighed. "Since we were wicked, do we have to clean out the garderobe?"

"Ye already *smell* like a garderobe," he told them. "But nay. I think we need to make a trip to the loch to get the stink off."

The lads cheered. They hated their weekly bath in a tub, but in summer, they were always keen to take a dip in a loch.

Before Brochan could exercise prudence, the lads extended an invitation to Cristy.

"Ye come with us, m'lady! Ye'll love the loch!"

"Aye, and ye can get the stink off ye too!"

Cristy hesitated. "I'm not sure your da—"

"Please, m'lady," one of the twins begged. "I want to show ye the frogs."

"And I can swim. Ye have to see how I can swim."

After that, despite Brochan's qualms about inviting a lass to bathe with them, he knew she could hardly refuse.

"Fine. I'll come."

At first, frolicking in the loch was fairly harmless. Since their clothing was coated with muck, the lads waded in, fully dressed, to rinse it out of their trews and leines.

But the lads were unaccustomed to swimming in their

clothes. So they very quickly and unabashedly peeled off their soaking garments, tossing them atop a boulder at the water's edge, and returned to swimming and splashing about like a pair of naked kelpies.

The lads took turns showing Cristy how well they could swim, and she praised their efforts. Of course, though she could wade into the water, she dared not go too deep. Her drenched wool skirts would pull her under. So she stood waist-deep in the loch, washing her face and loosening her braid in the sunshine.

While she watched the twins, Brochan watched her.

It seemed like Cristy had blossomed in the last few days. That first night, her face had been full of fear and hate and anger. But now she was radiant. Her eyes were joyful. Her head was held high. Her smile was wide and open. She was truly beautiful—in body and in spirit.

He wanted to keep her...forever.

Then he was struck with a bolt of guilt. That was the promise he'd given his wife.

Besides, it was a foolish wish. Cristy didn't belong to him. Even if her kin refused to negotiate for her return, he couldn't help but believe that, deep in her heart, she longed to go home.

The kiss they'd shared had been an accident, something fleeting and meaningless. The last thing a carefree young lass like Cristy wanted was to be tied to a man with two wee sons, two old servants, and a holding he could barely manage.

So then what was he going to do with her? He'd delayed her leaving, both to salvage her feelings and because he selfishly wasn't ready to part with her yet. But he couldn't keep up the pretense of holding her hostage. At some point, he had to let her go.

He knew that. So why did it agonize him so much to think about it?

Cristy smiled at the lads, clapping her hands in approval as they showed her the pebbles they'd collected from the loch bottom.

His chest ached as he thought of no longer having her in his life. True, he'd only known her a few days. But in that short time, she'd already become fast friends with his sons, and she'd already made a place for herself in his heart.

It wasn't the place his wife occupied. No one would ever have that place.

But he'd grown undeniably fond of Cristy. And since he cared about her, as much as it pained him, he had to tell her the truth. It was the right thing to do.

With a resigned sigh, he called out, "Lads, are ye good and clean?"

They groaned in protest. If it were up to them, they'd swim in the loch all day.

"Ye need to get back to the tower and give Mabel your wet clothes."

"But, Da…"

"Please, Da, we want to stay."

"If ye stay, ye won't get your chores done. And if ye don't get your chores done, ye won't get to see the comet tonight."

"I don't mind," Colin said. "I've seen the comet."

"Me neither," said Cambel. "I'd rather stay here and swim."

Brochan could honestly say he didn't blame them. Cristy's company was much more engaging than a star hanging silently in the sky. But he needed some time alone with her.

Remembering that persuasion was better than force, he said, "I'll make a bargain with ye. If ye get into dry clothes and finish your chores, I'll tell ye another story tonight."

"The Oak and the Reed?" Cambel asked.

"Nay, *The Tortoise and the Hare!*" Colin cried.

"Ye always get *The Tortoise and the Hare,*" Cambel complained.

"Whoever gets to the tower first can pick the tale," Brochan decided.

The lads sprang out of the loch, dripping, grabbed their clothes, and skipped toward the tower house, naked as newborns.

"Don't go near the cattle!" he yelled after them.

"We won't!" they called back.

He watched them scamper away for as long as he could, loath to confront Cristy with the painful news he had. When he could delay no more, he turned back...and froze.

Her clothes were in a pile at the loch's edge. Afloat in the water, letting the current lap at her bare shoulders, was beautiful Cristy, wearing naught but a smile.

He didn't know whether to be pleased or horrified. Fairly quickly, his body made up his mind for him. Within his trews, he felt a swelling as he continued to gaze at her and imagined what lay hidden beneath the waves.

"Are ye goin' to stand there all day?" she teased.

He gulped. "Maybe."

She obviously didn't know the power of her own beauty. There was no way to have a serious discussion with the lass while she was naked and so damned tempting.

"Why?" she asked sincerely. "Don't ye know how to swim?"

"O' course I know how to swim."

"Then come join me," she cooed, playfully twirling in the water.

She bobbed up briefly enough for him to catch a glimpse of a pair of lovely, pale breasts with dark points just beneath the surface. His mouth went dry.

"Ye aren't afraid o' me, are ye?" she teased.

He scoffed, though it came out as more of a croak.

But aye, he was afraid of her. She made him think of mad things, like forgetting his marriage vows, kissing her again, and holding her hostage forever.

Bloody hell.

"Ye're not afraid I'm a kelpie, here to lure ye to your doom?" she said with a laugh.

That was exactly what he was afraid of.

But he couldn't very well turn down her perfectly innocent invitation. She didn't mean anything by it. And he wasn't a coward.

With a sigh of defeat and determined to keep things as casual as possible, he began stripping off his clothes.

CHAPTER 9

Cristy's invitation was anything but innocent.

She wasn't unaware of the effect she was having on Brochan. She wanted him to kiss her again. And she knew that men, like cattle, could be more easily moved when they were guided along. Just as he'd said, persuasion was better than force. So she intended to persuade him.

What she didn't expect was the effect Brochan would have on *her* once he started undressing.

When he whipped off his leine, her breath caught in lusty surprise. His bare chest was taut with muscle, his stomach ridged, narrowing to a trim waist. His shoulders were broad, and his arms were massive. No wonder he'd been able to pack her off to the tower house with such ease that first night.

She swallowed hard as he hastily untied and stepped out of his trews to reveal powerful thighs and lean calves. For a startling instant, she imagined those legs tangled in bedsheets with hers, and a sudden twinge of need pulsed at her core.

Then he began untying the linen braies beneath. Anticipation sent a curious heat through her, humming around her head and diving deep between her legs.

All at once, his braies were undone. In one swift motion, he cast them off and headed toward the water.

A single fleeting glimpse of him sent a bolt of lust arcing through her. He was magnificent—bold and confident and strong—and something about the pure male energy of his body called to her womanly yearning. Though she'd never lain with a man before, she craved Brochan, longed to feel him beside her and, aye, within her.

That burning desire was instantly doused when Brochan entered the loch with a great surge of water that went over her head.

She came up choking and sputtering.

"Och, my apologies," he said, though there was a betraying twinkle in his eye. "Are ye all right?"

She answered him with a punitive splash of water. "Ye did that on purpose."

"Who, me?"

"Ye big..." She stopped to cough out the last of the water. "Whale."

He laughed. "Did ye just call me a whale?"

"I did." She stifled her own laughter.

"Well, if ye didn't swim like a cat..." he teased.

Her mouth gaped open, and she almost got a mouthful of water again.

"See?" he said.

She narrowed her eyes in feigned fury. She didn't swim like a cat. Using both hands, she started splashing him relentlessly, keeping up a barrage of water.

At first he held up his arms in defense. Then he sank beneath the surface.

Suddenly something pinched her toe, and even though she knew it was him, she yanked her foot back with a shriek. He grabbed her other toe, and she yelped, kicking it out of his grasp.

Then they collided, and she clearly felt his leg brush the side of her hip.

Startled, she thrashed around, and her hand grazed his chest.

When he broke the surface of the water, he was facing her.

Though there was still a residual smile on his face, his eyes sobered as he realized how close they were.

Panicked, Cristy raised her hands with the intent of splashing him away again. He caught her wrists to stop her.

And then the levity of the moment was gone. Time seemed to stand still.

This close, she could see the veil of desire muting his bright green eyes and the subtle flare of his nostrils as he gazed back at her. Water dripped with slow sensuality down the stubbled plane of his face and onto the wide expanse of his chest. But it was his mouth—his beautiful, delicious mouth—that truly tempted her.

When his eyes lowered to her lips, she parted them with a gasp. The craving in his gaze fueled her own. As they drew closer and closer, the water lapped sensuously at their bodies. And as they stared at each other, a powerful current snapped between them, shocking her to life.

She wanted him—all of him.

She let her eyes drift closed and tipped her head back, waiting breathlessly for his kiss.

He didn't disappoint. When he released her wrists, it was only to delve his hands into her hair and bring her near. His lips claimed hers with barely contained ferocity, sending an erotic shiver up her spine.

She moaned against his mouth and snaked her arms around his neck, reeling at the divine sensation of flesh on flesh as she melted against his muscular chest. Their tongues swirled together in the language of lust. And when she brazenly thrust her hips against his, she felt his bold arousal making its own silent demand.

When his lips left hers to nuzzle her cheek, she tipped back her head, and he rained kisses along her neck. He licked the sensitive spot beneath her ear, and she quivered, digging her fingers into his back.

Beyond reason, beyond care, her focus was drawn to the fiery yearning between her legs. Pure instinct made her grind against him, seeking to alleviate the burn.

He groaned and shuddered.

Buoyed by the water and using his shoulders for leverage, she lifted herself, entwining her legs around his waist. The warm skin of his torso felt heavenly against her inner thighs. But there was still an intense ache at her center, an emptiness longing to be filled.

In some remote corner of her mind, Cristy was mortified by her own wanton urges. But this new woman she'd become was beyond thought. Driven by passion, she followed her instincts without shame. And those instincts were telling her to join with him. Now.

Brochan had never wanted anything as much as he wanted Cristy at this moment. Maybe it was because of long abstinence, but he feared in another moment he'd explode. Every inch of him was aroused. Every nerve was on fire.

He was fast losing control. And if he lost control, he might do something foolish. Like consummate his desire with a woman who was not his wife, a woman who was probably a virgin.

So with every ounce of fortitude he could muster, he pushed down his carnal cravings and resisted her seduction, not because it was what he wanted, but because it was the right thing to do.

He eased her luscious legs from around his waist and loosed her arms from his neck, setting her away from him.

He thought she'd be grateful. After all, he was doing the responsible thing. He was taking charge of their indiscretion and guarding her maidenhood.

He couldn't have been more wrong. Instead of relief, her face was etched with betrayal and disappointment. She assumed he was rejecting her.

How could he explain that he was releasing her, not because he didn't desire her—bloody hell, how he desired her—but out of honor, duty, propriety, and for her own welfare?

Naught was going to smooth the crease of disillusionment from her brow—at least naught he could *say*.

But he could *do* something to reassure her, something to convince her that she was worthy and desirable and seductive and irresistible.

Ignoring his own raging lust, he engaged her again, kissing her pouting lips and caressing her ear between his thumb and finger. She succumbed almost at once, closing her eyes and leaning into his embrace.

He let his fingertips trace the throbbing vein along her throat. He grazed her bosom with the back of his knuckles. Her breath was ragged against his mouth as she arched her back, urging him to venture farther.

Inch by inch, he complied. Despite his unrequited arousal, he relished her increasing desire. At last, he brushed the stiffened points of her nipples, eliciting a gasp of wonder from her. He kissed her again as he cupped her lovely breasts, weighing them in his palms, stroking her wet, velvety skin.

Then he made a trail of kisses down her throat, nibbling at the place beneath her ear until she squirmed with pleasure. When his mouth drifted down to her bosom, she held her breath in anticipation.

Her hands tangled in his hair as he locked his lips upon her breast, feeding upon her ecstasy.

While she reveled in that delight, he moved his hand lower,

into the water, sweeping over her ribs, venturing across her stomach, and playing in the soft curls that guarded her maidenhood.

All the while, her sounds of sensuous distress were driving him mad. With every fiber of his being, he longed to lie with her.

So he did the next best thing.

Lifting her in his arms, he conveyed her across the water to the shore. There he lay her down in the shallows where the water was warmer and he could rightfully worship her beautiful body. Answering the question in her eyes, he stretched out beside her, holding her hand in his and letting his free hand follow a sinuous path toward the target of her need.

She flushed with amazed pleasure as his fingers slipped through her womanly curls and between her swollen nether lips.

His smile was strained as his body responded with painful force to what he was touching, imagining all too well how those soft folds would feel around his rigid staff.

Cristy felt like she was adrift in deep, uncharted waters. But though the feelings were dangerously new to her, she felt safe in Brochan's arms. Lying back on the soft bank in the shallow waves, she was soothed by the lap of the water even as she was aroused by the lovely movement of his fingers upon her most secret place.

She throbbed with need, and what he did was intensifying that yearning. She locked her hands behind his neck, squeezing her eyes shut as her body strained and swelled until she thought she would burst. Sharper and sharper her desire grew, centering at the spot where he stroked her with nimble skill. At last, able to endure no more, she stiffened, and the breath stilled in her lungs.

For what seemed an eternity, she hung in silent weightlessness, like an angel soaring high above the earth. And then, all at once, she plunged downward at breakneck speed, clinging to Brochan for dear life as she thrashed beneath him in the throes of ecstasy.

When she finally recovered, gasping for breath and glowing with relief, she opened her eyes to slits and peered up at Brochan.

There was a look of feral hunger on his face. His jaw was clamped shut. His brow was deeply creased. Like a bull ready to charge, his nostrils flared and his eyes darkened.

She wouldn't have believed it possible, but his expression sent her passions rising again. She suddenly longed to quell his craving the way he had hers. And though she knew it was improper to think such things, she wondered...if he could bring her to such a lovely anguish with only the light touch of his fingers, what could the rest of him do?

She had to act quickly, before too much reflection could make a coward of her. Having no idea what she was doing, she acted on impulse. While he was yet fully aroused, she positioned herself to accept him. Then she wrapped her legs around his hips and arched upward.

His groan startled her, but not as much as the sharp slice of pain inside her, followed by an impossible fullness. She gasped and winced. Then she looked askance at him.

His face was troubled. Had she hurt him? Had she damaged herself?

"Och, lass, I'm sorry," he wheezed out, as if it were his fault. "Are ye hurt?"

She furrowed her brow. "Did I do somethin' wrong?"

"Nay, but..." He squeezed his eyes closed and moaned again. She felt him pulse inside her.

"Did I hurt ye?" she whispered.

He broke out instantly into the most curious grin—part

amusement, part disbelief, part regret. Then he shook his head. "'Tis the furthest thing from hurt," he assured her.

She gulped with relief.

"But Cristy," he breathed. "I didn't mean for ye to get hurt."

She gave him a small, reassuring smile. Already the pain was fading.

"If ye'll let me," he promised, "I can make it better for ye."

She nodded.

He did make it better. He caressed her breasts with a delicate hand and breathed gentle encouragements into her ear as he slowly moved inside her. With painstaking patience and exquisite languor, he pushed against her until his breath grew uneven. Gradually, her pain diminished into desire. Soon, she was answering the dance, moving her hips and digging eager heels into his buttocks.

Again, her senses spiraled upward. And she could tell, peering at him through her lashes, that he was experiencing the same unbridled yearning. They suffered together, gasping for breath, moaning in glorious torment, until they could climb no more.

With a great primitive cry that called to Cristy and shook her to the core, Brochan erupted, spilling his seed into her with all the force of his passion. She joined him on that sensual skyward journey, and they rocked together until they fell softly back to earth.

As Cristy lay spent on the shore, she couldn't help but smile. She'd never been more content. The sun shone gently upon them. The loch plashed in playful waves around them. His hot breath rasped against her ear. His skin was warm and slippery against hers. And joined as they were, she felt as if she'd become one with him, as if they would never again be apart, as if she finally belonged.

Silently, Brochan cursed his carelessness. How could he have done something so dishonorable? He'd let lust get the better of him.

Aye, he'd never felt such pure elation, trysting with Cristy. He was ashamed to admit he'd never shared such depths of passion, even with his wife. But it wasn't right. He'd taken her virginity, for God's sake. Worse, he hadn't even taken precautions to make sure he wouldn't give her a child.

He would never believe it was Cristy's fault, even if she had impaled herself upon him. He knew better. He alone was responsible. He should never have put her in such a risky situation.

When he raised his head to gaze into Cristy's eyes—her bliss-filled, shining eyes—he was filled with remorse.

The men in her life had abused her. Her uncle beat her. Her cousins treated her with scorn. He couldn't join the ranks of those who inflicted damage upon Cristy. He couldn't deflower the innocent lass and turn her out into the world, a victim of his recklessness.

He had to make things right. He had to do the honorable thing.

And if his heart quickened—imagining her in his arms every night, waking to her beautiful face every morn—he pushed those thoughts away. He told himself it was not a matter of replacing his wife. He was only taking responsibility for his actions.

"That was...magnificent," Cristy sighed, gazing up at him with lust-languid eyes.

He quirked up the corner of his mouth, but there was a guilty lump in his throat now that wouldn't let him speak.

He'd made a grave mistake. And decency required he pay for it.

He convinced himself he would have done the same for any lass he'd compromised. It made no difference that Cristy had delectable brown eyes, honey lips, and a body that made him feel alive. It didn't matter that she had a wicked sense of humor and a delightful laugh, that she was beloved by his sons and his servants, that she felt like a fresh summer breeze blowing into his world.

No one would ever usurp his first wife's place in his heart. He'd sworn to love her forever, and he was a man of his word.

As he tucked a hand behind Cristy's head, first to give her a fond kiss and then to lift her out of the water, he made a silent vow. When they got back to the tower house, he'd make things right. Though it meant yet another person to be responsible for, he would accept the burden of his sin and ask her to be his wife.

By the time they climbed the motte, hand-in-hand, Cristy's hair was almost dry. Her kirtle was still damp, but she felt so warm and glowing inside that she hardly noticed.

She wondered if she looked different. She *felt* different—transformed, just as Brighde had predicted. Certainly if she didn't stop smiling, Mabel would know at once what they'd done.

Halfway to the door, Brochan stopped. He clasped her hand between both of his and cleared his throat.

Cristy's heart leaped. This was it. He was going to ask her to marry him.

He'd tell her that he'd fallen in love with her, that he didn't think he could live without her, that he wanted to give her children, and that he promised to love her forever if she would only agree to be his wife.

She waited breathlessly.

"I've been givin' it some thought," he said, his face very serious as he stared at the ground between them. "What will happen if your uncle doesn't send the thirty cows? Would that be so terrible? From what ye say, there's not much for ye to go back to as his ward. My lads are in sore need of motherin'. And there's too much work here for Mabel to do on her own. What I'm askin' is if ye think ye might be willin' to stay here at the tower house."

Cristy blinked in displeased surprise. That wasn't the love-struck confession she'd imagined at all. "Stay? What do ye mean, stay? Ye mean, as your servant?"

"Och, nay," he said glancing up at her and then returning to scowl at the ground. "I wonder if ye might be willin' to...ye know, to live with me as husband and wife."

Cristy was stunned. Was that it? Was that his romantic proposal?

What was wrong with him?

Was it possible she'd misjudged him?

"Do ye love me?" she asked.

He gulped and took too long to answer. "I could *grow* to love ye."

She felt his honesty like a dagger in her chest. As much as she wanted to accept his offer and become Lady Cristy Macintosh, she couldn't wed a man whose heart didn't belong to her.

So she withdrew her hand. "Then nay."

"Nay!" His amazement was clear in his eyes. "What do ye mean, nay?"

"I won't marry ye."

"But we trys-..." He lowered his voice, in case the servants or his sons were about. "We trysted together. I took your virginity."

His words only made things worse. Not only did he apparently not love her. He was only asking her to marry him out of guilt and duty.

"Ye didn't take my virginity," she corrected. "I gave it to ye." Her own admission upset her. How could she have given her virginity to a man who didn't even love her?

"Ye won't marry me?" He seemed utterly astounded. "But why?"

If he was too blind to see that she was not interested in merely a marriage of convenience, she wasn't going to tell him. She gave him an irritating shrug.

"But what if ye're...with child?" he whispered.

She suppressed a gasp. She hadn't considered that. Was that the real reason he was proposing—because he thought he had to rescue her from shame?

"If I'm with child," she said with flippancy she didn't feel, "then I'll go back where I belong and raise it myself." Her voice caught on the word "belong," for she knew she didn't belong in the Moffat household—not really.

The shock in his face rapidly turned to frustration and then menace. "I...I forbid it. If ye're with child, 'twill belong to me." He crossed his arms over his chest, as if his word was final.

Her jaw dropped. Their conversation had taken a nasty turn. "Ye can't take away my child."

"*My* child," he said with an imperious arch of his brow. "And I won't allow a child o' mine to be raised in your savage uncle's household."

She narrowed her eyes at him. She didn't want a child raised in her uncle's household either. But she wasn't about to let cocky Brochan Macintosh order her about as if he owned her now, just because they'd trysted once. "Ye won't have any choice. Once ye get your coos, I'll be free to go."

It was a foolish statement. She knew about the missive. Her uncle wasn't going to ransom her.

But rather than admit her threat was empty, she wheeled and stomped off toward the door.

Just before she slammed it behind her, Brochan got in the last word. "He's not goin' to send any coos! He doesn't want ye back!"

CHAPTER 10

Brochan grimaced, regretting his words the instant they left his lips. He hadn't meant to blurt that out. The truth was he'd panicked. And it was the only thing he could think of that might keep her from leaving him.

And then reality hit him. He was terrified of losing her.

But why?

When he realized the answer, he staggered back a step, shaken.

God help him, he *was* in love with her. He was in love with Cristy Moffat.

As impetuous and improbable as it was, he'd fallen in love with the outlaw lass who'd reived his coos.

But then who wouldn't love her? She was sweet and spirited, playful and passionate, lovely and loving, all any man could want.

Why then was it so hard to admit that?

Why had he given her every reason for marrying him but that one?

Wrestling with his conscience, he turned, slogging back down the motte and toward the byre.

It was his wife, he realized.

He still felt he had to be faithful to his wife.

Of course, he knew that was naïve. His wife wasn't coming back. She'd left this world.

Besides, as Mabel ceaselessly reminded him, she wouldn't have wanted Brochan to be lonely. She would have wanted him to wed again.

That might be true, he thought, but would she have wanted him to *love* again?

He entered the dim byre, noting that the milk buckets were empty. The twins hadn't done the second milking yet. He'd send them out after dinner. He studied the sagging thatch overhead that would need to be repaired before winter. And he wondered what his wife would have thought of Cristy.

He closed his eyes and tried to conjure up his wife's image. But it was difficult. And that troubled him. Her face should be etched indelibly in his conscience. And yet the longer she was gone, the more indistinct her features became. Soon, he feared, she'd be but a wisp of a memory.

Yet maybe that was as it should be. Maybe life was kind that way, gently smoothing away the edges of a person's face, like water polishing rock, until recalling her was less painful.

Five years she'd been gone. Five years he'd been without a woman. And though his sons had kept him from despair, giving him something to live for, they hadn't brought him the companionship he craved, the love of an adoring wife.

He leaned back against the byre wall.

He decided his wife would have liked Cristy. After all, her sons did. And Mabel and Rauf, who had been his wife's most trusted servants, liked her as well.

Maybe it was time.

Maybe his wife would forgive him for loving another.

As he pushed away from the wall and ambled back up to the tower house by the fading light of day, he felt at peace for the first time in years.

Then he remembered the strange tavern wench and her prophecy.

Maybe Brighde had been right.

Maybe it was time to change his stars.

As he entered the hall, however, he first had to attend to his clamoring sons, who rushed up the instant he arrived.

"Da! I won! I won!" Cambel said.

"Aye," said Colin, "Cambel got here first."

"Colin would have won if he hadn't tripped o'er a dry coo pat."

"I did trip o'er a coo pat," Colin admitted with a shrug.

"But we talked it o'er," Cambel said.

"And we both want the same story," Colin said.

Brochan put a hand on each of their heads. But his attention drifted to the beautiful lass standing by the fire to dry her skirts. He could hardly believe she was the same eager and passionate woman he'd made love to at the loch's edge. She was staring silently into the flames. Her expression was distant and elusive.

Colin tugged on his leine. "Don't ye want to know what story we chose?"

"Aye," he said. "What story?"

They answered together. *"The Mice in Council."*

Brochan nodded his approval, but his mind was still on Cristy. He had to apologize to her. He should never have said such a hurtful thing. And somehow he had to convince her to stay. Most of all, he had to find a way to make her care for him the way he cared for her.

But just then Mabel announced dinner. Soon he became distracted by salmon pottage and bannocks, the babbling of his lads, and the servants' report of the day.

Cristy sat quietly between the twins, stirring her pottage, as if naught was wrong.

She wasn't hungry. Indeed, she didn't want to sit here at all. Part of her wanted to retreat somewhere to lick her wounds after Brochan's cruel reminder that her uncle didn't want her back. And part of her wanted to seize the stubborn laird by the front of his leine and demand that he admit to loving her.

She didn't dare do either. To leave would invite too many questions. Already, Mabel was eyeing her with suspicion because of her quiet mood. And Cristy didn't wish to upset the twins. So she only picked at her bannock and stared at her pottage while dinner continued around her.

"Da, can ye tell us the story now?" Cambel asked.

"Aye, Da, tell us." Colin tugged on Cristy's sleeve, and she looked askance at him. "Have ye heard *The Mice in Council* before, m'lady?"

She shook her head.

Cambel told her, "'Tis all about bravery."

"Don't spoil it, Cambel," said Colin.

"I won't."

"Because 'twill ruin the surprise."

"I know."

"Hush, lads," Mabel chided. "Let your da tell the tale."

Brochan took a drink of ale, then cleared his throat and began. "Once there was a great family o' mice that lived in the shadow of a very wicked cat."

Cristy tore off a chunk of bannock and dipped it into her pottage. She could tell by Brochan's voice that he wasn't in a storytelling mood. No doubt the disgruntled laird was unaccustomed to having his wedding proposals refused.

"Now this cat had a powerful cravin' for mouse meat. It seemed that every time a mouse crept out of its wee home, she was ready to spring out and snap it up in her claws."

"Da," Colin interjected, "do ye think we could get a cat?"

"Colin, don't interrupt," Cambel chided.

"I'm just wonderin'."

"A cat?" Brochan considered. "I suppose, as long as ye look after it and keep it out o' the doocot."

Colin cheered.

"Now where was I?" Brochan asked.

Cambel said, "Snappin' up mice in her claws."

"Aye. 'Twas so bad, all the mice were afraid to leave their homes. They decided to have a council..."

"A mice council," Colin gushed, as if the idea pleased him immensely. Cristy wondered if his opinion would change when his new cat started gifting him with dead mice.

"In that mice council," Brochan said, "they discussed the matter. One mouse suggested they kill the cat. But most o' the mice disapproved o' the idea. The cat, after all, couldn't help her nature. Another mouse declared they should have watch-mice set up at points along the wall to report when the cat was on the prowl. But then the youngest mouse—"

"Did the youngest mouse have a name?" Cambel wanted to know.

"A name? I suppose so. What do ye think 'twas?"

"Morris," Cambel decided.

"Right. His name was Morris the Mouse. So wee Morris stood up bravely before the others and said, 'I have a plan.' The older mice scoffed at him, for he was young and inexperienced in the ways o' cats. But they let him speak anyway. He said, 'Why don't we hang a bell around the cat's neck? That way, whene'er we hear the bell ringin', we'll know the cat is nigh.'"

It actually *was* a good idea. In fact, if Colin got his cat, Cristy would have to give him a bell to put around its neck.

Then she remembered...she might not be here when he got his cat.

The thought saddened her. She truly wished to stay—to watch the lads grow up, to help take care of the tower house, to look after the hardworking laird of Macintosh. But Cristy had lived long enough with men who didn't care for her. When she married, it would be to a man who loved her with all his heart.

"At first," Brochan continued with the story, "none o' the mice said a thing. Then, one by one, they saw the genius o' the idea and started exclaimin', ''Tis brilliant! How clever! What a bright wee mouse that Morris is!' But while they were clappin' Morris on the back and tellin' him how lucky they were to have him in the mice council, the oldest, wisest, most respected mouse arose. Now whenever he spoke, the others paid heed, and this is what he said. 'This plan that Morris has is very good. But let me ask ye one question. Who is goin' to hang the bell around the cat's neck?' The mice were struck silent. And as ye can well imagine, none o' them wanted the task."

Cambel giggled.

"The moral, Da, the moral!" cried Colin.

Brochan obliged him. "'Tis far easier to say a thing should be done than to do it."

Colin nudged her. "'Tis a good moral, aye?"

She nodded.

Cambel added, "Da says 'tisn't good enough to be a man o' words. Ye must be a man o' deeds."

"Speakin' o' deeds," Brochan said, "ye lads haven't milked the coos yet this eve."

"Come on, Colin," Cambel said, jumping up from the table. "Let's be men o' deeds."

"Will ye come with us, m'lady?" Colin said. "We'll show ye how we milk the coos."

It was on the tip of her tongue to tell him she already knew how to milk cows. Then she reconsidered.

There was one way she could find out if Brochan loved her. One thing that would prove beyond doubt that he wasn't after a marriage of convenience. It would take great skill and great courage on her part, like belling a cat. But she had to try, because...sometimes it was necessary to be a woman of deeds.

So she smiled and let the lads take her by the hand out of

the hall. She pretended not to notice Brochan's irritation with her for leaving before he had a chance to speak with her alone.

After several minutes of letting the lads show her their milking skills, Cristy left them to their cows, making the excuse that she had to fetch her missing arisaid pin from the dovecot.

Instead, with a backward glance, she stole quietly across the starlit slope, toward the burn that separated the Macintosh and Moffat properties.

If she'd been aware that the lads had seen her leave and would follow her, she would never have gone. By the time she discovered them, she was past the burn, down the road, past the tavern, and deep into the fields of her uncle's holding.

By then it was too late.

For the last mile, she'd had the queer sensation she was being watched. She'd quickly discarded the idea as nonsense. Nobody but her reiving cousins roamed the Moffat holding at this hour.

But the feeling didn't go away. When she heard distant footfalls behind her, she wheeled around, half expecting to see Archibald and the others.

Instead, Cambel and Colin were thrashing through the weeds, trying to catch up with her.

Her heart sank. What the devil were they doing? Why had they followed her?

Before she could hold up a hand to stop him, Colin yelled out, "M'lady, wait for us!"

Fearing discovery by her kin, she put a warning finger of silence to her lips and hurried to meet them.

She crouched before them, whispering, "What are ye lads doin'?"

"Where are ye goin', m'lady?" Cambel whispered back.

Colin's face fell. "Were ye leavin' us?"

Her throat thickened at his sad expression. "Nay, I was only..." How could she explain? "I'm just bein' a woman o' deeds."

"What deeds?" Cambel wanted to know.

She rubbed a hand across her lips. What was she going to do with the lads? She'd come too far to turn back now. And if Brochan discovered his sons had gone missing, another quarter hour would make little difference in their return anyway.

She was tempted to make them wait in the woods while she did what she'd come to do. She knew if they swore on their honor to stay where she put them, she could rely upon their word.

But if any of her clan found them in the forest, they'd turn the lads in to Douglas. And Douglas wouldn't hesitate to use the Macintosh lads the way Macintosh had used Cristy—as hostages.

"What deed, m'lady?" Colin repeated.

There was only one thing to do.

"A deed that requires a special talent, which is why I'm so glad ye came." She squeezed their shoulders. "I could use your help."

When Brochan walked inside the byre, he expected to see the lads dawdling over the milking as they shared their skills with Cristy. Showing off was one thing, but they'd been out there for over an hour. It was past their bedtime, and he needed to find a moment alone with Cristy to see if he could repair the damage he'd done.

What he did not expect to find were full, abandoned milk buckets.

He frowned. Where had the wayward lads gone?

His first thought was the comet. Maybe Cristy had taken them out to the field to get a better look at it.

But he scoured the hillside, to no avail.

Then he wondered if they'd gone to the dovecot. When he ducked inside, it was dark and empty.

Exiting, he narrowed his eyes at the herd of cattle. Could they be out there with the cows?

"Cambel!" he called out. "Colin!"

There was no reply.

A sickly fear prickled at the back of his neck.

Where was Cristy?

She'd been upset. Even at dinner, he could see she wasn't eating. He'd said that stupid thing about her uncle not wanting her back. He couldn't blame her for feeling hurt.

Was she hurt enough to seek retribution?

"Colin!" he shouted. "Cambel!"

He told himself she wouldn't do the lads any harm. They adored her, and she seemed to care for them.

But then he remembered what else he'd said. He'd told Cristy that no child of his would be raised in her uncle's household. He'd threatened to take her bairn away if she had one. And she'd been just as insistent that she wouldn't let him.

Was she upset enough to take *his* children?

A twinge of alarm twisted his heart. If she wished to wound him, she'd pierced him in his softest spot. The lads were everything to him.

He steeled his jaw. Normally, he was a peaceful man. But he'd once been a warrior. And when it came to his sons, he'd take on the entire Moffat clan for them.

Unwilling to waste another moment, he strode with determined haste to the tower to fetch his blade.

Once armed and ready, he stalked with purpose across his fields, past his cattle, and over the burn that divided the properties, his hand clenched around the hilt of his naked sword. Fear had no place in battle, so he pushed down the dread that threatened to unman him. As he covered the miles between the properties, passing the tavern and leaving the road to trespass onto Moffat land, he thought only of his sons and the brute into whose hands they'd been delivered.

Indeed, so intent was he on mustering his courage that he didn't even see the lads until he was almost upon them. When he finally spied them cresting a distant brae, coming his way, he was so filled with relief that at first he was blind to everything except Colin and Cambel.

With renewed hope, he sheathed his sword and bounded toward them.

Then he saw Cristy. And the cows.

Slowing his step, he frowned. What the devil was she up to?

While he watched them, he saw Cristy guiding the lads, keeping a careful pace behind them as they herded one, two, three, four, five cows.

CHAPTER 11

Cristy spied the approaching figure before the lads did. How had Brochan arrived so fast? She'd hoped to have his sons home before he realized they were missing. God's eyes, he was probably furious. She only prayed he'd have enough sense not to bellow at her while they were still on Moffat land.

"Keep the coos movin', lads," she murmured. "Don't look now, but your Da is comin' this way. We can't let him scare the cattle."

Colin whimpered. "Och, nay."

"He'll be so vexed with us," Cambel said.

"He'll be vexed at *me*," Cristy assured them.

"But he'll be glad to have the coos back, aye?" Colin asked hopefully.

She wondered. Once Brochan had his five cows, he'd no longer have an excuse to keep her. So if he wanted her to stay—and she was almost certain he did—he'd have to give her a good reason. And it would have to be more convincing than needing a mother for his sons, help for his housekeeper, or a last name for her bastard.

The closer Brochan got, the more furious he looked. When he

finally drew close enough to keep pace with them, his expression was tense, and his words were clipped. "Are these my coos?"

"Aye."

Cambel said, "M'lady is bringin' them back for ye, Da."

"I don't want them back," he ground out.

His words were meant for her, but the twins gasped in surprise.

"That was the agreement," she said. "Ye get your coos. I get my freedom."

"I won't take them back," he insisted.

She frowned. "Ye have to take them back."

"I refuse."

"Ye can't refuse."

"I do refuse."

The lads suddenly became far more interested in the argument taking place than guiding the cows. They halted, which made the cattle halt.

Cristy stopped, crossing her arms in challenge. "So ye'd rather keep me hostage than get your coos back?"

Brochan stopped, crossing his arms in defiance. "That's right."

"Why?"

He glowered at her.

"Ye've got your coos now and your sons," she said. "Why will ye not take them and let me go? Ye were happy enough before. Why not put things back the way they were?"

He averted his eyes and mumbled something under his breath.

"What?" she asked. "I didn't quite hear that."

His sons were staring at him, awaiting his reply. He scowled, squirming beneath their regard. Then he muttered something again.

She furrowed her brows. "I still didn't catch the words. Did ye, lads?"

The twins shook their heads.

"Perhaps ye could speak up a bit?" she suggested.

Her words might sound sincere, but he could hardly miss the mischief sparking in her eyes.

"Lucifer's ballocks," he said under his breath, shaking his head. Then he threw his arms wide and yelled at the top of his lungs. "Because I love ye, Cristy Moffat!"

She had no time to enjoy his heartfelt declaration. An instant after he shouted, chaos erupted. The cows, startled by the loud noise, scattered. In an effort to protect the lads, she scooped Cambel into her arms while Brochan swept up Colin.

They managed to keep the twins from harm until the cows had run off and they could put the lads down.

But in the next moment, she heard faraway cries of alarm. Moffat's watchmen had been alerted. They knew they were there.

"Run!" she hissed.

They wasted no time, bolting toward Macintosh land as fast as they could. They tore across the grasslands, leaped over rocks, and charged through clumps of heather. When the lads began to fall behind on the road that led past the tavern, Brochan picked them up and carried one on each shoulder. By the time they reached the burn, Cristy could make out a half dozen torchlights in the distance, following them.

They forded the burn and didn't stop running until they were well across Brochan's own border, halfway back to the tower.

At last, too exhausted to continue, Cristy stopped, bending forward at the waist and bracing her hands on her knees. Her lungs burned, and she could hardly catch her breath. Brochan wheezed, his chest heaving as he set the lads back on their feet.

Suddenly the situation struck her as uproariously funny. She couldn't believe she'd gone to all the trouble to reive back his cows, only to have Brochan scatter them all with one outburst. She stifled a laugh.

Brochan must have seen the humor as well, for he looked at her with a sheepish snicker.

She began to giggle.

He chuckled in answer.

One laugh fueled the next. Soon they were overcome with laughter, collapsing onto the ground in uncontrollable hilarity.

The lads frowned down at them.

"What are ye laughin' for?" Colin asked. "We lost the coos again."

"Aye, what's so funny?" Cambel demanded.

Neither Brochan nor she were in any shape to reply. They were laughing too hard. But apparently their humor was catching, because soon the twins joined in until they were helpless with giggles.

When everyone finally sobered, breathless and weary, they made their way back to the tower house.

"Da," Cambel asked when they were almost to the motte, "did ye mean what ye said? Do ye love m'lady?"

Cristy's heart melted when Brochan looked at her and said, "Aye, I do."

"More than coos?" he asked.

He grinned. "Aye, Colin, more than coos."

Cambel asked, "Does she love ye back?"

"Ye'll have to ask *her* that."

Cambel raised his brows to her. "Well?"

"I do," Cristy replied with a smile, adding, "more than coos."

"Are ye goin' to stay with us then?" Cambel asked.

"Are ye goin' to be our Ma?" Colin added.

From the corner of her eye, Cristy saw Brochan tense. And she realized why he'd had such a difficult time confessing his love. He may have lost his wife five years ago. But he was a man of loyalty and chivalry. No doubt it was difficult to let go of his vows, even those that no longer had meaning.

So Cristy crouched down to answer Colin. "No one will e'er be able to replace your Ma, lads. But if your Da will have me, I'll do my best to love ye like a mother."

When she glanced up at Brochan, she could tell by his grateful gaze that her answer pleased him. And when the lads began to cheer and dance about, she knew she'd said the right thing.

Brochan was silent as they climbed the motte and entered the keep. But after handing the twins off to Mabel and hanging up his sword, he took Cristy by the hand.

"Will ye tuck the lads into bed?" he murmured to Mabel. "Miss Moffat and I would like to watch the comet alone tonight."

Cristy couldn't help but shiver with anticipation at his suggestion.

Mabel, who was hardly naïve, took the twins in hand and gave Cristy a wink. "Come along, lads," she said, "and I'll tell ye the story o' *The Ant and the Grasshopper*."

As Brochan spread his gray woolen brat for Cristy on the crest of the motte, he felt like a changed man. Propped on his elbow beside her, gazing out at his woods, his fields, his slumbering herd of cattle, he no longer saw an overwhelming responsibility, but a shared vision. Now that he'd let Cristy into his heart, it seemed a weight had been lifted from his shoulders. He was no longer alone.

He threaded his fingers through hers as they looked up at the shimmering comet.

"Do ye think 'tis true?" she murmured.

"What?"

"That ye can change your stars?"

"I know 'tis true," he said.

She smiled. "'Twas the comet that brought us together, ye know."

"I know."

She leaned her head against his as she gazed up at the comet. "I think the star is starin' down on us now and smilin'."

He turned to kiss her brow. "Do ye think it might be willin' to close its eyes for a wee bit?"

Cristy grinned. "I think it would be more than willin'."

Brochan had never made love under the stars. But he was feeling transformed, and somehow it seemed the right thing to do.

He lifted Cristy's hand and kissed her knuckles. Her lips parted, and he leaned forward to capture them between his own.

His blood went from warm to fiery in an instant. A roaring rush of desire flowed through his ears. He felt the tug of need in his trews before the kiss ended.

But he didn't want to hurry. Their first tryst had been impulsive and frantic. He'd given little thought to anything but slaking his thirst.

He wanted this joining to be special. This time, he'd give her the patience and care she deserved.

Brushing the hair back from her face, he pressed a soft kiss to each eyelid.

She sighed in pleasure and placed a hand on his chest.

He kissed her sweet mouth again, letting his fingers drift along her temples, across her cheeks, and along her neck, leaving a trail of feather-light touches that made her quiver.

Slipping his fingers beneath the neck edge of her kirtle, he gently nudged it from her shoulder. Then, tipping her head aside, he placed a row of slow and deliberate kisses from the point of her shoulder up to her ear.

By the time he reached her ear, she was squirming in lusty torment. When he caught the delicate lobe between his teeth, she gasped. And when he let his tongue slip around the rim, she moaned with need.

He let out a worldly chuckle. She might grow impatient, but he still had a long way to go. They had all night, after all, and he intended to show the inexperienced lass every delicious enticement he knew.

Cristy didn't want to wait. She'd waited her whole life to belong. And now that she'd found the man with whom she could share her laughter, her tears, her fears and hopes, she didn't wish to waste another moment. She wanted to share her body with him. Now.

With desperate haste, before he could stop her, she unlaced her kirtle. She dragged it, along with her linen leine, down over her shoulders and past her hips, kicking the garments off her legs. While his jaw was still gaping, she lunged forward into his arms, rocking him onto his back.

The kiss she stole was full of passion and promise, fire and heart. It was the kiss she'd been saving all her life.

After his initial shock, Brochan answered her caresses, licking tenderly at her lips and weaving his fingers through the curtain of her hair.

The ache between her thighs was powerful and compelling. And now that she knew the joy to come, she couldn't help but wish to hurry.

She fumbled at his trews, eager to free that amazing part of him that would grant her relief.

He caught her fingers and unlaced his trews himself. Then, taking control again, he clasped the back of her head. Wrapping his arm around her bare waist, he rolled with her until she lay on her back at the edge of the woolen brat.

From here, she could see the stars sparkling overhead like raindrops against the peat-dark sky. But when she shifted her gaze, she saw something even more beautiful. Brochan's eyes were glistening with love and desire.

Slowly, he removed his own garments, and she felt the twinge of yearning with every inch of skin he exposed. He belonged to her now—this magnificent man with the broad shoulders and wide chest, breathtaking arms and towering legs, a chivalrous spirit and a loving heart.

When he came to her, their joining was tender. This time there was no pain, only fulfillment. And when they rode together on passion's heavenly comet, a pure white light seemed to bless their union. Faster and faster they shot across the sky until the brilliant light shattered and scattered into a thousand bright stars.

Afterward, they lay together, side-by-side and hand-in-hand, gazing up at the night sky. They spoke of dreams and plans and wishes for the future. They mused over the gardens they would plant, the animals they would keep for the twins, and the Macintosh bairns they would make. And they marveled over the strange woman it seemed they'd both met at the tavern by chance, wondering whether it had been by chance at all.

As Cristy stared at the curious comet that had crossed her path and changed her fortune, she couldn't help but believe in the magic of the summer star.

The End

More books from the Medieval Outlaws series:
Danger's Kiss
Passion's Exile
Desire's Ransom

the outcast

A Scottish Lasses Novella

A broken Scots warrior believes nothing can mend the wounds of war until a young lass stumbles into his cottage and heals him with the most magical power of all—love.

DEDICATION

For wounded warriors and incurable nerds
Everywhere...
I love you just the way you are.

ACKNOWLEDGMENTS

Special thanks to:

Tanya and Laurin for taking a wary Hobbit
on a special journey,

Lauren Royal for being a genius and a cheerleader,

my sister Jewels of Historical Romance
for their loving support,

The Crown Jewels—best street team on the planet,

Charlie Hunnam and Amy Acker for inspiration,

and my husband Rich
for fun-filled geeky discussions.

CHAPTER 1

Keirfield, Scotland
Late November, 1542

Biera blew out a frosty breath and narrowed her one good eye at the cottage door.

Never had she felt so full of doubt. For hundreds of years the wise old crone had served as the Guardian of the Winter Stone. She'd borne the honorable burden of passing the treasure from Keeper to Keeper all through the ages. And she'd never failed to find the right Keeper for the precious relic.

But this time, something felt wrong.

Still, the rare round crystal in the wooden claw of her staff glowed with soft assurance, illuminating the snowflakes falling gently in the dark around her. She lifted the staff for a third time to rap on the door.

Finally she heard a shuffling scrape from within the cottage. After a long moment, the door creaked open a few inches.

Through the crack, a scruffy blond-headed giant frowned down at her with groggy, bloodshot eyes of gray. She could smell the whisky on him.

She frowned back. His hair was the wrong color. His eyes were the wrong shade.

Also wrong were the features of the second head that suddenly jutted out just below his—grizzled gray hair with brown eyes. Worse, they belonged to a gigantic slobbering deerhound.

She grimaced.

There wasn't much time. The new queen was about to be born—the old king about to die. The Scottish army had just suffered a harrowing defeat at the Battle of Solway Moss. The fate of all Scotland resided in the Winter Stone. Putting it into the right hands was crucial.

Biera tightened her grip on the staff and lifted a hopeful brow. "Anyone else livin' here?"

Lachlan squeezed his eyes shut. A moment ago, he'd been asleep and dreaming. Before that, he'd been drunk. 'Twas hard to tell anymore what was real and what wasn't. But when he opened his eyes again, the old crone was still there.

"God's bones, woman," he growled. "What are ye doin' out on a night like this? Ye'll catch your death o'—"

"Time's a-wastin'," she interjected, dismissing him with an irritated wave of her hand. "Aye or nae? Is there another livin' here?"

Lachlan Mar wasn't in the habit of receiving visitors ever, let alone at this ungodly hour. Hell, he wasn't even dressed. He'd managed to slip a linen shirt over his head, and he'd pulled on his trews, but he hadn't bothered lacing them, and he didn't know where his doublet had gone.

He sighed. He knew he shouldn't have answered the door. Anyone who'd wander the woods alone on a snowy winter's eve had to be daft.

What had she asked him—whether anyone else lived here?

Someone else *had* lived here, but no more. Margaret had fled less than a fortnight after Lachlan came home from the war.

"A couple o' mice maybe," he grunted, half hoping to scare the woman off.

'Twas against his nature to let people into his cottage. 'Twas his refuge, his escape, a place he could drink away his troubles and hide from his past.

But the old woman didn't look like she was leaving any time soon.

And as indifferent as he wanted to be, 'twas also against his nature to let people freeze to death on his threshold.

He rested his forehead against the edge of the door. 'Twould only be till morn, he supposed. He'd let her warm her bones by the fire and then send her on her way at daylight. And that would be that.

Besides, 'twasn't as if she'd mock his...deformity. A one-eyed woman could hardly make a fuss over a one-legged man.

He took hold of Campbell's collar to keep the hound from charging and opened the door wider.

Her gaze immediately flew to his crutch and his abbreviated leg, and she gasped.

"Ye're crippled?" she bluntly exclaimed, then continued in a mutter, "Nae, that canna be right. Ye dinna have the right features. And ye're sotted to boot. Somethin's gone awry."

He clenched his jaw, tamping down the urge to tell her those were rather bold words coming from a withered, one-eyed old crone. At least she wasn't throwing rocks at him like the village lads used to...before he'd acquired his fearsome deerhound.

Finally sighing in surrender, he tried to coax her forward with a nod of his head. "Come in out o' the cold, grandmother, ere the frost cracks your frail bones."

A keen twinkle appeared in her eye then, and she let out a soft cackle. "These frail bones have withstood a thousand fierce winters. 'Twould take more than a wee bit o' snow to pierce my hide."

She was definitely daft, he decided. She looked ancient, aye, but a thousand winters? She couldn't be more than seventy years old. And no one could long endure the cold of a Scottish winter without the benefit of shelter. He was shivering just from the flurry of snowflakes that had swept in through the door. Even his hound had known enough to come in for the night.

Lachlan perused the crone slowly from the top of her woolen hood to the tips of her snow-covered boots as she studied him in return. Then he noticed the wooden staff she was holding. The claw at the top of it held a frosty white crystal in the shape of a perfect sphere. 'Twas glowing with a strange light.

At first he thought it must be his imagination. Sometimes when he'd been drinking, he saw things that weren't real. Maybe the old woman wasn't real either.

Then she made a grab for his arm, nearly knocking the crutch out from under him, dispelling that notion.

"Give me your hand," she commanded.

Stunned by her suddenly forceful manner, he froze.

"Your hand!" she insisted.

He unfurled his fist, and she tipped the staff toward him. The claw released, dropping the heavy, round crystal into his palm. It was cold and polished smooth, a milky white stone almost as large as a hen's egg.

Her eye snapped as she asked him, "Will ye be the one to take the Winter Stone to its rightful Keeper?"

He scowled. What was the woman blathering about? Winter Stone? Rightful Keeper? That sounded suspiciously like it might involve a journey. Was she jesting? On one leg, Lachlan could scarcely walk to the spring and back, let alone embark on a journey to deliver some trinket for her.

"Will ye?" she demanded, shaking his arm roughly. For a

wee woman, she was certainly strong. Perhaps madness did that to a person. "Answer me!" she spat, her gaze ferocious.

The corners of his mouth turned down. He supposed he wouldn't be able to pry his arm from her grip until he gave her an answer. He grumbled, "Aye. Why not? I'll take it."

"To its rightful heir? The one with dark hair and bright green eyes?"

"Aye. Fine." That should assuage the mad crone.

The old woman seized his hand then and peered closely at the stone. It seemed to throw off a curious rosy shimmer as she did so. Apparently satisfied by what she'd glimpsed, she nodded and grunted and closed his fingers around the stone.

"Then I'll be off," she stated. "'Tis in your hands now. Keep it safe. 'Tisn't a thing to take lightly. The Winter Stone has the power to change your fate."

"My fate, ach, o' course, I see," he said to placate her. Then he turned aside for a moment to pull Campbell out of the way. "Now that that's settled, be a good lass. Come in and warm yourself by the—"

When he turned back, she was gone, vanished like mist in the snowy night. If not for the milky round stone in his palm, he might have believed he'd imagined the whole encounter.

He called out loudly. He even sent Campbell to search for her, not relishing the idea of finding a dead woman in front of his cottage on the morrow. But the deerhound came ambling back with his head lowered in guilt, unable to find her.

"That's all right, lad." Lachlan scratched the hound behind his ears. "Ye did your best." He squinted into the dark night, but 'twas impossible to see more than a few yards. "God willin', she'll find her way to shelter." Under his breath, he added, "Or we'll be thawin' her carcass out come morn." With that unsavory thought, he tossed the round stone out the door and into the snow.

Campbell immediately raced outside after it.

"Nae, lad!"

His command had no effect. The hound spent several moments nosing around in the snow until he found the bauble, picked it up, and came trotting back to the cottage, depositing it on the flagstone floor before Lachlan.

Lachlan gave him a rueful smile. He supposed the poor pup was starved for play. A man with a missing leg was not the ideal companion for a hound accustomed to running down deer.

Maybe he should be kind to the faithful beast and hand him over to someone who could exercise him properly...someone who was still useful...someone with two legs.

A familiar sharp twinge seized his heart, taking him by surprise. After three months, he thought he'd be used to his infirmity, used to the frustration and hopelessness. But his wounds still ached. The real pain of his useless existence gnawed at him daily, just like the false pain of his missing limb.

He sniffed sharply, then picked up the stone and tossed it once in his palm. It looked changed somehow, its rosy glow darkened to a muddy shade. But change his fate? Nothing could do that. With a bitter oath, he cast the thing away, back into the frozen night.

Before he could stop the hound, Campbell bounded out the door and after it again.

Lachlan shook his head at the fool dog. Maybe the thick-furred hound could stand the cold, but *he* was beginning to shiver, standing in the open doorway in nothing but his trews and his linen shirt. And Campbell would doubtless bring half the snowdrifts back into the cottage with him when he returned.

The hound again brought the stone between his teeth, his panting making fog in the chill air. He lowered his head and set his treasure gently on the floor once more.

"'Tisn't a game, lad," Lachlan explained, retrieving the stone.

"Sit." The hound obeyed. "Stay." He gave the hound a stern look, and then heaved the stone as far as he could one last time.

To his astonishment, the normally obedient deerhound leaped up and out the doorway, pushing aside the door when Lachlan tried to close it, almost upending his master in the process.

"Campbell!" Lachlan shouted. "What the devil?"

He didn't know what had gotten into the dog. Campbell always followed his master's commands. He was a faithful beast and served Lachlan well, hunting down game to keep them both fed.

But it seemed as if a strange wind had blown in with the snowstorm, disturbing the natural order of things. What else could explain a midnight visit from a one-eyed crone, her curious glowing crystal, the woman's sudden disappearance, and now his disobedient dog? Something unusual was definitely in the air.

"Campbell!" he called again. He'd thrown the stone a good distance, and he feared his persistent hound might freeze himself looking for it.

But just about the time he'd decided he was going to have to grab his cloak and limp after the dog, Campbell trotted up proudly with his prize, thoughtfully shaking the snow off of his fur before he entered the cottage.

Lachlan smirked. "Fine." He bent to pick up the stone. He would have sworn it glinted blue for an instant before he closed his hand around it and shut the door against the swirling snowflakes. "We'll leave it here then." He hobbled over to the hearth and set the piece on the stone mantel, where it seemed to wink at him. He frowned. "Just don't expect it to change your fate, lad," he said, giving the hound a scratch on his damp head. "I'm afraid ye're stuck with me."

Campbell looked satisfied with that. He circled three times and settled down before the dwindling fire.

Lachlan couldn't settle down so easily. He poked at the coals, adding another log and stirring the fire back to life, igniting his own whirling thoughts as well.

As mad as the crone had seemed, he was haunted by her promise. He wished he *could* change his fate. Indeed, he wished he'd died along with his brothers three months ago at Haddon Rig.

That wish brought back painful memories, memories he'd fought hard to suppress. But tonight, with the world a bleak, frozen, isolated place, they hit him full-force. His throat ached with grief as angry tears welled in his eyes.

The words came to him as they always did.

He should be dead.

His brothers were dead—all four of them. They'd been killed on that bloody battlefield, slain by English blades, their bodies trampled beneath English horses. Lachlan had promised his father he'd look out for them, and he'd failed.

Why had he been spared? Why hadn't he died in glorious battle with them instead of suffering a grievous wound and living in lonely exile as half a man?

Children feared him. Men pitied him. And women? They recoiled from him, as his dear Margaret had, sickened by his hideous disfigurement.

This wasn't surviving. 'Twas punishment.

He *should* be dead.

He lowered himself onto his bed and stared into the harsh flames. There was only one way to cope with these fits of melancholy that turned him from the brave soldier he'd once been into the weepy, self-pitying wretch he was now.

He eyed the jack of whisky he'd left on the table. There was enough left to bring him drunken oblivion, maybe enough to make him forget for one night the horrific Battle of Haddon Rig.

Chapter 2

Alisoune Hay's heart pounded painfully. They were coming after her. She wheezed through her burning lungs, cursing her tight stomacher, and squinted in the bright morning sunlight as she floundered through the thick fallen snow. Her satchel flopped against her thigh as she hoisted her sodden skirts up with one hand and held her spectacles onto her nose with the other.

She could hear the irate shouts of the townsfolk as they pursued her. Some of them were calling her witch. Some were calling her blasphemer. And some of them were calling her things she pretended not to hear.

'Twasn't the first time she'd earned the disapproval of an entire town. As her parents had oft remarked, Alisoune's mouth was even bigger than her brain. And that was saying something.

Usually the people in the towns she passed through dismissed her opinions as the brash ravings of an impertinent young lass. But this time they'd taken her more seriously. This time, according to the awful red-haired priest who'd instigated the hasty proceedings against her, she'd spoken against common wisdom, God's will, and the very nature of the known world.

But that had been precisely her point. The world was *not* known. In fact, science had barely scratched the surface of the vast realm of knowledge. How could man possibly pretend to know everything about the universe?

She suddenly stumbled over her dark green skirts and fell face-down in the snow. She heard a shout behind her and felt an instant of panic as the ground blurred in her vision. Patting feverishly about with her hand, she finally located her fallen spectacles and perched them again on her nose. They were wet and covered with snowflakes, but at least she could see.

Scrambling to her feet, she surged forward. She hadn't expected the crowd to follow her so far. And by their growing rage, it seemed they intended to do something more dire than merely run her out of town.

Now that her parents had gone to France and left the business to Alisoune, she had no one to placate the townsfolk and assuage their anger. She'd already tried to explain herself in a reasonable fashion and even resorted to offering the priest money to withdraw his claim. But that had only gotten her into more trouble.

"Burn the witch!" she heard in the distance.

Her breath caught, and she tried to slog faster through the snow, despite the cold, throbbing ache in her chest. They couldn't be serious. Burn her?

What could she do? Where could she go? She quickly cataloged her options.

She had no horse, no cart. There was no church nearby for sanctuary. There wasn't even a troupe of players or a group of pilgrims to vanish into, which was her usual mode of safe transportation from town to town.

If only she owned a pair of those wooden planks the Danish soldiers attached to their feet, she thought, she might be able to glide across the snow and lose her pursuers.

Or even better...one of those man-carrying kites invented by the ancient Chinese that could allow a person to fly over the treetops.

But she had neither. And no matter how diligently she tried to employ that big brain of hers, she could think of no plausible escape.

She certainly didn't want to be burned at the stake as a witch. 'Twas an unpleasant way to die, especially if the wood didn't create enough smoke to asphyxiate her first and she was forced to endure the flesh-scorching heat of the flames.

She let out an involuntary squeak of remorse. Why did she always have to think in such exquisite detail? Sometimes she wished her brain wasn't quite so big and that she could wool-gather her way through life like more simpleminded lasses, without a care.

The shouting grew louder, and she increased her pace, wincing at the stitch in her side. But she'd already done the calculations. Despite her long legs, the weight of her skirts gave the men following her at least a fifty percent advantage when it came to speed. They'd catch up to her in a matter of moments.

Then she saw something she hadn't figured into the equation—a seemingly abandoned cottage nestled at the edge of the forest.

Maybe she could hide there.

Her instincts for survival renewed, she bolted toward the place.

Before she'd gone two yards, the door of the cottage opened wide, and out charged a great gray beast. As if propelled by rockets, it began running straight toward her.

She gasped. When it leaped at her, all she saw was a scruffy face full of gray fur and a huge gaping maw full of sharp teeth. The animal knocked her down with its paws. Once she'd fallen softly onto the snow, it began to mercilessly lick her face.

It never hurt her. In fact, when the hound—which was the biggest dog she'd ever seen—heard the men yelling in the distance, it growled deep in its throat and nudged her as if telling her to get up and move before they arrived.

She grabbed her spectacles and satchel and staggered forward. The hound enthusiastically bounded around her, guiding her toward the cottage.

At the threshold, she glanced back once to see that the mob of a dozen or so men had spotted her. They bolted forward, their snapping cloaks and foul mood a dark contrast to the bright snow.

Then she swept into the cottage with the dog, slamming the door behind her.

Lachlan, still half-asleep, winced and groaned as the cottage shook from the impact of the door slamming. He opened one eye. The other felt like it was sealed shut. His mouth was as dry as plaster. And his head throbbed from the aftereffects of too much whisky.

"Campbell," he moaned. Over the past few weeks, the hound had somehow learned how to open the latch on the cottage door and tended to come and go as he pleased.

But the scuffling didn't quite sound like his hound. And when Lachlan managed to pry open his other eye, both eyes went suddenly wide at the sight before him.

Instinctively, he rose up on his elbows. "Who are *ye?*"

The tall young woman in the green gown blinked in surprise, as if she didn't expect to see anyone actually inhabiting the cottage. At least he *thought* she blinked. 'Twas hard to tell, because her eyes were shielded by two round pieces of glass perched atop her nose.

Before she could answer him, there was a loud pounding at the door. She dove for the bed, sailing over him to wriggle beneath the bed linens and pull the sheepskin coverlet over her head.

He was still reeling in shock at her boldness when the pounding came again, accompanied by irate shouts.

She started at the sound, and he felt her cold, naked leg brush against his as her small icy fist burrowed beneath his hip.

He glanced down at the shivering mound of sheepskin beside him. The woman was clearly hiding from whoever was outside. And whoever was outside clearly knew she was here. The last thing Lachlan needed was to get caught in the crossfire.

The pounding resumed, louder this time, and the woman peeked out long enough to plead with him in an urgent whisper. "I beg ye, sir, hide me. I fear they mean to burn me at the stake." She was pale from the cold, but her cheeks were rosy from exertion, and she was quivering like a cornered mouse. Indeed, with her longish nose and those big spectacles, she looked a bit like a mouse. "Please, sir, please. Keep me safe."

Then he frowned. *Keep her safe.* He was the last person to be trusted to keep someone safe. His brothers had depended on him to keep them safe. Four gravestones were proof of how that had ended.

But Campbell was staring expectantly at the door. And Lachlan knew he had to answer it. If whoever was outside intended to burn the woman at the stake, they might be carrying torches even now. And they might decide to make quick work of it by setting his whole cottage on fire.

With as little fuss as possible, Lachlan eased his right leg over the edge of the bed, tucked his crutch under his left arm, and pushed up. As usual, he staggered, and his head started throbbing, but he managed to regain his balance and limp over to the doorway.

He snatched open the door. "What do ye want?" he demanded harshly.

At least a dozen townsmen crowded together, trying to peer past him into the one-room cottage. He knew the men, though in the last three months since he'd moved back to Keirfield, he'd kept mostly to himself. Now—whether 'twas due to his rough and ragged appearance, his stern scowl, or his growling hound—nobody answered his question.

"Ye hauled me out o' bed with your infernal racket," he bit out. "So what do ye want?"

Finally, Father Ninian, the red-haired parish priest, gathered up enough courage to raise his quivering double-chin, demanding, "Hand over the lass, and we'll leave ye to your affairs."

Lachlan wondered what on earth a wee lass could have done to incur the wrath of this mob. Two of the villagers had their daggers drawn, four more wielded spades, and all of them had feverish fire in their eyes. He didn't care if the woman had butchered their livestock and set their fields on fire. 'Twas an unfair fight, and he didn't like unfair fights.

"Lass?" he dared them. "What lass?"

The father narrowed his pale blue eyes and began shuddering with rage. "Ye know very well," he growled. "We saw her run in here."

Lachlan looked down from a considerable height on all of the men. "Did ye?"

The townsfolk muttered in agreement.

He cast a quick backward glance at his bed to assure the lass was well-hidden. Then he opened the door far enough for them to see the interior of his cottage. "Well, I don't see her now. Do ye?"

Father Ninian charged forward, elbowing aside his fellows. "Out o' my way. I'll find that Satan's spawn."

The deerhound growled.

"I wouldn't do that if I were ye," Lachlan warned. "I've seen Campbell here tear a man limb from limb."

'Twasn't at all true. Campbell was keen for rabbit and could take down a small deer. But he mostly just growled at strangers.

Still, Father Ninian didn't know that. So for the sake of

caution, the priest backed away. Then he stabbed a threatening finger at Lachlan and snarled, "Ye mark my words, Mar, 'tisn't the end of it. Ye're harborin' a daughter o' the dèvil, and I mean to see her punished for her blasphemy."

With that, the father spun on his heel, and the mob marched off with him, grumbling empty threats to the air as they made their way across the rutted snow.

Lachlan closed the door and turned back to the bed. Blasphemy? Daughter of the devil? God's eyes, what had the woman done? Maybe he'd made a mistake, not turning her over to them.

"They're gone," he said cautiously. "Ye're safe."

Tentative fingers crept out from under the sheepskin. Almost without knowing he did so, Lachlan braced himself for her gasp. Women always gasped when they first saw him, even those who tried to be polite.

When she threw back the sheepskin all at once, her spectacles went flying. But her face beamed as she sat up with a broad, grateful grin.

Lachlan arched a brow in surprise. Now that he could see all of her clearly, he decided that while she might be a trifle mouse-like, she wasn't an unattractive lass. Her hair was the color of dark, wet wood. Her smile was soft and sweet. And her eyes reminded him of the first tender grass of spring.

Indeed, he thought with mild irritation, she glowed like a beam of sunshine—a ray of blinding white light to awaken him from his comfortable, numb slumber.

He exhaled. She seemed like she might be the cheery sort who'd try to drag him, kicking and screaming, into her bright world, a world in which he no longer belonged.

"Oh, sir, ye were magnificent!" she crowed, patting the feather-filled mattress for her lost spectacles. "Threatenin' them with your hound. But that big, droolin' beast wouldn't harm a flea, would he?"

"Campbell? Nae," he grunted, eyeing her spectacles on the floor.

"I can't thank ye enough, kind sir." She hadn't gasped yet, but maybe without her spectacles she was blind. "I owe ye my life."

He stiffened, reminded of the dead men who'd trusted him with their lives.

She continued to rummage through the blankets for her spectacles. Lachlan was in no great hurry to return them to her. "If it hadn't been for your lovely hound and your quick—"

He snorted.

"What?" she asked.

"Lovely?"

"He *is* lovely," she said with a coy smile. "And so are ye...for keepin' me safe."

There 'twas again, that phrase—*keeping her safe*. Those were the same words the old crone had used for the strange crystal. *Keep it safe.* He glanced over at the mantel. The stone was still there, safe for the moment.

As for the lass, she hadn't gasped yet. In fact, she'd just called him lovely. Now he *knew* she was blind.

He couldn't continue to let her search in vain. Besides, though he'd held off the angry mob for the moment, he didn't want to harbor a fugitive, no matter how bonnie she was. 'Twas probably best she get her gasping over with and go on her way.

Leaning on his crutch, he bent down to retrieve her spectacles and put them into her hands, and then hobbled toward the hearth.

"Oh, thank ye," she said, fumbling them back onto her nose. "Honestly, ye'd think I'd told the priest that the world was flat or some such..."

By her hesitation, he knew she'd spotted his deformity. But she didn't gasp. Instead, to his amazement, she cooed in wonder.

"Ahh, ye've got a missin' limb!" She scrambled to perch on

the edge of the bed and began chattering with rapt enthusiasm. "A most fascinatin' circumstance! Ye can sometimes feel it as though 'tis still there, can't ye? 'Tis called phantom pain. Benedetti believes that nerves are like the roots of a tree. Yet no one has been able to discover why, when the root is cut, the sensation o' the limb remains long after..." She trailed off at the sight of his furrowed brow. "Oh, I'm sorry. I'm bein' impolite, aren't I?"

She *was* being terribly blunt. But for some reason it didn't trouble him. She seemed genuinely interested in his condition and, to his consternation, not at all appalled by it.

She fidgeted with the satchel that was still draped diagonally over one shoulder. "My mother always said I was cursed with too much curiosity and candor. She said I had no stopper on the keg o' my thoughts. Anyway, I didn't mean to offend ye, especially after all ye've—"

"Are ye hungry?" he asked suddenly, and then just as suddenly regretted his invitation. What the devil was he thinking? He barely had two sticks to rub together, let alone the wherewithal to entertain company. Besides, hadn't he just decided against harboring a fugitive?

A quick lick of her lips gave her away, but she said, "I don't wish to impose."

"'Tis no imposition," he lied. Even as he spoke the words, he thought he must be a fool for letting her linger. After all, no good could possibly come of it.

He limped over to the hearth and coaxed the smoldering coals to waken. Then he rummaged in his cupboard for his store of oats and raided the bowl of apples sitting on the shelf beneath it.

She patted her knees, summoning Campbell to her. Scratching the spoiled beast's shaggy head, she murmured to him. "That's a good canine. If ye vow not to tear me limb from limb, I'll share my breakfast with ye."

The hound licked her face, knocking her spectacles askew, and she giggled.

Somewhere deep inside, Lachlan felt his frozen heart thaw a little at her laughter. 'Twas a lovely sound, one he hadn't heard in a long while. It felt like the comforting heat of a winter's bath on a frosty day...which reminded him...it had been a week or more since he'd had a bath.

He had little reason to bathe. Margaret had left him. He saw no one else. He seldom went out. Besides, on one leg, 'twas an ordeal to fetch enough water for a bath.

He probably stank. His clothes were filthy. His overlong hair hung like tangled straw. He hadn't bothered to trim his beard in weeks.

Suddenly self-conscious, he pulled together his doublet and buttoned it over his rumpled linen shirt. He tucked his unruly hair behind his ears and dipped into the bucket of water to one side of the hearth, giving his face a quick scrub and rinsing out his mouth. Then, silently cursing himself for even caring, he set to work at the wooden table, preparing the oats and peeling and cutting the apple, occasionally casting sidelong glances at the lass, who seemed to be making herself at home in his shabby hovel.

She was almost as tall as he was, a bonnie, scrawny, gangly bit of a thing with narrow shoulders and a neck no bigger than the trunk of a sapling. Much of the long, dark hair she'd pulled back into a braid had come loose, and wild tendrils curled down her cheeks and across her small bosom. Her eyes were large and of a most unusual green that almost seemed to glow. But that might be due to the magnifying lenses of the spectacles.

What made his heart catch was her smile. 'Twas a smile of gratitude as she wordlessly thanked him for making her breakfast, a smile of acceptance as she perused his rundown cottage, a smile of pure joy as she fawned over his hound.

The Outcast

How anyone could think the bonnie angel before him was the daughter of the devil, Lachlan couldn't imagine. But he supposed he should find investigate further.

CHAPTER 3

Alisoune had never seen a cottage, or a man, so woefully neglected. He must live on his own, she decided, for no woman she knew would let a place, or a husband, become so untidy.

Cobwebs hung from every corner. Dust covered every surface. The ash was thick in the fireplace. And there were enough crumbs on the kitchen shelves and on the flagstone floor to sustain a healthy colony of mice.

Of course, it must be challenging to keep a house clean when one was forced to move about on one leg, no matter how otherwise robust one was.

The man was definitely robust. Though his linen shirt and trews were crumpled and his doublet stained, and though he was in sorry need of a bath and a shave, he was in splendid physical condition. Few men could match Alisoune's height, but this one was over six feet tall by her estimates, broad of chest and brawny of build. No doubt he'd developed those wide, muscular shoulders using a crutch to compensate for his missing leg.

As far as how he'd lost it... By the sword, shield, and armor tossed into one of the corners, she deduced he'd been a soldier.

Wounds like that happened all the time when men insisted on battling with barbaric weapons like sharpened claymores.

But she had no scientific explanation for the way her heart was pulsing unnaturally as she watched him prepare the porridge. Something about the way his disheveled hair framed his bearded jaw...his muscled forearms hung the heavy iron pot over the fire with ease...his silver eyes narrowed at the flickering flames...made her blood feel suddenly warm and her heart beat a wee bit fast.

'Twasn't an altogether unpleasant feeling, and she was content to have it continue.

When the porridge began to simmer, he stirred the apples into the pot and asked casually, "So how did ye manage to incur the wrath o' the good people o' Keirfield?" He popped a stray bit of apple into his mouth and chewed.

She eyed him uncertainly. There had been a sardonic edge to his voice as he said "good people," but she didn't want to risk incurring his wrath as she had theirs. Sometimes the things Alisoune found interesting, others found deeply disturbing.

"'Twas naught," she said with an insincere shrug. "I was only passin' on a kernel o' knowledge...somethin' that could change the manner in which we view the entire universe. That's all."

He stopped chewing and stirring and arched dubious brows at her. "What?"

She couldn't help herself then. 'Twas such an exciting piece of news. Keeping it secret was harder than keeping a jack in its box. Her eyes lit up as she told him about Copernicus's latest theory. "'Tis quite possible—highly likely, in fact—that 'tis not the Earth which is at the center of our galaxy, but indeed the Sun, and that all the planets revolve around it."

He swallowed the bit of apple, and his expression went from dubious to amused. But 'twasn't the sort of amused scorn to which she'd grown accustomed. 'Twas more like amused fascination. "Ye think so?"

"*Copernicus* thinks so."

He resumed stirring. "Copernicus."

"Aye, the Prussian astronomer. 'Tis his heliocentric hypothesis."

He didn't even try to repeat that. "How do ye know about matters of astronomy?"

She straightened with pride and gave him a conspiratorial wink. "A woman o' my profession has access to all sorts o' men in high places."

His smile froze. His spoon suddenly slipped, and he burned his finger on the pot's rim. Then, quickly popping the injured digit into his mouth, he mumbled, "Your...profession?"

"Aye." She hefted up her satchel. "I'm a spectacle-seller."

He seemed relieved. "A spectacle-seller. Oh. Aye. O' course."

"I've sold spectacles to some o' the most esteemed academics in Scotland," she said proudly.

"Is that so?"

"Aye. Would ye like to see them?"

He gave her a puzzled frown. "The academics?"

"Nay," she chided with a giggle. "My spectacles."

A soft shimmer came into his gray eyes, like a candle appearing in the fog, as she saw he was only jesting with her.

Nobody ever jested with her. People usually thought she wasn't quite right in the head. The fact that he was treating her like an ordinary person suffused her with a sweet warmth.

Lachlan knew he shouldn't encourage the lass. 'Twas pointless. Besides, he needed to send her away before...before he started getting second thoughts about sending her away.

Still, when she looked at him with that damned sunny gleam in her eyes, how could he resist? He left the wooden spoon in the pot, wedged the crutch under his arm, and hobbled toward the bed.

She popped up, pulled a small box out of her satchel, and opened it. A neat row of spectacles were nestled inside, between strips of cloth which he presumed protected the glass from scratches.

"The lenses come in various strengths, dependin' on the need," she explained. "Most buy cheap leather frames, which can be replaced when they wear thin. But for the more affluent patron, they're made o' metal or ox bone or, like this pair..." She carefully lifted out a special pair of spectacles and handed them to him. "Polished horn."

Lachlan pretended to admire the spectacles. But in truth, he found the lass showing them to him to be far more intriguing. As he handed them back to her, he tried again to see through the spectacles she was wearing. Her eyes had looked grass green before. But now they seemed to twinkle like emeralds.

She looked up to catch him staring. "Ah, ye've noticed my own spectacles," she guessed incorrectly. "And ye probably want to know why the spectacle-seller wears simple leather frames." She slipped him a confiding grin. "I'll tell ye a wee secret. In fact, the true value is in the lenses. 'Tis no easy task..."

She halted, probably because he was indeed staring at her, unable to tear his gaze away from her smiling face. How long had it been since a woman had looked at him without cringing in horror?

"No easy task," she repeated, "findin' the perfect magnification." Her eyelids dipped, and she gulped, speaking more slowly. "And once ye do..."

She was staring back at him now. Her eyes looked like deep verdant pools. "'Tis best to hold onto them," she said, her voice growing softer, "and...and..."

He swallowed hard. 'Twas so rare—a moment like this when he didn't feel like the village monster, when he felt like a man, whole and hale—that he didn't want it to end. He was afraid to move, afraid to speak, afraid to look away. He scarcely breathed the word. "And?"

"And replace the frames when they're..." she trailed off, lowering the spectacles in her hand.

He didn't think. He didn't plan. He simply reached up and gently removed the spectacles from her nose and looked deep into her eyes. Apple green. Fern green. The green of new leaves in May and soft moss in clear pools.

His gaze lowered then to her rosy lips. How long had it been since he'd had that sweet taste, since he'd felt the soft caress of a woman? It seemed an eternity since he'd shared a kiss...and he doubted he'd ever have another chance.

But his heart squeezed in pain even as he dared to hope. No matter how great his hunger, this lass wasn't his to have. He didn't deserve such sweetness anyway. And 'twas not his way to force himself upon a woman. He might have lost his leg, but he hadn't lost his honor. 'Twas disrespectful and unchivalrous to...

The lass suddenly dropped the expensive spectacles to the floor and surged toward him. Before he could blink, she caught his face between her palms and planted a hard kiss square on his mouth.

What had possessed her, Alisoune didn't know. 'Twas quite unscientific. All she could fathom was that there was a prime specimen of a man standing within reach, that he was mysteriously attractive to her, and that something about the way he was regarding her made every nerve in her body quicken.

Her brain suddenly seemed to shut off, and she couldn't summon up a single intelligent thought.

Some other part of her took over then, thrusting her toward him, compelling her to try something she'd never experienced before—kissing a man.

The sensation proved to be rather pleasant. His mouth was firm, his skin warm, and he tasted faintly of apple.

She didn't consider whether he'd like it. And indeed, considering his lack of response, 'twas possible he did not. His mouth was immobile. He seemed to be holding his breath, though she was too mortified to open her eyes to check.

Now she was sure she'd done the wrong thing. Acting on impulse was seldom wise. But how could she extricate herself with grace?

Her fingers trembled where she touched his grizzled jaw, and she started to pull away.

Then she heard his crutch fall to the floor. In the next instant, his hands came up to caress her face. He tipped her head to the side. With a soft growl, he pressed his lips to hers and deepened the kiss. His warm breath sent shivers through her as he began to feast on her mouth like a beggar feasting on bread.

A bolt of current speared through her then, driving the intense pleasure he bestowed upon her lips down through her body, straight through her heart, deep into her belly, all the way to the vulnerable spot between her thighs.

She moaned at the curious heat building there as he kissed her with growing desperation. Her heart was pumping hard. Her nerves felt on fire. A shimmering buzz encircled her head. Breathless with yearning, she returned his passion, opening her mouth and daring to explore him with her tongue.

He groaned, and for an instant, she imagined she'd hurt him somehow. But it must have been a groan of encouragement, for he swept one arm around her back to press her closer, crushing her breasts against him and letting his tongue tangle with hers.

Now the hot, tingling desire traveled slowly up from between her thighs to her abdomen, up through her belly to her breasts. Her nipples ached with exquisite need where they contacted his solid chest.

She wanted him even closer, though it seemed anatomically impossible. She weaved her fingers through his hair and drew his head down, arching up toward him at the same time, eager to be completely enclosed in his embrace.

But she miscalculated. She pulled too hard and began to fall backward. Though he staggered and thrust out his arm to try to keep upright, he lost his balance as well. Their mouths were torn apart, but she foolishly clung to him, not wanting to be separated from him for one moment.

Thankfully the bed was behind her. She landed with a painless plop on the feather mattress, and he twisted enough to wind up mostly off of her. The hound sat up and whined in concern, which made Alisoune giggle. But she wasn't about to let her own clumsiness interfere with this most enjoyable endeavor. Giddy with delight, she wrapped her arms around the handsome man's neck, eager to continue, and smiled up at him.

But he wasn't smiling.

CHAPTER 4

Lachlan had never been so mortified in his life. This was the reason Margaret had left him, why he never let anyone close, why he wasn't deserving of a woman.

For God's sake, he couldn't even stand on his own two feet.

He'd utterly humiliated himself. He'd carried on like a lovesick cow, literally falling all over her, and now she was laughing at him.

She was right to laugh. He was a disgrace. He couldn't bring himself to look her in the eye.

"I'm sorry," he mumbled, shaking off her hands and trying to lever himself up off of the bed with as little ado as possible.

"Ye are?" She sounded hurt.

"I should never have..." he began, casting a glance over his shoulder for his fallen crutch. "'Twas a stupid mistake."

"'Twas?"

"Aye, and 'twill not happen again."

"'Twon't?"

"I'm..." He couldn't think of a better word to describe what a pathetic excuse for a man he was. "Sorry."

"Oh." There was an awkward moment of silence, and then she said, "Well...I don't think I am."

For an instant, his foolish heart fluttered. She sounded sincere. But that was just wishful thinking. Surely she was only being polite. Who wouldn't be sorry to be knocked over by a clumsy cripple?

He retrieved the crutch and got it under him, pushing back up onto his good leg. Though he tried to avert his gaze, his eyes couldn't help but be drawn to the breathless beauty sprawled on his bed like a fallen angel. Her green skirts were askew and puffed up like a dark storm cloud against the pale cream sky of his bed linens. Her long chestnut-colored hair had mostly come undone and swept her face in loose curls. Her eyes looked smoky now, like mist over a green sea. And her mouth was stained a luscious shade of crimson, darkened by the pressure of his kiss.

But 'twas pointless to admire her. He was only torturing himself. Clearing his throat, he withdrew and turned toward the hearth, grating out, "The porridge should be ready."

He set down the tip of his crutch, put weight on it, and heard an awful crunch.

He wouldn't curse in front of the lass. 'Twasn't seemly. But he longed to spit out a string of the foulest words he knew.

Her soft gasp as she saw her prize spectacles crushed beneath his crutch was like salt in his wounds. God's teeth! He was an arse, an idiot, a fool unfit for company, better off alone where he could do no harm.

He spoke through teeth clenched in shame. "I'll...find a way to repay ye. I'm sorry for..." He paused and let out a sigh of regret. "For everythin'."

"Nae!" she hastened to assure him as he continued to limp toward the fire. She wriggled down off the bed and followed him. "'Tisn't your fault. I'm the one who...who..."

He lifted the bail of the pot and gave her a brief sidelong glance. She was blushing.

"I shouldn't have kissed ye," she admitted, her hands

clasped modestly before her. "But I'm not sorry. 'Twas a most... pleasurable experience, well worth the cost of a pair o' spectacles."

He closed his eyes. Surely she wasn't serious. She only felt sorry for him. 'Twas pity, not affection.

And yet...a part of him was stupid enough to hope she was telling the truth.

He opened his eyes again and lifted the pot from the hearth. He didn't speak while he filled two crockery bowls with the porridge.

She squeezed her clasped hands tightly together atop her stomacher and asked softly, "Are ye so angry with me then?"

He frowned, unable to figure out how she'd come to that conclusion. "Angry with ye?"

"For takin' liberties with ye."

He glanced up at her. Faith, she was serious. She thought he was vexed with her for...for "taking liberties" with him? He bit back a smile. Taking liberties wasn't usually the sort of thing a woman did to a man.

She mistook his pause for condemnation. "Ye *are* angry." Her shoulders sank. "But ye must know, kind sir, I meant ye no harm. 'Tis only that I've never kissed a man before, and I have a curious nature, so I—"

"Never?" That was a surprise. She seemed awfully good at it for a novice.

She shook her head and pressed a hand to her bosom. "I didn't know what to expect. I didn't realize my heart would pound so fiercely...my blood would run so warm...my whole body would burn with such a heat that I could no longer think straight or—"

"I'm not angry," he blurted out before she could say something to drive him even more mad with longing.

She bit her lip then, effectively silenced. He slid the bowls to their respective places on the table. She located and replaced her own spectacles, and then collected the shards of the ones he'd broken and threw them into the fireplace.

He had only one chair. Spotting his dilemma, she scooted the table over to the bedside and sat atop the mattress, leaving the chair for him.

Fortunately, he had two spoons. He gave her one, kept one for himself, and eased down into the chair. Then he sat staring at his bowl of porridge.

He had no appetite. All of his hunger was focused between his legs. It had been months since the beast in his trews had stirred, but 'twas most definitely stirring now. And now that 'twas awake and ravenous, there wasn't a damned thing he could do about it.

The lass spooned a generous mouthful of porridge into her mouth and closed her eyes in bliss. "Mmmm."

His groin tightened. He clenched his jaw, then stabbed his spoon into the porridge, shoveling it past his teeth.

"Mm-mm," she crooned.

He swallowed the porridge in one giant gulp. It sank to his gut like a stone.

"Mmmm." She licked her lips.

He gave her a pained expression. "Can ye not...that is...must ye..."

She looked at him with wide eyes, her spoon poised between the bowl and her delicious mouth. "Aye?"

He shook his head. 'Twas no use. The lass couldn't know what she was doing to his insides. He'd have to suffer in silence. Soon enough they'd be done eating, and he'd send her on her way.

Alisoune wasn't sure why he looked so miserable. Aye, she'd overstepped her welcome, grabbing him and kissing him like that. But it had been most rewarding...at least for her. Until she'd knocked the poor man over, he seemed to be relishing it as much as she.

She wondered if she could repair the damage she'd done. When men of science failed in their experiments, they usually scrapped everything and started over.

"Perhaps we could begin anew," she suggested. "Ye can forget my improper advances, and I'll forget the broken spectacles." She stuck out her hand. "My name is Alisoune, Alisoune Hay."

He stared at her hand in surprise as if she'd placed a dead mouse on the table. She withdrew it. Maybe she was being too forward again.

He sighed, seemed to think it over, and then gave her a nod. "Alisoune," he repeated. She liked the way her name sounded in his deep, rolling voice. "I'm Lachlan."

"Sir Lachlan, happy to make your acquai—"

"Not Sir," he interrupted. "Just Lachlan."

She glanced again at his battle gear in the corner. She supposed if she'd lost her leg in a fight, she'd like to forget she'd ever been a knight as well. "Sorry."

"Nae," he said with an apologetic grimace. "'Tis fine. I just...I won't be donnin' armor again. I'm just Lachlan."

Eager to move away from an obviously uncomfortable subject, she quickly said, "The porridge is quite tasty."

He gave a single soft bark of amusement. "Porridge is porridge."

"Not at all," she countered. "Ye have to have the right proportion o' solids to liquids, the right distance from the heat source, and the right time of exposure to the heat."

"Is that so?" The soft twinkle in his silvery eyes let her know that he found her engaging, if a bit odd. But then everyone found her odd. At least he didn't seem to think she was Satan's spawn.

They both went back to eating. Finally Lachlan gestured

toward her spectacles with his spoon. "Do those truly help ye see better?"

"Oh, aye," she said. "Without them, I'm as lost as a lamb in a snowstorm. But with them..." She studied his face for something she could point out. "I can see the tiny white scar ye have at the corner o' your mouth there." She nodded to the mark.

He lifted his finger to touch the spot, as if he'd forgotten it.

"Impressive," he said. Then a roguish glimmer shimmered in his silver eyes. "Can ye see the whiskers on Campbell's chin?"

She whipped her head around toward the hound, who was sitting by the bed, licking his chops, waiting for scraps. "Aye."

"What about his eyelashes?"

She narrowed her eyes. "Aye, just barely."

"And what about that flea perched on the end o' his muzzle?"

She squinted for an instant before she realized he was jesting. Then she erupted into bubbling peals of laughter.

CHAPTER 5

Lachlan knew he'd carry the sweet sound of her laughing with him to his grave. It had been a long while since there had been any joy in his life. 'Twould be a long while before he was likely to have any. So he stored the lovely sound away in his memory, to pull out on days when loneliness and despair got the best of him.

Meanwhile, Alisoune was enticing his hound with the dregs of her porridge.

"Did ye hear what your master said about ye, Campbell? He as much as called ye a flea-ridden mongrel. Come on now, pup. I'll give ye a wee bit o' my porridge to soothe your injured pride."

The hound lapped her bowl clean and then eyed Lachlan's.

"I suppose ye'll be wantin' mine as well?" he said. "Ye've spoiled my hound, lass."

"Oh, I'll wager he was spoiled long ere I arrived."

She was right. As Lachlan's only companion, the trusty deerhound lived in relative luxury. Lachlan set his bowl on the floor, and Campbell made quick work of it.

Alisoune rose then and gathered their dishes.

"I can do that," he grumbled.

"O' course ye can." Nonetheless, she made herself at home, pouring water from his bucket into the empty porridge pot and hanging it to heat over the fire again.

'Twas admittedly convenient having her help. Lachlan had let the cottage go, mostly because there was no one worth keeping it clean for. But he didn't want her to think he was helpless. He got up from the table, took his cloak from its peg, and picked up the empty bucket.

Murmuring, "I'll be back," he lifted the latch of the door with his elbow and nudged it open. Campbell eagerly nosed outside, leaving the door wide, and Lachlan limped out after him through the snow, heading for the spring that coursed through the forest.

The day had turned gray and frigid, but not frigid enough to cool the residual passion that simmered in his veins. A part of him wished that he and Alisoune *could* start over and that she'd never kissed him. 'Twould be hard to forget the honeyed taste of her lips.

When he reached the spring, he leaned his crutch against a tree beside the icy water. Holding onto the trunk for balance, he lowered the bucket, filling it slowly. Then, with his crutch under one arm and the bucket in the other hand, he made his difficult way back to the cottage, careful not to spill too much.

The dog had relieved himself by then and nudged the door open for him. But when Lachlan stepped with his snow-covered boot on the flagstones, it slid, and a lightning bolt of pain suddenly streaked down his missing leg. He caught himself on the crutch, but not before a wave of water slopped out onto the floor.

Embarrassed, he glared sharply at Alisoune. She was busy rinsing out the bowls and didn't seem to notice. The calf of his missing leg was throbbing now, which infuriated him. After all, it should be impossible to feel a limb that was no longer there. He hoped to God 'twasn't going to be one of those days that he spent clutching his stump in agony. Compressing his lips and ignoring the pain as best he could, he bent down to replace the bucket.

"Is it still cold out?" she asked without meeting his eyes.

"Aye," he said, hanging up his cloak.

"'Tis been an unusually frigid winter."

"Aye."

"It looks like another storm's comin' in, aye?"

"Maybe."

"So there'll be more snow."

He frowned. The pain in his leg was beginning to ease. "If a storm comes, I suppose so, aye."

"Ye'll be grateful for a big roarin' fire to sit by then."

Lachlan's brows converged. She wasn't just fascinated by the weather. Something else was on her mind.

He was fairly certain he knew what she was after. And he was just as certain he should deny her. After all, he'd already been more than generous. He'd hidden her from an angry mob. He'd fed her breakfast. He owed her no more.

But though 'twas against his instincts, his better judgment, and his will, in the end, he knew he couldn't refuse the lass.

Alisoune didn't want to ask Lachlan outright to let her stay. But she feared the stubborn soldier was never going to ask her himself. And if he didn't, she didn't know what would become of her.

If she returned to her room at the inn in Keirfield, 'twould only be a matter of time before the priest dragged her out of it and finished what he'd started. If she left, she'd not only be leaving behind all of her possessions—her coin, her clothing, her tools—but she'd likely be caught without a cloak in a winter storm before she could reach her home in Stirling.

Then again, why should Lachlan invite her to stay? He was

perfectly content as he was. For the moment at least, he had a roof over his head, a warm fire, and a faithful dog.

Besides, she'd doubtless annoyed him by breaking into his house and forcing her affections on him. And she'd probably bored him with Copernicus's theory and her collection of spectacles.

'Twas no use. She'd never convince Lachlan 'twas to his benefit to harbor an outlaw. She wouldn't blame him if he tossed her out on her heretical arse.

He prodded the coals on the fire and let out a lungful of air. "If ye're wonderin' whether I'm goin' to turn ye over to the villagers or out into the snow, ye needn't fret. Ye're welcome to stay...till the storm passes."

Relief welled in her heart as she said, "Oh, thank ye, sir. Ye won't be sorry. I...I'll make your meals and fetch your water and make sure your hound—"

"I don't need your help," he said rather defensively.

"Oh, I'm certain ye don't," she said carefully, though 'twas plain his cottage needed a thorough scrubbing from top to bottom. "But I don't have much coin left, and I can't stay here in all good conscience without earnin' my keep."

Before he could have second thoughts about letting her stay, she grabbed a rag and began wiping down his cupboards.

Meanwhile, he made up the bed with one hand, cut a generous piece of salted meat for Campbell from the slab hanging in the kitchen, and put another log on the fire.

"Ye know, I have to admire the way ye get about on one leg," she told him as she scrubbed at the porridge pot. "I mean, everythin' must be a challenge...walkin'...fetchin' water...carryin' wood. But ye don't seem to let your adversity stop ye."

"I don't have a choice."

"Well, a lesser man might give up." She pushed her spectacles up on her nose. "How long has it been since ye lost it?"

She had the feeling, from the grim look in his eyes, that he could probably tell her down to the minute. Instead, he mumbled, "About three months."

"Is that all?" She turned to stare at him in wonder. "And ye've adjusted that well already. Can ye still feel it?" Alisoune was admittedly intrigued by the concept of phantom pain. She'd never talked to anyone with a missing limb before. 'Twas the perfect opportunity to do some firsthand scientific inquiry.

"Nae," he grunted.

Her face fell. "Truly? Because I've heard that—"

"Ye can't believe everythin' ye hear."

"Nae, I suppose not."

Still, when she glanced at him hobbling toward the hearth, she could tell by the subtle tightening around his mouth that he did indeed feel some sort of pain. 'Twas just like a soldier to try to deny it.

She wondered if there was any ease for him, if there was any way to eliminate or diminish his suffering. She was in the habit of looking for solutions. 'Twas the bane, she supposed, of possessing a scientific mind.

But she also genuinely wanted to help the man. He seemed lonely and uncared for, living alone in this wee cottage far from town. By the melancholy cast of his eyes as he gazed into the fire and the deep lines etched into his forehead, it had been a long while since he'd had a happy thought or a kind word or a good laugh. Perhaps it had been a long while since he'd had reason to laugh.

She might not know yet how to ease his physical pain, but she thought she could probably coax a chuckle out of him.

She set aside the clean pot, and then returned to the bed and began riffling through her satchel.

"Come here, Campbell," she called. The dog obediently ambled over and sat before her. She pulled out her box of spectacles and found the biggest pair. Campbell was very patient. He sat quietly while she strategically perched the oversized spectacles on his nose.

"What do ye think, Lachlan?"

What Lachlan was thinking as he gazed absently into the fire was that he should never have told Alisoune his name. It sounded too enticing upon her lips. He was already having trouble keeping his mind off of the bright ray of sunshine who was, much to his chagrin and against his wishes, lighting up his cottage and warming his heart. But when she said his name...

He reluctantly lifted his eyes. What he saw made his face crack into a grin. His buffoon of a deerhound looked like a wise old scholar.

"Oh! Wait," Alisoune said, digging in her satchel. She nudged Campbell around to face her and tied a white coif around his head. To Lachlan's amazement, the dog put up with her machinations without moving a muscle. She tied a red ribbon around the dog's neck and sat back to admire her handiwork.

"There," she said, turning the hound toward him. "Laird Lachlan, Lady Campbell wishes to make your acquaintance."

A snort of laughter escaped him. The dog made the ugliest woman he'd ever seen.

She pretended to politely introduce the hound. "Lady Campbell, Laird Lachlan."

Lachlan shook his head. "Ach, Campbell, have ye no shame?"

"Shame?" Alisoune cried, affecting great affront. "Why, Laird Lachlan, Lady Campbell takes great offense at that. Don't ye, Lady Campbell?"

Campbell lifted his muzzle and gave a mournful howl, and Alisoune broke out in infectious giggles. Lachlan couldn't help but join in. And the more they laughed, the more Campbell howled, until the cottage was filled with a loud and eerie mix of misery and merriment.

Eventually, the dog shook off the annoying accoutrements and slunk off to sit at the hearth, sulking in humiliation.

Alisoune was still hiccoughing when she removed her spectacles to wipe her eyes.

Lachlan's belly was sore from laughing. How long had it been since he'd laughed, truly laughed? Half a year? More? It felt good, like flexing his sword arm after a long absence from the battlefield.

He was still smiling when she put her spectacles back on and flashed him a wide, radiant grin. He realized now that her beauty didn't come from her appearance. She was beautiful by virtue of her honest face, her kind soul, and her sweet nature.

There seemed to be no artifice in her. What she appeared to be, she was. What she said, she believed. 'Twould be a lucky man who laid claim to a lass so pure of heart.

That last thought dimmed his happiness. He would never be that man. Nae, a woman like Alisoune deserved a whole man— a man who could care for her, love her...protect her.

CHAPTER 6

For Alisoune, there was nothing quite as satisfying as finding the solution to a problem. 'Twas the reason she enjoyed selling spectacles. Choosing the correct lens and instantly improving a person's sight was gratifying.

But that wasn't the only reason Alisoune's heart swelled at her success in coaxing a laugh out of Lachlan.

The way his teeth flashed, the silver sparkle in his eyes, and the easy chuckles that started low in his chest gave her a glimpse of the man Lachlan used to be...before misfortune befell him. That man was kind and fun-loving, mischievous and merry. And Alisoune thought she liked that man very much...very much indeed.

She caught her lip under her teeth. Of course he clearly didn't feel that way about her, which wasn't surprising. Alisoune made most men uncomfortable. Not only was she odd-looking—tall and spindly and bespectacled—but she was also too clever and outspoken for her own good. Men were intimidated by her, which was why, of course, the good folk of Keirfield wanted to burn her at the stake.

Still, Lachlan hadn't wanted to burn her at the stake. And aside from the unfortunate kiss she'd forced upon him, he didn't seem to feel threatened by her.

She glanced over at him. He stood by the window now, peering out the shutters. His face had gone grim again, as gloomy and gray as the weather.

She bit her lip. 'Twould be a challenge, luring him out of whatever pit of despair he'd fallen into, lifting his spirits and returning him to the carefree man he'd been.

But Alisoune loved challenges. They taxed her scientific brain. If she could solve Lachlan's problems, if she could choose a lens for him that would make him see his world and his life with new clarity, 'twould be rewarding indeed.

She'd start by clearing out the cobwebs, literally. His cottage was sadly neglected, much like the man himself. Perhaps if he could see restoration in his living quarters, 'twould give him hope for himself. Smiling in determination, she snatched up the broom and set about sweeping the corners of the ceiling to dislodge the spiders.

Then, because she found it difficult to be silent with all the interesting thoughts constantly whirling through her brain, she began to muse aloud.

"A spider web—that's it!" she exclaimed, staring up at a heavily webbed beam. "Can ye see, Lachlan? Our galaxy is like a gigantic spider web. And we've been thinkin' all along that we're the great spider in the midst o' the web, that the other planets are like flies caught in the strands. But what if 'tisn't true? What if the *Sun* is the great spider, and we're one o' the flies?"

She glanced at Lachlan from the corner of her eye. Would he mock her as most men did? Or would he simply stare at her as if she were daft?

He did neither. He listened and frowned and seemed to consider her idea. "But how can that be? I can see the Sun goin' from east to west, circlin' around us."

"True! However..." She thrust aside the broom and sought out objects to illustrate her point, finally settling on one of his apples and a small round stone she found on the mantel. "What if 'tis only a difference in perception?" She held up the apple. "Say this is the Sun. 'Tis circlin' the Earth here, aye?" She moved the apple slowly around the stone.

He nodded.

"But what if 'tis reversed? What if the Earth is circlin' round the Sun?" She held the apple still and circled the stone in the opposite direction around the apple. "To our eyes, 'twould appear the same, aye?"

His brow furrowed, but a spark of enlightenment glittered in his eyes. "Hmm."

"'Tis the heliocentric hypothesis!" she said in triumph, replacing the apple in the bowl.

He scratched at his beard. "Is this why the priest thinks ye're a witch?"

"Well," she admitted, rolling the small stone between her palms, "men o' the church don't much like men o' science. It upsets them a great deal to have their doctrine questioned."

"No doubt."

"But ye don't think I'm a witch, do ye?"

"Nae." He reached down to scratch his hound's ears. "Campbell doesn't let witches in the house."

She smiled, tossing the stone up a few inches and catching it.

"Ye'd better be careful with the Earth there," he warned her.

She giggled, then cocked her head at the round stone in her hand. 'Twas most unusual. "Where did ye get this?"

He smirked. "From a witch."

Scolding him with a dubious glance, she held the stone up to the light. It looked like polished crystal, but it had curious cracks in the interior that made milky filaments in the stone.

"A strange old crone brought it to me in the middle o' the night," he explained. "She called it the Winter Stone. She said 'twas a magic relic that could change a man's fate."

"Magic? I don't believe in magic." She examined the crystal closer. It shimmered in a rainbow of hues as she rotated it slowly from left to right, confirming her suspicions.

"It seems to change color," he said. "I'm not sure about changin' a man's fate."

"If this is what I think 'tis, it might indeed change your fate. It looks like a rainbow crystal. The cracks inside create an internal prism, which refracts the light into various colors. Stones like this are very rare and quite valuable."

He snorted. "Then why would she give it away?"

The instant Alisoune looked up at him, an eerie tingling arose at the back of Lachlan's neck, stirring his memory.

Dark hair.

Bright green eyes.

Take the Stone to its rightful Keeper.

Could it be? Could Alisoune be the Keeper the old crone was raving on about? But how could she have known? After all, the lass hadn't arrived at his cottage till hours after the old woman disappeared.

Lachlan wasn't sure he believed in magic either. But 'twas hard to explain the events of the past day using reason.

"I think she meant it for *ye*," he said.

"Me? Pah!" She set the stone carefully back on the mantel. "Nae, ye should hold onto it. No doubt 'twill fetch a king's ransom."

A king's ransom. What would he do with a king's ransom? Coin meant nothing to him, not when he had no one to share it with. He'd gladly give up a king's ransom if he could only get his brothers back.

But that wasn't what the old crone meant by changing his fate. And he was sure the lass must be the one the crone intended to have the crystal. He wasn't normally superstitious, but he'd told the old woman he'd deliver the relic to its Keeper. Just to be safe, before Alisoune left, he'd tuck the stone into her satchel.

She continued to clean his cottage, wiping the counters, tidying up the food stores, sweeping the floor. While it pleased him to see his hovel being restored to order, it also made him feel guilty for having let it become so filthy.

He tensed his jaw. He felt as if he should stop her. Not only was it not her duty to look after him, but 'twas not something he needed. Why should he live in a nice home anyway while his brothers dwelt under the cold, hard, blood-soaked ground of Haddon Rig?

He narrowed his eyes at the sunny lass in the green gown, who was humming to herself as she swept the ashes from in front of the hearth. She was far too sweet to suffer his bitterness. He might want her to stop, but he didn't have the heart to disappoint her by refusing what she deemed a good deed.

"I'm goin' out for a while," he said, buckling on his belt and slipping his dagger into its sheath.

"Oh?"

He owed her no explanation. But she deserved one. "I'm takin' Campbell for a hunt."

She smiled and pushed the glasses back up on her nose. "Be sure to be back ere the storm starts."

"I will."

"And dress warm."

"Aye." He'd already pulled a floppy woolen cap down over his head.

"As for ye, beast," she added, bending forward to address the hound, "bring us back a nice fat rabbit, and make sure your master doesn't lose his way in the woods."

Lachlan shook his head as he grabbed his cloak. Lose his way? Alisoune sounded like a worrisome wife.

He shrugged on the cloak and opened the door. 'Twasn't yet snowing, but 'twould be soon. Campbell bolted out past him, and Lachlan hesitated in the doorway, giving her a meaningful look. "Be sure to latch the door shut after me."

Alisoune did so immediately. She doubted the priest would come after her again today, not after Lachlan's threat. But 'twas probably wise to err on the side of caution.

Meanwhile, she would see what she could do to make his home more accommodating.

She pried open the wooden shutters over the only window in the cottage and polished the dingy diamond-shaped panes until they were transparent again. She weeded good food from bad, throwing handfuls of hopelessly shriveled vegetables onto the fire. She chipped the wax from candles that had dripped onto the floor and used it to polish the two oak chests near the foot of his bed.

In one of the chests, she found clean bed linens, so she stripped off the old. She tightened the ropes beneath his mattress, which she managed to flip over with some effort, and then made up the bed with fresh linens. She fluffed his feather bolster until 'twas light and airy and spread his snowy sheepskin coverlet over the top.

After an hour of sweeping, scrubbing, and sorting, the cottage began to look livable. Now 'twas time to make it comfortable.

Mopping her brow with the back of her arm, she scanned the interior, imagining what 'twas like for Lachlan, managing with only one leg. She decided that the most difficult thing was probably getting out of bed on his crutch. What would be useful was a bracing mechanism of some sort, some kind of rail he could use to pull himself up, something strong attached to the wall.

Fortunately, tidying his house, she'd found all sorts of odds and ends—tools, scraps, bits of wood and metal and leather, rope, nails—everything she'd need to make modest alterations to his living quarters.

Giddy with excitement over this small alteration and how 'twould improve his quality of life, she located the perfect spot for the bracket, the vertical wooden beam near the head of his bed. She was scouring the room, considering what she might use for the bracket, when her gaze lit on the armor he said he no longer needed.

CHAPTER 7

Campbell had been in fine form today, Lachlan thought as he patted the dog's head and slung the third rabbit over his shoulder. 'Twas as if the dog knew they had an extra mouth to feed.

He glanced up at the sky. Heavy gray clouds had gathered now, blotting out the heavens and lying atop the pines like a thick sheepskin. The air was cold and still. The snowstorm would arrive soon.

He winced as he leaned heavily on his crutch. His leg, his *missing* leg, was burning again. No matter how many times he told himself 'twas impossible—one couldn't feel pain in a missing limb—his missing limb couldn't be convinced of that fact.

He wondered if the lass was right. He wondered if nerves *were* like the roots of a tree. He wondered if a tree felt pain when one of its roots was lopped off.

Then he chuckled to himself. With all this wondering, he was beginning to sound like the lass herself.

She certainly was a curious woman, asking questions about missing limbs and spider webs and the universe. He'd never met anyone quite like her. 'Twas no wonder the priest thought her a witch.

From across the clearing, he spotted the cottage, and for an awful instant, he feared the worst, for there was no smoke coming from his chimney. Had the townsfolk come after all? Had they taken Alisoune?

Then he heard a loud banging from inside, and he caught his breath. She was apparently still there, though God only knew what she was doing. What she *wasn't* doing was keeping the fire going.

He stamped his boots on the threshold and rapped on the door.

"Who is it?" he heard her call from inside.

"Lachlan."

"Do ye have a rabbit?" she called back. "Because if ye haven't got a rabbit, I'm not lettin' ye in."

Lachlan couldn't help but grin at the saucy lass. "Suit yourself then. Campbell and I will build a fire and feast out here."

She unlatched the door and swung it open. He thought he remembered how she looked, but memory didn't serve him. After trudging through the dull snow under a wintry sky for the past few hours, looking at her was like having a first glimpse of spring in all its warm and verdant glory. Behind her spectacles, her eyes danced. Her smile was dazzling. And her laughter was as clear and musical as a babbling May brook.

The fire had dwindled to red coals, but he could see she'd been busy while he was gone. In fact, seeing what she'd done to his cottage—the clean-swept flagstones, the tidy shelves, the freshly made bed—made his throat close with gratitude.

And yet it also quietly vexed him. What gave her the right to come into the life he was resigned to and try to change it? Why give him false hope?

Swiftly, before he could blurt out something he'd regret, something that would fill her beautiful green eyes with tears, he limped across the cottage and tossed the rabbits onto the table.

"Three?" she said, cheering. "Campbell, ye've done yourself proud!"

In a rare show of impertinence, the hound reared back on his hind legs and placed his front paws on Alisoune's shoulders, almost bowling her over. He licked her face, knocking her spectacles askew.

Not bothered in the least by the hound's familiarity, she grabbed his whiskered face and scrubbed behind his ears. "Aye, that's a good lad! Ye've earned your keep today, haven't ye?"

"Campbell, down!" Lachlan barked, just in case she wasn't as pleased as she sounded.

The dog instantly obeyed and Lachlan sent him to the hearth with a nod of his head.

Alisoune straightened her spectacles and immediately set to dressing the rabbits.

"I can do that," he said.

"Don't be silly," she countered. "Ye brought home the rabbits. 'Tis only fair I should prepare them." Then she gave him a curious glance. "Ye must be weary. Why don't ye take a wee nap while I'm makin' supper?"

"A wee nap?" He scowled, and his words came out harsher than he intended. "I'm not an invalid. I'm just a man missin' a leg."

She smiled shyly and went back to work.

Meanwhile, Lachlan silently cursed himself. Why had he snapped at the lass? 'Twas obvious she was trying to help. He hadn't seen his cottage so clean since the day Margaret left him. Alisoune was kind to his dog, and she was civil to him. He had no right to speak to her so rudely.

"I'm sorry," he mumbled. "I'm not used to...kindness."

'Twas one of the saddest things Alisoune had ever heard. How could anyone be unkind to a person who was obviously suffering already?

But she'd quickly learned that Lachlan didn't like pity, so she kept her tone light. "Ye'll want to taste my rabbit stew ere ye decide 'tis kindness."

He chuckled once.

"Ye *can* help me by fetchin' the big pot," she said. If he wouldn't lie down on his bed, perhaps he'd notice the device she'd made for him when he drew near the fireplace.

But though he stood right beside the beam where she'd nailed the metal bracket when he bent to fetch the pot, he didn't seem to notice it.

"And the fire could use more fuel," she suggested.

She cut the rabbits into pieces while he stacked more wood atop the blaze. Still he didn't see the apparatus.

She smeared a lump of butter onto the bottom of the pot. Then she broke a few eggs into one bowl and a bit of flour into another, dredging the pieces and dropping them into the pot. She peeled and chopped an onion and an apple and added them with pepper and a few dried herbs from the cupboard. Then she lifted the heavy pot and handed it to him to hang over the fire.

Still he took no notice of the device.

While the rabbit sizzled away, filling the cottage with a delicious aroma that made Campbell lick his chops, Alisoune tried again to draw Lachlan's attention to her handiwork.

"The stew isn't burnin', is it?"

He peered into the pot. "Nae."

"Are ye sure ye won't sit down for a bit?" she tried. "Ye've been on foot for hours."

"I'm used to it."

She wondered. Even on two legs, trudging through something with the surface resistance of snow wasn't easy. "Even Campbell's worn out. Look at him."

Lachlan did look at him...and nothing else. When Campbell lifted his head, it wasn't six inches away from the bracket. But the man saw nothing. 'Twas incredible.

"I hope ye don't mind," she said, carefully ladling water into the pot and scraping up the cooked bits with a great iron spoon. "I tidied up a few things while ye were gone."

"Aye, I see." But nae, he did not see. He gave the room a cursory glance, no more. "Thank ye."

'Twas almost comical that he didn't notice what she'd done. She decided to let it go. Sooner or later he'd discover it.

While she tended to supper, he kept himself busy, bringing in a few more logs from his dwindling cache outside and scraping the rabbit pelts clean to use later.

They dined on the stew, which had turned out to be edible enough, despite a dearth of the usual seasonings Alisoune liked to use—saffron, cinnamon, and ginger. Perhaps such spices weren't as easy to obtain outside of large towns like Stirling.

She made sure Campbell got his fair share, despite Lachlan's grumbling protest that he'd rather have a third serving than waste such good food on a dog.

'Twas while she was cleaning up the dishes that Lachlan finally lowered himself onto to his bed and began to take off his boot. She pressed her lips together, trying not to smile in anticipation.

"What the devil?" he muttered. "What's my targe handle doin' on the wall?"

She spun around, beaming. "Isn't it grand? It should fit ye perfectly, because...well, the shield was designed to fit *your* arm, o' course."

He looked puzzled and, if she wasn't mistaken, none too

happy. "Why is my targe handle nailed to the wall?" he repeated.

"Oh." She smiled sheepishly and rolled her eyes. "I should have said. 'Tis a bracket...for balance."

His brows came together.

Her smile faltered.

"A bracket?" He seemed upset.

"Aye." She took a few tentative steps forward, intending to show him how it worked. "When ye need to get out o' bed," she said, cautiously sidling past when he didn't move his knee out of the way and sitting beside him, "ye just grab hold like this..." She demonstrated. "And ye pull yourself up."

Some dark, fierce emotion raged in his silver eyes. She felt uneasy, the way she had when the priest and his followers had suddenly turned on her.

"My targe handle?" Lachlan's voice broke. That targe had served him in half a dozen battles and saved him in the last. He couldn't believe the lass had...had dismantled it.

"Ye said..." Alisoune's voice was a tenuous whisper. "That is...ye told me...ye didn't need your armor...didn't ye?"

Lachlan closed his mouth into a grim line. Aye, that was what he'd said. And 'twas true. What use did a one-legged soldier have for a suit of armor or a shield or a blade? 'Twas ridiculous.

And yet a small part of him had clung to the absurd belief that somehow he'd awaken from all that had happened as if from a dream, that he *would* fight another day, that he *would* go back to the man he once was.

"I'll put it back to rights if ye like," Alisoune said softly.

"Nae," he decided. She was right. He'd told her he was no longer a soldier. He just needed to accept that fact himself. A broken-down, war-wounded hermit had no need for weapons.

"'Tis no bother," she murmured. "I can change it back as fast as—"

"Nae," he said, forcing a fleeting smile. "'Tis fine. Thank ye."

He could see she was disappointed. She'd gone to a lot of effort, working the rivets loose from the targe and securing the handle to the beam at just the right height for him to pull himself out of bed. He had to admit, 'twas rather ingenious.

But it also drew attention to the fact that he was different, that he couldn't function like a normal man. Hell, there was a time when he could have hopped up out of a lass's bed before her father even started up the stairs. Those days were gone.

Perhaps he was well rid of them. 'Twas time he accepted who he was, what he was.

"'Tis more than fine," he assured her, willing the warm sunshine to return to her eyes. "'Tis brilliant."

She blushed, but managed a tiny smile as she gazed down at him.

"Let's see how it works," he said, reaching for the handle to try it.

"O' course," she gushed, stepping out of the way.

A strange shiver passed through him as he took the familiar handle in his grip. He realized he hadn't done so since he'd come home from battle. A flood of unpleasant memories abruptly assailed him, and his palm began to sweat around the iron handle.

But Alisoune waited expectantly, her hands clasped beneath her chin, a hopeful smile on her face. And Lachlan wouldn't disappoint her further. He refused to be debilitated by dead memories that couldn't be changed.

Slipping the crutch beneath his other arm, he pulled himself up by the handle.

Where before he'd strained the muscles of his good leg to stand up, only to hastily and painfully catch himself under the arm with the crutch, now he rose with ease, assisted by the strength of his arm. Where he usually dipped and swayed, trying not to fall, now he simply held onto the bracket until he was balanced.

He looked down at Alisoune in wonder. 'Twas such a simple device, such a humble gesture. But it made all the difference in the world. Gratitude made a thick lump in his throat as she smiled sweetly up at him.

Damn, he wasn't going to weep, was he?

Willing his tears away, he let the crutch fall back onto the bed, reached out his free hand to lift Alisoune's chin, and placed a chaste kiss of thanks upon her smooth brow.

At least it started out chaste.

But Alisoune apparently had her own ideas about what a kiss should be, now that she was an expert on the subject. She slipped her fingers into his hair, stood on tiptoe, closed her eyes, and pressed her mouth against his with all the passion of a long-lost lover.

CHAPTER 8

Alisoune had feared Lachlan would never kiss her again. She'd been wanting him to for hours now. Of course she'd told him they could start over and pretend it had never happened. But that wasn't what she truly wanted. She'd only said that to be polite.

All around her, the clan celebrated with feasting and cheering. Lively merrymaking filled the great hall. Laughter and music echoed from the rafters.

This breathtaking intimacy and the delicate yet powerful surge of desire that rose in her when their lips touched was too delicious a forbidden fruit to be denied.

There was no turning back now, no pretending it hadn't happened. As her mouth moved softly over his, she sighed. If she'd known how enjoyable kissing a man was, she'd have started long ago. Now she intended to make up for lost time.

And this time she didn't have to worry about taking liberties. After all, *he'd* started it.

His hand cupped the back of her head, tilting it slightly, and his fingers stroked beneath her loose braid as he deepened the kiss. She felt his hot, rapid breath upon her cheek, tasted the intoxicating ambrosia of warm apples and sweet desire in her mouth.

She melted against him, relishing the way his long hair brushed her face and his supple leather doublet pressed upon her breasts. This time, instead of forcing him off-balance, he relied on the bracket to keep him upright.

'Twas fascinating, the current that sizzled through her veins from the simple act of kissing him. She was well-versed in most of the sciences, but when it came to the science of courtship, her knowledge was a vacuum. Would the current intensify if she grew more bold? Would she overheat? How much more could she endure?

Eager to find out, she drew closer, running her hands down his throat and across his chest, and then sliding them around his waist to the small of his back.

He groaned low in his throat, and the sound sent a frisson of primal longing through her that lodged with a jolt betwixt her thighs. Answering with a soft moan of her own, she slipped her hands slowly down until they cupped his buttocks. She squeezed gently, and through his trews, she felt his muscles flex.

Then she felt something extraordinary. Where her belly contacted his, he began to swell, hardening, pressing against her with tangible need.

The primitive nature of such a response triggered her own desires, launching them to new heights, and she found herself aching to...to...

Lachlan tore his mouth free, even as his body cursed him for it. He withdrew his hand from her and hung his head, gripping the bracket with white knuckles and panting heavily from the rush of lust that had almost made him lose his mind.

Not since he'd lost his leg had his loins stirred like that. In truth, he hadn't been sure 'twas still possible. But there he was, straight as a lance and hard as a rock.

Yet to what end? Alisoune was not the sort of lass to be trifled with. She was a young thing, an innocent. He wouldn't take advantage of her inexperience for his own selfish ends.

When he hazarded a glance at her, 'twas almost too much to bear. The combination of desire and confusion in her eyes was alluring and heartbreaking all at once.

"Did I...do somethin' wrong?" she asked breathlessly.

A rueful chuckle escaped him. "Nae, lass."

"Then why...?"

How could he explain?

"Come," he said, lowering himself to the bed and patting the space beside him. "Sit."

She did, but when her gaze wandered with wicked interest to his groin, he tossed the sheepskin coverlet over his lap.

"Ye said ye'd never kissed a man before, aye?"

"Aye." Then she turned to him in concern. "Did I not do it properly?"

He smiled in spite of himself. "Oh, aye, ye did it properly." He scratched his beard, wondering how to proceed. "Ye just did it with the wrong man."

"What do ye mean?"

"Ye need to save your affections for the man ye mean to marry."

She furrowed her brows. "What if I don't mean to marry?"

"Not marry?" he scoffed. "A bonnie lass like ye? Half o' Scotland's bachelors must be knockin' at your door."

"Pah!" She blushed and swatted his arm. "And what about ye? Would ye be knockin' at my door?"

The corner of his mouth quirked up. Ordinarily he wouldn't have thought he could be attracted to such an odd, clever, scrawny mouse of a woman. But there was something about her—her charm, her wit, her sincerity—that did indeed draw him to her.

Still, she couldn't possibly be drawn to him.

Instead of answering her, he said, "'Tis easy to mistake lust for love." He felt as if he spoke for his own benefit as well. "'Tis only the heat o' the moment that's turned your head."

She gave him a dubious stare, then considered his words. "So ye think 'tis pure science? Basic alchemy?"

Nae, he didn't think that at all. But perhaps 'twas best to agree with her. "Aye, most likely."

"Hmm."

She didn't look pleased with that idea, but at least the heavy-lidded desire was fading from her face. Now if only 'twould fade from him as well...

Alisoune felt dissatisfied and disappointed. It seemed she'd been on the cusp of some important discovery, so close to the truth. Then, abruptly, all her theories were dashed.

She still felt an ache deep within her body, still felt the residue of current sparking in her veins. Was he right? Could the way she felt have nothing to do with rational thought or deep emotions, but rather be caused by a simple mixture of elements, an alchemy for passion?

She didn't think so. She might not be as experienced as he was when it came to kissing. But she'd been around men before. She'd never particularly wanted to kiss any of them, not like she did Lachlan. There was something different about the way he made her feel, something she didn't think could be explained away by science.

But she supposed 'twas pointless to think about it now. His mind was clearly elsewhere.

Lachlan had let Campbell out one last time for the evening and banked the fire. As ridiculous as 'twas, he refused to let her sleep by the hearth, insisting she take his bed. He'd listen to no amount of arguing, claiming that his chivalry would keep him warm. So she reluctantly acquiesced, leaving him to stretch out on the floor.

Still feeling unsettled, Alisoune took a long while to fall asleep, finally drifting off to the sounds of Campbell's snoring.

It seemed she'd only just closed her eyes when she heard a rasping sound in the dark. She frowned and lifted her head a few inches to hear better.

'Twas Lachlan. He was talking in his sleep. The sound was faint and incoherent. He must be dreaming.

She pushed up onto her elbows, getting her bearings in the dim firelight. Campbell was still snoring. The dog was probably accustomed to his master's nocturnal conversations.

But Lachlan's voice began to grow more and more urgent, and soon his breathing quickened. He suddenly flailed out an arm, startling her.

She bolted upright. She could see he'd dislodged the cloak he'd draped over himself. Now he lay gasping and twitching on the flagstones.

With a soft cry of worry, she scrambled out of the bed and rushed to him.

"Lachlan," she called gently.

His eyes were still closed tightly as his head rocked back and forth.

"Lachlan!" She touched his brow.

Campbell was awake now. He shot to his feet and trotted over, sniffing his master in concern.

Lachlan jerked and emitted a sleep-muffled scream.

Her eyes wide, Alisoune shook him by the shoulder. "Lachlan!"

But still he would not awaken, and he was shuddering as if with sickness. On instinct, she knelt down, wrapped her arms around him, and held him close.

Almost at once, he calmed. The furrow left his brow, his breathing slowed, and he relaxed back into the oblivion of slumber.

As she cradled him, giving him comfort, she wondered what horrible dream he'd had to affect him so. She suspected he dreamed of battle. Most soldiers did. She'd heard that some were never the same after they'd gone to war, that nightmares haunted them the rest of their lives. Was that true of Lachlan?

Campbell seemed to answer her as he sadly lowered his head and returned to curl up in his spot by the fireplace.

She meant to return to the bed after Lachlan fell asleep. Somehow she didn't make it.

Drifting slowly awake, Lachlan felt a warm, womanly body curled up against him, and he smiled. There was nothing like having his bonnie Margaret welcome him home from war.

His eyes still closed and a wicked grin on his face, he snuggled closer, teasing her soft, round bottom with his swelling dirk.

Then his smile faded. His brow creased. That was a memory from another time. That was before…

His eyes flew open, and he pulled back at once, waking her. Not Margaret. Alisoune.

"Aristotle's beard," she exclaimed sleepily. "How did I get here?" She stretched out both arms, yawned, and then turned to him with a smile.

Of course she *would* smile first thing in the morning. What else did he expect? The lass was sunshine personified.

"Oh, I remember now," she said, rising up on her elbows, which made her square neckline dip low on one shoulder. "Ye were havin' a nightmare."

He frowned. He didn't remember. He never remembered his dreams.

What he *did* remember in all-too-vivid detail was the way she'd felt nestled against him a moment ago. He might have imagined she was Margaret, but to the lusty beast in his trews, a woman was a woman. That part of him was still as hard as steel and expecting to be pleased.

The fact that Alisoune was only inches away, her hair sleep-mussed, her eyes softly sparkling, her gown threatening to fall off of her any moment now, didn't help matters.

"I should split more wood for the fire," he announced under his breath. Maybe hard labor and the bracing cold would extinguish the fire in his loins.

Was that disappointment he glimpsed in her eyes?

It didn't matter. She'd be leaving soon anyway. The storm would clear, and there'd be no reason for her to stay. Besides, he thought with black humor, if she left, he wouldn't need to trouble himself with taking a bath.

Aye, 'twas for the best, he decided as he began the difficult task of levering himself up from the floor.

"Here, let me help ye." She jumped up.

"Nae!" he growled, half in ire, half in shame. "I can do it myself." At her crestfallen expression, he added more gently, "I've managed alone so far. I'll have to manage alone when ye're gone."

If the words caught unexpectedly in his throat, and his eyes grew moist, 'twas probably just ash from the fireplace. That happened when you slept next to a fire.

As soon as he was up, he threw on his cloak, whistled to Campbell, and headed outside with his hand ax to split what little wood he had left. He'd have to fetch more before the day was done.

Lachlan's words haunted Alisoune. *I'll have to manage alone when ye're gone.* Of course he would. But it saddened her to think of leaving. And 'twas disappointing to think that her brief time with him would change nothing, that he'd forget her as readily as one forgot a squirrel scampering through the yard.

She wanted to help him somehow, to make his life better. She didn't want him to slowly let the cottage return to its former squalor. She couldn't bear to think of him moping in lonely exile.

She'd made that bedside bracket for him, which had pleased him enough to earn her a kiss. Was there anything else she could do for him?

Outside, she could hear him splitting logs as she poured oats and water into the porridge pot. His supply of wood was almost gone. He'd need more soon. She would have offered to collect wood for him, but she knew he'd refuse. He seemed determined to prove he could manage by himself.

Chopping wood must be extraordinarily difficult for him. Not only would it be hard to manage an ax while standing on one leg, but he'd have to make a number of trips into the forest to get enough wood to last even one day, since he could only bring back what he could carry over one shoulder.

She pushed the spectacles higher on her nose and tapped on her lip. She wondered...

Campbell was big and strong. And he had *four* legs. If she could construct a sled of some sort with a harness for the big deerhound, he could probably haul a good deal of wood.

Setting aside the pot, she scanned the room for something that could serve as a sled. Her gaze stopped on Lachlan's battle-scarred steel breastplate. That would slide easily across the snow and, later, across the grass. She could fashion a yoke and harness out of wood and leather and attach it to the breastplate with rope.

Giddy at the prospect, she whirled just as Lachlan came in the door. "Lachlan, I need to borrow Campbell."

"Borrow him? What for?"

"I..." She glanced at the half-empty bucket. "I need to fetch more water."

"Give me a moment," he said, placing chunks of wood on the coals. "I'll fetch it for ye."

"Ach, nae...ye...nae," she said, stumbling over her words. "I...I could actually do with...with a breath o' fresh air." She may have overdone it by fanning herself. "'Tis terribly hot in here."

He frowned at her as if he thought she were mad. She couldn't blame him. 'Twas a bumbling excuse. "I can open the door and—"

"Nae! Nae, nae, nae, ye don't have to..." She sighed. "To be perfectly honest...I..." She could think of no plausible reason to leave the cottage.

He asked quietly, "Do ye need to attend to...women's matters?"

"Aye, that's it," she said, beaming. "I need to attend to women's matters, aye. And...Campbell..."

"Will keep ye safe."

"Exactly." She grinned, grateful he'd supplied the perfect, if vague, excuse for her.

While he kindled the fire, she secretly stuffed some rope, wood, and leather scraps into her satchel. Then she swirled on her cloak, and, when his back was turned, concealed his great armored breastplate underneath it, staggering out the door under its weight with Campbell at her heels.

The snow was falling lightly now, and she found to her delight that the breastplate made quite an excellent sled. With Campbell frolicking beside her, she dragged it all the way to the edge of the woods and a spot shielded from snow by thick pines where she could work.

Campbell was patient while she fitted him with the yoke, as if he understood he was taking on an important responsibility. Once she had his harness in place, she attached it to the breastplate with two lengths of rope so 'twould drag behind him.

Then, because she couldn't resist the temptation, she had Campbell take her for a wee sled ride across the snow. There was only one mishap when he started too quickly and she took a tumble off the back of the conveyance.

By the time she returned to the cottage, smoke was curling up from the chimney, she was dusted with snow and flushed with pleasure, and Campbell's entire body was wagging with joy.

"Now don't say a word, Campbell," she whispered to the dog. "'Twill be a surprise."

She unfastened the yoke and sled and propped them against the wall where the stack of wood had been. Then, looking as casual as possible, the two conspirators entered the cabin to enjoy a steaming breakfast of porridge.

chapter 9

"**S**omethin' is up with ye two."

Lachlan was sure of it. He might not know the lass well enough to read her expressions, but Campbell's guilt was written all over his face.

"Why do ye say that?" Alisoune asked with wide-eyed innocence, spooning more porridge into her mouth.

"Because Campbell looks like he's been eatin' kittens."

She giggled, almost losing her porridge.

He clucked his tongue. He supposed he'd find out eventually what the two of them were up to. In the meantime, he tried to enjoy his porridge. 'Twas nigh impossible when his attention kept drifting to the rosy-cheeked lass, who this morning looked as rare and beautiful as a rose in winter.

He still couldn't believe she'd slept beside him last night on the cold flagstone floor. The softhearted lass had sacrificed her own comfort to comfort him.

No one had done that for him before. His nightmares had always frightened Margaret. 'Twas one of the reasons she'd left him.

He never recalled the dreams. But when he woke in a cold sweat, breathing heavily, crushed by a vague sense of despair, 'twasn't hard to guess what he'd been dreaming about.

To realize that this lass he hardly knew, who'd crossed his path by chance, might wish to understand his pain...

He swallowed his last bite of porridge and looked up at her through suddenly watery eyes.

How could he bear to have her leave?

Yet how could he be so cruel as to wish she'd stay?

She smiled back fondly, warming him instantly and making him feel like she'd known and loved him all his life.

He cleared his throat and pushed himself up on his crutch, turning away. "I've got to go...fetch more wood."

"Now?" she asked, springing to her feet.

Keeping his eyes averted, he shrugged on his cloak, pulled on his cap, and muttered, "Better now, before the snow's heavy."

"Well then," she said cheerfully, "Campbell has somethin' he'd like to show ye."

Here 'twas—whatever they'd been up to. He supposed he wasn't going to be able to make his escape just yet. He wiped his nose with the back of his sleeve and said with false cheer, "Does he?"

"Come on, Campbell," she sang out. "Show your master what a handy beast ye are."

The hound came to attention and began yipping excitedly, something he rarely did. When Alisoune opened the door, Campbell charged out, bounding crazily in the snow and snapping at snowflakes.

Befuddled, Lachlan shook his head. "What did ye feed my dog to make him so wild?"

She winked at him. "Kittens."

He smirked.

She called Campbell back to her and began attaching some sort of leather harness over the dog's shoulders. When Lachlan saw her drag his breastplate—his fine polished steel breastplate with the Lion of Scotland engraved on it—across the ground to secure it behind the hound, his jaw clenched. But he managed to hold his tongue.

And then all at once he understood.

"'Tis a sled." He laughed in delighted wonder. "To transport firewood."

She nodded vigorously, joining in his laughter.

He was amazed, truly amazed. "But how did...where did... what...?"

He grinned down at her. She smiled up at him. Then she closed her eyes and lifted her face, clearly expecting a kiss of thanks.

He gulped. He didn't dare kiss her. 'Twouldn't be fair to her. 'Twouldn't be fair to either of them. There was no future in a kiss between them. 'Twould only be a taste of something they couldn't have.

So as much as he longed to press his lips to hers, and as much as he knew it hurt her when he didn't, he turned away and feigned a sudden keen interest in Campbell's new conveyance.

Alisoune opened her eyes, and then frowned in discouragement. If she didn't know better, she'd think Lachlan didn't care for kissing. But his body certainly responded to it. So why did he deny himself what was so pleasurable?

'Twas only a wee kiss, after all.

Aye, she understood what he'd said about saving herself for her husband. She wasn't a fool. She knew that men preferred their brides to be unbedded. But at the moment they were nowhere near a bed.

She sighed in resignation and wrapped her cloak tighter about her, trying to take joy in the way Lachlan was experimenting with his new toy.

"Come on, lad," he called to Campbell after he'd dropped his ax into the sled. "Let's try out this new device."

He waved his hand and gave her a lopsided grin of gratitude before he set off with Campbell toward the woods, disappearing in the quiet fall of snowflakes.

At least she'd managed to coax a smile from him, she thought, if not a kiss.

He was gone for a long while. Alisoune cleaned up breakfast and straightened the bed linens. She washed her face and hands and rinsed her teeth. She even took out her disheveled braid, combed her hair, and replaited it. But still he didn't return.

Bored, she began investigating the cottage more thoroughly.

He had a small store of spices, and she uncorked each of the tiny vials and sniffed at them, identifying them by name.

The trunk at the foot of his bed was unlocked, and she dug through his clothing, which was mostly linen shirts, woolen trews, and one rich black velvet doublet, for special occasions, she supposed.

She more closely examined each piece of armor, forgetting that he must have been wearing it when he lost his leg, shocked by the dark bloodstains that peppered the dull steel and by the notable absence of one of his greaves.

Then, because for Alisoune, curiosity always outweighed horror, she began to wonder, since the greave was missing, what had become of the leg inside it. Had he left it on the battlefield? Had he buried it? Had he brought it home for Campbell to gnaw on?

Silently scolding herself for such irreverent and grotesque thoughts, she put the armor back where she found it and picked up the round crystal on the mantel.

'Twas a beautiful thing. She'd never actually seen a rainbow crystal before, and she discovered that as she rolled it back and forth between her fingers in the firelight, it did seem to shine in different colors. At the moment 'twas a bright green, but when she turned it in just the right way, it flashed violet.

What had Lachlan said—that the stone was meant for her? Why would he think that? After all, she'd only appeared in his cottage yesterday.

Still, it felt soothing in her hand, the perfect size, almost as if 'twere made for her palm. It shimmered blue as she replaced it.

Then, impatient, she decided to keep a vigil at the door. Lachlan had told her to latch it, but she was sure nobody would bother coming for her in this weather. After all, 'twas nigh impossible to burn a person at the stake while snow fell to extinguish the flame.

Besides, she thought as she swung open the door, ushering in a cloud of snowflakes, she'd just come up with another way to make the dour Lachlan laugh.

Lachlan's spirits hadn't felt so light in a long time. The sled worked perfectly. 'Twas just as well she'd made it from his breastplate, since he had no other use for it. And even Campbell seemed proud to be of service. With the hound's help, he was able to chop and stack enough wood to last several days.

He wondered why he hadn't thought of such a brilliant solution. He supposed, wallowing in his misfortune and distracted by grief, it had been difficult to think of anything else.

Alisoune, on the other hand, had proved herself a genius. She'd immediately ferreted out his need, designed an effective remedy, and produced it. This one wee change in his life would make a great difference.

He'd never met a woman like Alisoune. Hell, he'd never met a *man* like her.

As he limped home, with Campbell dragging the sled by his side, he thought maybe the crone had been right. This lass, this

Keeper of the Stone, was indeed a special individual. And it seemed, whether the stone had anything to do with it, Lachlan's life *had* been changed, just as the old woman predicted.

He was almost home, less than a dozen yards from the door of the cottage, when an object suddenly flew past his shoulder. He ducked aside, and then turned to look for it. Had it been a bird? A rock? Behind him was only snow.

He turned back in the direction from which it had flown, and at that instant, a second object hit him full in the face.

'Twas cold and hard, and it stung where it hit him. He wiped wet snow from his face with the back of his hand and tried to see who was assailing him.

So stunned was he to see a grinning Alisoune launching another projectile at him that he had no time to duck out of the way of the third snowball, which struck him with deadly accuracy. His cap flew off from the impact, and he almost lost his crutch.

"What the devil!" he shouted, brushing bits of ice from his eyebrows.

She laughed and lobbed another hard-packed snowball at his belly.

He turned sideways, but not swiftly enough to avoid taking a hard impact to his arm. He swore, but his grin belied his anger.

"Is it war then?" he called out.

She answered with another snowball that glanced off his hip.

"Ach!" His appetite for revenge was whetted now, and he muttered under his breath, grinning all the while, "We'll see about that, lassie."

She'd stacked up an enormous store of munitions. The lass was likely to pummel him soundly before he managed to pack a single snowball. But surely his aim was better than hers.

While he rapidly compressed snow between his palms, she

threw two more frosty missiles. One hit his neck, sending shivers of ice down his shirt. The other impacted harmlessly on his crutch.

"A-ha!" he gloated, rearing back his arm and hurling his snowball forward.

But the little minx was ready for him. She'd appropriated his targe. She fended off the blow with a glance of his shield, then fired her next missile over the top of it.

Clearly he was going to lose this battle. And Campbell was of absolutely no use. The hound, his mind still on his serious wood-hauling duties, took no interest in their foolish play.

Alisoune was laughing triumphantly now, firing snowballs as if she were storming a castle, while he only managed to land one feeble clump of snow that struck the top of her head, dislodging her spectacles and showering flakes down over her face and shoulders.

She squealed with the cold shock, and he grinned in victory.

But her recovery was quick. With a shake of her head that scattered snowflakes everywhere, she reseated her spectacles, and then picked up a hefty missile in each hand and threw them in rapid succession.

Somehow he managed to duck *into* both of them and ended up with white splotches on the side of his doublet and the front of his trews, which sent her into gales of laughter.

He'd never win this lopsided battle, he decided, if he played fair.

CHAPTER 10

Alisoune hadn't had so much fun in years. Not only was she enjoying the thrill of competition, but the challenge of calculating the most effective angle of trajectory kept her brain entertained as well. So far, she'd landed her strikes with impressive accuracy.

She hurled another snowball at him, which hit him smack in the middle of the chest. But this time the blow made him stagger backwards, and his crutch slipped out from under him. As she watched in growing dismay, his arms cartwheeled, and he lost his balance. To her horror, he fell back, hard, into the snowbank, where he lay...silent.

Her jaw fell open. "Lachlan?"

He failed to respond. She dropped the second snowball from limp fingers.

"Lachlan?"

There was no answer. She stared at him in dread, gathering her skirts in clenched fists.

"Lachlan!"

She stumbled toward him, whimpering in fear under her breath. What had she done? Was he hurt? Was he dead? What ever had made her think 'twas a good idea to pummel a crippled man with snowballs?

He still hadn't stirred when she reached him. He lay sprawled and motionless on the snow, like a beautiful dark angel fallen to earth.

"Oh, Lachlan," she breathed in fright, clapping her hand over her mouth.

But she couldn't let panic distract her from reason. Steeling her nerves, she rushed forward and knelt by his side, using her fingers to feel for the pulse in his neck.

To her great relief, his heart was still beating. But he wasn't awake. She furrowed her brow in worry. She'd heard that after a blow to the head, sometimes people could dwell in a state of deep sleep for days. They eventually wasted away, never regaining consciousness.

"Oh, Lachlan," she said in despair, shaking him gently. "I only meant to cheer ye. I didn't mean to hurt ye."

She bit her lip. If he didn't waken straightaway, she'd have to get him inside so he wouldn't freeze. But how? He must outweigh her by half.

She glanced back over her shoulder at Campbell. Perhaps she could unload the wood and use the sled to transport him.

While she was considering the best course of action, and before she could move a muscle, Lachlan rose up, grabbed her, and rolled her onto her back in the snowbank.

She gasped in surprise and relief. "Ye're awake!" But a closer look into his twinkling eyes told her the truth. "Ptolemy's ballocks! Ye played me false."

Pinning her by the shoulders, he grinned down at her like a wildcat with a mouse between its paws.

"Ach!" she spat. "Let me up!" The snow was cold on her backside.

"Only if ye'll cede the battle."

She was vexed with him. After all, he'd scared the hell out of her, and she'd been worried. But when she beheld the merry sparkle in his silver eyes and the flash of his snow-white smile, she couldn't stay angry.

She shivered. "'Tis cold, Lachlan! Let me up!"

"Oh, I *know* 'tis cold. I was lyin' there for quite a while myself."

"Ye brute!" she cried, grinning in spite of herself. "Let me go!"

"Do ye yield?"

"Ye cheated!"

"Ye gave me no choice." He shook his head and clucked his tongue. "What sort o' villain attacks a helpless cripple anyway?"

"Ye're not helpless, ye big oaf!"

"Now ye're callin' me names." He sighed in mock disgust. "'Tis appallin'."

She laughed and pounded on his chest, but he didn't budge.

"*And* beatin' me."

She tossed her head, throwing off her spectacles. "Campbell!"

He laughed. "The dog's not goin' to help ye, lass. Come on now, ye've lost the fight. Surrender."

"Never," she mumbled under her breath.

He cocked his head. "What was that ye said? I didn't quite—"

"Never!" she said, laughing.

"As ye wish." He shrugged. "I've no place to go. 'Tisn't my arse freezin' in a snowbank."

She gasped, then giggled.

The wet snow was indeed seeping into her skirts. But as she continued to gaze up into Lachlan's dancing eyes, 'twasn't long before she no longer felt the cold.

Lachlan watched Alisoune melt before his eyes like snow in sunlight. He knew that look. The lass was all hot and hungry again.

And this time—curse his male instincts—so was he.

When her eyes drifted languidly down to his parted mouth, he was so drunk on his joy and her laughter that he didn't hesitate or even think before kissing her.

She tasted as fresh and clean as the fallen snow. As she gasped against his lips, the light fog of her breath moistened his face. Her fingertips were icy as she touched his cheek, but her kiss warmed his blood so thoroughly that he hardly felt the cold.

Her body was soft and welcoming beneath him, and to his astonishment, he fell into her embrace as easily as laying his head on his own familiar pillow.

Her shoulders were bared by the wide square neckline of her stomacher, and he stroked her tenderly there with his thumbs. She moaned softly and arched up, inviting his caress with her pale bosom.

He obliged her, running one knuckle along the upper edge of her gown and delving beneath with his finger. Her skin was supple and impossibly smooth, like fine silk, and he sighed into her mouth with pleasure.

But she wanted more. She threaded chill fingers through the curls at the back of his head and drew him down toward her, then slipped her mouth aside and offered him her throat.

With a low knowing chuckle, he kissed her delicate jaw and then lower, making a burning trail beneath her ear and down the side of her neck till she shivered at the sensation.

His own body, meanwhile, had gone instantly rigid with desire. It wanted only one thing. And the more he kissed her lips, her throat, the upper curve of her breast, the more intense his longing grew.

She arched even more, as if commanding him to touch her where she willed.

He knew what she was asking for, even if she didn't. With a broad stroke of his tongue, he grazed her bosom, nuzzling aside the fabric of her white linen chemise to taste her sweet flesh.

Her hands made fists in his hair, and she squeezed her eyes closed in bittersweet yearning, turning her head aside to grant him access.

He gently tugged her stomacher down to reveal the pale perfection of her small breasts.

She drew in a shuddering breath and held it in anticipation. With a seductive smile, he teased one of them with the tip of his tongue and then, when she gave a little cry of need, enclosed her fully in his mouth.

He was sure there could be no greater heaven than this. She tasted like smooth honey mead on his tongue, mellow and spicy and intoxicating. And when he drank his fill and moved to her other breast, she dug her fingers into his back with ill-concealed lust.

He'd thought his body had forgotten how to respond to a woman. But he was wrong. He ached with yearning and thickened with purpose.

She squirmed beneath him, and he remembered she was lying on the frozen ground, probably soaking her skirts with snow. Kissing his way back up to her other ear, he reached a hand beneath the curve of her hips and lifted her, rolling onto his back with her so that he would bear the brunt of the ice.

Her cheeks as she gazed down at him were flushed with cold, but a raging fire burned in her eyes. That look alone made his blood surge, and he groaned with desire.

The impetuous lass attacked him then, raining kisses over his face and throat and the vee of his chest as if to sample every inch of his flesh. With breathless enthusiasm, she wrenched open the buttons of his doublet, and her hands slipped beneath his linen shirt, gliding over his shoulders, across his chest, and along his ribs.

It felt divine. For so long he'd been bereft of touch, bereft of affection. That Alisoune would give herself so freely and lovingly to him was akin to setting a banquet before a starving man.

He felt like laughing with delight as she boldly explored him. And then she pressed a brazen palm against the front of his trews, and the laughter stuck in his throat.

He sucked a breath through his teeth and closed his eyes in delicious agony. But just as the curious lass began to loosen the laces of his trews, he heard Campbell growl.

Biting back a curse at the interruption and careful not to alert Alisoune, Lachlan peered through narrowed lids to see what troubled the hound. Then his eyes widened.

In the distance, a dark figure stood, watching them. At Campbell's second warning growl, the man turned in a huff and lurched off in the direction of the village, his black cloak stark against the white snow.

The man was too far away for Lachlan to identify. But whoever 'twas had probably recognized Lachlan and would babble to all of Keirfield what he'd seen.

Lachlan didn't care a whit what the townspeople thought of him. But he had to protect Alisoune. Already, the lass had pricked the pride of Father Ninian. If that infernal priest heard that she'd been seen sporting with Lachlan in the snow…

As difficult as 'twas to end such a pleasurable endeavor, Lachlan forced himself to gently seize Alisoune's wrist, stopping her passionate pursuit. He retrieved his cap and her spectacles and whispered, "Let's go inside, lass."

Father Ninian's secretary, fleeing purposefully toward Keirfield, was so overwrought with religious zeal and righteous fervor that he could hardly scramble fast enough through the snow. He pursed his thin lips in disgust. The father would hear about this.

He'd seen Lachlan Mar fornicating with the witch. He was

sure of it. They'd been copulating shamelessly, right there in the snow, in plain sight of God...and everyone else, for that matter.

He licked his lips. 'Twould be a long while before he could scrub from his memory the sight of the crippled soldier fondling the spectacle-seller's undersized teats.

Mar probably wasn't to blame, he decided. 'Twas probably the fault of that scheming witch. She'd probably ensorceled the poor wretch.

After all, the soldier had kept mostly to himself after he lost his leg and his Margaret. He didn't go to church. He didn't strike up conversations. He only came to town for supplies. He wasn't the sort of man to carry on with a strange woman.

Besides, he was a cripple. God had punished him. He clearly wasn't meant to enjoy such worldly diversions. 'Twas sinful that a man with one leg should be encouraged to partake of pleasures he didn't deserve, of what rightfully belonged to pious men whom God had seen fit to bless with whole bodies.

Father Ninian was right. The lass was the handmaiden of the devil, and Mar was wrong to try to protect her from the fires of purification.

He didn't wish to be seen as too overeager. But he couldn't wait to tell Father Ninian what he'd witnessed.

By the time Lachlan unhitched Campbell, unloaded the sled, stacked the wood, and hung up his cloak, Alisoune realized his lusty mood had faded. He'd doubtless had enough time to reconsider their impulsive actions and he felt guilty now. He was stoking the fire on the hearth, but the fire in his heart no longer burned brightly. He seemed...distracted.

What he didn't realize was that she had no intention of giving up so easily. She'd never been intimate with a man before. The way Lachlan made her feel, she was positive she was on the verge of some soul-shattering discovery. And she meant to pursue it. Alisoune was nothing if not persistent. She could be as pesky as a flea.

Determined to seize the day, she loosened the laces of her stomacher and, leaving only her linen chemise, casually drew her gown over her head, ostensibly to dry it by the fire.

Though he said nothing, his eyes coursed over her with an obvious flicker of appreciation, and she saw his breath catch.

She draped the gown over the back of the chair near the fire. Then she turned to warm her own damp backside, strategically placing herself between Lachlan and the fire, where the light of the flames would silhouette her body.

He tried to ignore her...and failed. Guilt might be a powerful force, she decided, but 'twas no match for lust. His fist clenched on his crutch, and his jaw tightened as he stared intently past her and into the flames.

"I'm goin' to town," he finally muttered.

She raised her brows in surprise. "Ye are? Now? Why?"

"I have to...get some...supplies."

He wasn't a very good liar. Perhaps she'd been too seductive and was scaring him off. She crossed an arm over her bosom, self-conscious now. "When will ye...be back?"

"I won't be long."

His face was grim. He didn't meet her eyes as he shouldered his satchel and tied a pouch of coins onto his belt. The familiar jingle alerted Campbell, who jumped up to his feet, ready to accompany his master.

"Campbell," he commanded, "stay."

The dog reluctantly sank back down onto the floor.

"Latch the door," he reminded her, nodding briefly in farewell.

She gave him a timid smile. But inside, her heart was sinking.

CHAPTER 11

Alisoune stared in silence at the closed door for a full minute before latching it and then turning dejectedly towards the fire. Atop the mantel, the curious white stone caught her eye as it reflected the leaping flames, and she idly picked it up.

What had she done wrong? Why had he fled? In the snow, everything had seemed perfect. What had happened?

She cupped the stone in her palm, gazing down at it as if the answer lay there while a dozen possibilities raced through her brain.

She'd been too forward.

She hadn't been forward enough.

She was too tall, too awkward, too thin. Too smart.

He didn't like lasses with spectacles.

He didn't like lasses who made a spectacle of themselves.

As she looked down at the stone in her hand, it seemed dull now, just an ugly lump of worthless rock. Alisoune felt like that, ugly and worthless.

Sighing, she reached up to replace the crystal, but it slipped from her fingers and dropped with a hard smack onto the floor, and then rolled across the flagstones.

She gasped. What if she'd cracked it?

Campbell got to it before she could, bringing the stone back to her. She took it gently from between his teeth and examined it. Fortunately, 'twas unbroken. The only flaw in the stone were the cracks inside, which of course were what made it so unique and interesting.

As she gazed down at the crystal, she couldn't help but smile at the parallel. Wasn't that true of people as well? Wasn't it a person's flaws that made them unique and interesting?

The way the stone lay cradled in her hand now, it appeared to glow in a beautiful rosy color. Her thoughts likewise began to take on a more rosy cast.

'Twas true that most men seemed to feel threatened by Alisoune's flaws. They were uneasy around her. But Lachlan was different. He didn't mock her or shun her or think she was Lucifer's progeny.

He must have fled for some other reason. She furrowed her brows and rolled the stone between her hands.

Then, all at once, it came to her.

Lachlan might feel the same insecurities she did. He was also flawed—physically and mentally scarred. He might figure he was cursed by God, undeserving of kindness, not entitled to compassion or pleasure or love. Maybe that was why he had panicked and left.

With a lightened heart and renewed spirits, Alisoune carefully placed the crystal back on the mantel, where it flashed bright green before wobbling to a stop.

She knew what to do now. She'd send Lachlan such a strong message of acceptance and caring and affection that he'd *have* to believe it. Indeed, a brilliant idea was already forming in her head.

"How about if we go for a wee walk, eh, Campbell?" She grinned as the dog's tail began to wag. "Would ye like to show me where the spring is?"

Lachlan didn't know which was worse as he limped home through the snow—his pain or his anger. Damn it, there was no godly reason he should feel such agony in his toes. They weren't there any longer.

What had Alisoune called it? Phantom pain. Well, if 'twas phantom pain, he was a desperately haunted man.

At least he'd taken care of that meddling busybody who'd been spying on them. One glance at the black-cloaked secretary's ruddy cheeks and heaving chest, and Lachlan knew he had his man.

He hadn't needed to say much. Lachlan's size spoke well enough for him. But he *did* advise the squirming weasel as he held him by the throat that if he valued his continued good health, he should forget whatever he'd seen and stay away from Lachlan's cottage.

Satisfied he'd put the fear of God into the man and knowing Alisoune was safe enough with Campbell to guard her, he'd taken time to stop by the grocer to purchase a few onions, eggs, preserved figs, a bottle of sack, and, on an extravagant whim, a small box of sugared almonds.

The last time he'd made the trip into the village, there had been no snow. On one leg, it had taken him a long while. But this time 'twas a tortuous ordeal as he balanced the satchel of goods over his shoulder and battled through thick snowdrifts. Halfway home, the cursed pain returned with a vengeance.

'Twas a reasonable price to pay, he supposed, for surviving the battle, for living when his brothers died. Still he had to fight the urge to stop where he stood and lie down in the snow until either it passed or he froze solid.

But he had to get home. He had to get back to Alisoune. He may have cowed the secretary for now, but Lachlan was no fool. He realized that time had a way of dulling a man's fear.

By the time the cottage was in sight, he was grimacing at every step. Walking had made the ache worse, and he despaired of ever being without pain again.

At least he had Alisoune to look forward to—Alisoune with her sweet smile and gentle touch, her compassionate nature and her amusing antics. Indeed, her latest antic—the one where she'd oh-so-innocently stripped to her chemise, leaving herself nearly naked to his view—almost made him forget his pain.

Several agonizing minutes later, he finally reached the cottage. He brushed the snow from his shoulders and knocked at the door. Once it opened, he was greeted by Campbell's wet nose...and struck by the bitter realization that when Alisoune left, Campbell would be the only friend to ever greet him at the door.

His attempt to appear cheerful didn't fool her for an instant.

"What's wrong?" she said in concern, rushing forward to take the satchel from him. "Ye're so pale." She brushed his forehead with her thumb. "And ye're drippin' wet."

Her words made a lump form in his throat. The lass was fawning over him. Nobody fawned over him anymore. "I'm fine," he croaked.

"'Tis your leg, isn't it?" she guessed. "Ambroise Paré has a theory that when a nerve is severed, it becomes more sensitive to the cold." He had no idea who Ambroise Paré was, but he let her take his icy hand in her warm one just the same. "Come. I think I have just the thing for ye."

She drew him slowly forward. He glanced past her. There by the fire was his giant wooden tub, generously filled with water.

He blinked. How had she managed to fill it? That much water would take hours to transport. "How did...?"

She grinned smugly and nodded to another device she'd assembled while he was gone.

"'Tis a water transport. It fits over Campbell's yoke," she

explained. "He can carry two evenly balanced buckets o' water now. Between his two buckets and my two, it took only three trips to the spring to fill the bath."

Words failed him. 'Twas another ingenious invention. The lass had given him a gift beyond value. He'd have no reason to scrimp on water now. He could take a bath every day if he so chose.

"Ye thought o' this yourself?" he marveled, hanging up his cloak and combing a hand back through his hair. "I hardly know what to say."

She smiled. "Ye don't need to say a thing."

She began ladled boiling water from the pot over the fire into the cold water of the tub to warm it.

"What ye *do* need, however," she added, "is to get out o' those damp clothes."

He hesitated. Until he'd met Margaret, who cringed at the sight of a naked man, he'd never been particularly shy about his male anatomy. But that wasn't what gave him pause now. He was wary of letting Alisoune see the mangled stump of his leg.

She mistook his hesitation for modesty. "Ye needn't fret," she assured him. "I'll just take off my spectacles." She plucked them from her nose and tucked them into the front of her stomacher. "There. Now I'm as blind as an owl in daylight."

Mollified by her claim, he undressed. For Lachlan, standing stark naked in front of a beautiful lass, whether or not she could see him, had an immediate and dramatic effect. He was glad her sight was impaired, for if she'd looked at him now, she'd have seen that more than just his leg had become a shocking stump.

Alisoune suppressed a smile. Owls weren't actually blind in daylight, and neither was she. 'Twas only a myth. But Lachlan didn't know that. And she wasn't about to tell him.

Instead, she surreptitiously savored every delicious inch of him as he eased his magnificent body into the water.

She hadn't exactly fibbed. Her vision wasn't ideal. Things in the distance blurred into unrecognizable shapes. But when she was close to an object, or in this case a handsome man, her sight was only slightly impaired.

Indeed, 'twas good enough that the vision of his broad chest and wide shoulders emerging from the steaming water took her breath away. His body was covered in muscle, and he looked as brawny as a bull. He could have crushed her with his powerful arms, though at present, they were draped with leisurely abandon over the edge of the tub.

He closed his eyes and let out a long, blissful sigh. She was glad to see the warm water was doing its work. It had broken her heart to see him looking so pale and troubled.

She didn't want to get her gown wet, so she stripped down to her linen chemise. Then she pretended to guide her way with her toes along the flagstones, groping aimlessly as she settled onto her knees beside him.

Wetting the spicy-scented soap, she casually peered down into the water. But the clever knave adjusted his seat in the tub just then to lean forward, obstructing her view.

He cleared his throat. "If ye'll give me the soap, I can—"

"Do it yourself? Oh, nae, 'tis no trouble, no trouble at all. 'Tis the least I can do after ye walked all that way for... What did ye get anyway?"

She moved behind him, out of his reach, ere he could snatch the soap—and the pleasure of bathing him—from her.

"Onions. Figs. Eggs. A bottle o' sack. Oh...and sugared almonds."

"Ooh, sugared almonds," she cooed, adding coyly, "and do ye intend to share them?"

He shrugged. "Oh, I don't know. Campbell doesn't much like sugared almonds."

She scoffed and lightly thumped the back of his head. "Naughty rascal."

Then she wet the soap and began to scrub patiently at his scalp, humming softly and occasionally peeking over his shoulder to see if she could catch a glimpse of...anything. But the way his knee was bent, his broad thigh blocked her gaze.

She finished his hair, rinsing it with clean warm water, and then moved down to soap his back. His muscles rippled under her fingers, and their lean, sleek suppleness did something to her insides, making her heart race. Suddenly she wanted to sample *all* of his textures.

When she slid the soap up over his shoulder, her wicked fingers let it go. It slipped down his chest into the water with a plop.

'Twas only natural her hand should follow.

He sucked in a quick breath when she reached for it. But what else was she to do? She couldn't very well bathe him without the soap.

And of course, he should realize that without her spectacles, 'twould take a while to find it. She took her time looking, searching every delicious nook and cranny, apologizing when she happened to graze a sensitive spot.

"Ah, there 'tis," she said at last, finding it nestled against his lean buttock.

He emitted a shuddering sigh, and she resumed bathing him. She ran the soap down his massive arms, marveling at his strength. She weaved her fingers between his to wash them, enjoying the way they fit together.

'Twas when she moved to his legs that he tensed.

She paused. "Is the warm water not helpin' your pain?"

"Aye."

She resumed bathing him, soaping his good thigh and knee and calf. But when she moved to the other leg, he seized her wrist to stop her.

"What is it?" she asked.

His mouth worked as if he struggled to find the right words. "'Tisn't a fit sight for a softhearted lass."

"But I told ye I'm as blind as—"

"I don't believe owls are all that blind," he chided. "And I think ye know it."

She caught her lip beneath her teeth, aware she was blushing and unable to do anything about it.

He continued. "Just give me the soap and I'll—"

"Nae," she countered, pulling free of his grip. "I'm not some fainthearted, lily-livered maid to swoon over a man's limb."

"Ye've never seen a limb like this."

"A limb is a limb."

"'Tisn't a limb. 'Tis a stump."

"A stump then."

"An ugly, misshapen knob o' flesh that—"

"Oh, for the love o' Pythagoras!" she said in amused exasperation, rolling her eyes. "Give me your damned leg ere the water gets cold."

CHAPTER 12

Lachlan would rather bare his arse than his ugly stump. 'Twas something he kept hidden, something he didn't want anyone to see, especially not a woman he...

What? Cared for? He dismissed the thought at once. 'Twas foolish to go down a road that went nowhere.

He supposed he was being overly defensive. But he didn't want to see the affection in her eyes dimmed by horror.

Then again, why not? She was leaving anyway. What difference did it make whether she left in tearful apology as Margaret had or ran screaming from the cottage?

"Fine." With a resigned sigh, he leaned his head back against the edge of the tub and closed his eyes to slits.

Alisoune wasted no time, delving both hands into the water and lifting his thigh with all the reverence of a bear hauling a trout from the stream. He braced for her grimace of revulsion.

But it never came. Instead, she began studying him intently, turning her head this way and that, even donning her spectacles to inspect every horrifying scar and twisted sinew, all without so much as a wince of disgust.

"Remarkable," she murmured. "Does it still hurt?"

"A bit."

"Not as badly?"

"Nae."

"'Tis the heat o' the water," she said triumphantly. "Paré was right."

He wondered if he should send Paré a gift of some sort. 'Twas strange, but the more Alisoune studied his mangled leg, the less awkward he felt.

"Do me a favor," she requested, her eyes sparkling, "in the name o' science. Close your eyes, and tell me where ye feel my touch."

He looked at her skeptically, but saw no harm in humoring her. He closed his eyes.

She ran her palm down his thigh, rounding the spot above his knee where his leg had been severed. A sudden twinge coursed down his shin and into his toes. His eye twitched.

"Where do ye feel that?"

He didn't want to tell her.

"Lachlan?" she urged.

He sighed. "I feel it in my damned toes."

"What about this?"

He felt a soft pressure under his missing heel. He shook his head. "My heel."

"And this?"

He felt the whole bottom of his missing foot, but it didn't hurt or tingle or burn. It actually felt improved. He opened his eyes.

She was rubbing and pressing at the end of his thigh. "Better?"

He nodded.

"Aha!" She grinned. "Ye see? If your nerves can fool your brain into thinkin' your leg hurts, then you can fool your brain into thinkin' ye're relievin' the pain as well."

'Twas amazing. Not only did her touch ease his pain, but it eased his fears. She didn't find the sight of him abhorrent at all.

She found him fascinating...almost as fascinating as he found her.

As Alisoune resumed bathing him, her delight at having made an important scientific discovery began to pale in the light of a newer, more interesting revelation.

Lachlan was watching her. His eyes had softened, and his silvery gaze roamed over her. She felt it on her hair, on her lips, along the neckline of her chemise. He must have appreciated what he saw, for when she chanced to lower her regard, she could clearly see his ready response beneath the water.

The sight of him had a curious effect on her. Her nether regions began to ache, and her breasts tingled, remembering the sweet caress of his tongue. The more she touched him, the more aroused she became, until she craved something more than just bathing him.

Using her fingers, she combed the clean, wet hair back from his face. Then, on impulse, she caught his face between her hands and leaned forward to give him a quick kiss.

But 'twasn't quick at all. He replied with a kiss of his own, lifting his wet fingers to tangle in her hair and tilting her head to a more desirable angle.

She closed her eyes, dissolving into his embrace. So compelling was his kiss that she forgot about everything else. The outside world disappeared. All that existed were their lips, entwined in glorious counterpoint.

Her braid dipped into the bath, but she didn't notice. The sleeves of her chemise dragged through the water, but she didn't care. She was barely aware, when he wrapped his arms around her, pulling her closer, that she half-fell, half-climbed into the tub atop him.

With only her thin, drenched chemise between them, she could feel every inch of his muscular, bath-warmed body against hers. His hands slipped down her neck, along her shoulders, and then lower, to caress her breasts through the wet linen.

She gasped into his mouth, and he answered her with a bold stroke of his tongue. He moved one hand lower still, over her chemise, past her belly, as their tongues engaged in a lustful feast.

And then he found the spot where her need was centered. The instant he pressed his fingers between her thighs, intense pleasure zagged through her like a lightning bolt.

She groaned and moved against him instinctively. Heat flashed through her body, and her heart raced. Her breathing grew shallow and rapid. She clutched his shoulders and squeezed her eyes tightly, reveling in yearning, yet yearning for more.

All at once he broke from the kiss and, with his other hand, clasped the back of her neck. He held her head close to him and whispered roughly in her ear. "I want ye, Alisoune. Damn, how I want ye."

"Then take me," she sobbed.

He hesitated a long moment, then at last seemed to surrender. "All right, lass. I will. But not in the bath. 'Twill be better in the bed."

She nodded, giving him one last kiss of promise. Then she struggled up and stepped out of the tub, dripping as she stood before him. But she wasn't cold, not with the way Lachlan was staring at her.

In wet linen, she might as well have been naked. Hunger burned in Lachlan's smoky eyes as he perused her. He made a sound that was half-groan, half-sigh, a sound that felt as if it generated a sympathetic vibration in all her bones.

He pulled himself out of the water, using the bracket she'd made for him. As she gazed at him standing before her—tall and massive and muscled—she was struck by a sudden shiver of fear.

449

He'd seemed smaller somehow in the tub, smaller and less threatening. Now he looked like a great Roman statue...except none of the statues she'd seen were quite so...endowed.

He must have sensed her trepidation. Dropping his gaze, he lowered himself to sit on the bed and draped the sheepskin coverlet over his lap. "If ye don't want to—"

"Oh, nae!" she hurried to say. "'Tisn't that. I do. 'Tis only..."

He sighed. "My leg."

"Nae!"

"'Tis all right," he said, shaking his head. "I don't expect—"

"'Tisn't your leg," she assured him. "'Tis your...your..." She made a gesture like a caber-tosser casting a 20-foot caber, and she saw him stifle a smile.

"Oh, lass, if that's all 'tis," he said, his eyes brightening, "come here and let me soothe your fears."

He did more than soothe her. He was tender and patient, riling up her senses until she was practically begging for his touch. Then he held her close against him as they reclined together on their sides, face-to-face, flesh to flesh. Slowly and gently, with one guiding hand upon her buttocks, he pressed into her.

She sucked in a quick breath as a sharp, brief pain knifed through her.

His whisper in her ear was taut with passion. "I'm sorry, lass. It couldn't be helped. But 'twill get better, I promise."

The pain receded in a moment as he smoothed the wrinkles from her brow with his thumb. And then she only felt deliciously full.

He began to move within her, grazing her with long, easy strokes that tamed her the way that petting tamed a wild cat. For a while, 'twas pleasurable, a lovely friction that warmed her and wrapped her head in a comforting haze. An indescribable love for him washed over her, a love for this broken man who had bared his body and his soul to her.

But gradually her fondness for him became much more. His touch no longer soothed her, but aroused her. Affection became desire. 'Twas a smoldering coal lodged betwixt her legs that suddenly sparked like a flint, a coal that he coaxed to flame.

Her mind floated away. 'Twas a purely visceral experience, and for once she was without a thought in her busy brain. Her limbs tangled with his. Primitive groans of joy came from deep within her. And her heart beat to a strange new rhythm of desire.

When she peered at him through half-closed lids, the beautiful anguish on his face catapulted her to new heights of passion, and her heart swelled in her breast.

"Oh, Lachlan!" she cried.

"Almost, love...almost."

She didn't know what he meant until she suddenly felt a tiny pinpoint of light arise inside her at the place where they were joined. It brightened as it grew, spreading out like a pool of warm honey, bathing her flesh.

He nuzzled her ear, sending a shiver of lust through her as he breathed, "Aye, lass, let it come."

And then, like a molten fount bursting up through the earth, she erupted with a throaty cry, shuddering with sweet relief.

He followed her soon after, roaring his ecstasy against her cheek as he clung tightly to her and trembled with a forceful release.

She didn't mean to burst into tears. It just happened.

Still breathing raggedly, Lachlan caught her face in his hands and frowned in concern. "What's wrong, sweetheart?"

"'Twas beautiful," she breathed, overcome with emotion.

He smiled. "Oh, aye."

"And I just," she squeaked out between sobs, "Oh, I love ye, Lachlan."

She thought his eyes filled, too, but she'd never know for certain, because he pulled her close, cradling her head against his chest and holding her there for a long while.

Her last thought before she relaxed into the arms of slumber was whether he could learn to love her as well.

In the mellow aftermath of lovemaking, Lachlan drifted off with Alisoune in his arms. Moved by her heart's confession and filled with peace and relief, he slept more soundly than he had since the war.

'Twas morn when he next opened his eyes. What he saw in the dim light made him smile. Alisoune was sitting at the foot of the bed with a sheet draped over one shoulder, looking like a Roman goddess in spectacles. She was feasting on sugared almonds and inspecting a piece of his armor.

"Good morn," he croaked.

"Oh!" She gave a guilty start and dropped the greave, which clattered on the floor.

He smiled as she picked it up and propped it against the wall. "Did ye sleep well?"

She nodded, handing him the bag of almonds, and he popped a few in his mouth. He found her sudden shyness adorable. Also adorable were her sleep-mussed tresses, her delicate naked shoulder, and her bare feet.

"I haven't slept so well in a long while," he volunteered, reaching out a hand to entwine her fingers in his.

She nodded again, but averted her eyes, running an idle finger over the back of his hand. "Was that the first time...I mean...have you ever..."

He almost choked on an almond. He didn't know whether to be pleased or insulted that Alisoune believed he might be a virgin. "Nae, I've had a wee bit of experience." Though he'd left his wild days behind, he'd enjoyed the favors of at least a dozen maids in his youth.

"Were ye...married?"

He hesitated. Alisoune was the most curious lass he'd ever

met. But he wanted to be honest with her. "Nae, but I was betrothed once."

She seemed to consider his words. "What was her name?"

"Margaret." 'Twas the first time he'd said her name out loud since she'd left. 'Twasn't as painful as he'd expected.

"What happened to her?"

Her question was a reminder that, as with Margaret, his time with Alisoune was likely limited. "She left."

"Why?"

He sniffed. "She needed to wed a *real* man." Those had been her words, but they felt like his legacy now.

"What?" Alisoune furrowed her brows in righteous indignation. "But ye *are* a real man."

"She needed a man who wasn't a cripple, who could support her, protect her, give her a life."

"Hmph! It sounds like Margaret was the cripple."

Her assessment surprised and pleased him. Margaret *had* always been a rather helpless lass.

Alisoune rubbed the pad of her thumb across his knuckles, and her eyes turned soft. "I think she was a fool to let ye get away."

He swallowed hard. 'Twould be easy to fall under Alisoune's enchantment, because a part of him so desperately wanted to believe it. He wanted to believe, as she'd sworn last night, that she loved him. But he suspected the lass was confusing lust for love.

She'd tire of him once the novelty of lovemaking wore off. And when that happened, she'd realize he was only a helpless cripple who could do nothing for her.

Once the storm passed, she'd leave him, just as Margaret had and just as fate decreed.

But until then, he yearned to wring every drop of joy he could out of the time they had together. He might not have a future with her, but at least he'd have a sweet memory of her to warm his lonely nights.

"Lachlan?" She was drawing lazy figure eights on his thigh.

"Mm?"

"Would you want to…that is…if 'tisn't too much trouble…"

"Aye?"

She lifted her eyes to him, and he read her lusty request in their smoky green depths.

They needed no words. He grew instantly hard, she tossed aside her spectacles and her sheet, and they enjoyed a spirited breakfast in bed.

An hour later, the storm was in full-force outside. Wind whistled through the cracks between the window panes and rattled the door against its jamb.

The sound was music to Lachlan's ears. As long as the storm continued, Alisoune would remain with him. They could live in a blissful utopia and never face harsh reality.

Indeed, after their fourth bout of lovemaking, he decided he didn't care if the snow lasted till June.

CHAPTER 13

For two days, between snuggling with Lachlan under the covers, letting him bathe her in his great tub, and inventing novel positions for her new favorite pastime, Alisoune worked on a secret project.

With the snowstorm raging outside, they were stuck indoors. As Alisoune had explained to Lachlan, she'd go mad if she didn't give her active brain something to do.

And so, inspired by the sketches she'd seen by Ambroise Paré, she tinkered away on a new invention. But since she wanted to surprise Lachlan, she worked on it out of his sight behind the bed, giving him stern instructions that he wasn't allowed to peek.

Meanwhile, Lachlan kept busy, doing repairs he claimed he'd let go too long. He mixed clay to seal up the cracks around the window. He stitched up the clothing he'd let turn to rags. He washed his bed linens and hung them near the fire to dry.

A few last rivets, a bit of finessed carving, and some strategic padding, and Alisoune finished the project. By afternoon, she was ready to let Lachlan try it out.

At least that was what she intended.

But once she saw what he'd been doing for the past half-hour—shaving off his unruly beard, revealing his chiseled jaw and square face—she thought he looked more handsome than ever, handsome and irresistible. And she didn't feel much like resisting.

Lachlan awoke in the morn with Alisoune's tangled hair draped across his face. He smiled and inhaled deeply, loving the scent of woman, the scent of *her.*

Numerous times last night she'd made him glad he'd trimmed his beard. She'd brushed her knuckles along his cheek, marveling at its smoothness, and lavished kisses all over his chin. And then, with a lascivious growl, she'd pulled his head to her bosom, inviting him to nuzzle her breasts with his freshly shaved face. That wasn't all he nuzzled, and she'd been thrilled with the erotic adventure he'd taken her on.

That they'd missed supper was little surprise. And with Campbell's uncanny ability to come and go out of the cottage on his own, the hound hadn't awakened them in the night to be let outdoors. So the fact that neither of them had stirred until now wasn't unexpected.

What *was* unexpected was what Lachlan saw when he gently brushed Alisoune's hair from his face. A bright, cheery beam of sunlight streamed in through the window and pooled on the flagstones.

His heart sank.

The storm was over.

He'd known this hour would come. Indeed, he counted himself fortunate to have had this much time with her. He didn't deserve her, after all. Women like Alisoune and Margaret were too fine for a man with one leg and no future.

Still, knowing all that didn't make it any less painful. He'd lived in denial for days now. He'd allowed himself to forget he was a cripple. He'd convinced himself her love for him would never fade. He'd let himself believe they could go on living like this in his cottage forever.

'Twas a hard delusion to give up.

Before Alisoune even opened her eyes, she stretched and yawned with cat-like grace. Smiling, she made a sound of lazy bliss, then purred, "Good morn, handsome."

His heart felt as if it might break. But he wouldn't disappoint her. If this was to be their last morn together, he'd make it one to remember.

"Good morn, beautiful," he choked out.

She cupped his chin and grinned. "I have to say I like this new face o' yours."

"Do ye now?"

"Aye. I quite like it." She gave him a lusty perusal. "I particularly like it betwixt my—"

Campbell chose that opportunity to shove his shaggy head between them and lick at Lachlan's newly bare face.

"Ach, dog!" he said in annoyance, wiping his face with the back of his hand. "Away!"

Alisoune laughed. Then she popped up, her attention already distracted. "Oh! I never got to show ye what I've been workin' on."

Lachlan furrowed his brows. He didn't want to see it. Whatever she'd made for him, 'twould be a parting gift, something she'd leave behind that would remind him of their last hours together.

"Ach, lass, let's eat first," he said instead. "I'm starvin' to death. Ye never fed me supper last night."

She swatted playfully at his shoulder. "Am I your cook now?" Then she wiggled her eyes suggestively. "And by the way, I think ye're wrong. I recall ye had quite a nice feast last night." Then, shocked by her own lewd remark, she covered her mouth and erupted into giggles.

He smiled back, but his heart was aching. How he'd miss the sound of her laughter. "I never realized ye were such a naughty lass."

"It must be the company I keep," she teased.

He'd achieved his aim, at least for the moment. They'd have one last meal together ere he let her walk out of his life forever.

Alisoune bustled about the kitchen, cracking eggs and stirring porridge, preparing breakfast as if nothing were wrong. But if he'd looked closer, Lachlan would have noticed that her smile was shaky and her hands trembled.

She'd seen the sunlight flooding through the window.

The storm had passed.

Lachlan would expect her to leave.

And she didn't want to go. Not yet.

She loved him. She knew she'd said so in the heat of passion. But even now, with her brain fully engaged and her lust held at arm's length, 'twas true. She loved Lachlan.

She loved the way his silver eyes turned molten with desire. She loved the way he frowned in concentration when he was banking the fire. She loved how he romped with his dog, how his teeth gleamed when he smiled, how he raked the hair back from his brow.

Most of all, she loved the way he made her feel. Around Lachlan, she felt desirable and clever and beautiful. He took an interest in her interests and never appeared bored or irritated or dismissive when she spoke at length on some fine point of science that anyone else would find dull.

He appreciated her intellect, and he didn't mind her spectacles. He shared her sense of humor, and he thought her breasts were just the right size. He was amused by her sense of curiosity, and he seemed pleased by her willingness to learn when it came to lovemaking.

But she'd barely begun wooing him. If she wanted him to fall in love with her, she needed more time. She cursed the arrival of the sun, wishing 'twould disappear and not return for months.

She knew she shouldn't overstay her welcome. Lachlan had already been more than generous with his lodging, his food, his protection.

But if he could only realize how much more she had to give, how much love she could lavish upon him, how much better his life would be with her in it...

Maybe her gift would help. Maybe once he saw what she'd made for him—this unique gift of restoration given from her heart—he'd fall in love with her.

She tried to keep up a merry attitude all through breakfast, but she could see that he too seemed ill-at-ease. He was probably trying to think of how to politely ask her to leave.

She couldn't give him that opportunity. She had to keep him preoccupied—with conversation, with her gift, with her body, if necessary—to keep him from saying the words that would banish her from his cottage, and his heart, for good.

But in one of her rare quiet moments as they ate, Lachlan nodded to his hound, who was curled up in a patch of sunlight on the floor. "Campbell's missed the sun."

The porridge stuck in her throat. She had half-hoped he wouldn't notice the change in weather. Now his words, spoken aloud, seemed to hang like an ax over her head.

She rushed to fill in the deadly silence. "An interestin' thing about that... Leonardo would say the sun is a form o' *direct* light. But what we're actually seein' in the cottage isn't the sun. 'Tis *diffused* light, because it's passin' through the atmosphere." She glanced feverishly around the room, looking for something to make her point. Then she tossed her napkin onto the table and scraped back her chair, standing to pick up the stone from the mantel and holding it in the sunlight. "The light passin' through an object like this milky stone is a different kind altogether, and the fourth," she said, turning the stone until it cast a violet wedge on her palm, "is *reflective* light, the kind that bounces off the prism in the midst o' the stone."

She knew she was chattering, but she couldn't seem to stop herself. There was a sad cast to Lachlan's eyes that told her he well understood the significance of the sun, and it had nothing to do with Leonardo da Vinci.

The porridge sat like a heavy lump in her stomach now. She didn't want him to tell her to leave. She didn't want him to say anything.

In a cheerful panic, she rushed over to snatch the cloth cover from the project she'd been working on for the past two days. She hefted up the heavy thing, brought it over, and placed it in his arms, giving him a watery smile.

He frowned at it. "What's this?"

"A gift."

"But what is it?" He turned it over.

"'Tis called a prosthesis."

"That's my armor."

"Aye, but 'tis more than that." She took it back carefully from him and demonstrated. "Above the greave and inside the poleyn is a knee hinge with a dowel that runs down to the foot, the saboton, and at the ankle, there's a spring." She took the padding out and tipped it so he could look down the top. "See the wooden top there? I took the liberty o' makin' a mold o' your leg while ye were sleepin', and I carved the wood so it should fit. But o' course, ye'll want to keep the paddin' in for comfort's sake. And then these buckles here are made to attach to your swordbelt to hold it on."

"'Tis a leg."

"Well…" She blushed. "'Tisn't quite a leg. But it should serve ye well enough. I copied the design from Paré, who—"

"Ye made me a leg."

She bit her lip, feeling strangely unsure of herself. Honestly, she couldn't tell from his expression whether he was pleased or appalled.

CHAPTER 14

Lachlan had never felt so conflicted.

Moved by Alisoune's kindness and generosity, he felt his throat close with emotion. He was overwhelmed by her gesture and impressed by her invention, which, upon closer examination, appeared to be a spectacular creation of rivets and springs and hinges that faithfully replicated the movements of a real leg.

Yet how could he accept such a gift? His limb had been the price he'd paid for outliving his brothers. He'd willingly suffered that loss, knowing they had lost so much more. 'Twasn't right that he be restored, that his debt to them be so easily forgiven.

He didn't expect her to understand. How could she? She'd never been a soldier. She didn't have brothers to look after. She didn't know the guilt he carried for surviving the battle.

"Thank ye," he murmured, setting the piece aside.

"Aren't ye goin' to try it?" she ventured.

"Later," he lied. "I'm a bit...weary now."

Her smile faltered. "Weary?" Her voice cracked on the word, and for a moment she looked uncertain. But then she tucked her lip under her teeth and stepped closer to walk her fingertips lightly up his arm. "Well, if ye're weary," she whispered in invitation, taking off her spectacles, "maybe we should go back to bed."

'Twas what he wanted more than anything—one last chance to hold her in his arms, to join with her in that most intimate of embraces, before he had to set her free.

Their mating was bittersweet—gentle yet fierce, languorous yet desperate. He tried to memorize every detail, tried to fix her image in his mind. And then he tried, unsuccessfully, to let her go.

They were still entangled a few hours later when she finally nudged him and murmured, "Come on, lazybones. I want to see how your prosthesis works."

"I'm sure it works fine."

She poked him. "Ah, Lachlan, don't be a tease. Ye know I want to see it."

"Maybe later."

"Later? What do ye mean, later?"

"Later, after ye're..."

"After I'm...?"

"Just...later." He lowered his eyes. He couldn't bear to see her hurt.

"After I'm gone," she murmured. "That's what ye were goin' to say, wasn't it?" He could hear the pain in her voice. "Ye want me gone."

"I didn't say that."

"Ye didn't have to." She turned away from him in the bed, but he could see her shoulders tense.

"Ah, ye know 'twas never meant to be, lass." He said it for his own benefit as much as hers. "*We* were never meant to be. Ye'll find a man one day, a *whole* man who will—"

"Ye *are* a whole man," she insisted.

"A man who can provide for ye, protect ye, give ye a proper

life." He scowled. The thought of Alisoune with another man left a sour taste in his mouth.

She bristled at that, turning toward him with angry, tear-filled eyes. "I built ye a brace, made ye a wood and water carrier, and designed ye a prosthesis. Do ye think I need a man to provide for me? My parents left me their spectacle trade, which I've managed on my own for the last year. I'm not exactly helpless."

"I meant no insult. 'Tisn't that ye can't provide for yourself. But ye shouldn't *have* to." He rolled onto his back and stared at the ceiling. "Ye deserve better."

Alisoune's throat ached from holding back sobs. Better? She wasn't going to find better.

But she saw through his words. He pretended that her leaving was for her own good, but she knew the truth. He was only being polite to spare her feelings. He obviously didn't love her the way she loved him. And he didn't want to tell her that.

There was nothing she could do about it. She'd tried every weapon in her arsenal. She'd transformed his cottage into a warm home. She'd created tools he could use to improve the quality of his life. She'd made him laugh. She'd even given him the gift of her body.

But 'twas impossible to force a person to feel an emotion that didn't exist inside them. Love wasn't a hypothesis, to be proved or disproved by scientific fact, but neither was it something that could be altered by alchemy. If Lachlan didn't love her, there was nothing she could do to change that.

She got out of bed before he could hear the sob in her chest and see the stricken tears in her eyes. Gathering her discarded clothing, she dressed quickly, trying not to think about her breaking heart.

Even the hound knew something was awry, for he sat alert, keeping his distance and whining softly.

She couldn't blame Lachlan...for any of it. She'd burst into his cottage, after all. She'd imposed herself upon him. It had been her idea to kiss him and, ultimately, to make love to him. She'd instigated everything. He'd only followed her lead.

Behind her, she heard him rise from the bed and pull on his trews. She brushed a tear from her cheek with her thumb. With trembling fingers, she combed her hair into a rough semblance of order and gathered her things into her satchel.

"Ye'll need food," he said behind her.

"I'm not hungry."

"'Tis a long journey."

"I'll be fine."

He sighed. "At least let me pack ye some oatcakes and cider." He limped toward the cupboard.

Then she remembered—her tools, her coin, her clothing, everything she owned was locked in her room at the Keirfield inn. She couldn't just leave them behind. She might be able to travel home to Stirling, 'Twas only six or seven miles. But without her tools and with no coin, she wouldn't survive long there.

Her shoulders slumping, she pushed the spectacles up on her nose. She didn't want to impose any further on Lachlan. But she didn't know what else to do.

"I hate to trouble ye," she said quietly, "but I can't leave quite yet. All my things..."

"They're in Keirfield?"

She nodded.

"I'll fetch them."

"Thank ye."

Their talk was so stilted, 'twas hard to believe that only an hour before, they'd been in bed together, locked in a lovers' embrace.

He continued to assemble food for her as if he provisioned her for a pilgrimage.

Campbell ambled up with his head lowered, and Alisoune scratched him behind the ears. Her eyes grew moist. She'd miss the silly hound as well.

Once Lachlan finished packing the fare and knotting it into a great linen cloth, he threw on his shirt and doublet and began tugging on his boot.

Determined not to cry, the most Alisoune could muster was a wee hopeful smile as she held out the prosthesis to him. "Maybe ye can try out your new leg on the way to Keirfield."

He paused in his labors, sighed, then resumed them. "I can't accept it."

"What?"

"The leg, I can't accept it."

"What do ye mean, ye can't accept it?"

"Maybe ye can save it for someone else."

"Someone else?" 'Twouldn't fit anyone else. Besides, 'twasn't as if one-legged men were around every corner. "But I made it for *ye*."

"I don't need it."

She flinched. "Ye're not even goin' to try it?" All the hours she'd spent customizing the armor—measuring the steel plate, carving the wood, adjusting the spring tension—and he was refusing it? She felt crushed.

He hastened to assure her, "'Tis brilliant. Ye should show it to one o' those brainy scientist fellows o' yours."

"But why wouldn't ye...?" she choked out. "I mean, I made it for ye...to make your life better."

"That's just it," he muttered under his breath as he wrenched up his boot the rest of the way. "Maybe my life shouldn't be better."

She blinked. "What in the name o' Pythagoras are ye talkin' about? Don't ye want to be happy?"

"'Tisn't a matter o' what I want. 'Tis a matter...a matter o' what I deserve."

"What?" she said, incredulous. "Why wouldn't ye deserve to be happy?"

He slipped the crutch under his arm. "Ye wouldn't understand."

"I might understand."

"Nae, ye can't," he said, pulling himself up. "Ye're not a soldier."

She crossed her arms. "I'm not a dog either, but that doesn't stop me from knowin' what pleases Campbell."

"That's different."

"How?"

"Damn it! Dogs are their own creatures. They only look after themselves. They don't have a...a king to fight for or...or fellow soldiers to watch over. They don't have young men entrustin' them with their lives!"

His voice cracked, and for an instant, she thought he might break down. But he steeled his jaw and stared at the flagstones. Eventually, his eyes grew distant with memory.

When he finally spoke, his voice was as bleak and chilling as the edge of a sharp sword. "The battle where I lost my leg, the battle at Haddon Rig, they said we won it. 'Twas a great victory for King James." He shook his head. "Not for me. My four brothers were killed in that battle. I should have been killed as well." He sniffed. "But nae, that would have been too easy. Better to leave me alive, lamed and worthless, to suffer." He frowned. "My father bid me watch over them. I failed. Because o' me, all o' my brothers are dead. And I have to atone for that."

Alisoune swallowed hard. She didn't know what to say. To lose four brothers in one battle...

"So ye see why I cannot accept your pros-..."

"Prosthesis," she breathed.

"'Tis my penance." He turned aside and hobbled off to fetch his cloak. "Payment for their souls."

Her jaw dropped. Surely he didn't believe that.

"'Twasn't your fault they were killed," she said, "was it?"

"I made a vow to my father to keep them safe."

"A vow impossible to keep. How could ye watch o'er anyone in the chaos of a battle?"

He punched the wall suddenly with the side of his fist, snarling in frustration. "I could have! I could have saved them. I could have clapped them in irons or...or ordered them home...or gotten them too drunk to stand. If I'd kept them from the fightin'...they'd still be alive."

"And they'd hate ye for keepin' them from the fightin'."

"Maybe. But they'd be *alive* to hate me."

"Ye can't blame yourself, Lachlan," she insisted. "'Twasn't your fault. Even your brothers wouldn't condemn ye. I'm sure ye did your best to protect them. What ye're feelin'—all this guilt and sufferin' as if ye're somehow to blame... Can't ye see? 'Tis like your phantom pain. 'Tisn't real."

"Ye don't know that. Ye can't know that."

"Your penance and sufferin' is not goin' to bring them back, Lachlan, any more than wishin' for your leg will grow ye a new one." She approached him cautiously and offered him the prosthesis again. "The best gift ye can give your brothers is to live your own life."

He shook his head as his eyes filled with tears. "I can't. I don't deserve a new leg." He snatched the cloak from its peg and flung open the door. "And I sure as hell don't deserve ye."

With that, he set out at a limp for Keirfield, slamming the door shut behind him.

Lachlan's sight blurred as he headed for the village. He wiped away a rogue tear that rolled down his cheek.

Alisoune's words haunted him all the way to town. *'Twasn't your fault.* How could his brothers' deaths not be his fault?

He was the eldest. He was supposed to look after them.

And yet she'd stumbled upon the truth. 'Twould have been almost impossible to keep his brothers from the fighting. The Mar lads were brave and brawny, and their father had raised them up to be warriors. Sooner or later, whether Lachlan willed it or not, they'd have taken up arms in some war or another.

Then why did he feel so guilty? Why couldn't he accept their loss as just a casualty of war? Was it only because he hadn't been killed with them?

Maybe Alisoune was right. Maybe all his suffering was like his phantom pain—a cruel trick of his mind.

By the time he reached the inn in Keirfield, paid her bill, and collected her things, he decided it didn't matter if he blamed himself or not. Alisoune was leaving, taking away his only hope of happiness.

Halfway home, his leg began to throb. Remembering how Alisoune had said that cold triggered the pain, he took the liberty of digging a few rags out of her things to stuff into the knotted knee of his trews, hoping to insulate his leg against the cold.

It seemed to help, but 'twas still a long journey home. He didn't arrive at his cottage until well into the afternoon. And when he opened the door, the sight that met him made a hard lump form in his throat.

Alisoune was fast asleep, curled up on the floor in front of the hearth with her arms around his hound. Campbell raised his eyes when he saw his master, but didn't lift his head, seeming to know not to disturb the lass. Lachlan smiled ruefully, wondering which of them would be more upset when she left.

Not wishing to trouble her, he closed the door carefully behind him and quietly added a log to the fire. Then he sat on the bed with his bottle of sack, gazing down at her.

She was so beautiful to him now. He no longer saw her as a gawky, awkward, skinny lass, but as a lovely, kind, desirable woman. His heart ached when he thought about her walking out of his cottage door and never coming back.

For that reason perhaps, he felt in no hurry to wake her, instead letting his eyes drink their fill of her as she slept. He took several pulls of the sack, hoping to numb the pain—of his leg and his heart. And because she lay there for so long, with Campbell snoring beside her, perfectly content to let her remain there, Lachlan himself grew drowsy watching them slumber. Before he knew it, he was fast asleep.

CHAPTER 15

"I saw Mar leave town not an hour ago," the secretary confided to Father Ninian, arching a smug brow. "I learned from the innkeeper that he paid the woman's bill and gathered her things."

The father tapped thoughtfully at his pursed lips. When the secretary had come to him with the tale of Mar and the spectacle-seller copulating in the snow, he'd dismissed it as the ravings of the man's overactive imagination. After all, according to Margaret's last confession, Lachlan Mar was incapable of such things.

But now the issue with the spectacle-seller had become complicated in ways the secretary wouldn't understand.

"'Twould be a failin' on my part were I to allow her to spread her heresy to other villages," the father said.

The secretary nodded. "Oh, aye."

That was what he claimed—that he feared she might infect other towns with her ideas. But the truth was more personal than that.

He'd expected the furor caused by the woman's impious ravings to have died down by now. After all, he'd run her out of town, and no one had seen her in days.

But this morn he'd overheard several of his flock *still* discussing her claim—the claim that that mad Prussian Copernicus had put forth about the Sun being the center of the galaxy—as if such a heretical notion might have true merit.

And if the townspeople started questioning the nature of the universe, 'twouldn't be long before they began to question the nature of God and, more significantly, the role of priests in such a world. Father Ninian held a certain comfortable authority in Keirfield, and he couldn't afford to lose it because of a spectacle-seller...a spectacle-seller, for God's sake!

"Why, even the woman's trade is an insult to the church," he decided, stroking his flabby chin. "Imagine the effrontery—claimin' to correct the vision that God gave us, as if 'twas somehow less than perfect."

"What will ye do, Father?" the secretary asked eagerly.

Father Ninian steepled his fingers as if in pious thought, and then sighed. "What I should have done before. God's will. Purify the heathen witch with holy fire." He made the sign of the cross. "An example must be made of her. 'Tis up to the church to prove that science is the handmaiden o' the devil, that anyone who dares challenge the will o' God must face the flames o' purification."

"But how will ye fetch her? The soldier—"

"He's a cripple," he scoffed. "By the time he comes hoppin' to intercede, the deed will be done."

The secretary rubbed uncertainly at his throat. His recent unpleasant altercation with Mar had apparently left him shaken. "And the hound?"

The priest shrugged. "Toss him breakfast—meat spiced with belladonna."

He didn't much care for dogs. They were often depicted as consorts of the devil. True, Mar might well starve without his hound's hunting skills. But that would be in the hands of God.

The man probably should have died alongside his brothers on the battlefield anyway.

The first thing Lachlan noticed when he woke the next morn was the cold. He opened his eyes to see that the door stood half-open.

"Campbell," he muttered to himself. A chill wind had slipped in like a thief, stealing all the warmth from the cottage.

Then he sat up and saw that Alisoune was gone.

His heart sank to the pit of his stomach. He'd known the lass was leaving. Hell, he'd sent her away himself. Still, 'twas a blow to discover she'd left with no word of farewell...and no kiss goodbye.

They'd parted on bitter words. He wished he'd made peace with her before she left. It wouldn't change anything. She'd still be walking out of his life forever. But at least her last memory of him would be pleasant.

With a heavy heart, he rose from the bed, using the brace that every morn from now on would remind him of Alisoune.

He adored her, he realized. 'Twas absurd. He hardly knew her. But in a harsh and stifling world where a man was judged, not by his measure, but by an accident of warfare, Alisoune, who took him as he was, was a breath of fresh air.

He wedged the crutch under his arm. Then he happened to glance toward the kitchen. Alisoune's satchel and the bundle of food he'd prepared for her were still there.

His foolish heart flipped over. She hadn't left yet after all. Perhaps she'd only gone outside with Campbell. Cursing himself for having false hope—after all, she *was* leaving, whether 'twas now or later—he nonetheless hobbled eagerly to the door and opened it wider.

As he squinted against the sun-bright snow, he could make out the dark shape of his dog several yards in front of the cottage. It looked like the deerhound was stretched out on the icy slope.

"Campbell?" He frowned. "Campbell!"

The hound barely lifted his head, but wouldn't come. That wasn't like him at all. Something was wrong.

"Campbell!" he yelled, limping toward the dog as fast as he could.

God's wounds! What had happened to his beloved hound? Had he been gored by a stag? Charged by a boar? Attacked by wolves?

Halfway there, he could see Campbell's heaving sides and the clouds of mist he huffed out with each labored breath.

"I'm comin', lad!" he called out. "Hold on! I'm comin'!"

But his crutch slipped on a patch of melting snow, and it went out from under him. He fell hard on his hip, and it took him a full minute of cursing to get his limbs under him again and retrieve the crutch.

By the time he got to Campbell, the poor beast couldn't lift his head at all. He was quaking, and his pupils were reduced to pinpoints. Beside him on the ground was a small pile of dark berries. Lachlan didn't know what they were, but his gut told him 'twas no mistake they were there. Someone had poisoned his dog.

Biting back a snarl of anger, he patted the dog's neck and murmured, "Ye'll be fine, lad."

He hoped he was right. If anything happened to Campbell...

He clenched his jaw, trying not to think about it. Nothing would happen to Campbell. He'd make sure of it.

Yet that was what he'd thought about his brothers. He'd been certain he could keep them from harm. He'd been wrong.

Still, he couldn't let fear make a coward of him. Choking down dread, he forced himself to reason.

First he had to get his dog inside where 'twas warm. Fortunately, the wood carrier Alisoune had made for him would be useful for that.

Loading the big limp hound onto it was no easy feat, but he finally managed and was able to drag Campbell back toward the cottage. All the while as he trudged through the snow, an unthinkable question teased at the edges of Lachlan's mind. Where was Alisoune?

Just before he entered the cottage, his gaze snagged on a reflective object in the snow near the threshold. A small half-circle of broken glass stuck out of the white drifts.

His breath caught in his chest. Alisoune's spectacles. They were broken.

She wouldn't have been so careless. And she'd never go anywhere without her spectacles.

Not willingly.

All at once, he knew what had happened. His heart began to pound like the drums of war.

Steeling his nerves as best he could, he wrapped Campbell in blankets near the fire and put a bowl of water nearby. But a dire thought kept echoing through his brain... If they'd poisoned Campbell, what had they done to Alisoune?

He was afraid he knew the answer, what they'd intended all along—to burn her at the stake.

For the love of God, he had to save her. But there was no time. And the devils who'd taken her had known that. They'd poisoned his dog, but they hadn't bothered waylaying *him*, because they knew a one-legged man was no match for them. They'd be done with their unholy business before he could even limp into Keirfield.

Seething with rage and frustration, Lachlan pounded his fist against the hearth, knocking the round stone from the mantel. It fell and rolled to a stop beside Campbell.

With a curse, he threw his useless crutch across the room. It clattered over the flagstones and landed at the foot of the steel leg Alisoune had made for him.

At first, Alisoune had been angry with herself for falling so easily into their trap. Campbell had let himself out of the cottage, as was his morning custom, but he was gone a long while. Naturally, she ventured out to see what had become of him.

They'd caught her instantly, gagging her ere she could cry out, tying her hands behind her ere she could fight her way free. And that was when she saw that they'd also hurt Campbell, done something to make him crumple to the ground, unable to move, unable to come to her aid.

When they picked her up to carry her away, her spectacles fell off, and she heard a crunch as one of the men stepped on them. And for Alisoune, not being able to see clearly was almost as frightening as thinking about what they intended to do with her.

Now, however, anger had given way to terror. She was in Keirfield proper, where a stake had been erected and stacked with kindling in the town square. While two men held her captive before a crowd of villagers, the priest went on and on about the will of God and purifying fire. He was making no logical sense whatsoever with his strange ravings about witches and demons, the heretic Copernicus and the evils of spectacles. And then, as if his lack of logic wasn't frightening enough, all the townsfolk joined in, echoing his sentiments, embracing his condemnation of her as if 'twere an absolute truth.

If only he'd remove her gag, there were arguments she might make in her favor, scientific evidence that could prove she was no blasphemer. And yet she knew her voice would not be heard over the rabid fervor of the crowd. What men couldn't understand, they feared. And what they feared, they sought to destroy.

As helpless as she was, she couldn't quiet her feverish brain as the men sliced her dress from her, leaving her shivering in her chemise. Why, she wondered, did the priest not just let her go? She'd been planning to leave Keirfield. Surely he knew that. He'd never see her again. So why had he brought her back to burn her at the stake? Why was he so intent on killing her?

All at once, it came to her. The priest wasn't just killing her. He was killing science. Science threatened his control over these people. In the same way men believed the planets revolved around the earth, Father Ninian believed his flock revolved around him. He viewed Alisoune as an intruder who had upset what he considered the natural order of things. And the only way he could restore that order was to convince his flock that Alisoune was a witch, that science was blasphemy, that knowledge was evil.

She fought back a sob as the men wrenched her forward toward the stake.

If only she hadn't stepped outside to look for Campbell...

If only she hadn't delayed her departure, hoping Lachlan would change his mind...

If only she'd told him how much she loved him, how she never wanted to leave him, how she knew they belonged together and how happy she would make him...

Now she'd never get the chance.

Her eyes filled with tears as they tied her to the stake and acrid smoke rose from a flaming brand.

Even if Lachlan woke to find her gone, he wouldn't be able to save her. There wouldn't be time. She'd be dead before he got halfway to Keirfield.

Lachlan's stump hurt like hell. But now that he'd mastered the steel leg, it worked like a perfectly engineered crossbow. With a naked sword in his fist and a bloodthirsty sneer on his face, he covered the mile to Keirfield in long, determined strides.

No battle had ever fired up his blood like this. No enemy had ever stirred such rancor in him. His force of will was sharpened to a fine edge, and nothing could turn aside his blade now.

When he entered the town and first beheld Alisoune—a frail angel in white bound to a blackened stake—he let out a loud roar and raised his sword.

The man holding the brand hesitated. The crowd wheeled his way. Lachlan strode forward with menace—his face grim, his manner merciless.

Suddenly, the air was filled with gasps. Mothers grabbed their children. Men staggered backward. The secretary's jaw dropped. And Father Ninian clutched his chest.

As Lachlan made his way through the parting crowd, he heard whispers of speculation around him.

"His leg's grown back..."

"'Tis a miracle..."

"The spell of a witch..."

"God's own hand..."

"The work o' Satan..."

"Impossible..."

"Bewitched..."

"Blessed..."

Lachlan didn't care what they thought. He didn't care if they believed his restored leg was a gift from God or a curse of the devil...as long as they didn't stand between him and the beautiful lass he meant to rescue and hold onto for the rest of his life.

EPILOGUE

"**S**low down!" Alisoune called after Lachlan, laughing. Now that he'd had a few weeks to practice walking on his prosthesis, he sped along the streets of Stirling as if he'd worn it all his life.

"Hurry up!" he retorted. "I want to take the stone in ere the shop gets busy."

She grinned and shook her head. She wasn't quite sure what he intended to do with the rainbow crystal. But she supposed he'd never get over the notion 'twas some sort of magical relic. When they'd returned to the cottage on that awful day the villagers had taken her to find Campbell with the stone under his paw, completely recovered from his poisoning, Lachlan claimed the old crone had been right. The Winter Stone had changed the dog's fate.

Alisoune didn't really care what he believed about the crystal. She was just happy he believed in her love and in himself again.

They'd decided to leave Keirfield forever. There was still disagreement in the town as to whether Lachlan's new leg was

478

the work of God or the work of Lucifer. Alisoune didn't dare try to convince them 'twas just a work of engineering.

So they sold his cottage and moved into her house in Stirling. She made spectacles in her downstairs workshop. And 'twasn't long before Lachlan's skills with the sword got him work training young lads to fight.

"Here we are," he announced, tugging on Campbell's leash and stopping at the shop where a wooden sign embossed with a gold cup proclaimed it *John Gilder, Goldsmith.* Unfortunately, the door was closed. It appeared John Gilder wasn't in residence. Lachlan frowned. "Damn. Where can he have gone?"

But Alisoune was never one to make assumptions. She required empirical proof. So she banged loudly on the door. Sure enough, a few moments later, a key turned in the lock, and the door opened a crack. Out peered a lass of no more than fourteen, dressed in a blue smock. She was a bonnie young thing with dark hair, a dimpled chin, and big brown eyes.

"Is the goldsmith here?" Alisoune asked her.

The lass looked undecided for a moment. Then she nodded and opened the door wide. "Aye. Come in."

Beautiful gold pieces were displayed all around the shop, some with jewels, some with enamels, some with pearls. The handiwork was amazing.

"I have a stone," Lachlan said, pulling it out of his coin pouch. "I'd like to have it set."

"Oh!" the lass exclaimed. "'Tis a rainbow crystal."

Alisoune lifted a smug brow at Lachlan.

"Can the goldsmith do it today?" he asked.

"Today?" the lass squeaked.

"Aye." Lachlan had gotten very superstitious about the stone. He didn't want to be without it for any more than a few hours.

"Well..." the lass said, casually reaching over to scratch Campbell behind the ears. "John Gilder is away for a few days."

479

Her eyes lit up as she confided, "He's gone to see the new queen, to present a gift to her."

"The new queen?" Lachlan asked with a frown.

"Aye, sir. Have ye not heard?" She could barely contain her excitement. "The babe was born today. She's called Mary, after her mother."

"A lass," Alisoune said in wonder. Both England and Scotland had possible female heirs to the thrones then.

Lachlan sighed. "So it can't be done today?"

"Well..." the lass said, catching her lip under her teeth. "There *is* another goldsmith here who could do the work."

"By the end o' the day?" he asked.

"Aye, sir."

"And 'tis quality work?" he asked.

"Aye, sir." She fetched a tray full of intricate pins, brooches, and rings. She lifted her chin as she said, "'Tis the same goldsmith who made these."

He nodded his approval. "Fine."

As he went on to describe what he wanted done, Alisoune narrowed her eyes at the lass, taking note of her apprentice's smock. Then she asked with a knowing smile, "Would ye be the goldsmith's daughter...and his apprentice?"

The lass gulped in guilt. "Foster daughter, aye. My name is Florie."

"Well, Florie," she said with a wink, "I think we'll be very pleased with the results."

As it turned out, Alisoune *was* very pleased, particularly because Lachlan had had the Winter Stone mounted into a pendant for *her*. 'Twas a wedding gift, he said, which she gleefully accepted.

If he wanted to claim that the Winter Stone gleamed bright blue with peace and contentment as he fastened it around her neck, she didn't bother arguing 'twas only the prism inside that made it so. For Lachlan, 'twas a reminder that one's destiny could be altered, that all wounds could be mended, and that love was the most powerful healer of all.

The End

More books from the Scottish Lasses series:
MacFarland's Lass
MacAdam's Lass
MacKenzie's Lass

ᴄʜᴀɴᴋ ʏᴏᴜ ꜰᴏʀ ʀᴇᴀᴅɪɴɢ ᴍʏ ʙᴏᴏᴋ!

Did you enjoy it? If so, I hope you'll post a review to let others know! There's no greater gift you can give an author than spreading your love of her books.

It's truly a pleasure and a privilege to be able to share my stories with you. Knowing that my words have made you laugh, sigh, or touched a secret place in your heart is what keeps the wind beneath my wings. I hope you enjoyed our brief journey together, and may ALL of your adventures have happy endings!

If you'd like to keep in touch, feel free to sign up for my monthly e-newsletter at www.glynnis.net, and you'll be the first to find out about my new releases, special discounts, prizes, promotions, and more!

If you want to keep up with my daily escapades:
Friend me at facebook.com/GlynnisCampbell
Like my Page at bit.ly/GlynnisCampbellFBPage
Follow me at twitter.com/GlynnisCampbell
And if you're a super fan, join facebook.com/GCReadersClan

ABOUT THE AUTHOR

I'm a *USA Today* bestselling author of swashbuckling action-adventure historical romances, mostly set in Scotland, with over a dozen award-winning books published in six languages.

But before my role as a medieval matchmaker, I sang in *The Pinups,* an all-girl band on CBS Records, and provided voices for the MTV animated series *The Maxx,* Blizzard's *Diablo* and *Starcraft* video games, and *Star Wars* audiobooks.

I'm the wife of a rock star (if you want to know which one, contact me) and the mother of two young adults. I do my best writing on cruise ships, in Scottish castles, on my husband's tour bus, and at home in my sunny southern California garden.

I love transporting readers to a place where the bold heroes have endearing flaws, the women are stronger than they look, the land is lush and untamed, and chivalry is alive and well!

I'm always delighted to hear from my readers, so please feel free to email me at glynnis@glynnis.net. And if you're a super-fan who would like to join my inner circle, sign up at http://www.facebook.com/GCReadersClan, where you'll get glimpses behind the scenes, sneak peeks of works-in-progress, and extra special surprises.

www.ingramcontent.com/pod-product-compliance
Lightning Source LLC
Chambersburg PA
CBHW020240120726
47904CB00001B/40